CHEST OF TIME

BOOK 3, THE AFTERWORLD CHRONICLES

VICKI STIEFEL

For Subsidiary Rights, Live Events, or other questions contact Paula Munier, Talcott Notch Literary Services, LLC at pmunier@talcottnotch.net

✸ Created with Vellum

To Blake and Ben, My Beloveds
You make my world turn

Time is too slow for those who wait, too swift for those who fear, too long for those who grieve, too short for those who rejoice, but for those who love, time is eternity. —Henry Van Dyke

PRAISE FOR VICKI STIEFEL

THE AFTERWORLD CHRONICLES

"*Chest of Stone* is a fast-paced urban fantasy with plenty of action and eclectic, vibrant world-building. Ms Stiefel's... writing is very original, it just flows, always in the moment, always unconstrained. There was nothing formulaic about *Chest or Stone*, and I thoroughly enjoyed that. — Nocturnal Book Reviews

"I was completely caught up with *Chest of Stone's* skillfully woven, fast moving story ~ and totally in awe of the author's spare but hard-hitting prose. And high praise for the credible and heart-moving romance between Clea and James ~ wow-oh-wow!" — Parris Afton Bonds, Goodreads, author of *The Calling of the Clan*

"The story is fast-paced, with non-stop action. The plot is complex and intriguing with unpredictable twists." —Sujitha Alexander

"*Chest of Bone* was full of action, magic, suspense and deception. The magic was mysterious and intriguing, and the way it was described was beautiful. I highly recommend this book if you're a lover of the fantastical with loads of mystery and lots of explosive kisses!" —Tiffany Roberts, author of *Dustwalker* and Isle of the Forgotten series

"*Chest of Bone's* writing style is innovative, the world is very interesting and provocative. It's a great story! I's a bunch of crazy, but it's GOOD crazy, with some super vivid scenes and fascinating characters." —Nocturnal Book Reviews

THE TALLY WHYTE SERIES

"This is an amazing thriller with action on almost every page. The paranormal elements fit right into the storyline... The heroine is strong, independent and sees things nobody else does... Vicki Stiefel writes a brilliant psychological thriller." —Book Review.com

"Tally is a compelling protagonist—edgy, compassionate and vulnerable—with a clipped narrating style that keeps the tricky plot in focus. Stiefel's latest shows—again—that she can hold her own against genre heavyweights like John Sanford and Patricia Cornwell." —Publishers Weekly

"Compelling, touching, and a pleasure to read." —Robert Parker

"Three words describe the Tally Whyte series: Intense. Addictive. Chilling. Tally's personality will draw you in as surely as the mystery does in this series. Supporting characters are multi-layered and intriguing, building a world you'll want to know." —Fresh Fiction

"An interesting read that concludes in an unexpected, dramatic fashion." —RT Book Reviews

"High on suspense, this wonderfully gripping tale is just about impossible to put down." —New Mystery Reader

A DYING MAGE

A Dying Mage.
A Wrathful Monster.
A Desperate Mission.
And a Time-twisting Tale of Love.

When her teenage ward goes missing, truehearted Mage Clea Reese must confront a duplicitous fae adversary who steals the Chest of Time - but not before an accident leaves Clea near death. With her life now at stake, Clea's allies must retrieve the Chest before death takes Clea. For if the Key Mage falls, a new Key will arise - one whose brutal ambitions spell a dark end for humankind. Clea's fierce lover James leads the multifaceted team on a quest that takes them through lands both Magic and Mundane to battle the vengeful fae and The Union. But their greatest enemy? Time itself.

PROLOGUE

She kneeled on the bank of a sluggish river the color of merlot, the sun bright overhead. *It* was there. She was sure. How she knew eluded her. Was it a call? A pull? A song?

Silence surrounded her. No caw of birds or buzz of insects cut the air. Even the grasses on the small verge before the wood were hushed.

The opaque water drifted by. Her knees ached. She'd been kneeling a long time. She dragged her fingers through the russet water, shamed by her vacillation. Palms open to the river, she moved her hands to the left. No, that wasn't correct. She shifted them to her right.

A bright crystal note chimed in her head. She plunged her hands deep into the river and pulled *It* out. She rocked back on her heals.

But, it couldn't be...

A storm ignited in her mind, her heart, burrowing insistently into her soul until it unmade her.

The world snapped off.

Hours later—Days? Millennia?—she lifted heavy lids. Dizzy.

It rested on her belly, and her mind failed to fathom what she held. Was it brown or purple? Square or oblong? Stone or wood?

Why couldn't she *see* it?

She sat up and shook her head to clear it. Something was different. She stretched her arms above her head, body stiff, muscles aching. Odd. Her fighting leathers felt tighter across her breasts and hips, but looser at her waist. Crazy. Her braid pulled at her scalp, and she reached back to unleash it.

Longer. Her hair was definitely longer. She went to pull a clump to the front.

The crack of a branch stilled her hand. The sound had come from up the hill, within the scrim of trees.

She ponytailed her hair, plunged *It* back into the river, and leapt to her feet. Adrenaline vanished the aches and pains, and with precise motions from years of practice, she reached back, unfastened her bow, unfolded it, and strung it. Found her quiver and clipped it to her belt, her arrows now easily accessible. She carried twenty-five of them, firing fifteen per minute, wishing she had her full complement of fifty. But the remainder were back at camp. It would have to do.

Now she'd wait, an arrow nocked, prepared for the inevitable attack. It wouldn't come from the purple-grassed hill, with its scents of lavender and honey. No, they'd slink beneath the stand of red-barked oaks with polka-dotted leaves of white and green shielding them. The gollups weren't stupid, but disgusting things of oily blackness and sinew and bone.

The black sand shifted beneath her feet. Nerves. She wished to move, needed to. That would be the smart thing to do. But if she did so, her absent companion's fury would result in more of her blood spilled, more vile bruises and deepening heart pain.

She cast her eyes left, center, right, her ears pricked for each crunched leaf, every sloughed breath. Oh, the gollups were there, right at the periphery of her senses.

Sweat dotted her upper lip, and she wiped it away with her

gauntleted forearm. She lowered her bow and arrow to her side, allowed her muscles to momentarily relax, her body to regroup.

The gollups would attack, all right. They always did. In pairs or trios, seeking what she'd found. The Chest of Time lay beneath that turgid wine-dark water.

She and her... She refused to even think the word, it prompted such sadness. They'd searched years for the chest and had stumbled upon its location by accident. Correction. *She'd* stumbled upon it. *She'd* found it. And as was typical, *she'd* been left alone, *again*, to guard what was more precious than a sliver of the true cross.

She didn't want to *be* here anymore, in this strange land of unexpected killers and miraculous sunsets, where time passed in trickles of days or tsunamis of years. She could never be sure which was which anymore, only that it hurt.

A tickle to her nose, one not near as good as the shifters, but good enough. The creatures' scent drifted on the air just before the soft breeze batted it away. There, to her left—*gollups*. How many? She raised her bow. While her stance remained face forward, her eyes slid in their direction.

She was ready, her quiver filled, her mind disciplined by her companion to utter stillness. The last was a lie, but it amused her. She wasn't *that* easily cowed.

Movement. A shadow darker than the red bark of the oak closest to the stream.

Sweat tickled her spine. Would this be the day she missed? Would this be the day the gollups devoured her? Would this be the day she ceased to exist?

Her arrow flew. A howl of pain. She'd already nocked a fresh arrow even as the shadow creature crumpled to earth, its taloned fingers reaching for something it would never obtain.

Over the years, she'd gotten inhumanly faster. Ha! Poor word choice—she'd never been human.

She caught movement from the corner of her eye and swung around as two more rushed her, one dead center and a second on her right.

In a flash, she let fly a barrage of arrows, felling one. But the other, too close now.

She unsheathed her knives. Death flew at her on swift feet, bearing pointy teeth and razored claws.

And for what? Forgiveness? Pride? Love?

She braced for attack.

1

All we had to do was get into the rental van that awaited us outside our hotel in Charleston. How hard could that be?

Apparently near impossible.

When James swung our weapons pack into the back, he bumped Alex. *Shit.*

"What the hell, Larrimer?" Alex clamped his hand around James' throat.

James punched it away. "Asshole."

"Me?" Alex laughed. "Look who's talking."

Testosterone flared to nuclear levels. Alex might rule the Arctos pack, but James commanded the Five. James might be stronger, but Alex had bigger teeth. And they were staring death at one another, Alex's gold eyes glowing and James' nanoteched muscles bulging.

"Stop it." My words, unsurprisingly, had no effect.

I looked to my companions for help. Melike's wolfie teeth had elongated, too. Neddy bounced on the balls of his feet, fingers lengthening and turning pink. Rae grinned. *Damn* that mage, he was enjoying this.

We had one purpose—to find my rebellious, beloved 16-year-old ward Lulu and bring her home. Days earlier, she'd run away. From me. From the wolves. From safety.

Alex raised a clawed hand. Now it was James' turn to laugh.

I wasn't putting up with their crap, not when my frickin' fae mother had already lobbed her first salvo. Hands at my sides, palms out, I dug deep to covertly unleash my fireflies, the pleasure-pain pinching my nerves.

Golden motes swirled from my palms to surround the men.

They froze.

"Good move, boys." My Flow wasn't hurting them. But it could, and they knew it.

How to diffuse this? What to say? "My mother knows we're coming."

The tension popped like a burst balloon. The two men swiveled toward me, and I fisted my hands, cutting off my fireflies. Five pairs of angry eyes speared me. Ouch.

"What did you say, Clea?" My lover's iced voice shivered down my spine.

"When I hit terra firma after we landed. In my head. She repeated what she'd said after I killed Tommy."

Rae snorted. "*Repeated?* Since y'all haven't seen fit to tell us, sugah, what might those words be?"

"She screamed, *You killed my son!*"

"And you didn't tell me because..." James, so quiet, his honied-granite voice tight with suppressed anger.

"Or me." A growl rumbled up from Alex's chest.

Melike just snarled.

I spread my arms. "Because I knew you'd all react *poorly*."

James barked a laugh. "Since when are you given to understatement?"

"So now she knows we're here," I said with a glibness I wasn't feeling. "Big whoop."

"It changes things, Clea," Neddy piped up in all his boyish innocence.

"We'll work it out, Neddy," I said. "We always do."

"But I'm *worried* about you." The boy ran a hand through his tousled curls.

I gave him a hug, then snagged his eyes. "Look, we can't do anything about it now, right? What we can do is fix James and Alex."

"*Fix*?" the two men chorused.

Melike and Neddy laughed, and Rae rolled his eyes before he slipped into the driver's seat.

"Yes, I said *fix*. You two are acting like playground children. Get over it."

"She's right," Melike said, who grinned at Alex's dour look.

James rocked back on his heels. He thrust out a hand to the alpha wolf. "Truce, for the duration."

Alex eyed it, then gripped James' hand in his and shook. "Agreed. We settle this after we retrieve Lulu."

Before James climbed inside the van, I tugged at his shirt and brushed his chin with a kiss. His response was to take me in one so passionate, I forgot our mission, forgot the world, and reveled in his arms banding me, the heat of his lips burning me, the demands of his tongue delving me. Our song rose, his thread speaking of love and devotion, twining around mine, which spoke the same. Together. Partners. Home.

Good thing he kept his arm around my waist when we came up for breath. "Wow."

"It was either kiss you or smack you." His Pacific-blue eyes blazed. "Next time, talk to me, Clea. Tell me."

I'd hurt him. I hadn't meant to. "I will. Promise. Was the cherry on top Alex watching?"

He flashed that devilish grin of his.

I lay a hand on his chest, stood on tiptoe, and whispered, "You're my one and only, Dragon Dude. For always."

ONCE WE'D ALL PILED into the van, Rae turned in his seat and caught the eye of each of us. "Here's what we're all gettin' into. Ever since the French and Gaelic fae invaded America in the eighteenth century, they gathered a shit-load of magic to create their primary court in America—Charleston. First stop, the Angel Oak, ya'll."

"A thin space," James said, surprising me.

Rae nodded. "Ya'll been doin' your homework. It's the portal to their court, which remains in the mundane realm."

"But with all that magic, Charleston's faeland can't be mundane." I said.

"Correct," Rae said. "Nor is it the same as in the magic lands, sugah. The Fae Court's one of the few lands with merged magical and mundane worlds. Ya'll be prepared for weird, hear?"

WE DROVE ACROSS JAMES ISLAND, then over another river onto Johns Island, home of the Angel Oak. All the while, I couldn't stop thinking about Lulu. Just three days earlier, she and I had giggled and swooned when we rewatched *Wonder Woman* and *The Princess Bride*. My empathic senses had devoured her exuberance and joy. And it hurt, to think how she'd been preparing to carve a hole in both our hearts.

My emotions ping-ponged from angry to sad to worried and back again. Why had she left?

In that note we'd found, she'd said she needed *"to prove to you that I'm worthy."* I mean, c'mon. Worthy? Lulu had never been *un*worthy! She was precious and beautiful, smart and feisty, and full of fun. She had opinions and spine, and, yeah, sometimes she was a pain-in-the-ass teen. Weren't they all? But she'd triumphed over her kidnappers and her father's tragic death and come into her own. I was so proud of her.

Worthy, my ass. Geesh, Lu, why?

My eyes burned with tears. I wouldn't let them fall. I had *failed*— to mother her, to understand her, to make her feel her worth in a way *she* understood. If I hadn't, she wouldn't have left. *I'm sorry, Lu.*

I'd fix it. I had to.

Now, the six of us were on our way to a strange land I'd targeted as Lulu's destination because her bitch of a birth mother had lured her there. The place had to be a minefield, especially because Lu was a mutt like me—part fae and part mage.

Once I found Lu, I'd hug her like crazy. I'd throttle that bitch mother of hers, too. The woman had abandoned Lulu when she was just a kid, the same as my mam had done. Hugging and throttling settled in my gut with a pleasing thump.

Suburban houses, industrial buildings, lots of trees and other vegetation rolled by. James slipped his hand into mine, threading our fingers together. His head dipped and his breath warmed my ear. "We *will* find her, Clea."

"What if I'm—"

"You're not wrong. And if you are, the hunt continues until we bring her home." He squeezed my hand. I squeezed his back. It felt good, right, our fingers entwined. A comfort.

We made decent time and parked on a street much like any other. After we weaponed up, we walked the short distance to Angel Oak Park's entrance. Which is where I slammed into a wall of power. I staggered, as did Rae. Neddy stumbled, and Alex caught him. Neither Alex nor Melike seemed affected by the surge. Maybe because the Arctos pack had lived so long in the mundane world? Or perhaps because they were shifters? Unsurprisingly, James hadn't budged.

"Did you feel power surge?" I asked him.

"Yes. But I expected it. The wyvern warned me."

Now he was *talking* to the wyvern who lived inside him? A progression I didn't like.

We walked across a carpet of browned leaves that covered the mulchy soil. A small cabin stood to our left, but the focal point was the massive live oak said to be the largest tree east of the Mississippi. I'd swear I smelled magic on the air.

The oak was shorter than I expected, not near as tall as full-growth northern oaks. But from its mighty, moss-covered trunk, branches sprawled nearly two hundred feet from end to end, so huge they would drape the ground had they not been elevated by wooden blocks. Some said the oak was 400 years old, others said fifteen hundred, still others alleged it was eons old. The city of Charleston claimed ownership. I suspected the fae did the same.

Like giant octopoid tentacles, the oak's limbs seemed to reach for us. A soft breeze pushed at our backs, prodding us toward the trunk. The push might be faint, but the pull toward the tree was exquisite and inexorable. Were those whispers? From whom?

I raced forward.

Shouts behind me, but the more ground I covered, the more the whispers rose, a sea of spirits urging me onward. I had to find them. I ran farther, faster.

An arm clamped around my waist stopped my forward movement.

I blinked, paused. "James?"

He stared, all sleepy-eyed and calm, cheekbones sharp, jaw tight. I knew that look. It meant the monster was about to emerge. Oh, not the wyvern, but James' own, personal one, which was scary as shit. "What's wrong?"

He leaned down, nuzzled my ear. "You went somewhere else. Stay with me, baby."

"I…" I shook my head. "Didn't you hear the whispers?"

He cocked an eyebrow.

Those whispers… Ghosts? Fae? Other? "Strange stuff."

"Yup."

Which is when I realized… I wiggled my gold finger, the one crafted by Rae to replace the digit lost to the Chest of Stone. "I can *feel* it, sensation in my finger."

He rubbed his thumb across the mechanical digit.

"Wow," I said.

"I'm betting that's the least of it."

"Y'all fixin' to move?" Rae said. "We've got three days to find her, we agreed. Only three."

I rolled my eyes.

Rae wagged a finger. "You've got to find the remaining chests, sugah, or soon the world, it's gonna splinter into a million pieces."

"I know. I know."

We strode toward Rae, around the immense trunk, and away from the tourists who, oddly enough, ignored us. The sky lightened, the air redolent with gardenia and hints of the exotic.

"We're at the gate, y'all hear?" Rae said. "We're gonna hold hands to get through. It won't be easy." Rae clasped Neddy's and Melike's hands. Alex came beside me opposite James and took my free one.

I squeezed their hands as we walked forward following Rae's group.

The air grew viscous, each step challenging our forward momentum. We pushed, and I held tightly to my companions. Instinct told me they couldn't move forward without my half-fae aid. No, I'd bet James, with his fae spark and wyvern blood, could.

We pressed harder, muscles straining, our clasped hands slick with our mingled sweat. I leaned, muscling my way forward.

The pressure ended so abruptly we crashed to our knees.

I caught my breath. Once we regrouped, we peered down a seemingly endless drive, the red earth hard-packed beneath our feet.

"Everybody okay?" James said.

Distracted murmurs of assent, their preoccupation obvious.

Live oaks draped with Spanish moss lined the drive, except they grew alongside strange pines with periwinkle needles and black-barked trunks. Tiny alien violet flowers carpeted the earth, interspersed with clumps of taller red bee balm. Ruby-throated hummingbirds drew nectar from tall red flowers, the birds replicas of those at my feeder. But the brilliant pink, blue-throated hummingbirds feeding alongside them were hawk-sized.

Is this what our world would look like when the magic and mundane completed their retwining? I'd been to the magic realm. This place was different—a mashup of both.

Here, the air redolent with florals and spices, evoked feelings of calm and harmony. So unlike our world, where the retwining was discordant—chaotic at best, disastrous at worst.

If I successfully retrieved all five Chests of Unity, our world could be like this—harmonious and beautiful. Which would never happen if Tatianne or The Union had their way. My imaginings grew bleak. My task weighed on me.

We moved into what James called the wedge formation—a triangle, with James leading as point man. Rae fanned out to the left behind him, with Alex on the right. Melike took the base of the triangle's left, I took the center, and Neddy the right. We didn't expect trouble. Nonetheless, we'd prepared. As soon as we'd crossed into their land, the fae had to know we'd arrived. But James insisted we should present some sort of tactical formation to the fae. Expert archers Melike, Alex, and James carried bows at their sides, their quivers strapped to their backs. Of course James also carried his katanas. We all carried various weapons. But Rae had assured us the fae, renowned as archers, would use bows.

"Pick up your pace, hear?" Rae said.

I glanced at Melike as we walked toward faeland. "Do you feel the difference in the air?"

She nodded. "*Oui.* It's thinner."

"Cooler, too," Neddy chimed in.

"Like we're at a higher elevation," I said. "The scents are incredible."

Neddy flexed his bicep, muscle bulging, and laughed. "I'm stronger, which is really neat."

I reached for my power. It slammed into me like a bullet train. "Whew, me, too."

MY GUT SAID we were being watched, and I was sure the others knew. We'd discussed that contingency and decided we'd ignore the fae until they made the first move.

Up ahead, James peered over his shoulder. "The wyvern demands to speak with you."

"*Now?*"

His brows crashed together. "So he says."

It disturbed me how much the wyvern was talking to James. "Let me in?"

"You don't have to ask."

"It's polite."

He snorted. "Your good behavior worries me."

"Don't worry. It won't last." I grinned, stilled, and dived inside James. Deep, past the radiant fae spark that I'd once seen nearly extinguished, deeper still to the wyvern.

How was I able to do this? I never knew, yet each time I ended up at the wyvern's "den."

And there he was. The rounded scales of his immense red-gold body glowed with health, as did the spikes along his spine and the golden horns curving above his triangular head. He was magnificent.

His green eyes flashed open. They pulsed with excitement. Uh oh. He grimaced, and I took the rows of knife-edged teeth he revealed as a smile.

Welcome, Clea.

His voice resonated in my head. *Hello, Wyvern. You wanted to talk. Are you okay?*

Okay? I'm fabulous.

You've been talking to James?

Of course.

Bullshit. He never used to talk to his host, not until me. Not until I took away the wyvern's pain those many months ago. Since then, he seemed to have grown in strength and awareness.

You haven't visited me for ages, he said. *You don't call. You don't write.*

He'd also acquired a strange new attitude, not to mention hipness. *It's only been a few days.*

He dipped his head closer to my essence. *An eternity.*

He'd saved my life, so I'd forbear the snark, but talk about hyperbole.

I reached out to pet him and he...purred? *Gotta go. Fae Court stuff and all. We've come for Lulu.*

His majestic head bobbed. I'd seen the wyvern in the flesh, when he'd emerged and taken over James during battle, something he'd liked way too much. For him to assume his physical form in the mundane world, I'd had to "command" him out, per his instruction. I sure as hell hoped that was true in this blended half-mundane/half-magical world.

I know about the Lulu girl, he said.

It's upsetting.

Yes, my Clea, deeply. You are being shadowed by the fae.

I assumed, but thank you. I really have to get going. I patted his head again.

A moment. A warning. Do what you came to do and leave.

Of course we would leave. *Okay.*

Heed me. I sense—

Shouts, growls.

I careened back to awareness, crouched on the ground, surrounded by our group. Arrows rained around us in a circle, forming a pattern, but no fae were in sight.

None of our group were firing back and no one had been hit. Yet. Apparently this was some idiot fae welcome. A nasty one. We'd compressed the triangle, backs to each other. I leapt to my feet and stepped forward to stand between Melike and Neddy. She'd raised her bow, as had Alex and James.

I raised my hands, palms out, and called my fireflies. A massive surge of pain-and-pleasure as they flew from my palm, tiny motes of power, incandescent and beautiful.

They formed the triple-chains knitted stitch pattern, a beautifully protective one, as if my spirit chose the best pattern for my need. Much like a fisherman would cast a net, I threw the gorgeous motif over my companions, not hemming them in, but shielding them from the arrows.

Oh, hell. Neddy's fingers had turned pink, black clawed, and elongated. His snout had lengthened, too, and was dappled with shiny pink flesh and tufts of fur. Even as I watched, smoke curled around him, while his body grew taller. He was transforming into the Pinky.

"Neddy, no!"

His head whipped around, a snarl blooming from huge drooling lupine jaws.

"Neddy." I squeezed his shoulder. "Don't do this now. We've got this."

His leaf-green eyes began to clear. The Pinky-boy swallowed hard and nodded, his features reforming into all boy.

The rain of arrows abruptly ceased. Still no fae. A glance over my shoulder showed Alex and James with their bows drawn. Beside me, Melike's was the same, while Rae's black motes swirled around his hands in a figure eight.

Needless to say, I kept my firefly shield in place.

I wanted to soothe Neddy's fears. "It's all good."

"Yeah?" Neddy said, voice wobbly.

"I don't want them to see you as the Pinky yet, okay?" Awkward it might be, but I leaned in and kissed his cheek. "You're terrific."

"Yuck, Clea."

I laughed. Our strong, courageous Neddy was back.

"Fae sure are a pain in the ass," Rae muttered.

A soft murmur, then a dozen fae stepped from the trees lining the drive, arrows nocked, bows aimed at our group. *Charming.* Much like Charlie the fae, they were tall and slender, pointy-eared men and women except for one curvy, six-foot female whose face bore a dangerous grin. They wore jeans and colored t-shirts, some with leather vests. *Lord of the Rings* they weren't. Gee, they could've at least dressed up for their attack. A few had different length, pearlescent horns protruding from their skulls, like Charlie's, the longest about three inches.

All were stoic faced, except for the grinning woman, who winked at me. I wasn't sure what to make of that.

"Drop your shield," said a gaunt, gray-haired fae. His brown eyes gleamed with malice.

"No," James said. "Lower your bows and we'll consider it."

He gave us teeth.

I sensed James behind me.

"How long can you last?" he said with little more than a whisper.

"Long enough."

"Good. We wait for the leader."

"He isn't here?"

"*Her* spark's behind the oak to your right," Rae said.

I forced myself not to look.

A rustle through the fae, and with their bows still aimed at us, they dropped to one knee.

And...here's Johnny!

Their commander stepped in front of me. I hadn't seen her move. She was just...there.

Not Johnny, but Wonder Woman. She wore knee-high, lace-up combat boots over sprayed-on brown leather pants. Her gold bustier resembled WW's, but with a peplum that belled over her hips. Gold armbands climbed from her wrists to her elbows. Wow —she'd sure be a hit at a cosplay event. Her auburn hair, woven in braids atop her head, was capped by five-inch pearlescent horns that curved away from the crown of her head. The longest horns I'd yet to see, which I assumed reflected her position as commander.

She moved panther-like as she stalked toward us.

Cold silver eyes fastened on me like claws. She betrayed nothing, but I *felt* her pleasure when she couldn't probe my inner shields. Weird.

Her unpainted lips widened into a smile of gleaming white teeth and lethality.

Oh, no. Nonono. Awareness shot through me. I knew that smile, had seen its twin many a time on my grandmother Bernadette's face.

My mam was the troop's commander.

Gee, maybe she'd flay me now for killing her precious son. Or barbecue me later. *Hell.*

She stepped close enough to touch the fireflies draping my body. No acknowledgement. Nothing. In a blur of movement she fisted my scarf and pulled. My fireflies fell, bouncing on the earth like pingpong balls.

James arm snaked around my waist, and he shoved her hard with the other, flinging her backwards.

She shouted, "Hold your arrows!"

But one arrow flew true.

Melike screamed. Alex...falling to his knees, an arrow to the chest, blood staining the green parrots on his Hawaiian shirt.

I raced to Alex, feeling slow and clumsy as he slumped toward the ground, only to be caught by Rae. They became Michelangelo's Pietà, Alex draped over the mage's lap, one limp arm brushing the ground.

His heart. Had the arrow pierced his heart?

"Rae!" I screamed. "Heal him!"

His smoky eyes rose to mine. Moist, they held a grief I'd never seen before. "Can't. Their arrows... Can't."

I whirled on the fae, my fireflies a terrible thing as they poured from both palms. I would burn them, fry them, kill them all.

We can save him.

My mam's voice in my head.

With a reluctant twist of my hands, I halted my Flow mid-air and speared her with my eyes. "Is this your bullshit?"

No. I speak truth.

Should I trust her? Did I have a choice? I squeezed my fists, ending my Flow in a shower of falling stars.

"Do it, dammit!" I turned to kneel beside Alex and stroke his beloved face, the tanned skin now leached of color. James and Melike loomed over us, swords drawn.

You are an arrogant little pissant, daughter.

I jerked, giving the golden bitch a narrow-eyed glare.

She nodded to the large fae woman, who ran to us and dropped to one knee. Melike hissed, raising her sword.

The large fae woman grinned up at Melike. "I am Ozille, the chief healer. Just try it." Ozille turned back to Alex, her hands surrounding Alex's wound. They began to glow with an etherial blue-violet light. Face taut, the fae's eyes shuttered.

"Remove the arrow," she said in a lilting Southern voice.

Slow and sure, Rae drew the arrow from Alex's chest while the fae's steady blue-violet light pulsed. Blood welled, but the alpha wolf remained still as death, his long hair a river on the red-clay earth.

Ozille pressed her glowing hands atop the open wound. Blood oozed between her fingers. After endless minutes, the flow slowed. Was his heart ceasing to pump or was he healing?

The healer's dusky face grew as pale as Alex's, but she remained still.

Alex's eyes fluttered, but didn't open.

"Alex," I said. "We're here. Please stay with us."

"It's not workin'," the healer said. "Not healin' him. Not enough for him to survive." She expelled small pants of breath. "His shifter magic's different from ours. He's losin' too much blood." The healer cast a dark look at the woman I refused to call "mother."

"Maybe my fireflies..." I raised my hands.

Rae gently pressed his hands to mine and lowered them. "Not with fae magic in the wound."

My mother stood before us. "Let me take him. I can port to other healers who can give him what Ozille alone cannot."

I hesitated.

"I don't care if he lives or dies." My mam shrugged. "But you do, correct?" She stretched out her arms.

"Think on this, Commander," I said. "He is alpha of the Arctos pack. If he dies you will greatly regret the haste of your archer."

James lifted the unconscious Alex and transferred him to my mother, who held the taller man with ease. I wanted to protest, but James was right. We had to do this.

In a poof the golden bitch and Alex disappeared.

2

We followed the fae warriors down the road, winding through dense forest. As we neared what I guessed was the Fae Court, faint sounds of pipes sang in the distance. The gossamer melody held notes of James' and my song.

Here in faeland, my binding with James felt stronger, almost tactile. Though we walked side by side, it was as if our flesh touched, head to toe. Charlie had said our individual fae sparks were both of the Protector line–as opposed to the warrior or healer or others—which is why we'd mystically tethered so swiftly. Of course, we'd fallen in love, which helped.

The road spilled us into a halcyon meadow dotted with clumps of tall birches and tiny flowers of blue and red blooming amidst the impossibly green grass. Beneath the birches, lily of the valley clustered, their scent perfuming the air. The burbles of streams and the lowing of farm animals punctuated the distant piper's song, while a light breeze caressed our faces.

My worry for Alex and longing for Lulu rode me hard. Faeland was all too bucolic, and I wanted to scream.

The dirt drive narrowed to stone paths. We forked left, then left again, and soon began seeing other fae, most dressed in jeans or khakis, button downs or t-shirts. A few of the women wore flowy gowns and some of the men looked like they were dressed for a Renaissance Faire in tunics and leggings, swords belted to their waists.

My eyes scanned every face hoping I'd catch a glimpse of Lulu. No luck.

All of this passed like a surreal movie, while my mind carouselled with fear for Alex. The further we walked, the more the wood changed. Leaves on the birches now shimmered with silver and gold—some dotted with tiny white flowers—bringing to mind Lothlórien's wood. Mundane-world beech mingled with other-worldly copper-leaved and -barked trees that shadowed the path, as did the black-trunked pine with their periwinkle needles.

We'd walked what felt like miles.

"When will we get to our wolf?" James said, voice firm, betraying nothing of the seething anger that poured off him like flames.

The gaunt fae male who led us halted. "Shut up, abomination."

"*Connard*." Melike spat at the fae.

I pivoted to face him. "Don't you *dare* say that again. Ever."

James crossed his arms. And watched. And waited.

A sneer marred the fae male's face. "Or you'll do what?"

I smiled, a nasty one. "Wanna see?" I wiggled my fingers in front of his face, fireflies darting like tiny Tinkerbells. His eyes snagged on my golden index finger.

He bent at the waist to go eye to eye with me, his hatred icing the air.

"You stupid..." He abruptly straightened, eyes unfocused, as if listening to a voice only he could hear. Silence, his face trans-forming into that of a man who'd eaten a bucket of lemons. He bowed. "Apologies."

"To *him*," I said.

The fae's fists clenched, but he swiveled to James. Again, he bowed. "Apologies."

As he turned away, the gaunt fae's lip curled.

James snorted, and bent close. "Interesting man. Your challenge wasn't necessary."

"It was *very* necessary. I am not taking any of their fairy crap. Rae calls the fae uppity. He says they feel superior to the other magical races because their blood is so pure. What a crock."

The fae led us beneath a treed passageway with a twined canopy to a large tented building of wood and white silk. We passed through the open doorway into an airy room floored with dark wood decorated with silver runes. A blackened stone hearth stood to our left against a wall, fire blazing, and in front of us rested three finely netted bowers with more runes painted on the netting.

Golden light infused the room, warm and comforting.

An immense wolfhound padded over to Melike and sniffed. She reached out a hand to pet the dog, which snapped at her. Her returned growl flattened the dog's ears, and it dipped its head. An incongruous long-haired black-and-white chihuahua appeared at my feet, tongue lolling, mouth open in a happy grin. I crouched down to pet it, caught a whiff of eucalyptus, and the dog poofed into my lap. I set it down and stood, wary in the extreme.

A weight thumped on my shoulder, eucalyptus. When I probed, my fingers met silky fur. Okay. The little dog immediately began to lap my ear. I reached up and plucked the dog from my shoulder. "Rae?" I held out the dog to him.

He shook his head. *Ya'll nuts if you think I'm taking that thing.*

At a loss, I tucked the creature under my arm and turned to the gaunt fae. "Where's Alex?"

He pointed to the first bower, turned, and left along with his fellow warriors, just as Ozille stepped through the bower's curtains. At her somber expression, my blood froze.

She held up a hand. "He lives. For now."

"He *must* live," I said, and laid a hand on James arm. The damned little dog reappeared and leaned against my ankle. Beside me, Rae slung an arm around Neddy, while Melike stood white-lipped, her eyes haunted.

James cupped my chin. "He's too stubborn to die."

I nodded.

He stepped toward the fae healer.

Ozille took a step backward, fingers clenched on the curtain, mouth open, but gave him a tremulous smile.

Before James could respond, a haunting melody drifted from the bower.

"Our *Sangestre*," the healer said.

"What does that mean?" I said.

"Songstress. She's using her song to help heal him."

I didn't recognize the words. Gaelic? Celtic? Welsh? But the tune I knew well. The old Scottish ballad "Loch Lomond."

Remembering Lulu's haunting song hurt my heart. She'd sung it for me after I'd been injured by Tatianne in the magic realm. In English, of course. But this singer's transcendent quality was similar to Lulu's. Perhaps...

We all paused, a moment out of time. When the final note drifted into silence, we stepped through the curtained door.

My eyes locked on Alex, the breath leaving my body. He lay supine on the huge bed, far paler than his pale-gold hair that fanned across the covers. He was naked, but for the sheet draping his groin and legs. His cheeks were pink with fever, his unbandaged wound puckered and red.

Seeing him like this nearly undid me, and I dug my nails into my palms wishing for the pain to bolster my courage.

I glanced toward the singer, with the hope that she was Lulu, and glimpsed a swish of moonlit-silver hair leaving through the opposite curtained door. Disappointment collapsed my hope. Lulu's hair was copper colored, her frame shorter than the singer's. Then the bowered room held only our companions and Alex.

Damn. Melike stared down at her alpha, her dark-honey skin a sickly gray.

I notched my chin toward her and headed outdoors. She scrunched her forehead, but together we left the bower and walked into the wood. I halted about twenty-five yards away from the bower, beneath the canopy of golden birch.

"Let's sit," I said.

"What is all this, Clea?" She bristled with energy, a fierce warrior who was never still.

But she sat on the soft, loamy earth beside me. "I'm worried about you."

"Eh? No one worries about me. It's my job to worry about you and the others."

"Alex does. Worry about you, I mean."

She ran her hand over a tuft of psychedelic-green grass. "*Oui.* It's his job as alpha."

"It's more than that, and you know it." I held my friend's shoulders. "Stubborn woman. I see your eyes when you watch Alex. His injury is devastating you."

"*Oui.* He is more than my alpha. His kindness and strength when Paul was killed... Bah, the words come hard in English. He made both my boys little wolves out of clay. Years ago, when I had more trouble with my English, he found me a kind teacher with patience, something Carlos never had." She smiled, gesturing wildly with her hands. "One day I come home to find the three of them, Alex, Paul, and Bron, eating PB&J sandwiches. The kitchen was a wreck! He'd allowed the boys to make their own."

I grinned. "He can be a menace."

"He saved Carlos and me when we would have drowned after Paul... Yet now, I am powerless to help him."

"Your pack bonds—"

"Aren't enough!"

"But they still help. Let me smooth—"

"*Non.*" Her hand sliced the air. "I've watched you with others, and what you do is powerful. A good thing."

"Then why not?"

Her face tightened into a warrior's mask. "Because I *want* this pain. I need it. Alex deserves it as my alpha and my friend."

Melike's refusal might frustrate me, knowing I could ease her pain, but I got what she said. In her own way, she was honoring Alex. I couldn't dispute that. Nor did I want to.

WE'D SURROUNDED Alex for hours. We'd talked to him, petted him, even sung to him, although our voices couldn't compare to that of the songstress. They'd set up a table for us, brought in some hassocks and chairs, where James sprawled. All of us were hollow-eyed.

The man who'd become my friend, who'd saved me from the Cardillo, whose charm and surfer-guy persona masked an implacable will and a mighty heart, was dying.

His large frame appeared to shrink before our eyes, while his once-tanned skin grew sallow, his hands icy, his lips bloodless.

Healers came and went. The large, smiling chief healer, Ozille, again and again sent her healing magic into Alex with little success.

"The singer?" I said to her at one point.

Ozille frowned, snorted. "That one. But an angel's voice. She'll return, but not when you're around. She doesn't cotton to strangers."

Melike's drawn face found mine. "It's time."

I nodded and turned back to Ozille. "We need to speak to your queen."

She gave me a queer look, one between shock and curiosity. Then she honked out a laugh.

Gods, I thought all fae laughter tinkled or something.

"They are holdin' a banquet in your honor tonight," she said. "You'll see her then."

I glanced at the wolf. His jaw had tightened, lines of pain scored his forehead, his breathing shallow. I picked up his hand, now balled into a fist. "He's getting worse, isn't he?"

Ozille remained silent.

"Healer?" I said.

"Yes, ma'am. He is."

A ping. I descended onto a puffy hassock, folded my legs, closed my eyes. Knowledge spiraled through me, sinuous as curling smoke.

I gasped.

I stood, taking James' hand. "We'll be back, guys."

WE BRUSHED through the draped door, and the smell of eucalyptus tickled my nose as we entered the forest.

"And we're going where?" James said.

I shook my head to hush him.

Was it real? Yes. I clenched my belly, though the hum was more like a soft buzz draping my shoulders.

James slid his arm around my waist, and we walked beneath the birches, their leaves rustling as we passed. The strange little Chihuahua followed on our heels. A shifter? Gods knew.

A fat gray bunny hopped into our path, nose a-twitch. I smiled... until an arrow arced into its side.

A fae I didn't recognize, clad in jeans and a tie-dyed tee, stepped from the wood, plucked the arrow from the dead bunny, and lifted it by its ears.

His grin was wide, but his eyes held secrets, cruel ones. "Dinner." He eyed the Chihuahua.

I moved in front of the little dog. "Enjoy your meal."

When he loped off, I whooshed out a breath. "I don't like being here. Don't like these people. I guess it was too much to hope we'd be in and out, get Lulu and leave."

He tugged me over to a bench made of twigs and branches, with tendrils of those same branches curling to the floor of the wood and into the earth. So much beauty existed here, and so much cruelty.

When he sat, he pulled me onto his lap. "Clea mine, something's troubling you beside the wolf."

He spoke in a whisper, and I did the same, resting my hands on his shoulders. "It's *here*."

"*It?*"

I shook my head. "One of the remaining chests. It's here in this half-mundane/half-magic land. In fae." My mission as The Key was to recover the Five Chests of Unity. Only when they were returned to their guardians and reunited would the magical and mundane realms recombine in a smooth and orderly fashion. Now? Strange and chaotic Events were erupting around the world, and the chaos would only get worse. I'd recovered two chests, but the three others remained lost.

"Fire?" James said. "Time? Earth? Can you tell?"

"Hard, but Time is theirs. The faes'. It called, and that scares me."

"Because it called to you."

I jumped to my feet and paced. "No. They sometimes do, but that's not what's disturbing. The chests act differently in the magic realm, which is why I believe the council transferred them to the mundane one. Rae said that in the magic world, the Chest of Time's innate properties often alter its surroundings, things, people. What if—"

"We're not in the magic realm, Clea."

"No, but there's plenty of magic here. What if it changes me? You? Time itself?"

"You're The Key. Charged with reuniting them."

I plucked a blade of grass. "The fae haven't said a word about my being The Key, which is odd."

He nodded and began to speak, and I pressed a finger to his lips. The thread I followed confused me. "Maybe they don't know I'm The Key. And whoever has the chest, well, I doubt he or she knows the chests call to me."

"The damned things are frustrating as hell." James swiped a hand across his face. "This one could be a box. A spear. A fucking plant."

I picked up a rock clear as glass with orange crystals beneath its surface and smoothed my thumb across it over and over. Maybe even a rock. "They hide in plain sight. With a chest here and Alex so injured, Rae's three-day time limit is moot. My sensing the chest is way too coincidental."

His eyes gleamed. "Neither of us believes in coincidences."

"This changes things. I've kept my empath senses tamped down. I might be half fae, but I don't *want* to feel them."

"Then don't."

I straightened. "Of course I will."

He chuckled softly. "Must you always be so contrary?"

"Am not!" The laugh he barked when straight to my heart.

"What you're not, baby, is boring."

I scooched next to him on the bench, and he swung an arm around me. "Nor are you, Dragon Dude." I tucked my head against his shoulder. The whole idea of a chest here, *now* felt overwhelming. We *had* to get Lulu back and Alex healthy. Add in the chest and... "I'm just so damned sick of the stupid chests and my *mission*."

He captured my eyes with his. "Why do you constantly fight against it?"

"I don't." Except... "Well, maybe. I should be thrilled a chest is within easy reach. Instead, I'm pissed and frightened. Why, James?"

"Because you've never accepted your role."

"But I have. I..." I'd been given a job that mattered. The gathered chests would set the combining worlds to rights, save millions of lives, bring harmony to the natural world. "It all feels so abstract."

I snuggled closer. "I always imagined I'd live a small life, you know? A partner, a family, a home. Even working for the FBI wasn't that much. I was a cog in their machine. And then I met you, fell in love... Finding the chests is a Big Thing."

"You never wanted big, did you?"

"No."

He brushed my crazy hair away from my face, his hand butterfly gentle. "You're a warrior, Clea. Never forget that. You were made to battle big things."

I raised my head to scan that beloved face. He set my world in motion. I lifted my fingers and traced his lips, his cheeks, his scars. "*You* are what matters to me. You, my family, my friends."

"You'd die protecting me or them."

"I would." Keeping them safe from harm. Yeah, that wasn't working out so well. I rasped a laugh.

"What?"

"You." I kissed him, and lost myself in the joy of James, his lips, his tongue, his scent. When we parted... *Gods*, he looked at me with such love. How did I deserve that much love? Just being with him gave me joy. He saw me. All of me. Listened with intensity and focus. He was like that.

Finding words for the love I felt for him always eluded me. It was huge and complex, full of nooks and crannies I continued to discover. It was *everything*. If I could hide us away, I would. Except that would be letting him down, letting my friends down, people who had risked their lives for me and my mission.

"When Dave told you to 'acknowledge and accept,'" he said, "I suspect you did neither." His warm smile took the sting from his words.

Guilt flushed my cheeks. "I said the words, but I guess I didn't mean them."

"You've acknowledged," he said. "That much I know. But you haven't accepted, have you?"

"Perhaps not." My hands flapped. "Accepting is such a large thing. The fate of the world on my shoulders? I sound ridiculous. Me? I'm not—"

"You're everything you need to be, Clea."

"Am I? I feel inadequate and second best. Not up to the task. Not even *wanting* the task." I stared at my lap, almost afraid to look him in the eye. He'd see me as less, know I wasn't up to snuff.

He cupped my chin, raised my face, and captured my eyes with his. His granite-honied voice rumbled deep and low. "Yes, you are exactly who you're supposed to be for this task. You are protective and loving. Courageous and steadfast. Unlike me, you care about people. *All* people."

His eyes shined with truth. He believed it. He really believed I was *that* special.

His belief wove through me, and our song rose, the most exquisite feeling of pleasure and completeness in the world. I might be The Key, but James was the pivotal element I needed to see this through. To *accept*. In that moment, I knew with unremitting certainty that the mission was *mine*.

An overwhelming pulse throbbed through my body, and a geyser erupted from my toes to my head, making me dizzy. It rose through me—my flesh, my blood, my bones...my soul.

When I opened my eyes, the world was brighter, the sounds louder, the scents stronger. *I* was stronger. I sucked in a deep, cleansing breath. As always, I looked to James, whose eyes warmed and steadied me with their love and constancy. "Good thing I've got you by my side, mister."

"Always." He smiled, and I treasured each one.

"Remember the first time I called us partners?" I said.

"Of course. You were puking your brains out after eating—"

"Don't say it. That was *so* gross. Partners. Yes, we are. It's beautiful." I blushed. He was looking at me with that singular focus again, his laughing eyes turning hot and hungry.

He slid me back onto his lap, cradled my head between his hands, and took my lips with an intensity that stole my breath. James *always* stole my breath. His tongue delved deep, slow and leisurely, and mine answered. Time ceased to matter.

When we surfaced for air, his cock pressed against my bottom, and I was wet and restless and eager for him to be inside me. "Let's go—"

"Eyes, Clea." He nipped my lower lip. "Not here. Not now."

"Fine, Mr. Pragmatic."

"One of us has to be, baby."

He was correct, damn him. But I felt lighter. I'd owned finding the elusive chests and making the worlds *right*. His gorgeous black hair was wild and damp with sweat. I scraped a hand through it, pushing back the long locks from his forehead. "It's all good. And maybe someday we'll have that family, that white picket fence."

A look of horror skated across his face. "*That* I can't picture."

"You will."

"I don't even know if this nanoteched body can give you children."

"So? We'll work it out. We always do."

"Perhaps. I know that I would try."

Come quick, sugah. Rae, in my head. *We've got a problem.*

WE RAN, and when we neared the bower, shouts and swearing pelted the air. James flipped back the curtained doors and strode inside. "What?"

His bellow silenced the room.

Backs to us, Ozille held a spear at the ready, while two fae soldiers brandished swords. Our companions faced them. Neddy's jaw and hands had elongated, Melike's sword was raised, and Rae's fingers swirled with lethal black motes.

"What's going on?" James said.

Our companions stepped aside, revealing the empty bed.

I got very calm, my fireflies encircling my hands. "Ozille, where is Alex?"

"These idiots won't tell us shit," Rae said.

"*Where?*" James said, the word a command.

Ozille stumbled back, eyes wide. Then that blank look came over her, as if she were talking to someone in her head. "To the magic realm. We can heal him better—"

I got in her face. "That will kill him."

Her eyes narrowed. "It *won't.*"

"*Oui!*" Melike spat. "We Arctos have lived so many generations in the mundane world, we can no longer travel to the magic one without death."

Ozille's mouth became an O. "I can tell her! Wait." Ozille tilted her head, blinked rapidly. Her look was desperate when she caught my eyes. "She's not answering!"

I grabbed her shoulders. "So find her!"

WE RACED through the sylvan wood behind Ozille, up grassy knolls and down treed valleys. "Faster, you guys," I said, breathless. "Don't wait for me."

Rae and Ozille stuck with me, but James and the shifters raced ahead.

The air grew thinner, the magic stronger.

I hate the fuckin' fae, Rae said in my head. *They think they're the goddess's gift to the magic realm.*

James and the others were far in the distance as they zoomed up a hill peppered with birches and pine. At the top, something white lay on the ground of a grassy knoll. Alex. I could pick out soldiers and the commander in her WW costume. Did she not have any normal clothes?

The commander waved her arms, and a haloed nimbus grew behind her, surrounding what looked like the sun.

Oh, shit. James and the others weren't going to make it.

I ceased running, Rae jerked back to stay by my side, as did Ozille. "Wait!" My chest heaved, but I focused my mind, opened my shields. Went deep. Deeper still. *Stop!* I screeched. *Stop! You'll kill him!*

Atop the hill, the fae soldiers fell to their knees, as did Ozille beside us.

The commander kept waving her arms.

Rae and I ran.

3

My mental screech also brought Melike and Neddy to their knees, but James crested the hill in a blur of motion. The commander leapt in front of Alex's supine form, her fingers lengthening into saber-like claws.

From somewhere a song began, the woman's haunting melody gaining in power until she stepped onto the crest of the hill above us. Although too far away to make out her features, the silver hair and affecting voice told me she'd been the singer in Alex's bower. The fae's *Sangestre*. The kneeling fae soldiers stirred. Rae and I dipped downward into a hollow. My legs pumped with fury, earning me a stitch in my side. I couldn't see, *damnit*. When we finally raced out of the hollow, crucial moments had passed. On the hill's peak, the singer was gone and the golden bitch was throttling James, who now held Alex in his arms.

Shit!

We flew up the hill.

James' grin was feral, his face turning crimson. Red-gold smoke writhed around his feet.

"No!" I screamed. "James!" As I flew to them, I cast my fireflies, encompassing the commander, James, Alex, and myself in a protective bubble where her soldiers couldn't reach us.

Tremors shook James' frame, his neck tendons bowstring taut. He threw his head back and roared. Smoke cycloned around him, from legs to torso, until it encompassed him and Alex completely.

Oh, no no, no. "I'm here, James. Stay! Please *stay!*"

Two heartbeats, then three passed. The smoke dissipated, beginning with his very human work-booted feet.

I took a deep breath. He'd won. My *human* James stood cradling Alex's limp form.

Except my mother buried her claws deep into James' neck, rivulets of blood running down his throat and chest. "What *are* you?" Her face was ravenous, her silver eyes pulsing, her teeth elongated to fangs.

James had no options. He couldn't release Alex to get at my mother or he'd possibly kill the alpha.

If I tugged on her arms, she'd rip out James' throat. A human would already be dead from her assault. "Stop, damnit!" I punched her in the gut. "Taking Alex to the magic realm will kill him."

Her soldiers reacted, but my protective bubble kept them off us.

The commander stepped back, deliberately ripping those deadly claws from James' throat.

"James!"

He staggered, but remained standing. "I'll be okay."

What she'd done would have killed a mundane. Blood streamed from his neck down his shirt, painting it red. Tight lines bracketed his mouth, but he didn't falter. The blood flow was lessening, his torn flesh beginning to knit together. Keeping my fireflies going with one hand, I took James' handkerchief from his jeans pocket and dabbed at his throat. "What do you need? How can I help?"

"A mosquito bite."

"Drop the barrier," my mother commanded. "I vow we will not attack you."

A fool to believe her? No, she was done. For today at least. I clenched my fist, ending my fireflies.

My mam pivoted, clawed hands flashing inches from my face. "Whatever your creature is, he has no manners!"

Thank the heavens she had no clue about the wyvern. Gods knew what she'd do then. "Manners? Look who's talking. You stole Alex from the bower."

Her claws receded, and she fisted her hands on her hips. "I didn't *steal* him, foolish girl. I was trying to help him."

"You would have killed him."

"Like you killed my son?"

Shit. Now everyone knew she was my mam. I hadn't mentioned it because... Well, I just hadn't.

I gave her a one-fingered salute. "You mean my *twin*. Because he was about to kill us. I loved him, unlike you who abandoned both of us. Tommy became a *monster* under the thumb of that creature Tatianne. He murdered Dave Cochran, kidnapped Lulu, directed James' and my torture. And he killed your mother."

Horror skated across her face, and she crumpled.

Yeah, well, welcome to my world, lady.

She turned her back on me, hands dropping to her sides.

"Let's get out of here," I said to James and Rae as Melike and Neddy joined us.

My mam's shoulders straightened. She tilted her head, so her face was in profile. "My anger burns *hot*. Thomas may have been a monster, but he was *my* monster, *my* child. You ended him. You had no right."

My Tommy. I would remember him for always as he once was, his death a part of me forever. I took a long breath. "I had no choice."

The sun glinted off her armbands as she made a cutting motion. "His death is not something I choose to forget. Nor is it easy to forgive." With a wave to her soldiers, she stalked off.

We huddled around Alex.

James quirked an eyebrow. "Your *mother*?"

I shrugged. "Yep."

"Anything else you've 'forgotten' to tell us?"

My grimace wasn't pretty. "I don't think so." I ran a hand down his arm. "James?"

"I'll be fine, my Clea."

"Thanks to you, so will Alex," Melike said.

I cupped the alpha wolf's cheek and a thrill washed through me. He no longer burned fever hot. *Thank the gods.*

Rae completed the healing of James' throat wounds, took Alex from James, and poofed back to the bower.

"Handy, that," James said as we walked.

I threaded my fingers through his. "I've never been so glad of your nanoteched flesh as when dear old mom ripped half your throat out."

He squeezed my hand.

"You controlled the wyvern."

The muscles of his face tightened, jaw bunching, but he remained silent.

"I bet both of you wanted to eat my mother, though."

"We still do," he said, utterly without inflection. "But I doubt she'd taste very good."

My giggle was most undignified. "Trying to make me smile?"

"Perhaps."

"Um, did you *ask* the wyvern to emerge?"

"No."

The wyvern was gaining power. He'd started talking to James. Now, in this magical-mundane land, he could emerge on his own.

We left unspoken what that meant for the man I loved.

I bent over Alex's bed and ran a hand across his forehead. He looked better. His color had returned and his face was free from lines of pain.

The *Sangestre's* song was either helping to heal him or his shifter DNA was doing its work. Either way, Alex was getting better.

I finally allowed my tears of relief to fall.

An hour later, after we'd bathed away the day's adventures, we dressed in clothes provided by the fae. All except Melike, who proclaimed them disgusting, and Rae, who'd donned his own brand of crazy.

He was a *she*, something he/she did with regularity. An Asian woman this time, a sexy one who wore a tight-fitting cheongsam in red, matching Chinese slippers, and hipster spiky black hair and bangs. That would go over big with the fae. I, of course, loved it.

I wore a one-shouldered flowy thing in spring-bud-green chiffon and copper sandals, sadly without nail paint. Any minute I'd break into a Regency quadrille. James—towering and massive—looked delicious in his black tunic, belted at the waist where he'd hung one of his katanas. "Yum. Love how those tights show off your thighs."

He poked a finger under my nose. "Don't. They're legging things that tie. It was either these or the bloody jeans and shirt."

I sidled up to him, my voice smoky low, and said, "Maybe you should wear your leathers."

"You know well that I would if I could for tonight's little affair."

My fingers tiptoed up his leg to his ass, and rubbed.

"Behave," he said, voice a granite rumble.

But, ah, that twinkle in his eye. I squeezed his oh-so-beautiful butt. "Never."

He tugged me to him and swooped in for a kiss.

"No!" I pushed at his chest. "You'll wreck my makeup and dr—"

"You started it. I plan to finish it."

AMIDST REAPPLYING MAKEUP—*so* worth the mess we'd made of it—James loomed behind me. "Dragon Dude, we don't have time for—"

"Here." He held out his hand. A pair of gold Celtic-knot earrings with a dangling pale leaf-green stone nestled in his palm.

My heart stuttered, eyes burning. *Geesh*, tears would wreck my makeup yet again. James hadn't given me gifts. We hadn't had *time* for gifts. "Thank you," I said, voice watery.

I slipped them into my ears.

"They reminded me of your eyes." Hands on my shoulders, he leaned down to kiss the nape of my neck.

"They're beautiful. I'll treasure them."

"*You* are *my* treasure," he said.

I hugged him, pressed my face to his chest, inhaled deeply. I suspected this was our last moment of calm before the shitstorm we planned to unleash that night. We'd been told most of the fae community would be attending the banquet. If we didn't spot Lulu, we'd demand to see her. Once we spoke with her, and found the chest, she would return with us. Once she knew we'd come for her, she'd see how much she meant to us. She'd come home. She *would*.

DUSK LAY an ethereal cloak over this land of mingled magic and mundane. The air carried scents of juniper and gardenia and pine, the light like that of Scotland's gloaming, but enhanced by the fae glow-torches along the path. We arrived at a large wooden open-air building, winding living trees creating a branched canopy clothed in gold, silver, and copper leaves.

James walked beside me on my right, and to my left, the strange little dog kept pace. She could be a spy, a shifter, or simply an odd dog. I had no clue why she'd attached herself to me, as the wolfhound had to Melike, but her antics made me laugh.

I looked down at the little long-haired Chihuahua creature. "Why are you here?"

Her jaws opened, her tongue lolled out. She grinned.

"Really? Just don't poof onto my shoulder tonight. Got it?"

A yip, which I took as either a yes or a no-way. Which was as good as it was gonna get.

Neddy and Rae followed behind us, while Melike, accompanied by her wolfhound, took up the rear. She'd told me she wanted to keep the huge dog. Just what we needed.

A fae directed our group to a weapons depot bearing dozens of fae swords and long knives hanging from the wall. James seemed untroubled as he hung his katana beside a fae sword. I suspected he cared little since *he* was the weapon. Melike grumbled, but followed James' example. I didn't bother unstrapping my ankle knife. My long dress covered it, and it gave me confidence.

I wondered when I'd feel that way about my quirky fireflies, although lately they'd been behaving admirably.

We entered the hall, with a long aisle dividing two semi-circular banquet tables that faced each other, while at the far end, another semi-circular table took point. Most of the fae clustered in conversational groups, glow-torches illuminating their faces and burnishing the horns of those who bore them to a warm shimmer. Those tiny violet flowers I'd seen when we'd entered faeland carpeted the earth.

I kept my smile to myself. The hall looked like a stage set for *Lord of the Rings*. Then again, there were the dogs, the fae's horns, and my resurrected mother. Yeah, Tolkien had never envisioned *her*.

Conversation continued as our escort led us down the aisle, gesturing to the smaller round tables in the corners that held drinks and what I assumed were appetizers.

As if on cue, my stomach grumbled.

I remembered an old story, about how eating or drinking in fae compelled the person to remain in that land.

"Can we eat and drink?" I whispered in Rae's ear.

The fae leading us looked at me and winked, which told me his hearing was just fine.

Rae pursed her luscious red lips. "Y'all'll be okay." Her singsong voice hinted of laughter. "But I'd avoid the shrimp puffs. The fae do weird shit to them."

I poked her in the side. "Don't be a wiseass."

Her chuckle prompted several of the fae to stare, to which Rae replied with a sexy smile and swish of the hip.

Please let me survive the evening. My eagerness to leave this strange and alluring place was only trumped by my longing to find Lulu.

I didn't see my mam. Oh, but I was betting she'd appear wearing some sort of Wonder Woman outfit, her golden bustier polished to a high sheen. Most likely she'd be accompanied by her lieutenant, that stern gray-haired fae. I spotted Ozille, who waved at me. She was one of the few likable fae we'd encountered.

At some silent signal, the fae took their places at the long tables.

Our guide seated us at the head one, on one end, and soon the little dog nestled at my feet. I ducked my head and wagged a finger. "Remember to behave." The jaws opened, the tongue slipped out, but she stayed silent.

My palms caressed the velvet-smooth table. I'd always loved wood, and this solid piece of reddish burl, with its live edge, mellow sheen, and faint scars, spoke to me.

I leaned toward James on my left. "We should get a table like this for our house."

His eyes slammed into mine. "Our *house*?"

Shit. Nothing like foot-in-mouth disease. Our lives had been so filled with crazy, we'd rarely talked about our tomorrows, at least not normal ones. Now I'd done it twice in one day. "I, um…"

The tinkling of a thousand bells cut off our conversation. Everyone in the hall rose, so our group followed suit.

Oh, goody. A parade.

All dressed to the nines, what I supposed were the fae nobility entered from a side door. I was sure I'd see my mother, obviously a higher-up in the fae pecking order.

The gray-haired gaunt man entered first, along with others I didn't recognize. Then came a tall young woman wearing a long black dress with a trumpet skirt, emerald gems studding the silver hair piled atop her head. Her hair really was *silver*—less a color than a precious metal. The singer. Each entrant stood behind a chair. Another woman entered, older than the singer, and how I knew that confounded me. The fae aged so slowly it was hard to tell their true years. I sucked in a breath. She wore a diaphanous red gown, her impossibly long black hair banded by a single white lock that framed her exquisitely beautiful face. Cruella, or so I'd called her as a child, didn't have that white streak in her hair back then. Boy, was that old nickname prescient. I almost laughed aloud. She was Dave's missing wife. Lulu's mother. When I'd known her, her hair hid her pointy fae ears. Not tonight.

Which made me wonder why only *some* fae ears were pointed.

I hadn't seen her in twenty-something years, yet she looked the same—like my mam, a woman in her mid-thirties. Her true age? Incalculable.

Her eyes locked on mine, venom-soaked and deadly.

Nope, Maurelle hadn't changed one bit. I grinned, one of those Jack Nicholson crazy ones that said we had scores to settle.

She jerked, and I widened my smile as she took her place behind a chair at the table.

Behind her, the final person in the processional entered—Charlie! He'd provided James with his fae spark and betrayed us to Tatianne. He'd also saved us from that monster, twice, and had given me the fae knives in order to end my brother's life. He was as capricious as the winds, and yet I couldn't help but like the damned fae.

As Charlie walked, he limped, his right leg stiff. When he raised his eyes to mine, he winked. Curse that rascal, I'd almost laughed out loud.

The procession ended, and when Charlie took his place behind his chair, all the fae raised their voices in a harmony of notes, much like a chant.

So where was the golden...

Oh, no. No, please, no. *Shit. Shit. Shit.*

My mam glided across the hall, her white gown shimmering with golden threads, her chignoned hair studded with diamonds. Another huge diamond rested on her forehead. I'd swear it mocked me.

Viviane, my mother. An impossible sea of emotion washed over me. The woman who'd abandoned me—who'd let me believe she was dead—was the freaking fae *queen*.

The little dog sitting at my feet yipped.

WE ATE some flowers-and-mousse concoction for dessert—okay, so it tasted delish, but my temper rose with each spoonful. My mam hadn't looked at me once during the meal. Charlie had, plenty, and I'd even spotted Cruella and the gaunt fae sneaking peeks. But dear old Viviane? Nothing.

Maybe she was still pissed that I'd given her the finger.

I tossed my spoon aside and stood. So did the singer, so I abruptly sat back down. She raised her arms, palms up, and sang a wordless tune that set my inner fae spark humming.

A sylvan meadow. Trees with barks of silver. A grassy verge painted with purple and gold. A taste of the sea. The sea. The sea. Waves crashed, foamy with brine, against rocks night-black and jagged.

A bower, where two lovers entwined. James. Me. We radiated light. Copper tears streamed from my eyes onto the downy grass.

A shadow above us. Dark. Fierce.

The swooping of colossal wings.

Anger. Hatred.

I reached to pluck it from the sky.

Talons bit into my skin. Pain. Blood.

I screamed.

Flesh warm in my hand, hot breath on my face. "Clea."

I blinked a couple times to find James staring at me, my hand gripped in his. "Oh."

His eyes surveyed the room, his face taciturn and deadly. I followed his gaze.

Swell. All of the fae were staring at me.

I did a finger wave, not knowing what else to do.

"What did *you* see?" I whispered to him.

"The hills of Montana." Longing filled his voice. "I was galloping on a huge roan with wild eyes. I was *on* the horse, but I saw through the horse's eyes, too, with you riding alongside me on a paint."

"Sure wasn't what I saw."

"What—"

"No." I rose. "Screw this. I'm tired of waiting for the queen." I stormed over to her seat at the table's center, James at my back. He always had my back.

I stood beside her, foot tapping, and waited while she ignored me to finish the last of her mousse thing. She didn't bother to look up, but I caught the two fae soldiers who'd raised their bows, arrows nocked.

I sweetened my voice and projected so it would reach the entirety of the hall. "Hello, *Mam*. Or should I call you, Queen Mam?"

Murmurs through the crowd.

She carefully set her spoon aside and stood. Bernadette's hazel eyes peered back at me. We were of a height, both shrimpy. I sort of liked that. I donned a sad face and quoted the wyvern. "You haven't called, haven't written."

She stretched out her arm and her index finger bayonetted James. "First, get rid of the thing."

I made a point of stabbing right back at her with my gold metaled one. "We're a package, Mam."

Her "nasty face," as I'd termed it as a child, tightened her skin. She pursed her lips. "Still reckless and disobedient, I see."

"The gifts of free thought and encouragement come courtesy of Da. You remember Da, right? You left him, too."

Her eyes turned bleak, which she swiftly masked with derision. "You always turned to your father."

"He loved me."

"Love has many forms, daughter."

"So it does." I took a breath. Now shouldn't be about my mother and me. "I don't want to fight. We're here for Lulu. Where is she?"

A hint of discomfort slipped through her shields. She waved the archers away and did the same to the host of fae diners. "Go!" In seconds the hall cleared but for the head table. Melike, Neddy, and Rae moved to stand beside James, while the fae at the head table assembled behind their queen.

All we needed was the chime of a bell and a free-for-all would commence.

"Lulu?" I said to my mother.

My mother nodded. "You've seen her."

"No, I haven't."

"Yes," someone said, voice smoother than satin.

My mam's eyes traveled to the singer. "You have."

Impossible. Lulu was sixteen, her hair copper-colored. The singer's silver hair glowed like the element itself. But... I took a step toward her. I hadn't been this close to the singer before or seen her face so clearly. Lips of ruby. Pale skin, finely boned, a few freckles. Tall. Maybe five-foot-ten or -eleven. High cheekbones beneath angry eyes that...

Those eyes. Those glorious violet eyes.

My bones liquified, but I bucked it up. I walked forward until I was inches from the *Sangestre*, and I caught the singular bubblegum and cashmere scent that was Lulu.

My eyes traced the adult Lulu's face. "But you can't be—"

She dipped her head, an oddly regal gesture. "I am, Clea."

Murmurs from my companions even as my world topsy-turvied. Absurd. *Days* ago I'd been with sixteen-year-old Lulu. This woman was at least twenty-four.

My eyes lied. They *had* to lie.

But she wore Lu's face, matured by years and, I suspected, hardship. It was a honed face of great beauty, the freckles across the bridge of her nose bringing a burn to my eyes.

Cruella moved to the singer's side and took her hand.

The girl...the woman, Lulu, shrugged off her mother and stepped closer. "You didn't *come* for me, Clea."

"But we did." I opened my empath senses wide. And there she was. My Lu. My ward. And she churned with a toxic mixture of anger and hurt.

"But..." I reached for her. "But we did come. We *did*."

She looked down her nose at me, stared at my hand until I dropped it.

"Don't *ever* touch me again."

JAMES and I sat in the living room of the queen's home. As we'd entered, I'd glimpsed the stately reception room with its throne of gold and silver living trees. We'd been seated across from each other, on one of the leather chairs and a sofa, which sat atop Persian-style rugs. A fireplace commanded one end of the room, while an incongruous flat-screen dominated the opposite wall. The room was warm and inviting, with bookshelves lining one wall, sconces lending a soft glow to the wood paneling.

I took it all in, cataloguing, my dazed mind failing to process my deeper thoughts. James hadn't said a word, his stoic mask firmly in place.

What was there to say? My mother was queen. Lulu was an adult. What did that all mean?

The queen had dismissed Melike, Rae, and Neddy, along with the rest of her entourage, except for Lulu, Cruella and Charlie. I'd drawn the line at James, and so he'd stayed, much to my dear mam's disgust.

I'd never understand why so many judged him an abomination or monster before getting to know him. The wolves had once done it, though that perception had changed, and now the fae were reacting the same way. Their smallness and prejudice disgusted me, with their knee-jerk reactions to someone they didn't understand. Why was the unfamiliar so frightening to them?

At least the wolves had a valid misconception of his monstrosity. The fae? Nothing justified their feelings.

At some point, coffee and a liqueur that looked like golden light had been delivered, but thoughts of Lulu, the *new* Lulu, so distracted me I had no idea when.

The queen, Charlie, Cruella, and the silver-hair woman entered the room. That could not be our Lulu. Yet she was. How to comprehend the incomprehensible?

James remained silent, watching, waiting, preparing for gods-knew-what.

Where had the teenaged girl I'd known mere days ago gone? Feeling a horrible kind of desperation, I rummaged in the pack I'd had a fae attendant retrieve, stood, and handed Lulu Blue Monkey. "I thought... I thought you'd like to have him."

Lulu's eyes blazed, and that fury was oh-so familiar. She ripped Blue Monkey from my hands and hugged him. Then she gave me teeth. "You left me here for *ten years*. You didn't come. You didn't *care*. Why have you come after all this time?"

"Ten years," I whispered.

"I barely survived." She stole a glance at Viviane. "If it hadn't been for the queen, I would have withered and died."

She still liked drama, for sure. "Lulu, I—"

"You think I want to hear it *now*? After all this time? Go away."

I forced calm and warmth into my voice. "Lulu, please listen."

"Get out." She didn't scream, didn't shout, her voice a low harmonic sizzle of rage. "As soon as Alex is healed, you will leave."

WHY HADN'T I FOUGHT? Why hadn't I insisted she listen? Why hadn't I demanded answers about her aging? It was all a blur as we'd left without a word. Now we sat around Alex's bed. He might be pale, but he was awake and sitting up. James had given the others details of our brief convo at the queen's home, while I raked my hands through hair I wanted to rip from my head.

I stopped. "Holy moly." I pulled a lock of hair in front of my face. "My dreads are gone." I examined another hunk. Long, loose blond curls spiraled from my scalp. "This place is nuts."

Alex wheezed. "I'll second that."

"No denying we've got a consensus," Rae said, once again a black male in jeans and a tee.

The bower's flaps moved. So did James, katana in hand. Ozille stepped inside, and he lowered his blade, but didn't re-sheath it. Her fear tasted sour, yet low notes of empathy meandered beneath, along with a few grace notes of anger.

She held her hands before James in a placating gesture. "Don't cut off the messenger's head, please."

A rumble low in his throat, but he said no words. In fact, he'd said almost nothing since the banquet.

"What do you want, Ozille?" I said.

"The singer needs to work on the shifter." Her eyes darted between me and James. "She wants all of you to leave."

"The *singer*," I ground out, "is my ward. We're not leaving."

She shrugged and turned toward the entrance, muttering, "That's what I told her. But would she listen? No. Of course not."

I fisted my hands. "I don't understand. I don't. How could she age *ten* years?"

"I've been cookin' some ideas, sugah," Rae said.

Melike whirled on him. "Stop cooking and share, you annoying mage."

He grinned. "Yeah, that's me. I need to see Lulu. Smell her."

Lulu glided into the room. Even in jeans and a peach t-shirt, she held herself like a princess, head high, shoulders back. "No one is smelling me, Rae." Her eyes found mine, then locked onto each person in the room. "Now get out. All of you."

That was it. I was done. "You know, you're acting like a real bitch, Lu. Whatever happened, whatever changed you, we're sorry. We *came* for you mere *days* after we defeated Tatianne and Tommy." I leaned forward, got in her face. "You will show us some respect."

Her look transformed to a guilty one reminiscent of the teen, the one we all cared about, the girl we loved, the girl we'd die for.

It hardened all too quickly. "You don't deserve my respect."

My vision went nuclear, and my hands shot out to shake some damned sense into her.

I was swept off my feet and hauled out of the bower.

4

The five of us sat beneath the starry blanket at a round table alive with vines and leaves the color of English ivy. I plucked at a leaf, focusing on its slubby texture. Lulu's song haunted the air, and the beauty made it hard to keep my anger close.

Neddy huddled on the bench beside me. I held his hand, an attempt to reassure the boy that all would be well.

"Being here," he said. "Um, am I going to age fast?"

"Nope," Rae said. "I've been here a time or two. Even brought a mundane friend once. Nothin' happened, age-wise at least." His grin was lascivious.

Relief washed over Neddy's face. "Good thing. I want to play ball in college."

"So tell us your thoughts on Lulu." James directed his request at Rae.

The mage stroked his chin. "Yeah, yeah. I've got a theory." Pause.

Melike slapped the table. "*Mon dieux!* You with the drama."

Rae's laugh grated. "Stop pitchin' a hissy fit, wolf."

Gurrr. "Please, Rae," I said.

"Darlin', I've been ponderin'—"

James fisted Rae's shirt and lifted the mage five feet off the ground. "Now."

Rae swallowed. "You know I can turn y'all into a porcupine, right?"

A laugh burst from James, and he set Rae down. "Christ, Rae, get on with it."

"All right. All right." He flapped his hand. "Don't want to get that dragon's knickers in a twist."

James crossed his arms.

The mage leaned forward. "See, this idea I've got, it's a strange one. It takes craft, and not in a good way. You feel me?"

I waved for him to speed it up.

"If someone took Lulu to the magic world, well, time there is fluid. Not all the same streams, if you get my drift." He stretched out his arms, made a wavy motion. "The magic world's different from the mundane when it comes to time."

Neddy snorted. "Yeah, time and everything else in it."

"Point taken, now hush," Rae said. "See, different time streams flow there. Not everywhere. Only in certain parts, mind you. Why, I remember when —"

"*Rae*," I said.

"A person's got to know where these streams flow and how to use 'em. They're not easy to find, though sometimes they find you. But if Lulu lived inside one of those streams for years, then returned here, well, time coulda flowed by there, but not here. I'm thinkin' that's what happened, y'all."

"But what about her hair?" I said.

Rae tugged on his lip. "If she handled the chest, and it's the Chest of Time, that could change her, too. Age her faster, make her younger, older, change her hair, her body. You met Maurelle as a kid, right? Does she look older to you? Is anything different about her?"

I might have been young, but I remembered her well. "She doesn't look older, but that white streak in her hair is new. Maybe that's from the chest, too."

"Could be," Rae said.

Melike's hands fisted. "*Merde*. If our Lulu was in the magic realm for ten years, whoever took her there robbed her."

"Yes," I said. "But why doesn't Lulu know that?"

The quiet startled me. Lulu's song had ended.

"I'll be right back," I said. "Stay here and don't interfere." I raced back to the bower. Dammit, Lulu *would* listen to me. I would make her believe how we'd come for her right away. She'd been cheated, and I had a good idea who'd done that to her.

I FLEW into the room to see Lulu's palms on Alex's shoulders as she struggled to hold him down.

"You will *not* get up, mister," she said.

Alex's hands banded her forearms and pushed. She flew across the room, landing on her butt.

"Alex!" I said.

He whipped off the covers. "No one fucking tells me what I will or won't do." He stood, in all his naked glory. And it *was* glorious. Holy shit.

His chest bellowed and he reached for one of the posts to steady himself. His glowing gold eyes lanced Lulu, who'd gotten to her feet and was brushing herself off.

"No one," Alex said, the alpha resonating in his voice.

She slapped her hands on her hips. "You're still the same pain in the ass, Alex."

His grin was of the demonic variety.

"Why you shitty—"

"Stop it!" I said. "Both of you!"

Their eyes flew to me. Then Alex's eyes rolled back in his head and he thudded to the floor.

Well, *hell*.

Lulu and I stared down at the unconscious man. The very beautiful unconscious man, whose muscled chest and other *parts* faced us.

"Think he hit his head?" I said.

"Wouldn't hurt him," she said. "He's too block headed." She peered around the room. "So where's James? He can lift Alex easy."

I looked over my shoulder, shrugged. "I told everyone else to stay put. C'mon, I'll take his shoulders. You get his feet."

I hefted Alex's shoulders, trying not to look at his man bits. "One."

"He's big!" Lulu looked down, then her eyes darted to me, cheeks aflame.

"Two."

"Maybe this is a bad idea," she said.

"We can't leave him on the floor."

She bit her lower lip. "He has really long...toes."

"Toes, huh? Focus, Lu."

She nodded.

"Three!"

We surged upward. Except I wavered, his shoulders like a bag of rocks. Lulu wobbled. Alex's head tipped to the side, as did his lower appendage. Lulu giggled, which set me off, and we teetered.

We went down in a tangle of naked man legs and arms. We laughed, which was horrible, awful. And hilarious.

"He would kill us if he were conscious," Lulu said, said between hiccoughing guffaws.

I wiped tears from my cheeks. "Tear us to shreds with those claws and teeth."

"A-yup. He *is* beautiful. Gorgeous." She sighed. "He's like sunshine, y'know. A good guy, someone you can count on. And fierce!" She rolled her eyes. "He could be such a pain when he'd tell me what to do. Except I pretty much worshipped him."

"He was kind to you. And patient."

"Boy, were you pissed when he taught me to surf."

"I wasn't pissed, I was—"

"Scared?"

I held up a hand. "Guilty as charged."

Her eyes wandered to Alex, his blond scruff now an almost-beard. She sighed. "I bet he's a player."

"He really isn't like that, Lu."

"No? But he always seemed so..." Her brows scrunched together. "What about with you? He was pretty obsessed."

I laughed. "Once, maybe. When James returned, things changed. Fortunately, we're only friends now, dear friends, but nothing more."

"I bet James would have something juicy to say about that."

"Oh, he's fine with our friendship."

She laughed, her eyes bubbling with disbelief. "No way."

"You're so much like me," I said, pointing a finger at her. "Contrary to the bone. And you're wrong."

"Am not."

Which got us giggling again.

"C'mon," I said, resuming my former position at Alex's shoulders. "If the others find us like this, we'll never live it down."

That got her moving.

"One," I said. "Two. Three."

We managed to swing Alex up and onto the bed's edge. Then we pushed, straightened him up. Lulu pulled the sheet to his waist, while I finger combed his hair.

I surveyed our handiwork. The wolf looked near angelic.

Lulu bowed backward, stretching. "Killer."

"Yeah." I walked over to the table holding wine and poured a glass.

"Hey, how about me?" Lulu said.

But she was... No, she wasn't sixteen anymore. "I was about to offer."

We sat across from each other in chairs that flanked the table, both flushed, hair a-tangle.

"To achieved objectives." I raised my glass.

She went to do the same, halted. "You left me here, in this strange place for so long."

I held that violet gaze and hung on. "Please. Give me five minutes."

Her lips thinned, but she nodded.

"We left the Arctos compound three *days* ago, just a few days after I obtained the Chest of Stone."

The muscle in her jaw tightened.

"Five minutes," I repeated. "Three days ago. Which was four days after you ran away."

Her spine stiffened, and she gestured at herself in a "ta da" motion. "Does this look like four days ago?"

"No, it doesn't. Think about this, the fae are long lived. They age slowly. But if you left faeland to visit the mundane world, *our* mundane world, you'd see I spoke the truth."

She leaned forward. "That's some impossible bullshit you're spouting."

"Really?" I said, voice deadpanned.

Her head tilted in a move so reminiscent of her father, my throat closed. Then her face hardened. "*No.* I spent nine long years searching for something for *you.*"

"Why? Why did you do that?"

"You'll see. And I hated it. *Hated* it! We traipsed around the magic realm. Jeepers, talk about weird. These things called gollups got wind of us. No idea how." She took a swig of wine. "They're obsessive creatures, never giving up until they're dead. They were horrible, awful looking, with talons for fingers and gross long nails like razors. They're oily and black and evil. They wanted to devour us and..." Her face lit up. "I got kickass at archery. You should see."

"I'd like to."

"Mother's spells worked okay to keep them away from us. Mostly. She spelled my arrows, too, which helped." She picked at one of her already-ragged fingernails. "But she'd go off and leave me alone to deal with them, and everything else that came at us."

Now it was my turn for a deep pull on my wine. How had teenaged Lulu coped? Obviously she had, but at what price?

Another sip, then, "The years passed. Long ones. Boring. No movies or TV or video games. No friends. Just Mother and me." She shot me a look, brow furrowed. A splash of sunlight caressed her face, and I realized her brows had retained their copper color and darkened to ruby.

"Lu?"

She rested her chin on her fisted hand. "Mother isn't a very nice person."

I almost blurted out agreement.

"She'd get abusive. Hit me. Call me horrible things. Mean things. Is it wrong not to like your mother?"

I barely heard her words through my fury. How *dare* Maurelle hurt my Lu. I was going to...

"Is it wrong, Clea?"

I rubbed my fingers across the back of her hand. "Oh, sweetie, no, not if that person is cruel and abusive." I was so incensed at Cruella, I looked away so Lulu wouldn't see my fury. Hummm. What would my mam do if I eviscerated Maurelle?

Lulu finger-tapped my head, and I turned to see her bright, fake smile. "It wasn't all bad. Sometimes we'd stay in a village within our search area, and that was cool. A few were really primitive, but others felt more like our mundane realm, even having some electronics and stuff, like..." She giggled. "One woman had a vacuum cleaner she'd gotten from our world. It was old, like from the '50s, and she had this setup I didn't get that generated electricity to run the thing. The vacuum was pink!"

"Pink?"

"Yup." She sighed. "I was missing college, I knew I was, so I'd go to the village library and read and read and read. Some of the books made no sense to me, others were written in languages I didn't understand, but a bunch were in English, and my fractured French, as Melike likes to call it, came in handy, too. It's odd, but a lot of the magic realm's languages seem to match up with the ones in the mundane." She blew a loose strand of hair out of her eyes. "Anyhoo,

I learned a little about magic, and a ton about literature and math, even some science. Well, bio, really. The best part, some of the village singers would teach me. A few were amazing. My song magic evolved. It grew a lot."

"So did you, dear Lu. I'm so proud of you. You turned an awful situation into a positive."

Her eyes drifted downward, her voice small. "I did it for *you*. But you never came."

She sounded sixteen again, and so very sad. I wanted to ask her about the chest, her hair. But all I could think of was Lu's suffering. I knocked back half the glass of a damned fine merlot. How to get through to her about the time slippage without taking her out of faeland? *Of course.* My gears finally clicked into sync. "*Geesh*, Lu, look at Neddy."

Amidst raising her wine glass, she paused, a few droplets splashing on the table. "Neddy?"

I dabbed them up with a tissue. "How *old* is Neddy?"

She stared at me as if I'd sprouted two heads. "I don't know!"

"Remember when you went on a date with him?"

"Some date. Yeah, I remember. Ancient history."

"We adults haven't changed much. But that makes sense. Adults don't age the way kids do. When you left Arctos, which was ten years ago *to you*, Neddy was sixteen. *Neddy is still sixteen*. He looks the same as when you left. If I was lying, he'd be the same age as you, twenty-six."

Her face blanched, freckles standing out in stark relief.

"He's the same age, kiddo, as when you last saw him. When *we* left the compound to come after you, *three days ago*."

"No." She shook her head, voice roughened, tears glistening her eyes.

The old Lulu would have let them fall. Not this woman.

"Yes," I said.

"*Yes*," came Alex's voice, strong and alpha sure.

Lulu's wine glass fell to the floor and shattered. With a desolate look at Alex and me, she fled.

Moments later, James, Rae, Melike and Neddy crowded inside the bower.

James came up behind me and laid a hand on my shoulder.

I placed my hand on his. "Hey."

"That was illuminating, baby."

"Poor Lu," I said.

He leaned close and whispered in my ear. "Yes, but she'll recover. Not so sure Arctos would if he knew of your shenanigans.

"You *heard*?"

"And saw." Melike wiggled her brows.

James brushed my ear with his lips. "The Clea, Lulu, and Alex show."

I whipped around. "You're telling me you guys watched!"

Rae giggled. "I was so distracted, I almost peed my jeans."

I wagged a finger at them. "I can't believe you guys didn't help."

"My friend, you told us not to interfere," Melike said, eyes twinkling.

A rumble from Alex. "What the hell are you guys yapping about?"

I narrowed my eyes at each and every one of them, then looked to Alex. "Nothing. You feeling better?"

"Yeah," Alex said. "So you and Little Miss Princess were—"

"Don't call her that." I held in my temper, poorly. Gurrr. "Her dear mother took her on an *ex*-plore, as Pooh would say, to find something for *me*. Now what little treasure could that be?"

James sat and pulled me onto his lap. We didn't usually go in for public displays, but he was warm and large, and I drew comfort from the circle of his arms.

The rest of the gang sat around the table, while Alex turned on his side to face us, his head resting on his palm.

Rae cupped his chin. "Sugah, it's obvious."

"*Non*, it's *not* obvious," Melike said.

"Get on with it, Rae," Alex said, voice a raspy growl.

"One of the remaining chests."

A cool wind brushed around me. It spoke of primeval forests

and jagged peaks, of skies filled with dragons and a sea cruised by leviathans, of the time before time, when the world was young and the Queen of All ruled. My vision misted. I saw a hexagonal prism of light take shape, scored with runes carved by magic into the sides and top.

Neddy tilted his head. "I thought only Clea could find the chests."

"No," I said, my voice oddly dreamy. "Anyone can find them. But I'm the only one who can reveal their true natures and activate them." I blinked. "Lulu has found the Chest of Time."

WE DIDN'T SEE Lulu again that night, nor did we try to pursue her. She needed space, and at least we could give her that. The following morning, I snuck out of the hut where we were staying. I wanted to talk to Lulu on my own. Except I ended up trooping across fae whateverland accompanied by James, who stuck to me like a tick.

We easily found Lulu's house, one made of living trees. I kept wondering if the threaded branches of birch and beech were also home to spiders and other unappealing critters.

"She's here," I said to James.

"You know this because...?"

"Hard to explain. Over the missing ten years, Lulu's essence changed. Earlier, when I sensed the singer, I didn't realize it was Lu. But now that I've identified the essence as hers, I can sense her. I'll go in. Just me, okay?"

"Not okay," James said.

"*Fine*," I said, his bossiness making me petulant.

James and I walked across the threshold into a single large room. Lu sat crosslegged on her bed in jeans and a T-shirt, headphones on her head, body bopping, book opened in front of her. Along with the bed, the room included a pin-neat kitchenette, two worn comfy chairs, and not much else. A smallish flat screen sat across from the bed playing a music video, minus the sound, which I suspected was because most fae would find Judas Priest anathema.

Lulu's pose, the music, both made it hard to believe she *wasn't* sixteen years old anymore. My heart stuttered, reminded of how she'd once been. Now, she was this odd combination of poised woman and hipster teen.

James was a dark shadow, his banked anger hot and smoldering. He wanted to get Lulu and the chest and leave, pronto.

My feelings were the same. Our time spent in the vicinity of my mother served to remind me of the chasm that separated us. Had she mourned her mother's passing? Given a thought of what it had done to me? Had she even missed me for all our years apart?

I didn't know. Didn't want to know, either. Right. Too bad I couldn't sell that lie to myself.

As evidenced by her actions, my mam was one cold, autocratic bitch.

Lu was apparently oblivious to our presence, so I raised my voice to penetrate the headphones. "Lulu!"

She threw them off and stared at me wide eyed. "By Oona's crown, you scared me shitless." Her smile was quick and sweet. "Hi, James."

He tipped his head, frowning. "Lulu."

"You're pissed at me," she said.

"You hurt Clea," he said.

Lulu nodded. "Perhaps, but she's tough."

A dart of pain. I might be tough in some ways, but I was sure a mush in others.

James said nothing, but his anger simmered a little hotter.

Since no chairs were offered, I plopped on the edge of the bed. "We're here to—"

"Stuff it." She lifted the remote to switch off the TV. "I know why you're here, and I don't have it."

A few fireflies swarmed my fisted hands. "What I was going to say was we'd like you to come home with us." Why hadn't her mother, or mine for that matter, told Lu the mundane world had only aged three days?

Her finger twirled one of her long silver locks, another gesture reminiscent of the copper-haired teen. Except four days ago, her hair had been dyed and cropped short. This was so messed up.

"Will you come home?" I said.

She shrugged. "Probably not."

"You like it here?"

Her eyes fizzed with anger. "It's okay. My mom's here. And Aunt Viviane."

"*Aunt* Viviane?"

"Hello? Mom's the queen's sister."

Gobsmacked. The only word for what I was feeling. "Cruella is my mother's sister?"

She folded her hands on her lap and widened her eyes. "Quick, aren't you. And her name is Maurelle, for your information."

She'd always be Cruella to me. "I don't need your sarcasm." I took a deep breath. "Do you feel you belong here, Lu?"

Her pale, long-fingered hands twined together. "Yes."

It didn't take an empath to hear her hesitation. "Everyone wants you to come home. The mutts miss you. So do Ronan and Calico Kitty and Gracie. All the wolves. James. Most especially, me. We love you."

She smirked. "You're just saying that so I'll tell you where *it* is. You're full of shit." She tugged a hank of hair. "How do you think I got this? We'd been in the magic realm nine years. But once I touched the thing, my hair changed, my boobs got bigger, and so did my ass!"

Ouch. "You're still slim as a reed. What about your mother's white streak?"

"While I held the thing, she touched the chest with one frigging finger." She scowled.

And I just bet Maurelle knew the properties of the chest, too, which was why she didn't handle it. She had a lot to answer for.

From the corner where he'd been a dark wraith, James stepped into the light that fell from the window. "Clea's sick at heart, Lulu. So cut the act and be straight with us. Why are you so bent on remaining here?"

Lulu had trouble looking at him. He'd saved her life. Hell, I'd saved her life. But in her world, that was many years in the past.

She clutched Blue Monkey to her belly. "All right. I promised Mother if she let me help her retrieve the chest, I'd stay here with her."

My hand gripped hers, and even though she tried to shake it off, I hung on. "Dammit, Lu, she can't make you stay."

"Oh, yeah, she can. And anyway, I won't break my word."

Her freckled face tightened with apparent resolution. But her eyes, those gorgeous violet-blue eyes, darkened with pain and desire. Oh, she wanted to come home all right.

"Sometimes, our words need breaking," I said. "Come with us."

Spine stiff, she said, "I made a vow."

"To a crazy woman who's manipulating you."

"She's my mom." Her chin tipped up. "Anyway, I made my promise when Aunt Viv was there. Mother told me it's binding."

Screw that. We'd just have to un-bind it.

SOFT LIGHT FILTERED into the medical bower where we'd set up camp, having moved all our stuff from the hut we'd been given. A fae suggested we return to our digs, but Alex still needed the bower's healers and we wanted to stay together. We'd respectfully declined.

I kicked one of the pallets the fae had laid for us on the floor. And, yes, they were fine, comfortable even. But I had to take out my anger on something.

Lulu *would* return with us. The poor kid...woman...must be hurting so bad. She'd been deceived by those she trusted. If I thought too hard on it, I'd strangle them. We also needed to find the chest. So I'd walked to my mother's palace to talk to her. I'd been refused admittance by her fae guard. Nice. After much back and forthing through one of her minions, she'd agreed to see me the following morning.

Extra nice.

After all these years apart, I couldn't believe I needed to make a frickin' appointment with my godsdamned mother. An *appointment!*

I paced. I brooded. I swore.

At least Alex slept peacefully in the bed, oblivious to my fury. Melike, Rae and Neddy had vacated the premises when they saw the volcano brewing inside me. James sprawled in the chair by Alex's bed reading, calmly waiting for my temper to simmer down.

Every time we left the bower, the fae looked at us like we were aliens. I'd even seen a fae start to draw his sword, which was when James had a chat with him. A few were kind, including Ozille, but we *had* to get Lulu and the chest out of there, and we had to do it *now*.

James cleared his throat. "You think your fury has to do with Lulu and the chest?"

"Isn't it obvious?"

His index finger traced the long white scar on his face. "Nope."

I slapped my hands to my hips. "Really?"

A lip twitch. "Really."

How dare he sit there legs sprawled, utterly relaxed? I took a deep breath. "What's that supposed to mean, Mr. Cryptic?"

He wrapped his hands around my waist and pulled me forward between his legs. A singular eyebrow arched.

I sighed and plopped my butt onto his thigh. "You gonna tell me or play guessing games?"

He remained silent, but his vibe screamed patience. He was so damnably patient sometimes.

I leaned forward for a kiss.

"Clea," he said, drawing my name out in a way that said no kissing until I talked.

"Fine!" And now I sounded like a sulky Lulu. Shit. "Okay, Mr. Shrink-ola. Yeah, so maybe my feelings *might* have something to do with my mam's abandonment."

He nodded.

I scraped a hand through my long curls. Stupid curls. Which I wanted to cut except my hair grew faster than weeds. Which sucked. Everything sucked. "I can't see her clearly, you know, not from back then. But my head and my heart tell me my mam wasn't unkind. But she was a hardass. Maybe it was because I expressed as a mage, like my da, and not fae, like her. Whatever. Although I can't see much about those years, my feelings of never measuring up to her standards of excellence are crystal clear."

"You hurt."

"Like Lu said, I'm tough."

"Yeah? I don't see the tough Clea—only the whiny one."

I leapt off his lap. "Damnit, James."

"The tough Clea *thinks*. You've got all this anger and resentment inside you. So why did she leave?"

"I was told she and my da died in a car accident. And, yes, eventually I knew Da had most definitely died in a different way."

I pictured his death and shivered.

He leaned forward, elbows on knees. "You saw the goblin rip his head from his body."

I sure-as-shit had. I'd held his head, for gods' sake, and at three years old I'd commenced to destroy the goblin, my father's remains, and our house in one fireflied burst. Except I hadn't remembered that wee "incident" for twenty-something years. When Dave fully reawakened my magic, the memories had started to trickle in. Strange memories. Funny ones. Horrible ones.

At the time I'd been too busy finding a killer to think about what had become of my mother after the fictional car accident. Everything about my past was messed up. Hell, I'd thought my beloved Tommy was simply my foster sibling, not my frigging twin.

I flopped onto the floor and crossed my legs. "I guess I need to talk to her, don't I? And I don't mean about the other stuff, but about us, about her and me, and why she left."

In one large stride he was on me. He lifted me off the floor and slung me over his shoulder.

"What the fu—"

"I'm not making love to my woman with the wolf sleeping near-by." His long strides ate up the ground.

"Who says I'm up for it?"

He shook with laughter. "Aren't you, baby?"

Of course he was right.

5

W ith me still slung over James' shoulder, he paused before an immense live oak, its Spanish moss swaying in the soft breeze. "Hang tight," he said, and he began to climb.

"Wait. What?"

"A surprise."

Yikes, he'd gone all caveman on me.

As he climbed, the tree's majestic branches waved in a sinuous dance, while the cascades of moss played peek-a-boo with the late afternoon light. I felt a little drunk.

He climbed and climbed.

"This isn't a good idea," I said, wheezing through a diaphragm compressed by his shoulder.

"Sure it is."

"The moss has chiggers, James. Put me down. C'mon."

He didn't.

"They're these mites or something. And they bite and make you itch. Stop it, now!"

He didn't.

"I'm not making this up. They're red and disgusting. I read about them in one of those Charleston magazines. Put me down now."

He dropped me to my feet, and his eyes, those gorgeous eyes, held a wild light. I could drown in them and die happy. His mouth slid into a fierce grin. Where were we? On a tree branch? Floating in air? I didn't care.

I stood on tiptoe and slid my hands up his chest. He was so tall, for me to kiss him, he'd have to bow his head. He always did. For me.

Our kiss was a hot pressing of lips, swirling of tongues, clinking of teeth, we were so hungry for each other. Impossible to ever get enough. Our song surged around us, through us, a divine double helix of otherworldly musical notes that built and built.

He nibbled his way down my neck, the feel of his soft lips sending shivers along my spine. One large hand slipped beneath my shirt, my bra, and he ripped them over my head and tossed them. His hands covered my breasts. My head fell back, reeling at his warm, firm strokes, the scrape of his callouses heightening my pleasure. He took my lips again, plucked my nipple, and I rubbed my crotch against his hardened cock. I wanted to free the hard length of him from his jeans and suck.

His eyes captured mine. He didn't say a word, but his love poured into me like a raging river. With care, he set his own weapons aside. He dropped to one knee, unbuttoning, unzipping my jeans, and tugged them with my panties down my legs, not bothering with the knife sheathed at my ankle.

Oh, gods, here? Now? But I wanted his warm, clever tongue on me so much.

He pressed his face close and inhaled, then parted my nether lips. I scraped one hand through his hair, my other clung to his shoulder and held me upright.

Touch me, touch me.

My beautiful man. My beautiful love.

His tongue flicked out and I moaned.

This was part of who we were, our hearts so engaged it threaded through our love making as the sweetest ache, our song notes of golden honey.

Tongue pressing harder, faster, fingers delving inside me, flicking and...oh, gods, he suckled my clit, my knees wobbling, pleasure a slowly building geyser. My hands squeezed, clawed, I ached to touch all of him.

More. Faster. Yes! Oh, James.

I panted as he brought me down slowly. When I opened my eyes, he stood naked above me, his proud cock glistening with moisture. He tossed my jeans away, and I leaned up, but he pushed me down and covered me, his warm flesh fitting me perfectly. His tense face a mask of purpose, muscles bunched, velvet-covered steel, he slowly eased into me. A sob broke from my lips.

He was my home. My safety. My passion. My love. A man so complex that each day with him became infinitely more fascinating and intense.

I wrapped my legs around his hips and squeezed him tight, his slow moves increasing the after-pleasure of my orgasm.

He rested his forehead on mine. "You are my light in the long dark night of life. You give me far more than I should take, but I take it anyway because you make me a stronger, a better man. I wandered so long in a bleak world devoid of joy."

The pace of his hips increased, and a sweet ache again built in my belly and groin.

Tears burned, sliding across my temples. "James, I—"

A finger to my lips hushed me. He continued to move, sliding in and out of me faster, building our pleasure.

His face tightened. "I can't make your world perfect, but I can travel it with you every step, every breath, every heartbeat. Clea mine. Clea mine."

He pistoned into me, electrifying every cell of my body. His moans mingled with mine, the sweetness of our pleasure incalculable. He dipped his head, suckling, nipping my breast.

Almost there, almost there.

"Beloved," I say.

Our song burst forth, my climax rocketing through me, around me.

With a shout of release, James threw back his head, neck tendons strained, muscles clenched, and he pumped once, twice, thrice more.

He collapsed on top of me, and I reveled in his weight. Sweat greased our bodies, his dripping from his hair. He lifted, but I held him to me.

"Too heavy," he said between pants.

"No. Perfect." I combed my fingers through that beautiful hair. The promise on his face squeezed my heart, and I curled my arms around his shoulders, nestling my head in the curve of his neck.

"For you, all my forevers, James."

"And mine for you, Clea."

In the not-far-enough distance, someone cleared their throat. James stiffened, and not in the good way, and the realization that I was abruptly lifted aloft in his arms didn't surprise me. Our mating had a way of blocking out reality.

Another throat clearing.

James set me on the wooden platform built over two sturdy branches of the live oak. The smooth boards held a couple of jewel-colored pillows, a soft nest of blankets, a bucket holding a bottle of wine. James melted me all over again.

"This is perfect." I smiled up at him.

He most definitely wasn't smiling. "I'll be right back." He pulled on his jeans.

"We've got a problem down yonder," came the voice from the base of the tree.

Rae. Gods, he had the worst timing in the world.

"What the hell do you want?" James said, peering over a branch.

"Don't y'all take that attitude with me."

"I'll take any fucking attitude I feel like. What's the problem?"

"Neddy got into a fight with some fae kid. He went all Pinky. Didn't hurt the kid, but y'all know what he looks like when his Pinky erupts. Now he's in a cell and they won't be letting him out anytime soon. You feel me?"

I'd gotten dressed while James talked. I tossed him his shirt and handed him his weapons. He wrapped an arm around my waist and leapt. We almost landed on Rae, who stumbled back, tripped over a branch, and fell on his butt. "If I wasn't so worried about Neddy, I'd fry yo' ass."

James smirked. "You could try."

He offered Rae a hand up, and the mage took it, leapt to his feet, and brushed himself off.

"How did you find us?" I said.

Rae plucked at his lower lip, but his smoky eyes held unholy laughter. "Oh, I don't know. Maybe it's because you broadcast yo' song to every fae in this place that you two's doin' it."

My mouth fell open. "No."

"I heard it myself, sugah, so I just followed the music."

JAMES, Rae, and I ran down another forested path while the sun dipped low on the horizon. After we'd checked on Alex, Melike keeping watch, the three of us were headed to the fae prison.

As our feet ate up the acres, the forest darkened. The leaves blackened and curled, falling to the earth like spent embers. The clack of branches, the skitter of creatures, the shapes of shadows—a malevolent miasma that clung to my skin. I fisted my hands and ran faster.

A damp chill brushed my cheek. Sounds became muffled the closer we got to the prison. A boggy stench wove beneath the land's sweet, gentle smell, the scents reminding me of when I'd been attacked by the Cardillo. The earth took on a soggy texture, as if we might sink through its pores.

I shivered, tossed it off, refusing to allow the faeland's theatrics to rattle me. We weren't in the magic world. The fae only had so much power over the earth here in this magic-mundane realm, and while they could harm me, it wouldn't be with spooky tricks.

James jerked to a halt, wrapped an arm around my waist, and pulled me close. He peered down at me. "You're cold. You good, babe?"

I leaned into his shoulder. "I am."

Except for this latest disaster with Neddy. The kid had been through so much. Changed into a Pinky thing by Rolf's demented scheme, he'd come back to us as a boy, which was wonderful. But he'd lost his wolf form to that of the Pinky—a monstrous seven-foot-tall creature of shiny pink skin dappled with wolf fur and immense jaws filled with equally huge teeth—who wasn't quite sane.

We'd stopped at the edge of the trees. Before us in a clearing stood a hut built of sturdy wood, windowless and tiny. A guard sat outside the hut eating a sandwich. He put it down when we stepped into the clearing.

The guard rose, and James moved forward. "You have my boy inside. Why?"

Two more soldiers appeared from the wood, carrying swords and wearing jeans and t-shirts. Of course they knew we'd come, but I so wasn't up for a major confrontation. At least until we got Lulu and the chest.

I finally realized what bugged me so much about the fae. Few were kind and many were narcissistic and self-important. My least favorite kind of people.

A third man appeared, the gaunt-faced fae with those commanding brown eyes and an obvious dislike of our group. He nodded to us. "Let me introduce myself. I'm Commander Iron Heart, and I'm afraid your creature has broken several laws of our land, thus he'll remain incarcerated until you depart."

James crossed his arms. "Exactly what laws?"

"He initiated a conflict with one of our young."

Rae stiffened. "No, Commander, I must demur. He did not."

Leave it to Rae to lose the Southern speak for that of a Federal judge on the bench.

Iron Heart scanned Rae from the bottoms of his flip-flopped feet to the top of his orange-and-brown dashiki. The fae's lip curled. "He did."

I stretched my empath senses and read the group. The gaunt

fae's disdain was a piece of cake, but the simmering fear that ran beneath the other three surprised me. They were ready to go off on us with their swords. Yet Iron Heart seemed almost lackadaisical.

James did that, too, just before he pulverized somebody. When we'd met on the road into the fae court, Iron Heart had seen what we could do, knew we could take these men and him, and retrieve Neddy.

But not without shedding blood.

James' eyes glittered, but his voice was calm when he spoke to the commander. "Were you there?"

"No." His eyes shuttered. "But I received a full report."

James notched his head toward Rae. "*He* was. Your kid started it. Goaded him. Threw the first punch."

The leader's slow smile taunted us. "You are here in our land, by our sufferance. We take our people's word over strangers, who tend to lie effusively."

"We don't lie." James scraped a hand down his scar. "We'll see him now."

The fae nodded, all faux serious. The bastard was gleeful that we'd given up so easily. Yet my senses told me his caution remained, as did the jagged edges of his disdain.

With a wave of his hand, he led us to the hut, handed James a flashlight, and opened the plain wood door.

When we stepped inside, the door closed and darkness surrounded us. No light, no sound, no sensory cues of any sort. The fetid room was suffocating, with a deathly blackness so profound, my flesh goosebumped.

The click of James' phone, and a light illuminated walls of raw boards and a dirt floor.

A deep ululating growl echoed around the room.

"Neddy?" I said.

The sound of chittering, a Pinky's chittering.

James' light swept the tiny room. We spotted Neddy-Pinky, and walked to the boy-creature huddled in the corner.

Ropes of drool dripped from his elongated Pinky jaws, and he glistened with sweat. Black-clawed feet and hands which could rip out a spine were trembling now. Bruises darkened his muzzle, as well as a cut above one eye. The chittering sound escalated.

This wasn't a jail, but a sensory deprivation cell, which they were using to torture a sixteen-year-old kid.

James handed me the phone. He remained standing, but turned to face what I assumed was the door. Rae and I kneeled before Neddy beaming the light on him, but not so close it would blind him.

Immensely larger than in his human form, Neddy was over seven feet of muscle, teeth, and claws. He'd fisted his fingers around the claw and tooth that hung on a leather cord from his neck.

"Neddy, it'll be okay." I reached out a hand to stroke that terrifying head.

He snapped at me, which I prayed was more reflexive than dangerous. I snatched back my hand. His maw opened, jaws widening, drool dripping from his purple tongue, to reveal rows of gleaming teeth. Spiky teeth. Gigantic teeth. Oh, boy. Neddy's growl purred across the room.

I captured those leaf-green eyes, their color so like mine, as I wrestled down my anger at what the fae had done to him, and projected warmth and safety.

Neddy's jaws widened further. His lips curled back from his distended muzzle. "Neddy, it's us. Rae. James. We're all here for you."

"What y'all doin', kid?" Rae said.

They were good friends, pals. The boy's eyes moved to the mage. Neddy's head darted forward, jaws swiping at Rae's throat.

Rae scooted back.

I held out my hand and stroked Neddy's immense one with the tips of my fingers. His head swiveled to mine. Low growls reverberated from his throat. We were eye to eye, his aggressive with fury and fear.

I moved my fingers up and down his hand, gently, in a soothing way that complemented the warmth and love I was pouring into him.

Neddy's black-clawed hands opened and closed. A dollop of drool landed on my thigh.

A creak. The door. As if to open.

Shit!

I whirled the light, caught Rae's motes pressed against the door to keep it shut.

"We're not done here." James' granite voice boomed through the room.

"Come out." The disembodied fae voice barked an order. "Now!"

"We're not done." James stepped closer to Neddy and me.

"Ten more minutes," the fae said. "Then we blow the hut wide open."

I returned my focus to Neddy. Too much time was passing. The hut smelled of sweat and fear, the air thick and cloying and still. We had to get him out of that awful place or he might get trapped in his Pinky form.

James crouched in front of Neddy, who snapped at him, too. He wrapped his arms around Neddy and gripped him tight.

"James!" My shout rattled the walls.

Maybe that's what saved him, my yell so startling Neddy-Pinky that he didn't bite through James' neck.

"You're safe, kid." James' voice was granite hard and filled with command. "We won't leave without you. Got it? Come back to us."

The boy's body shook, and James held on tight amidst Neddy's growls and fae shouts from outside.

"Neddy, please," I said. "We love you. We need you."

James pushed on the boy's shoulders, held them tight, and peered into Neddy's eyes. "Come back to us."

"Five more minutes!" shouted someone through the door.

"Shut yo' pie hole," Rae barked.

Neddy sniffed James' neck, his shoulder, his hair. A whine. Then he looked up at me. "Cle-ahhh."

I shuddered. "Yes, Neddy, it's Clea. And James and Rae."

"Cle-ahhh."

"Are you ready to leave here?"

He nodded.

James leaned back on his haunches, but kept his hands on Neddy's shoulders. "Good."

I smiled. "We're ready to leave, too."

James' large hand gripped the boy's muzzle, eyes laser bright. "To do that, you have to change back to Neddy."

The boy closed his eyes...and nothing happened.

The noise, the smell, the tension, Neddy's fear—all were contributing to his inability to transform. Corralling the boy's gaze, I delved deep inside myself, spiraling down to find the soul place where my magic lived. A fire that didn't burn, a light that didn't sear, a place connected to that genetic harmony that made me mage. I raised my hands and gently poured fireflies onto Neddy.

"Do it, Neddy," James said. "Change now."

Smoke rose in the beam of the phone's light, and I released my fireflies, leaned back, and watched in awe, as I did each time a shifter went from animal to human.

James stood and backed up a step.

Within the whirling smoke, light pulsed inside the leaf-green of Neddy's eyes, flickering bright inside that smoky barrier and accompanied by Neddy's scent of neatsfoot oil and cherry.

The breath I'd been holding whooshed out of me.

And there he was—a brown-haired sixteen-year-old in dirtied and ripped jeans, a bloodied t-shirt, and workboots. His face was scraped, his jaw swollen, and his eyes...haunted.

"Oh, sweetie." I pulled him to me, hugged him hard. He rested his head on my shoulder and sighed.

"Y'all havin' an emo moment." Rae squeezed Neddy's shoulder.

"Let's go," James said.

A bolt slamming shut. "Out of time!" said Iron Heart's disembodied voice. "The queen has commanded you remain until the Lady arrives to release you. She will then decide the pink creature's fate."

"I'm... I'm sorry," Neddy said. "I didn't mean—"

"We know." Rae clenched his fist, his motes dissolving. "It's all good."

"Damn her," I said. "James?"

Outside, the fae had quieted.

James reached for the door. It didn't budge. "This is a bad idea," he said through the heavy wood.

Silence answered his shouted words.

Neddy grabbed my hand. "You...you're taking me with you...right?"

"Always."

"Open the door or suffer the consequences." Again James' bellow shook the walls.

Silence. The door didn't move.

Rae snorted. "Fucking fae." He raised his hands, palms out. "This is a pain in my ass."

Black motes of fury erupted from his hands, sparking with rainbow colors as they attacked the door.

And fell like chips of obsidian to the ground.

Rae swore. "They warded the door. Should'a thought about that. Those fairies probably warded the whole damned hut."

"Let's see." I unleashed my fireflies on a wall. They lit the ten-by-ten room as they formed the labyrinth stitch, a thick heavy weave that arrowed to the wall on my right. They met the same fate as Rae's motes.

James backed to the far wall, and hands in front of him he ran straight into the opposing wall. The place shook as if it were made of paper. The walls didn't budge.

"Takes a nuclear amount of power to break those wards." Rae frowned. "They're all waitin' for old queenie."

James squeezed Neddy's shoulder. "We're not, are we, kid?"

Neddy dug his hands into his pockets. "Um, I guess not."

James laughed, and his eyes boiled with the same demonic glee when he charged into battle. *No, no, no.*

Rae snickered. "Never show a fae your weakness."

"Not helping, Rae."

The phone's light winked out.

Eager to see you, my Clea. The wyvern's voice.

Oh, shit! The wyvern had initiated our dialogue. In my head.

I wrapped my hands around James' bicep, his skin already boiling with heat. "Don't do this."

"Do you see any other way?" he said.

I liked the wyvern. A lot. But I feared his desire was to subsume James. He was immensely powerful and so...other. I kept imagining losing him to the wyvern. Ridiculous, and yet it felt true down to my bones. Losing Dave and Bernadette, even Tommy, tore holes in my heart that would never fully mend. Losing James... Unthinkable. There had to be another way. I leaned my head against his chest. Choices. We had few. Wait for my mam? When hell froze over.

On tiptoe, I pulled James' head toward mine. My kiss held all my love and trust, and he answered fully. When we broke apart, I said, "Whatever you want to do, I'm with you."

He chuckled. "Good. Unless you're willing to spend the next hundred years in this box waiting on the queen." He kissed my forehead. "Neddy. Rae. Get beside Clea."

I shook the flashlight, and it blinked back on. After Neddy and Rae complied, I beamed the light on James. "Where should we stand?"

"Back up until you hit the wall. He won't hurt you, Clea."

I wasn't worried about *me*. We moved to the wall and waited.

James rasped out a breath. "He's frustrated. Say the words, Clea."

Which gave me a small surcease from worry.

I went fast and deep, so deep into James... And there he was, the red-gold beast. Already roused, he blinked, twice. I held those glittering green-gold eyes. *Now, wyvern. I command it. Now.*

My mind flew out of James, and I rocked back on my heels.

In the faint beam of light, it began.

Red-gold smoke swirled until it obscured him. The column rose high to the ceiling, curled forward until... A roar.

The hut's boards rippled outward, the ground beneath our feet atremble, and the roof flew off.

Green flame shot upward from the dissipating smoke.

My gods. The wyvern's glow seared the room, his light near blinding me, his pulses of magic melting over my skin. His long sinuous neck scraped along the ground, curling back around a red-gold body bristling with three-foot-long spikes down his spine. His rounded scales glistened.

We were pressed against the wall, but still the wyvern's immensity shoved at us, broiling hot. His neck undulated like a snake's until his triangular head wove back around to point directly at me, eyes aflame with anger.

"Hello, wyvern."

My Clea. They've tried to confine us in this imprisoning space. Fools.

I pet the ridge between the two golden horns projecting backward from his head. "I know. Idiots."

You appear worn down.

"I've had better days."

Rae's mouth was agape, while Neddy's shocked eyes saucered at seeing the wyvern for the first time.

"Wyvern," I said. "How about we vacate this joint?"

His laughter held the arrogance of a creature who knew he was *the* apex predator. *Don't move. Please craft one of those impenetrable shields you do.*

"Oh, right." I'd forgotten. In the presence of the wyvern, I forgot most everything.

I fireflied a shield, not a great one given my exhaustion, but it would protect our mortal flesh.

That's better.

Then the wyvern raised his immense head and flamed the place to cinders.

Long moments passed until the sparking dust particles finally settled. It was all that remained of Neddy's prison, and, apparently, the fae wards.

What have you done!

Not the wyvern. Nope. That was mommy dearest, in all her glorious bitchery.

Don't you dare blame us! I thought at her.

Naturally, she didn't answer, and I had no idea if she had heard me or not.

The smoke dissipated. At last we could see the glittering stars above us, the gibbous moon, the crystalline night. Neddy's happiness at his freedom washed over me, and a rightness settled. Before us stood the wyvern—fifteen feet high, twenty feet long, eyes bright with smug satisfaction. His chest bellowed in and out, and each exhale sent a puff of warm smoke into the night air.

He was a creature I no more understood than I did the stars above. An ancient being of beauty and terror and mystery whose life had been stolen by The Union and who somehow existed within the flesh of the man I loved.

What I did know was that he had needs and desires, and only with reluctance would he return James to himself.

"Yes, my friend." I bowed with a flourish. "You are a badass."

I am.

"Now what?" Rae said.

Good question. Should I ask the wyvern to return James or not? Which aspect of James would deal better with my mother, who I was sure was hightailing it over here?

The glade where the hut had stood was empty of fae. They must have fled at the wyvern's explosion. I sent a prayer to the gods than none had been harmed.

The wyvern would antagonize the queen, I didn't doubt. She'd be furious he'd entered her realm. She'd be afraid, too, as well as concerned for her subjects. He could defeat the fae, but at what cost?

If James were James, he wouldn't provoke my mam, not the way the wyvern would, with his peculiar, mercurial nature. He'd also discovered snark and innuendo, which, given his arrogance, was not a good thing.

I inched closer to his supernova heat. "Can I touch you or will I burn?"

His internal laughter disconcerted me. *You will not burn. At least, not that way.*

Gods. "Would you like a scratch?" Oh, shit. I hadn't meant it to sound like that.

He chuckled. *Of course.*

Dip your head.

He did as asked, and I scratched behind his horns.

James?

As I've said before, he is with me, and I, with him.

Don't go there. Please.

"You two." Rae walked over wagging a finger. "Y'all chit-chattin' on your own bandwidth? Havin' a tea party or what, sugah?"

The wyvern's head snapped around, muzzle raised with a growl. His nostrils puffed smoke into Rae's face.

Fire will be next, for that one.

"Let me handle this, Rae," I said over my shoulder. *Wyvern, I need James to return.*

He rested his head on the ground and puffed out a smoky breath. *Clea. You know how much I relish this form.*

I sat beside his head and leaned into him, touched his muzzle. *I do, and you are beautiful, powerful. But it will be best if James returns before my mother arrives.*

Do not imagine I don't know what you dread.

I forced my eyes not to look away, kept my hands on those beautiful, silken scales. *Is it justified?*

When the magic and the mundane complete the transition, you and I will be together, and we will fly.

Fear spiraled to my core. *Now... I need James now. Please, wyvern.*

It shall be done. Stand back.

I herded Rae and Neddy to the tree line as red-gold smoke rose from his clawed feet to tornado his gargantuan frame. Just before it enclosed his proud head, he winked. *See you soon, my Clea.*

I wrapped my arms around my waist in an effort to stop shaking.

Moonlight bathed the clearing as the smoke dissipated. James stood before us, wearing the same jeans and t-shirt as before.

I ran forward and leapt into his arms.

He swayed catching me. "What was *that*?"

I nuzzled his neck. "Me. Happy you're back."

He shook his head like an awakening animal. "What a fucking ride, looking out eyes fifteen feet in the air."

I clung to him like a monkey. "Do you remember any of it?"

"Bits. Pieces." He took my lips hard and fast. I wove my fingers through his hair, giddy with his return.

"Guys?" Neddy said.

James squeezed me tight, then released me. My legs dropped to the ground, but he kept one arm around me, firm, solid, there. He was there, I was happy, and my mam could go screw herself.

The little black-and-white dog padded into the clearing, looked around, and poofed onto my shoulder.

"What are you doing here?" I said to the creature.

She licked my cheek, probably getting a mouthful of ash in the process.

"Y'all, that pompous ass of a queen is on her way." Rae stepped to Neddy, slung an arm over the kid's shoulder.

I started when two shadows emerged from the wood to join our group. "Melike! Alex!"

Melike notched her chin toward Rae. "That mage got in our heads and called us. As if we were his to command. Bah!"

Before I could comment, a phalanx of fae walked into the glade.

Our group faced them—James and I in the center, Rae and Neddy to our left, Alex and Melike on our right.

My mother stepped forward, flanked by Iron Heart, Lulu, and Maurelle, who held Lulu's hand.

"You haven't changed, daughter." She scanned the clearing, left to right. "Still crafting chaos."

I nodded, smiled. "Finally, a compliment from my mother."

Her horns gleamed in the moonlight as she tilted her head.

"Bringing a wyvern and that pink thing into my domain is anathema."

The little dog growled. So did Alex.

"I should kill you all." She tapped a finger to her lips.

Was I crazy or was that humor in my mam's eyes?

James' fierce grin summed up our sentiments.

"But I will not, considering my daughter is The Key. But it's time for your ragamuffin band to leave."

"Not without Lulu." James' gave her teeth, then he actually winked at my mam. "Or the chest."

She stepped forward and flung out her gauntleted arm toward James. "*You*. You will not transform to the wyvern again while in my domain."

He was getting ready to throw some shade. I squeezed his hand.

"I will not," he said. "But you will give us the chest and allow Lulu to leave fae."

My mother nodded, but her eyes burned with fury. "But of course."

Whoa. *What?*

6

Charlie the fae awaited us when we reconvened in the queen's living room, my mam nowhere in sight. James insisted on moving the sofa so its back faced the wall, and we sat, the persistent chihuahua between us. I'd tried to leave the dratted dog in the clearing, but she kept poofing back onto my shoulder.

Neddy and Alex slouched in two chairs, while Rae and Melike stood sentinel flanking the sofa.

Lulu and Charlie sat to the left of the queen's empty chair, which held court beside the blazing fireplace, the focal point of the room. Lulu scanned the room, her face sober.

Melike caught Lulu's eye and growled. "How can you stand this place?"

Lu grinned. "It grows on you. Like warts."

"More like hives," Alex said.

Lulu huffed. "What's wrong with warts?"

Melike leaned down and whispered in my ear. "They are like comic relief, *non*?"

"*Oui!*" I replied.

I tried to catch Charlie's eyes, but he refused to look at me.

How would my mam present us with the Chest of Time? What

did it look like? How would it affect me? And would she simply let us walk out of her realm with both the chest and Lulu? My skin itched with suspicion.

The doors yawned open.

Let the games begin.

Iron Heart preceded his queen into the room and stood beside the empty chair. The queen nodded to him, then sat, a tall and straight woman with an imperious presence. Apparently Maurelle wasn't coming, for which I was thankful.

One fae guard closed the double doors, and the pair stood legs akimbo in front of them.

We were quite the group, bubbling with animosity and other unpleasant emotions. So where was the chest?

Viviane surveyed her "guests," the room hushed. When her eyes bored into Neddy's, disgust hardened her features.

Yeah, I'd had it with her prejudice. "You're so predictable, Mam. Kindness would serve you better than cruelty."

Contempt filled her eyes. "You've quite a collection of abominations."

I forced my face into pleasant lines. "I'm drawn to unique individuals. Kindness and character are my barometers. As they were Da's. Can we lose the posturing and get on with our business?"

Woman's up to somethin'. Rae's voice in my head, loud and clear. I nodded.

A knock, and the doors opened. In waltzed Maurelle, face smug. She wore a black velvet pants suit and carried a foot-high, matching velvet-covered something in her arms.

She crossed the room and handed the package to Viviane.

The Chest of Time. I noted how she wore gloves. Yeah—in case the chest might change her in this half-magic land. Hypocrite.

As with the other two chests I'd recovered, this one would mask its identity until I touched it. Oddly, the Chest had grown silent. I had no sense of what my mother now held. But already I ached to touch it, to feel it with my flesh, to see if they'd actually found the real deal.

My mam drew back the velvet to reveal a beautiful sweetgrass basket. Perhaps eighteen inches in diameter, its rounded sides met a split handle that joined to form a perfect arc above the open basket.

Baskets fascinated me, and this one was no different. Stunning. The coiled baskets were a famous Lowcountry craft, the tradition descended from African slaves. Also called Gullah baskets, Charleston was known for them. The basket my mother held was incomparable, its symmetry perfection. A beautiful thing in and of itself, but I ached to see the chest's true shape.

"Y'all, I've got a question," Rae said.

This should be good. With reluctance, I dragged my focus to Rae.

"If y'all claim this here basket's the chest, how'd you recognize it?"

Maurelle flicked her hand at him. "Fool. It spoke to me in the magic realm."

"Spoke, did it?" Rae tapped a finger to his lips. "Ah. And in the magic world, could you open it?"

Her lips thinned.

His sardonic laugh filled the room. "Couldn't, could you?"

She shrugged. "That wasn't the point."

Rae held up a finger. "One more question. Y'all claim to have found this 'thing' in the magic realm, so how come Tatianne didn't find it first?"

Of course. Tatianne desperately wanted the chests and to subsume me in order to control them. The memory of my hair's-breadth escape made my stomach cramp. A powerful and knowledgeable monster, she had a vicious intent to keep the worlds of magic and mundane separate. I wished I knew more about her history. Apparently, over the years she'd "ingested" aspects of shapeshifter and mage, possibly even vampyre. She'd been my brother's lover, had almost killed me several times, and relentlessly and ruthlessly sought the chests. That she couldn't enter the mundane world was a saving grace.

I peered at Maurelle, curious as to how she'd answer. If only I could peer into her twisted mind. She gave off an unpalatable vibe, a cocktail of avarice and anger, with low notes of...*insecurity*. Odd. *Why* had she gone for the chest, and why take Lulu with her? It certainly wasn't out of motherly affection.

The queen turned her head. "Well, dear sister?"

Maurelle's fingers smoothed across her velvet pants. "I met someone."

"Who?" Rae said.

The queen glared at him.

"*Someone*," Maurelle spat. "I vowed not to reveal his name, and I take my vows seriously, unlike some others in this room. He's an incredibly powerful mage."

The roll of Rae's eyes said it all.

Lulu's mother never lost a beat. "He suspected the chest remained in the magic world, in a time stream unknown to Tatianne, since she hadn't found it."

Her tale sounded fishy. Anouk had told me all the chests were in the mundane world, lost to the magic one. My bullshit meter went into overdrive.

"He couldn't fetch it himself," Maurelle said. "But *I* could do so. It took me years to find the correct time stream, then more years to find the chest. Dear Clea, I thought you'd be pleased. I did your job for you."

I boiled over. "It took you and *Lulu* years. You stole ten years of your daughter's life! You *needed* her to find the chest, didn't you? Lulu found it, right? Not you. And for what? The least you could've done was tell her about the timestreams, and how touching the chest might change her."

Maurelle's sly look made me want to throttle her.

"Maurelle!" Viviane said, face white with fury. "You didn't tell my niece?"

"No," I said. "She didn't. She deliberately hid it from her. Since their return, Lulu's been here in happy faeland, with no idea that only a few days have passed in the mundane realm."

Maurelle shrugged. "So? The mundane world means little. If

Tatianne possessed the chests, my bitch of a sister would destroy everything."

My world rocked yet again. *Sister?* I looked back and forth between Viviane and Maurelle. Their matching expressions of chagrin told the tale.

My mam waved a hand. "Tatianne *was* our sister. Once. Now? Now she is many things. Sister is *not* one of them."

Holy shit, Tatianne had been screwing her nephew. *Ewww.*

Alex's fury, Melike's disgust, Rae's distrust—emotions swirled in a thick sludge of tension, chaotic violence simmering just beneath the surface. My skin felt stretched too tight for my body, the downside of my empath "gift." Where was this going? Who was the choreographer? What was the endgame?

Scenes like this washed over James like a soft rain on a summer's day. I put a hand on his arm, soaking up his calm and certainty of purpose.

James leaned forward. "Give us the chest and Lulu, and we're gone."

Maurelle notched her chin. "You can't have Lulu."

Claws sprang from Alex's hands. "We already do. She is ours."

"I am *not* yours, Alex Arctos. I'm not yours either, Mother." She poked a finger at her torso. "I choose *me*."

Maurelle's hand covered Lulu's. The girl...woman...snatched it away. "*I* choose, Mother. You deceived me and stole precious years while we traipsed around that other world."

"Of course I didn't." She brushed back a wing of her hair. "You wanted to come. Insisted upon it."

"You forgot to mention I was going to lose ten frigging years in that screwed-up place. I was an idiot sixteen-year-old. A kid. What did I know?"

"Hey," Neddy chimed in. "I'm sixteen, and I'm not a kid."

"Quiet!" commanded the queen, her talons sprang out and dug into the arms of her chair. She surveyed the room, her face wreathed with an imperious smile. "Do remember in whose presence you are. *I* decide what will be done."

Her smile flattened when she turned to Maurelle. The other woman cringed.

"You told me *nothing* of this particular time slip, sister," Viviane said. "You well knew where you were taking my niece, which you failed to mention to me. Had I understood Lulu would age, I would never have permitted her attending you. How dare you?"

Maurelle crossed her arms and looked out the windows to the wood beyond.

"Maurelle!" barked Vivianne. "Why did you take her? Answer me."

She turned, spine straight, chin notched. "Without her mage essence, I would never find the chest."

Lulu's eyes widened. "But I expressed like you, as fae, not Dad's mage."

"But it's within you, daughter," Maurelle said. "Just as fae is within your...*cousin*." She stared at me, eyes sparked with hate. "The chest rightfully belongs to The Key, which is why I thought to do Clea a service and fetch it for her."

"You can't stand Clea," Lulu said. "Why would you try to help her?"

Maurelle sniffed. "She might be a blight on this earth—"

"Careful, Maurelle," Viviane said.

"She is The Key, after all." Maurelle turned to her sister. "Shall I present the chest to your daughter, Viv?"

My mother paused for long moments, then waved a hand. "Get on with it."

With reverence, Maurelle lifted the basket and carried it to me. "Lose the dog. This is a ceremonious moment."

"Why?" I pet the pup's head. "She's just a pal."

Viviane nodded, and a fae guard hauled off the pup. I suspected no more poofing until we left the queen's presence.

Maurelle held out the sweetgrass basket. "Will you take it?"

Once I touched it, the chest would metamorphose into its true form. But I would still have to activate it, and I had no intention of doing so before this crowd of onlookers. Time enough when we returned to the Arctos compound where I'd activate it in the secure room that held the two other chests.

I cradled my hands around the chest's curved sides.

Eiderdown brushed my flesh, along with pulses of warmth. The soft stroking traveled from my palms, across the backs of each hand, tickling up my forearms to my shoulders, my throat, my face. Heavenly.

My wrist tattoo spiraled to life, the glowing light moving up my arms. Fireflies escaped my hands where I held the chest, and I almost screamed when a vise of power gripped my flesh. I fought to keep my muscles relaxed.

I inhaled deeply and prepared for what was coming.

The basket tremored, began to alter shape as pinpricks danced across my body. The insidious pain almost made me close my eyes. But I didn't. I had to see.

Light surrounded the shifting basket, so bright I strained to watch the hexagonal glass-like box take shape within the prism.

Rainbowed colors shot outward. The six-inch box pulsed to match my heartbeat. Gold symbols and runes streamed across its face, its sides—an ouroboros, a dragon, an eye—to encase the crystal. Once covered in symbols, it stilled.

I shuddered, dizzy from the chest's transformation.

An awed hush infused the room.

"Well?" Maurelle's hungry eyes ate me up.

"Stuff it, Maurelle." I ran my fingers across the chest's lid, and sighed. The chest's hum rose within me. A song infinitely familiar and utterly unknowable.

My fingers reached to raise the lid, to see inside...

Callused ones held them back.

I stared at James. "What?"

He leaned close, his breath warm on my ear. "Don't open it."

"I must."

"Wait." His roughened voice was a low whisper. "Please."

His somber face jarred me. But...this was my mission, my task. "Why, James?"

"Because I'm asking." His eyes were darkened pools of blue, deep and mysterious.

He seldom asked, more comfortable giving orders than making requests. My heart squeezed. I so wanted to agree, to bow to his plea. The warmth in his eyes fed my soul. I loved him so completely. He was my other half, the answer to all my dreams and wishes and desires. The chests paled in comparison. I gave him a tremulous smile. "Okay."

I raised the chest to hand it off to James. It would again become a basket and we'd prepare it for travel.

The glint of a golden rune caught my eye.

My fingers stiffened. I lifted the lid.

Someone may have touched my hands, warm, yet irrelevant compared to the wonders before me.

Reality lay in the fathomless chasm, in the scents of ozone and jasmine. I had to know, to understand. Tiny stars flashed and dissolved, surfacing and vanishing as if in an ebony snow globe. Yes. *Yes.* I dove.

I saw nothing.

I saw *everything*.

Dawn rising...Moon setting...Scents of bergamot, heliotrope, peach...James, Bernadette, Viviane...Alcyone, Aegina, Callisto... Rowan tree, hawthorn, elder...Opal, ruby, emerald...Sidhe, Tuatha Dé Danann, Tylwyth Teg...Wings, watersongs, waterfalls...Acorn, pine cones, autumn leaves...Caves, crystals, bells...Stallion, fawn, ewe...Oona, the queen; Dagda, the king; Tara, the home...banshees and burial mounds...bees and honey...days and decades, tomorrows and yesterdays...the wyvern—wings spread, muzzle agape...James armored, arms wide...A roar. *His* roar. No. Wait! *No!* The Storybook, the Queen, the *souls*...Amber fireflies swirling, dancing—a galaxy, a spiraled nebula, a fireworks of stars—and worlds upon worlds upon worlds upon...

～

"CLEA, WAKE UP!" Jame said, his voice a guttural growl. He *willed* her to awaken. His Clea would. She *must*.

She lay limp in his arms, and he cradled her close, her blonde curls tumbling across his thighs. "Wake up, baby." He whispered sweet words in her ear, cajoling, demanding, pleading. How much time had passed since she fell? A minute? A hundred? A thousand?

Her face was slack, but her eyes were frantic beneath closed lids, as if the world she viewed blazed by. Not his world. Only hers. He clutched her tighter, to anchor her, keep her with him, never let her go. "Clea."

Someone cleared their throat.

Not *Maurelle,* the bitch! No, she'd vanished after ripping the chest from Clea's hands. Clea had slumped into his arms, and *she wouldn't wake up.*

He raised his head. Each creature seated around the room got his cold, flat stare, which wouldn't reflect the panic pounding his heart.

Clea's she-devil of a mother half-stood, hands white on the arms of her chair. Had she orchestrated this? He'd rip her apart. Lulu shook, face wet. Tears. Neddy whined. The kid looked panicked. Alex's thrumming growl pissed him off. The wolf should shut up. The others...

He scoped the room. Who else was a traitor?

Who the fuck cared?

Easy enough to kill them all.

Just like he'd kill Maurelle. Damn that shit-fuck.

And now Clea wouldn't wake up. He stared down, memorized her face for the millionth time.

He should've seen it coming, protected her, but he'd been too slow, *too slow,* and Clea was...

James seethed, the wyvern screeching for him to *do* something. He could unleash his fury, end them. Every. Single. One. The red haze was blinding, the wyvern's shrieks incessant.

A hand on his shoulder. He whipped around, teeth bared.

"Calm, Larrimer, calm," Rae said. "We need to talk. All of us."

Talk? What good was talk? "Get. Back."

Rae jerked away plenty far enough. *Smart move, mage.*

Clea, limp and still but for those restless eyes. He shifted her across his lap. She'd be more comfortable that way. His hand traced her cheeks, her brow, her lips. Warm. Alive. *Gone.*

His eyes snapped up, left, center, right. No one better come near again.

A howl built in his chest, and he released it. His Clea was *gone.*

When he came back to himself, he narrowed his eyes at the intruders. They should leave, get away from him. The faces peered back at him, eyes full of fear and questions. Like he'd know what to do.

Fucking what to do?

Did Maurelle have an accomplice? Who? Charlie? James' fae maker had betrayed them before. Perhaps Iron Heart, the steely fae who despised them? Clea's mother? Viviane had sheltered her sister and was one cold, imperious bitch. Was she jealous of her daughter's power?

"What...what happened, Larrimer?" Lulu said, in that unfamiliar grown-up voice.

He growled at her question. "What the fuck do you think happened?" She shivered. Good.

What did they know? They never *saw* him. Only Clea did. Only Clea.

Neddy sprang across the room to kneel beside the sofa. James reached out to toss the kid across the room for daring to touch his Clea.

No, James, that's not you. A memory. *Her* words. It had once been him, but he was no longer that machine-man. He was more. He was Clea's and she, his.

The boy's trembling hand gripped Clea's. Hers was small, but she was proud of the callouses she'd gained from practice with the katana.

Christ, he was losing his mind.

"Clea," Neddy said, voice wobbly with tears. "Come back, Clea.

Please." Neddy looked up at him. "Where did she go, Larrimer? Where?"

"She's stuck, Neddy," Rae said. "Stuck inside that crazy-assed world."

The queen cleared her throat. "When Maurelle stole the Chest of Time, my daughter's consciousness was trapped inside it. Did you see how it returned to its basket form when Maurelle touched it? As The Key, only Clea's touch can transmute the chest into its true form. Without her transformation of the chest, she will be forever imprisoned within."

"Why did she open it?" Lulu said. "Why?"

"Does it matter now?" Alex said.

Viviane straightened. "The chest always compels The Key to fall. While the journey is arduous, The Key always finds the strength to return. But without the Chest of Time in her possession... That is impossible. She is lost."

Not for long. He'd find that damned chest. He raked a hand through his hair. His mind was fuzzy, brain muddied. To save Clea he needed a clear head, razor precision, and cunning thought.

The crimson mist thinned enough for him to regard the gathering with dispassion. He went to that cold place inside himself, the one he used for command and in battle. The one emotions barely touched, where clarity of thought ruled.

What *exactly* had happened? While everyone babbled, he went back in time to recreate Clea's actions with the Chest of Stone.

They'd been in that warded room at the Arctos den. Easy to recall the scene. He'd seen every movement she made. Heard each word. Clea touching the necklace. It's transformation to a rectangular box maybe five inches in diameter, and made of an iridescent stone, its lid curved. She'd lifted the lid, fallen, and returned. The process had been challenging, but she'd accomplished it. And after her return, she'd 'activated' the chest. That's what she'd called it. Without activation, she'd told him, the chest remained inert.

Next, he reexamined her actions today, moment by moment.

She'd done all those things, except... She hadn't had time to *activate* the chest before Maurelle ripped it away. A smile formed on his lips.

"Larrimer, y'all are smilin'!" Rae said. "Y'all be goin' even more crazy ass on us?"

"No." Unless the damn thing was switched on, it was useless to the person who possessed it. Maurelle had stolen a fucking basket. That was all. He had some time. To get the chest back. To save Clea. He started to laugh.

"*Mon dieu!*" Melike said. "Larrimer, he is *démentiel!* Crazy!"

James caught Alex's eyes.

"I don't think so," Alex said.

The wolf had been there when his Clea activated the previous chest. "Remember, Arctos. Remember the last time."

Alex head tilted, then he slowly nodded. "She didn't..."

James pressed a finger to his lips. They'd find Maurelle, recover the chest, save Clea. Anticipation filled him, shattering the ice around his heart.

WELL, hot damn. Alex ducked his head, so no one caught his smile. They had something to work with, a way to return Clea to herself. Ha!

Hope infused Alex, a drug that said they could make it right. He prayed like hell Larrimer didn't go wyvern on them. He was one badass monster.

Pressure squeezed him—his alpha nature telling him to take command, take on Larrimer who was holding Clea like she was only *his*. Godsdammit, she was his packmate, she was his friend, she was *family*. Alex's aggression spiked, making him want to gut the big bastard, which would give Clea a shit fit. Except she wasn't here to bitch at them, but somewhere weird and terrible. Damn, she was so vulnerable, on some Key trip that he couldn't get his head around. He drew in a deep breath.

One thing was crystal—Larrimer would never leave Clea's side. No way.

It was up to Alex to get the chest.

Now. He'd leave now. He stood.

The fae guards drew their weapons. So did the general. All aimed at the room's non-fae inhabitants.

Man, these fairies were idiots.

He looked at Larrimer. *Here it comes. The shitstorm.*

JAMES BRISTLED with more power than he'd ever felt. *Fuck, it felt good.* So much power, he took extra care keeping Clea steady.

"We're leaving your domain," he said to the queen.

"I think not." The queen swept an arm upward, and the crazy fae raised their puny weapons. "My daughter is safest here."

In control now, James clamped down his shields, mind tight and clear. He handed Clea to Rae, then manacled the queen with his stare. "Then you think wrong."

The queen's lips pursed. "We need to discuss our next move."

"*You* have no next move," he said.

Her spine straightened. "We're going after my sister."

He paused, working various strategies. Denying her now would lead to a fight. People would die, perhaps Lulu, Melike, Neddy. Clea would hate that. He might, too. He wasn't sure.

Clea's safety was paramount. Number one, get her away from these fucking traitorous fae. The queen had no clue how bad the wyvern wanted to scrape her heart from her breast with his talons. *Or I could burn her to a crisp. Satisfying.*

Shut the fuck up.

Let me out!

No. I'll handle it. Nostrils flaring, he stalked to the queen.

"Stay back!" The tip of the general's sword halted an inch from his chin.

His hand clamped the blade and snapped it in half. A pleasing sound.

"Stop!" the queen ordered.

He opened his bloody hand and dropped half the blade onto her luxe carpet. He smiled.

The queen recoiled.

He'd bet the wyvern shined through his eyes, maybe puffed a little smoke out his nose. His smile widened.

Lulu darted forward and wound a white cloth around his hand.

"Auntie," Lulu said. "Stop this."

"Quiet!" the queen said.

The girl halted. Woman. Whatever the hell she was now.

"Auntie?"

"This isn't your concern," the queen said.

"It is," Lulu said in a soft voice. "My mother did this."

Viviane's lips pulled into a snarl. "How do I know you weren't a part of her scheme, niece?"

Lulu blanched.

Christ, they could yap forever. Enough. "We go to the bower, and we're taking Clea with us."

Viviane sneered. "My daughter remains here. In my home." She waved a hand, as if dismissing them. "Take your people and go."

James didn't need this shit. What he needed was to get Clea safe. Threats would make the queen more volatile. He could kill them all. Tempting, but he was unsure how Clea would react to him ending her mother. "Clea's soul is twined with mine. She stays with me."

The queen's eyes widened, before her mask slipped back in place. She hadn't known. He liked it.

"You will abide here, in my home, with my daughter. She belongs with us. She is blood of my blood."

A snort. Rae. "Queenie, you just make my ass itch. Y'all sure ignored your daughter for twenty-some years. Hell, y'all abandoned her in the first place."

Viviane rose half out of her chair. "How dare you?"

Rae tapped a finger to his lips. "Any a what I said untrue?"

The queen had the grace to remain silent.

James needed to figure Viviane out. Why was she reluctant to let

Clea go? Was she a bargaining chip? Was this about control over activating the chest? Or was she concerned about her child? Against all odds, he suspected the latter, but it wasn't a surety. He didn't trust the queen. He and Clea would make tracks out of here fast. He grunted. "Have you considered there may be other traitors in this realm beside your sister?" A gasp from Lulu. "*Not* your niece. Are you that big a fool to leave Clea prey to them?"

"I must think." Her face cold, her eyes swept the room.

Either she'd concede or he'd unleash his wyvern. The beast flared within. His body began to heat. Hands on hips, he waited. Heat flushed his face and smoke spiraled up his legs. He didn't try to stop it.

He gave his back to the queen and stepped toward Rae, arms lifted to take back his Clea.

"Iron Heart goes with you to the bower," the queen said. "As do three more of my guard, along with Ozille. Perhaps she can make my daughter more comfortable."

With effort, he shut down the wyvern. "Agreed."

He took Clea and left.

7

Alex hated seeing Clea lying so still on the bed he'd used to recuperate. Neddy sat beside her, a devoted wolf. At the boy's feet sat the strange little dog, which he doubted was a dog. He suspected who she was. So why wasn't she revealing herself?

The others had pulled chairs into a circle, and he'd been entertained when Larrimer, eyes aglow, had forced the soldiers and Iron Heart outside the bower. A powerful incentive, that. What would Clea think of the new form her lover's eyes had taken?

He snorted. Clea'd probably get off on it.

"We've got a good plan," Rae said.

Lulu was convinced she knew where Maurelle had gone. Some gods-forsaken desert in Texas he'd never heard of. Since they had zero other options, they were going with it.

Alex nodded. "The plan's not bad. Not perfect, but I agree." That vise pressing for control rode him again. Growls rumbled his chest.

"I'll have to change." Lulu plucked at her dress.

"No," he said.

She gave him that pissy look, the one that made her eyebrows look like wings.

"We take our weapons," Larrimer said, "but otherwise go as is. If they get a hint of us leaving, it'll end in violence."

"Violence sounds appealing," he said.

Larrimer's smile evoked the monster. "I agree, but Clea wouldn't like it."

"Point," he said.

"I'll get us cloaks," she said.

"Do you only think about clothes?" Alex said.

Anger smoked her violet eyes. A shame she didn't fear him. She never had, this girl with more passion than sense.

She smiled, her little white teeth flashing. "They're magic. They blend, conceal. They'll help us escape."

He'd concede she was right, but she was still a smartypants. Her now sinfully curvy body might've changed. *She* hadn't.

Larrimer nodded. "Thank you, Lulu. Good idea." He eyeballed all of us. "In an hour."

"Agreed," they echoed.

"NOTHING, AUNTIE, NOTHING!" Lulu wanted to curse. Seated in the luxurious leather wing chair, she flung her arms wide. Unlucky that on her way to get the cloaks, she'd been summoned before the queen. She made certain her inner annoyance didn't reach her face. The ever-aggravating Alex had predicted she'd get all pissy. He'd been right, but she was hiding it well, and she'd never tell him he'd been spot on.

Aunt Viviane had insisted on meeting her in the palace library, fire blazing, a snifter of brandy for each of them. What a strategist. She'd be toast without her ability to lie to her aunt, a talent few possessed. She blithely smiled at the woman who'd taken her in all those years ago after she'd run from the Arctos compound.

She appreciated her aunt's generosity, even if coming to the Charleston fae had ended up royally screwing her.

As good as her aunt's truthsense was, Lulu's abilities at deception were better. Probably one of her mother's "gifts," since she'd convinced her that entering the magic realm wouldn't affect them at all. Her treacherous, duplicitous mother.

Why hadn't she listened to Clea back then?

Because she was a sixteen-year-old idiot who paid attention to no one. As the years had passed, it was hard to even remember that girl.

Self-recrimination was useless. She slumped into the chair's soft leather. A pose. She modulated her voice to sound tired and weepy. "Can I go now?"

Her aunt pursed her lips. She loved the woman, but not the way she loved Clea.

Oh, Clea. Lulu might have been stuck in the magic world, but Clea... She was trapped in that awful chest. *My mother's actions have damned you.*

Which brought genuine tears to Lulu's eyes.

Auntie nodded. "Yes. Go. But report anything they do out of order to me or to Iron Heart. They plan to take my daughter. I'm certain of it. Where, I can't imagine."

I can. Don't let it show. Don't let it show.

Her aunt gave her a long look before she stood. "Charlie will escort you."

Charlie stepped from the shadows. Dressed in jeans and a green linen button-down, she hadn't even sensed him. She was a blockhead.

Now she'd have to escape *him*.

"Thank you," was all she said, when she wanted to scream. She had to get the damned cloaks.

LULU AND CHARLIE traversed the wood on silent feet. Moonlight glittered onto the silvered leaves and grassy carpet beneath them. She stole a glance at the mysterious Charlie, a man she knew had betrayed the fae, yet somehow he'd been enfolded back into their bosom, and into the queen's good graces. Perhaps into her bed? She'd wondered about that.

Handsome, as were most fae, lithe and tall, with those pearlescent horns she found so hot. He'd shorn his hair to his shoulders, a little rebellion the queen apparently tolerated. Surprising.

She puffed out a breath. She *was* tired. She hadn't lied about that. And she still had to retrieve the cloaks from the armory.

He bowed to her at her door.

"Thanks for walking me home."

His soft laughter like crystal bells set the leaves fluttering. "Oh, I don't think so. You wished I was to hell and gone."

"Why would you say that?"

He remained silent.

She lifted the doorlatch.

"I'll be watching." He disappeared into the night.

She *did* change into her fighting leathers, no matter what Alex thought or said. With perhaps too much force, she stuffed jeans, shirts, essentials, and Blue Monkey into her pack. She only gathered a single short sword and a few knives since she was pretty mediocre at using them. Ah, but her row of bows... Those sang to her. She'd learned on the classic longbow, and loved it still. Her crossbow appealed, but hers was heavy, not meant for long treks, which she suspected they'd be taking. She reached instead for her favorite, the one she'd acquired in the magic realm. Crafted from a wood not found in the mundane world—light, flexible, and incredibly strong—the recurve bow had amazing reach, yet folded into a lightweight, portable package. She plucked it and her quiver with arrows from the wall. Yup, she was full of badassery with those in her hands. She attached them to her harness and slipped it onto her back, then strapped her bracer onto her left forearm. The few dollars she'd need, she shoved into the pouch at her waist.

When she donned her cloak, she made sure to fasten all the buckles. The better to hide herself.

She lifted the hood and stepped out the back door.

"Hi there." Charlie leaned against the post to her studio, one leg crossed over the other, lounging. He tipped an invisible hat.

Shite. Unlike Clea, she wasn't good at all this intrigue crap. "Go away."

In the soft light, his silver eyes sparkled. "I will accompany you."

"No you won't."

His lips tilted upward. "I'm glad you're not playing games, little one."

"Don't call me that."

He glided closer. "I am going with your band of merry men." He kept his voice low and conspiratorial. "You and the others plan to find you-know-what. I..." He ran a hand across one horn. "I must accompany you."

She shook her head. "You're just a spy for Aunt Viv."

"No. She won't miss my presence until we're long gone."

Her snort echoed in the stillness. "Then why insist on coming?"

His silver eyes darkened to storm clouds. "I have wrongs to right, particularly concerning Clea Reese and James Larrimer."

"I don't believe you."

"Believe what you will. I shall meet you at the Angel Oak in an hour."

She wanted to roll her eyes. But in the years she'd spent in the magic land with her *dear* mother, she'd learned to mask and conceal.

"Be sure to be there," he said. "One hour. If not... Remember, Viviane is all about sovereignty, as you should know so well."

He dematerialized in a whoosh of power, his version of a threatening postscript.

Now, to get her companion's cloaks.

ALEX MISSED CLEA. She might have become more sister than lover, but she was ever in his thoughts. His glance slid to Larrimer, whose one-armed fireman's carry of her looked damned uncomfortable, but was for the sake of reaching the katana strapped beneath his concealing cloak.

The seven of them were shadows in the night as they walked the wood. All wore the cloaks Lulu had provided, as well as wax stuffed in their ears, which drove him near insane. Not having that sense equaled a limb cut from his body. A necessary loss in this case, as Lulu sang the Song of Sleep across Viviane's domain, one of the talents she'd acquired in this cursed place. If their group heard her song, they'd grow drowsy, too, just like the little dog who'd shadowed Clea.

They'd debated about taking the pup, and decided, whether friend or foe, bringing her was too risky. So they'd left her in the bower, snoring beside the Wolfhound.

If what he suspected about the Chihuahua was correct, that decision would bite them in the ass.

Given Larrimer's precious burden, Rae led the way. Alex wanted to lead, but his injury left him with no memory of the paths and roads. It stuck in his craw. This half-fairy land had eroded his temper to a jagged edge. Melike took up the rear, with Neddy, Lulu, Larrimer, and Clea in between.

Any minute they'd emerge from the tree-lined path onto the dirt road, the same one they'd used to enter this crazy-weird land. Eager as he was to see the last of this place, he nonetheless waved them to a halt at the tree line.

He tipped his head toward Rae, who removed the wax from one ear and swirled his motes around the three of them, he guessed as a barrier for Lulu's song.

"We're fully exposed here," Alex said. "If they find us, they'll use those damned poisoned arrows. Just a nick and..."

Lulu shook her head and kept singing.

They'll be wantin' to capture us, not kill, Rae said in his head. *After y'alls reaction? I'm bettin' no, too.*

"Some bet," Alex muttered. "How far, Rae?"

The mage held up two fingers.

Two miles. "Lulu, can you sing if we run?"

She shook her head "no." Exhaustion drooped her shoulders and shadowed her eyes, but she kept singing.

Walk it was, then.

Rae replaced his ear plug and dropped his motes. He directed them to the road's edge, where they'd at least have some sort of escape route. Maybe.

The moon waned, which gave them a little more cover. But they were damnably vulnerable.

The group picked up their walking pace, and Alex wanted to rip out the damned earplugs. Instead, he filtered through his companions scents and found no others. They remained alone in the wood. Yet he was certain they'd be attacked. The only question was when and where. Lulu's song might make them drowsy, but there were so many fae, the song wasn't powerful enough to put them all to sleep. And from his own experiences as wolf alpha, he knew things like songs and spells affected some more than others.

The road curved after about a mile, and in the distance, the Angel Oak stood proud and massive. Once there, once out of this half-magic land, they'd have the advantage over any pursuing fae.

The mundane was his world, and he bristled with anticipation.

Closer. Closer. Almost...

Larrimer's muffled shout thumped like a bass drum. He ripped the plugs from his ears. They ran.

Lulu cried out, and Alex doubled back to help her stand, even as arrows cascaded from the sky.

Larrimer bent over Clea to protect her until Neddy arrived in full-on Pinky mode to guard her. Larrimer, already pincushioned with arrows, started lobbing stones from his pack at lightning speed, while Rae flung those mote things, deflecting the fae's assault. Father Fenrir, Lulu was on one knee and she was shooting arrows, too. Melike... *Fuck.*

"Run," Rae shouted. He was blocking enough of the arrows so that they could race to the oak.

Alex ran back for Melike.

Time...time became thick and tacky, sticking to him, holding him back as four fae grappled Melike to the earth in her half-shifter form.

"Go!" she screamed, and bit a fae on the arm.

A dozen fae circled her. Too many. But how could he leave Melike? He could not.

He leapt toward the fae.

"Too many!" she screamed. "Go! You must!"

Truth. The arrow's agony from days ago couldn't compare to this heart pain at losing Melike. Midair, he twisted, shifted, and raced toward the oak.

DAWN FINGERED the dark as they sprawled beneath the Angel Oak's massive branches. Once they'd reached the tree, the fae had fallen back.

The fae wouldn't hurt Melike. He had to believe that.

They'd had little trouble reentering the mundane world, as if it welcomed them back. Not like their struggle when they'd entered faeland.

All but Clea and Lulu had taken hits with the fae arrows, and Alex thanked Father Fenrir that they didn't contain the poison that had brought him low.

Lulu pulled two arrows from Rae and three from Neddy, who remained in his quicker-healing Pinky form. The girl hadn't even blinked at the sight of Neddy's altered shape. Good thing Rae was working some spell to cloak them from any pre-dawn tourists.

When Lulu walked over to Larrimer and reached for an arrow, he growled. Asshole. She huffed out a breath and walked away.

Now she stood before Alex, weaving on her feet, but with narrowed, flashing eyes. "Can I take care of you, or will you growl at me, too?"

He tilted his head in assent. Until the arrows were out and the healing began, he wouldn't shift back to his human form. At least Rae and Lulu'd been right. If the fae had used their poisoned arrows, he'd be one dead wolf.

She moved to his side, placed her palm on his shoulder and pulled. *Fuck, that hurt!* A growl spilled out.

"Oh, shut up."

He hadn't meant to growl.

Then she lay her hand on his butt and tugged the second arrow from his flank.

Shit!

"You're a baby."

He snapped at her and she bopped his nose. *Just you wait, little Lulu.*

She stumbled back to Larrimer and kneeled. "Are you all right?"

The monster nodded, his eyes focused on Clea, now draped across his arms.

"Can I take the arrows out now?"

"Do it." Larrimer's face tightened, but he didn't make a sound.

When she'd finished, she washed and wiped her hands, then ran her fingers down Clea's cheek. "We're on our way, Clea. We'll find it. You'll be back with us in no time."

Alex's mind filled with Melike, a soldier to the end. *His* soldier. He had to go back for her, free her. It was his duty as her alpha. With the arrows gone, he'd be back to full strength soon.

Lulu pushed to her feet, and returned to him, cloak flapping in the damp breeze. She peered down at him. Not that she had to look far. His wolf form came to her ribcage.

"I know what you're thinking," she said.

Foolish girl. A child, really.

She ran a hand down his fur. "You want to go back for Melike. You can't."

He whooshed out a breath. A laugh. As if she could understand the need driving him.

Lulu's violet eyes took on a sharp gleam. "There were too many of them. They would have held you hostage, too, and where would that get us? Listen to me. I know them. They'll keep her safe. She's a bargaining chip, so they won't hurt her. Aunt Viviane's no dummy. With Melike as prisoner, my aunt is assured we'll return. She wants Clea back, too. I told her that a fae force going after my mother would only complicate things, not that she listened. But she understands stealth. We're a powerful group, and she knows it. Now that we've gone, I suspect she'll leave us to our own devices."

When had Lulu gotten so smart?

He shifted, not that he wanted to. Smoke surrounded him, pulsing with a warm golden light, and he drew in the scents of sea and sun as his body reformed, this time with quite a bit more pain than pleasure. He uncurled to his full height. Lulu might be tall for a woman, but he had a good six inches on her. He looked down at her face, which was creased with concern.

He didn't like his choices, knew the dangers of leaving Melike with the fae. She would lash out—it was her nature—and possibly be injured or worse.

"You, me, Neddy, and Rae," she said. "We can do this. We can find the chest for Clea. Don't you see, Alex, we must."

His eyes were drawn to Clea, her form still as death.

"Look at me," Lulu said. "We all have to talk."

"Let it wait until—"

"No. We talk now. It's important."

The urge to free his packmate rode him hard, but he'd think on Lulu's words, even as he fought the urge to fly on four legs to the queen's lair. He followed Lulu over to where the others sat beside Larrimer, Clea now cradled in his lap.

Control. Must keep control. "What's so urgent, Lulu?"

LULU THREADED HER FINGERS TOGETHER, knuckles white. She didn't want to tell. Rae, always moving like a kinetic sculpture, sat cross-legged, fingers tapping his knees, eyes pinned to her. She was glad Larrimer was so preoccupied. He'd be disappointed in her.

Neddy shifted back to his boy form.

"Smooth," Alex said to the boy.

Neddy's eyes fell. "In that hut, I was—"

"It's fine, Ned," Alex said squeezing the boy's upper arm. "What's so urgent, princess?"

Neddy gave Lulu a wary look, and Alex... The alpha's cold gaze made her want to run and hide, but she'd never do that again. Never.

"Charlie's coming," she said.

"That pain in the ass fae?" Rae said.

"Yes."

She waited for swear words that never came. They all sat there looking at her like she was speaking Gaelic. She sighed, and the story poured out.

"So where is he, darlin'?" Rae said.

Lulu's eyes went to the sky now painted a gray-gold. "He'll be here in fifteen minutes."

"Fifteen minutes." Alex sprang to his feet, face tight, fists curled. "Let's go. Now."

So Alex had made his decision to hunt with them, to not go back for Melike. She hoped she'd spoken true when she'd said the fae wouldn't hurt Melike. She'd meant every word, but... She was glad Alex was staying. He might be imperious and annoying, but she didn't want him trapped by her aunt, too.

The others flowed to their feet. She wobbled. They had no idea how the Song of Sleep exhausted her.

James handed Clea to Rae and stalked behind a large tree limb. It seemed nature called even for him.

Alex stared at her for long moments. "You all heard Larrimer say he'd take Clea to the Arctos compound to wait. Lulu insists she's coming on our hunt for the chest, so there'll be four of us. "

"No," Neddy said, hands fisted.

Oh, dear. Neddy had just contradicted his alpha.

Alex swung around to the boy, power pouring off him. "What did you say?"

She was shocked to see Neddy tilt his head, exposing his throat in submission, then he straightened, strong and proud.

"As my alpha, I know you can make me, Alex," Neddy said. "And I know you think it's right the four of us go for the chest. But I should go with Clea and Larrimer. He's got to carry her the whole way." Neddy's toe scuffed the dirt at his feet. "I can help with that, so he can defend us against any threats. We'll have to rent a car. We can't get on a plane with Clea passed out. He's strong, but he needs to eat, and Clea, you know he won't leave her. She saved me, Alex. She's...she's like my big sis." He went quiet. "Please."

Neddy stood proud, shoulders back, ready to take whatever his alpha dished out. He'd been through so much, yet here he was, strong and beautiful. If Lulu were younger... But she wasn't. Ten years of her life, gone.

Alex raised a hand, and she hoped to gods he wouldn't hit the boy. He thumped his hand on Neddy's shoulder and nodded. "You're right, Ned. I agree, you go with Clea and Larrimer back to the den. She'll be safe there."

Lulu stood there feeling like a fool while everyone gathered their weapons. Larrimer returned and slipped Clea back into his arms. "Guys, we can't leave before Charlie gets here. He can find us, me. He'll tell my aunt our plans. Everything."

Alex shrugged. "So you stay. Wait for him."

"Oh, that's a really bright idea. You won't find my mother without me."

His mantle of alphaness descended on her like a hammer. "I will."

She flung up her hands. "You're not going without—"

A crash through the oak's branches. She snapped up her head. Larrimer handed Clea to Neddy and drew his katana.

"Shit," Alex said.

Draped across one of the Angel Oak's massive lower branches lay Charlie. Blood covered his head and dripped onto the leafy ground below. In the distance, a clock chimed the hour.

Alex scrambled up the tree to the branch and passed the fae down into Rae's waiting arms.

She gasped. "His horns. Auntie sliced off his horns."

LULU SAT beside a sleeping Charlie and breathed in the stale plane air. The book in her lap sat untouched, and she tried and failed to stop glancing at the fae.

He'd been passed out most of the time, but regained consciousness long enough to tell them what had happened, to walk through security, and onto the plane. Her aunt's monstrous punishment for Charlie's refusal to speak of their trip didn't surprise her. He was ever contrary. His horns would take years to grow back, and their lack diminished his powers.

No, she wasn't surprised. But she hated this, all of it. The violence, the lies, the crazy, as Clea would call it. The world she now inhabited was the opposite of the one she'd once lived with her kind, gentle dad. He'd filled her world with safety and warmth and love. The cruelty of this one hollowed her out.

Alex and Rae sat a few rows in front of them, Alex now wearing another of his crazy Hawaiian shirts, reminding her of one he'd worn years ago. Or to *them*, days ago. She shook her head, unable to get her mind around the time slippage.

Clea, Alex—back then they'd angered her, and she resented them for not caring enough to come after her for so many years. When, in truth, they'd come for her right away.

He was a good leader, a good wolf. She respected that, and she should keep it in mind when he made her want to stab him. Over the months she'd lived with Clea, she'd watched her guardian grow in patience. Time to take a page from Clea's playbook.

She texted Alex on one of the burner phones they'd bought, along with a bunch of other gear she hadn't paid much attention to. She needed to know when they'd arrive, and she'd lost track of time trying to sing Charlie back to a semblance of health.

Now, she was so tired she couldn't even...

You should be asleep, pinged Alex's text.

Her fingers tapped the screen hard enough to break the phone. *Are you going to tell me when to pee, too?*

Maybe. To answer your question, we arrive at 6 p.m.

Hours yet. She sighed. Arguing stole more of her energy. He

couldn't help his autocratic manner. She knew that. *Thank you,* she texted back.

Are you sick? he replied.

Of you. She smiled, and finally dozed off.

ALEX PRAYED LULU WAS RIGHT. Though they were going to Texas, they'd landed in Albuquerque, the closest airport to where they were headed. The SUV and camper he'd rented for the drive to the mountains was middle of the road, and less likely to draw attention during their stay in the national park. He increased the pressure on the accelerator as they drove onto the highway.

The location was strange—Nowheresville Texas? But Lulu was sure her mother had traveled to the Guadalupes, to the man who controlled her. They all were banking on Lu's certainty.

Most of the flight, he'd spent reading about Guadalupe Mountain National Park and arguing with Lulu via text, which had been the fun part.

He'd been texting with Larrimer, too, as their trio drove west toward California, the Arctos compound, and safety.

Clea...limp in Larrimer's arms, her long hair a waterfall of curls. He couldn't let go of the image. She should be with him, under his pack's protection. Yet he admitted she fit with Larrimer, which surprised him. Worse, when he tried to picture Clea with him, he saw a long fall of silver instead of Clea's blonde curls. Ridiculous.

He raked his hair, forgot he'd braided it, and swore. No matter where Clea belonged, by Váli he would avenge her.

"Y'all lookin' pissy as hell," Rae said.

He glanced at the mage sitting shotgun, and laughed. "I *am* pissy as hell."

"Stop that now, hear? Y'all got to get your cold alpha on."

"When the time comes, no worries old friend. Pretty much 24/7, he's clawing to come out."

IN THE BACK SEAT, Lulu rearranged Charlie for the umpteenth time, wishing the sleeping fae wouldn't keep flopping his head onto her shoulder. That hat they'd bought him itched, too.

She was anxious. She hadn't been in the mundane world for more than ten years—*her* time she amended. She'd been full of bravery and bravado that now leached away with each passing desert mile.

Talk about feeling like an alien.

It was as if she were hurled back in time, to her own past, a place she'd once inhabited eons ago. Everything felt familiar, yet distanced by a remote wall made of the life she'd lived and the events she'd experienced.

Her hands curled into fists. She'd helped her mother perpetrate this atrocity. Shouldn't she have caught her deception? Her hunger for her mother's love shamed her. Her need for Clea's approval when she'd run away looked foolish in retrospect.

If Clea were here, she'd offer Lulu a tiny violin, one perfectly in tune.

"What are you smiling at?" Alex said.

"Who said I'm smiling?"

"It's called a rearview mirror, princess."

She stuck out her tongue. Pain in the ass wolf.

ALEX'S GUT eased once they left Albuquerque, headed for the wilds of Texas. Tough to picture Maurelle anywhere but enjoying a spa day at the Ritz. But Lulu assured them she'd come here. That girl. That woman. Whatever she was, she kept things lively.

They sped through Los Lunas, Belen, Socorro, past pecan and post oak, on to Truth or Consequences, then to the desert's rolling earth around Las Cruces, with its cholla, agave, and the occasional tree. Damn, but he loved the desert, which was ridiculous according to his lieutenant, Erick. After all, they were Arctic wolf shifters.

As they turned onto Route 375, acres of desert flowed wild and wide like the Pacific. Alex couldn't stop glancing back at Lulu. Once clear of the Franklin Mountains, she'd finally fallen asleep. He again peered in the rearview mirror. She sat next to Charlie, lips slightly parted, snoring softly. An adorable picture, one he could get accustomed to.

And where the hell had that thought come from?

8

James and Neddy nearly made it to Indianapolis. James had been driving for twenty-four-hours because he'd taken twisty back roads, rather than the eleven-hour straight shot. Lack of sleep seldom bothered him, but his concern for Clea had gnawed away his energy.

He pulled the SUV into a lonely rest stop to stretch his and Neddy's legs and take a whiz. The kid had been out like a light, head resting on the window. Clea lay across the back seat, still as death.

The kid wasn't a talker, and he liked that. He felt an odd kinship with the boy. They'd both been altered in fucked-up ways. They were both monsters. They were both loved by Clea.

He touched the boy lightly on his shoulder. "Neddy."

The boy whipped around, claws extended.

He grasped the boy's wrists, stopped his attack. "Neddy."

"Sorry." The kid blinked a couple times, relaxed. Neddy didn't have to say aloud how he was struggling, how Clea's unconscious state was fraying his control.

"It's okay, kid. We'll work on it."

Neddy looked over the seat at Clea, then left the car and disappeared into the fringe of wood that ringed the rest stop. He'd wait until the boy returned before he took his break.

James got out, slipped into the back seat, and unsnapped Clea's makeshift seatbelts. He slid her carefully onto his lap so as not to dislodge the line of fluids and nourishment that kept her body from dehydration and starvation. She'd lost a little weight, but that wasn't what bothered him. She felt different. Lighter, less corporeal. Like she was fading. He caught himself running his finger down the scar on his face, a tell he couldn't seem to break.

"Clea, we're getting you back to the Arctos compound." The wyvern then piped up, telling him to kiss her.

Now that the damned creature had started talking to him, he managed to intrude at absurd moments. It sucked having another being inside himself, a semi-psycho, sentient one.

Kiss her!

The thing was shouting now. *Your yelling's going to drive me insane. You know, wyvern? And if I'm nuts—*

Then I'll have this body all to myself.

Yeah, well, I'll kill myself first. So fuck off.

The wyvern chuffed a laugh.

But he did kiss Clea, soft, insistent. He tried to burrow inside her mind. Her shields weren't up, but she was...gone. He leaned back, closed his eyes, and sighed.

Minutes later, the snick of a gun, close, outside the window. Two heartbeats, one fast, the other measured. With Clea resting on his lap, this could be an epic clusterfuck. He was fast enough to shield her, and the bullets wouldn't hurt him much. But he didn't want to leave two bodies beside the road and draw attention to themselves. For all he knew, even this desolate a rest stop had cameras.

He cranked open his eyes, slow, as if he were just waking. A fleshy thug stood outside his door, pointing an old Walther P5 semi at his face. Scruffy beard, drug-crazed eyes, and arm tremors. Shit fuck. Behind him, a taller, skinnier guy waited, hands in the pockets of his biking leathers.

James held the fingered peace sign, then cracked the door and eased Clea back onto the seat. He didn't want to step out. His size alone would intimidate these bozos. He'd have to wait to make his move until he was well away from the car and Clea. Simple enough then to render them unconscious and book it.

"Easy, boys," he said, as he widened the door.

"Get out," said the gun-toting idiot.

He did as requested, shut the door behind him, and uncoiled to his full height.

Fleshy Guy with the gun flinched. Skinny Guy held his smirk.

"Whatever you want." He spread his arms. "It's yours." He took a step away from the car.

"Don't do that," Skinny Guy said, eyes heavy lidded as he looked at Clea with a hunger that made him want to throttle the bastard. Larrimer almost sighed. So that was the way it was going to be, eh? He had to move now. Fleshy Guy was a disaster waiting to happen. Skinny Guy found it funny. Not for long. He coiled his energies to spring just as Skinny Guy reached for the door and for Clea.

"Larrimer?" came the shout.

Hell.

And then a seven-foot Pinky launched himself at the two men.

JAMES STOOD QUIET, while his mind processed different scenarios. A fine mist cooled his face, the product of a day turned from steel-gray to a soft rain. They had no garbage bags to clean up the mess. Fleshy Guy had blown out two tires in his wild, fear-induced bid to save himself. They had one spare.

He glanced at Neddy, still all Pinky. Gore covered him, head to toe, and he was eating the face off Skinny Guy. Any minute another traveler could drive in.

"Stop eating his face."

Larrimer turned on the car so Clea wouldn't suffer in the late afternoon chill. "Anyplace we could wash, Ned? Maybe a stream or a pond back there?"

Bloody drool flew as he shook his head.

"Here's what we're going to do. You will carry these pieces of meat into the woods. You will leave them, not feed. Got it?"

Neddy narrowed his eyes, then shook his head.

"Yes, you *will* do this."

The boy finally rose, clawed hands fisted on hips. He shook his head.

He kept his voice low and controlled when he said, "Do you want Clea to suffer? We need to get her safe away."

Neddy slumped, and after minutes of apparent thought, he nodded.

"Good. Now do it, while I use the spare to change one of the flat tires."

Twenty minutes later, the tire was changed and Neddy was semi-clean, having washed using the rain, most of their water, and several large bottles of Mountain Dew to get the glop off himself. He'd finally turned back to human, and his clothes were pristine. He avoided thinking about the rest of the kid. James had re-strapped Clea into the seat and rechecked the fluid lines running into her weakening body. Ready.

They could do little about the blood on the pavement. Or the bastards' car in the lot.

He put the SUV in gear, and they thumped back onto the road due to the remaining flat tire.

In the rearview mirror, his eyes repeatedly flicked to Clea, her IV bags swaying.

"I'm sorry," Neddy said. "I shouldn't have attacked. I should have waited for you to take care of them."

"Yes, you should have." He expected the kid to give some excuse for his precipitous actions.

"When I'm scared or pissed, I can't manage my other form, not like I could the wolf."

"No, you can't. I would have handled those men differently."

"I know," Neddy said, voice a whisper.

"So this is something we can work on. I can train you so you can control your other form. You can learn to manage those impulses and to channel them, to focus them, so they help, rather than hinder you. To chain the beast."

"How can you be so sure?" Neddy said.

A small smile lifted his lips. "Been there, done that."

Neddy laughed. "Got the t-shirt?"

James smiled as they drove across the muddy landscape, headed for a town with a low population, a gas station, and showers.

LULU COULDN'T BELIEVE how much dust billowed from the tires as they sped along the road toward the distant Guadalupe mountains. She and Rae battled over the truck's radio while Charlie dozed. Alex had been conspicuously silent.

"Both of you *shut up*," Charlie mumbled. "Switching channels and arguing over classical and hip hop for the past hour. I thought I'd go mad."

"Hello to you, too," Alex said. "Glad you're in one piece."

"*Almost* in one piece." Charlie began to raise his hand to his scabbed horn stumps, then dropped it.

Lulu glanced at the fae.

"I don't need your pity," Charlie turned away from her to stare out the window.

They'd arrive in a couple of hours. Lulu was eager to get going, to get this over with so Clea could recover. But if she were honest, she was scared to death, too. Not of the physical. In the magic world, she'd proven herself by staving off the gollups, those creatures of shadow and avarice. Yet her fear lived inside her like an alien being. It hadn't existed...before her dad's murder and her kidnapping and her trip to the magic realm. Before Tommy had tried to kill her and Bernadette had died as a result.

Who would she be had she lived a safer life? What would she feel?

She pressed her lips together, saw her mother's face twisted in anger. Pain for Lulu, either physical or psychic, almost always accompanied that face.

If any of her companions learned how her mother had treated her... They *never* could find out. She was so ashamed.

Alex reached back and took her hand. "What's wrong, Lu?"

She snatched it away, disturbed by the reflection in the rearview mirror of the concern darkening his eyes. She made sure her smile was plenty perky. "Just thinking of stuff."

He returned his focus to the road. "She won't get to you. Promise."

A laugh bubbled up, more manic than she would have liked. "Wolfie promises. I know all about those."

"We'll keep you safe," he said.

"Sure you will." As if he'd have a chance against her mother.

"Guys, I've been studying up," Alex said.

"And..." Rae said.

"I've formed a bunch of conclusions. The Guadalupe mountains are a thin space, where the magic realm has bled into the mundane for years."

"Like Charleston?" she said.

"No," Charlie piped up. "Charleston was a thin space, there was some magic, but we fae created that realm with deliberation."

"Hush everybody!" Rae turned up the radio's volume.

The Mt. Vesuvius eruption came with no warning. The volcano was quiet before a massive explosion rocked it at three a.m. this morning. Explosions fountaining at the crater have produced a high-volume lava flow. Satellite images depicting a deadly pyroclastic flow of hot gas and volcanic matter shows the cloud moving away from the volcano toward Naples at an unprecedented speed of 500 miles per hour. More than three million lives are threatened, and reports are coming in of thousands injured and dead due to this unprecedented event.

"Shit," Alex said. "The worlds' chaotic retwining?"

"'Spec so," Rae said. "It'll only get worse. I'm goin' to sleep. Wake me when we get there."

A growl rumbled from Alex's chest.

"You should hear this, Rae," she said. "You can sleep later."

Rae flapped his hand and closed his eyes. "Ah can listen with my eyes closed."

"Pain in the ass mage," Alex muttered. "Good thing you're one of my oldest friends, or I might shoot you. Charlie's right. The Guadalupes are different. Natural. Pockmarked with magic."

"What do you mean, pockmarked?" Lulu said.

Alex rubbed a hand back and forth across his face. Lulu remembered him picking her up from ballet class, after he caught her elbow when she tripped. His hand was calloused and strong, and... Oh, heck, what was she thinking?

"This is all speculation," he said. "But I'd equate it to the Arctos challenge."

"What's that?" she said.

"A course we set up for our young wolves. We fill it with traps, danger, disasters. I suspect the Guadalupes are like that."

"Oh, funsies." She wanted to crank the window, to breathe real air, but the temperature was blistering.

"So listen up." Alex waved toward the desert. "When we arrive at the campsite, it'll look like this. Scrubby—rocks, yucca, cactus, you know. Your mother and her *friend* could be holed up in one of several spots. We have to figure out which thin space they're using if we have any hope of catching them unawares. So first we're going to check out Smith Spring. From what I can tell, it's dark and dense. Mysterious."

"My mother loves water," she said.

"A perfect spot for Maurelle and her merry band of thieves," Charlie said.

Alex nodded. "McKittrick Canyon's another possibility. A strange place for Texas, it looks like New England, especially when the leaves change in fall. There's a stream, a grotto, an abandoned lodge, and a hunter's shack. Pretty nice place from the pictures. I can see your mother hunkering in there, Lu."

She shivered.

"Is he her lover?" Alex said. "Your mother's friend. The one who talked her into doing all this."

Wow, that was a yucky thought. She didn't know. Maybe. *Ewww.* It was hard for her to picture her elegant mother and some guy. Any guy. Even her dad. If he were here, he'd know. He always was wise to her mom's shenanigans. To Alex, to everyone else, her dad had been gone less than a year. To her? So long ago. "I don't know if he is her lover. But when we find her, we'll catch on pretty quickly."

"All right. The Guadalupes have plenty of arroyos, perfect for drowning in a flash flood. Tons of rattlers and other unfriendlies. But I figure if we leave them alone, they'll ignore us."

Lulu snorted. "Mom won't be anywhere near those arroyos. She hates creepy-crawlies."

"*She's* pretty creepy-crawly," Alex said. "Watch out for the trees, princess."

"Don't call me that. Why the trees?"

"The rattlers fall asleep in them and drop to the ground. One might land on top you."

She punched him in the shoulder.

"Hey!"

"Stop making stuff up."

He grinned. "Sorry to say, I'm not, little Lulu."

"Don't call me that, either," she said in her most haughty voice.

The mountains loomed closer and closer. The windows were closed, the A/C cranked. Even so, she felt the magic press against her skin like plastic wrap. It wasn't friendly.

"Last place to look," Alex said. "The Bowl's a prehistoric alpine forest about 7,000 feet up. Huge pine trees, Douglas fir, some aspen, meadows, elk, black bear and mountain lion. Acres and acres. A lot of drama. It looks more like Montana than Texas. My bet is that's where they'll be."

It would be good if there was a sign with a big, fat arrow proclaiming Bitch Mom Here.

NIGHT HAD STOLEN day's final rays. After Alex gassed up and had an argument with Rae that pissed off his wolf, they decided to spend the night at a nowhere motel, rather than take on the mountain. The following morning, they downed a hearty breakfast and made good time to the park.

Alex hopped out of the truck alongside the Pine Spring Visitor Center near the park entrance. Today was a roaster. Bright morning sunlight reminded him of home, of pack, of Melike. He shoved those distractions into one of his mind-boxes and inhaled. The air was rich with desert smells and thick with magic, as well as the human scent inside the building. He'd braided his distinctive hair, and now he tucked the braid beneath an Albuquerque Dukes ballcap he'd bought on the way. He opened the door, savored the cool air for a second, then sidled over to a long counter running opposite a wall of books, pictures, and other park odds and ends. No one in sight, so he dinged the metal call bell.

Seconds later, a short brunette in a national parks uniform bustled out from a back room. When she stood directly across the counter from him, he smiled. "Hey, I'd like to purchase some park annual passes."

She tilted her head, and he'd swear he caught the faintest whiff of magic. Not hers, but...

"How many are there in your vehicle?" she said.

"Me, and three other adults."

From beneath the counter she withdrew a clipboard with papers and pushed it toward him, along with a pen. He brushed her fingers as he took them. *She* wasn't magic, but mundane. That much was a certainty. But he'd be damned if she hadn't been around magic users lately. So he'd cast out some breadcrumbs to see if they led him anywhere.

He paid the fee, then completed the questionnaire with the verifiable, but false information he kept in reserve.

"Do you need guidebooks?" She waved at the shelves. "We've got a great selection."

He shook his head. "We bought them online. But, thanks. We thought we'd stay at the Pine Springs campground."

She grinned. "Plenty of room."

"Good."

"No fires of any kind."

"We have a propane stove."

"That works." She scratched her upper arm.

Something about this woman was fishier than a dead mackerel. More breadcrumbs needed. "We plan to climb Guadalupe itself, but we'd also like to hike to Smith Spring, McKittrick Canyon, stuff like that."

Her chin bobbed up, her brown eyes sharp. "All good, except The Bowl near Hunter Peak is closed. We had some trouble up there a few days ago, so the Park Service closed it for a week."

"Is that so?" he said. "What happened?"

Her fake smile didn't reach her eyes. She again scratched her arm. "Some dummy lit a campfire up there. It did some damage. We're still looking for him."

"I see. Let me grab a few maps, and I'm outta here."

By the time he walked out the door, that ranger girl wasn't the only itchy one. Now to see if his breadcrumb trail bore a nice, fluffy loaf of bread in the form of a fae or mage.

Alex filled in his companions on the ranger and the tidbits he'd tempted her with as they made quick work of setting up camp. Along with their SUV and camper, a tent and a pickup were the only other signs of life at the campsite. Not a popular time of year, he supposed. It was also possible Maurelle's mysterious mage had cooked up a keep-away spell, one that didn't affect his group in the least.

After they'd all used the facilities and showered at the camp's small washroom building, they piled into the camper where he'd spread maps of the park across the camper's banquette table. He circled the three sites they'd targeted with red pen.

"I'll go with Lulu to McKittrick."

She nodded. "Should I bring my bow?"

He shook his head. "Not this time. Just some concealed knives. No overt displays of weaponry for our first foray." He focused on Charlie and Rae. "You two take Smith Spring. We'll meet back here. Be thorough, but be careful as you clear your site. They might have set magical snares and watchers."

"We know how to be sneaky." Rae winked at Charlie.

The fae straightened, his expression dour.

"We'll meet back here tonight and make plans for the four of us to explore The Bowl."

"Rae and I can apparate the four of us in," Charlie said.

"I'm thinkin'," Rae said, "that after your powwow with the ranger they'll know we're comin'."

Alex nodded. "Agreed." His grin encompassed them all, and he squeezed the fae's shoulder. "But we've got this guy up our sleeve."

Charlie started, then a slow smile bloomed across his face, his soft laugh like the tinkling of bells.

For the hike to McKittrick Canyon, Lulu had dressed in her lightest cargos and tank, but after five minutes sweat coated her arms and face.

So what? Nothing mattered but that she was afraid, which was so *stupid*. But she couldn't get rid of the feeling. Now that she was back in the mundane world, she realized how safe she'd felt with the Charleston fae. Whether Aunt Viv realized it or not, she'd shielded Lulu from her mother's cruelty and manipulation. Many of the fae even admired and respected her. She'd been protected, the same as she'd been by Clea after her father's death. Even when she'd been kidnapped, she knew Clea would come for her. And she had.

Now, for the first time ever, she was on her own.

Boy, her mom had sure done a job on her. Ten years of her mother's invasive manipulation felt like she'd been split open and hollowed out.

It was simple, really. She'd have to get over it and get her confidence back. She wasn't sure how she'd do it, but she vowed to work on it each and every day until she *owned* it.

For now, she'd continue her "bold and brave" act. Who knew? Maybe the act would become truth.

"Speed it up, Lulu," Alex said.

"Coming."

The access road they hiked into McKittrick Canyon was smooth and groomed, yet she stumbled.

She might not be like Alex or Rae or Charlie, but she wanted to be.

She *had* to think positive. She had her Song. Now all she needed was a lick more courage.

Alex pivoted to peer back at her. "What's wrong?"

"Nothing."

"You're full of a lot of 'nothings' lately."

"Bite me." She grinned, having perfected faking it.

He resumed their hike, ignoring her.

She stumbled again, but not because of her clumsy feet. McKittrick Canyon nestled like a precious emerald in the heart of the raw desert. The trees. She loved trees and had read all about the native flora. They sang to her—heavy-leafed walnut, ash, maple, and oak mingled with choke cherry and the cool-barked madrone. Every shade of green imaginable in the mundane realm. Here, in this parched desert. Amazing. She walked toward the stream that cut through the canyon. It bubbled happily over rocks, forming tiny whirlpools and riffles and eddies. The water danced with life.

Dryads and naiads. And elves, those cousins to the fae. Their essences brushed her throat, her neck, her arms. But the touches were old, almost dissipated, as if they'd left their trees and water and rock for other realms.

"This place speaks to you," Alex said, moving to stand beside her.

"Yes." She parted her lips to sing, to the trees, to the water.

"Don't."

"But I... "

"You'll alert our enemies. They know someone's here. They may not know our identities yet. Got it?"

Of course she got it. "Yeah, I do. I forgot for a moment."

With his eyes intense on hers, he gripped her arm. "Well, don't forget again. Or you'll be a homing signal for your mother."

She tugged her arm away. "I *know*."

They continued down the serpentine trail that paralleled the stream. Miles later, he said, "We're getting near the Pratt house. Stay behind me."

Hadn't that been exactly what she *had* been doing? Gods, she was in a foul mood. "All right."

He waved her forward, then he jerked and shoved her deep into a clump of bushes. Thorns bit her bare arms. *Ouch.*

"Stay there," he hissed, as he remained on the path.

The earth shook. And a smell, like rancid cheese. Stilton.

She peeked around the bush.

Three creatures stood on the path. *Damn.* Each was a good seven-foot tall and were built like sumo wrestlers, slabs of muscle covering their purple bodies. The trio wore leather pants and bandoliers that held swords at their backs. A red sash bound the presumed leader's waist. Their lower jaws protruded, with tusks that curved upward to lethally sharp points. She knew about the points because she'd met their cousins in the magic realm.

Goblins.

The leader took in Alex and grinned. "Well, lookie here. Dinner."

Alex snorted and crossed his arms. "Man, you guys smell bad. Bathe much?"

The leader winked. "Won't matter to you."

"But it will!" Alex said. "I'll have to get up close and personal to kill you."

All three goblins laughed.

Shit! Didn't Alex know what these creatures were? They loved eating flesh off the bone, especially if that flesh was still alive. Her mind raced with possibilities of how to get them out of there. A distraction. Something. Alex could take one, but all three? Impossible.

The leader flicked his hand. "Turn back little shifter, and we won't eat you." He made a snuffling sound. "Or that lurker in the bushes over there."

She parted the bushes and stepped onto the path behind Alex.

"You smell familiar, girl," the leader said.

"We've never met." At least not this particular goblin.

"Move aside," Alex said. "We'd like to continue our hike."

"You wish." The leader scratched his chest, turning his black marble eyes on her, and gestured to one companion. "Take her."

Alex began to morph into his half form, claws extended, muzzle elongated.

"Halt!" She shouted, pressing Voice into that one word.

The goblins and Alex froze. It would only last a minute or two, but that should be enough.

There was something important she should remember about goblins, something... *Yes!* If these responded as the ones in the magic realm had, she might pull off a coup. If not, well, she had her knives, Alex his claws and teeth. Yeah, they'd be dead.

She swallowed, her throat so parched with terror she coughed. But appearances were everything, or so her mother claimed. Her gambit wouldn't work if she couldn't sing, so she repeated a mantra Clea had taught her as she gulped mouthfuls of water. After she replaced her canteen, she notched up her chin and stepped forward toward the goblin leader, all eyes glued to her. The surprise on Alex's face had been worth it, even if she did get eaten.

Alex twitched a finger.

Her Voice command had begun to dissipate, which meant a slow return of their ability to move. She held up her hand, the smile she planted on her face small and sly. "I heard a rumor about you guys, one that may or may not be true. Curious?"

The leader leaned forward, close enough that she smelled his unappetizing cheese scent and fetid breath. "Perhaps."

"I'd like to make a bet with you three." Good timing because her Voice command was almost gone.

The leader straightened. He looked at his companions, and all three pairs of eyes glowed with excitement and avarice.

"Someone sent you here to guard the path. Eating us would be a bonus, right?"

The leader neither acknowledged or denied her claim.

"You might defeat us. Or you might lose and die. Either way, you'll be in a world of hurt at the end of our little contretemps."

"Our what?" Goblin Three said.

"Fight," barked the leader.

She was dying to look at Alex, to see his reaction. She didn't dare. "My wager is a pretty simple one, really. I'll make you cry."

The goblins guffawed, slapping their knees and punching each other's shoulders. They thought she was a riot.

Alex stood stiff as a frozen popsicle. Her Voice might have worn off, but her lunacy had paralyzed him.

"And if you lose?" the goblin said.

"We'll go with you to your leader without a fight."

"We're going to kill you and the shifter, little girl."

No, they wouldn't kill her, not if she told them who she was. But their mission would end in disaster. They still might try to kill Alex, but... She couldn't think that way. She just couldn't. "Oh, I know I can make you cry. Bawl like babies, in fact."

Two of the goblins snorted with laughter. But the leader only narrowed his eyes.

"If I win," she continued. "You let us go. You're so certain I'll lose, where's the risk? My sources tell me goblins have their own kind of honor, especially when it comes to bargains."

The leader notched his head toward the trio, and they stepped off the trail to talk amongst themselves in their strange guttural language.

Alex stepped close. "What the hell are you doing, Lu?"

"Trust me? Just let me play it out." She was risking a lot, and not just their lives. Even if they scraped out of this with a win, things would be damaged and lost. What else could she do?

"Fuck me." But he moved beside her, shifting back to his fully human form.

"We, too, have heard things." The leader approached them. "That shifters are deceitful. And that little fae girls lie, too."

"So what? If I'm lying, you can still kill us." She grinned. Alex's bristle of fury scraped her senses raw, but he remained silent. "But isn't this more fun?"

The leader came nose to nose with her, and she forced herself not to flinch.

With his impossibly long tongue, he licked a tusk. "It will be, little fae. For us."

Alex's gut tightened until he thought it would implode. What the flying fuck was she playing at? Make three goblins cry? *He* hadn't cried since he was six. He doubted these creatures had *ever* shed a tear.

Lulu was going to sing, that much he understood, which would alert her mother to their presence. Others, too.

If he had a choice, he'd spirit her away. He'd seen the hungry looks on those goblins. They might intend to kill him, but they had other plans for her. Ones that made his nostrils flare and claws prick his fingers.

She sat beside the stream, her palms resting on the earth. He hunkered down beside her. The stream was deep enough, fast enough that he could toss her in. She could escape.

He tried to remember his ancient history lessons. Did goblins hate water? Memory failed.

She waved her hands at the trio in an up and down motion. "Sit. Sit."

They complied, squatting across from her.

"Good," she said.

Her fingers dug into the earth and she closed her eyes. Then her expressive hands lifted as if in supplication and sang.

"There was a time when men were kind..."

Her voice rose, amplified, expanded into another dimension. He stiffened, his body fighting the flood of emotion, the urge to close his eyes. He narrowed them on the goblins.

Bodies stiff, fists clenched, they too fought the rush of emotion.

His fight lasted longer than theirs as he watched their muscles relax, their eyes close, their lips move as if in prayer.

He'd heard her songs before, some funny ditties she'd sing at the den or lullabies to quiet a child. In the wood, a song of healing, of silence, of sleep. But this... No, he'd never heard its like.

He crumbled, pressed his hands to his eyes as if to stopper the tears at the tragic melody and words. The battle was futile. He sobbed.

When his eyes flew open, realizing what he'd done, he saw that the goblins had wrapped their arms about their torsos and rocked, while rivers of tears cascaded from their eyes.

The song went on and on, Lulu's face a beautiful porcelain mask, the need to comfort her, cherish her, overwhelming.

When the last note hung like a dragonfly in the air, he sucked a breath into his lungs he hadn't known he'd needed.

Two of the goblins sat motionless, while the leader reached into air as if to capture that final otherworldly note.

Her violet eyes bore the calm of a person totally connected to her essence, her truth. It could be a mask or real. Didn't matter, when all he wanted to do was crawl inside that peace and hold it tight.

"More," the leader ground out, voice thick with emotion.

Her "Danny Boy" brought on the goblin's tears again. He'd heard it enough times that he could stopper his, but not without effort. But she leveled him again when she sang "Loch Lomond."

Then she broke into Johnny Cash's "A Boy Named Sue." The goblins transformed from tears to confusion to laughter as they listened, and her finale, "Grandma Got Run Over by a Reindeer" had them snorting with laughter. By that time, her voice had grown hoarse, the drooping of her eyes the only indication of the huge amounts of energy she'd expended.

For two heartbeats, when her song ceased, the world around them kept silent. Then a cacophony of bird chirps and squawks said her audience had gone beyond goblin and shapeshifter.

Her eyes held the leader's. "The bargain is met. The bet won."

He moistened his lips, and when one of his fellows went to speak, his silenced him with the slice of his hand. "That it is. And I have never heard its like." As he kept Lulu's gaze, his eyes, those beady black orbs that promised death, softened. "You *do* realize you've tied your own noose, child."

LULU KEPT her mouth closed as they hiked back to the campsite. She'd expected Alex to shred her. Instead, he hadn't said a word. Why didn't the damned man do anything she expected?

Not to mention how their plans with Charlie apparating them into The Bowl had gone all to hell when the goblin told them about the wards. The special ones. He'd been almost *nice,* waiting to speak to them after he sent the other goblins to mark the path by peeing on it.

Alex abruptly stopped beneath the shade of a madrone. *Now what?* He snapped around to face her, gold eyes aflame. *Here it comes.* His face, taut with emotion boded ill for her safety. Maybe she should run. Her muscles clenched to do just that.

He stepped forward, body bow-string taut, so close she smelled his sweat and that sunshine-and-sea aroma of his. She stepped back, a tree helping her stand as her legs jellied. His eyes locked onto hers, and his fingers clamped around her chin. He leaned in. She swallowed.

He took her lips in an angry, punishing kiss.

She stood there stiffly, not knowing what to do, how to react. Was this his punishment for disobeying him?

Then his kiss softened, his tongue licking the seam of her lips. Her mind might be wrecked, but her body liked it, liked him, and she opened. He delved inside her mouth, nibbled her lips, explored her mouth once again.

His desire, honey, bathing her in the sweetness of his kiss. She ran her palms up the ridges and valleys of his muscled chest, her fingers curling into his damp t-shirt. She held on, her sea of confusion drowning in an answering emotional storm.

He finally pulled back. A moan. Hers or his she wasn't sure, the loss of those warm expressive lips a terrible thing.

Drunk with his kiss, she could only stare at him. The flare of his nostrils said he'd been affected, too. Maybe even as shocked as she. What had begun as a conquest turned into something very different.

Questions riddled his eyes, as the pads of his fingers traced her swollen lips.

She ran.

In her head, Clea's admonition, *Never run from a predator.*

Except she couldn't help it, couldn't stop, her legs pumping with panic-fueled adrenaline.

Over the rise, down the road, thump, thump, thump. The campsite ahead. Their truck and camper. Charlie and Rae lounging in the shade of the camper's awning.

She veered off, snaked into the washroom, darted into the women's section. She pressed her hands to her knees, panting as if she'd run miles, rather than yards.

What was she going to do? She wanted to kiss him again. And again. And again.

ALEX KNEW EXACTLY what came over him. Understood it down to the very cells of his being. It was wrong. Lulu Cochran might have a twenty-six-year-old's lush body, but she had the emotional age of that lost sixteen-year-old. And he was doomed, his fate sealed.

"Hey, man," Rae said as Alex walked into camp. "What's got your ass in a twist? The little girl just bolted into the lav. Eh?"

The little girl. He swiped his face, tugged the band on his braid to release it. He needed to run. He needed...

His shift, swift and sure, unleashed his wolf. He tore off down the path, submerged in the power, the rhythm, the beat of his paws on the dusty soil. He ran and ran and ran.

Hours later he was more settled, more comfortable in his human skin. While the wolf might feel the pull toward Lulu, the man could control both his and his wolf's urges. Control was everything to an alpha, and he wasn't about to lose it.

After he'd showered and dressed, the camp's cooking smells made his mouth water as he left the washroom. Man, he was starved. He trotted across the hard-packed earth and sank into an empty camp chair beside Charlie.

Someone had set the chairs in a semicircle beneath the unrolled awning.

"Where are the others?" he asked Charlie.

"They moved the cooking stuff around to the other side of the camper. Something about creatures of the night."

Which made him think of vampyres. He hadn't seen one for years, as most seldom ventured from their islands.

"Hey, y'all," Rae said, rounding the rear of the camper. "Alex, y'all grinnin' like a possum eatin' a sweet tater."

"Potatoes aren't my favorite."

Rae chuckled and set a platter of steaks and one of corn on the cob on the low table. Alex swiped a hand across his face. "Damn, but I could definitely eat a bear."

"Sorry, but bear's not on the menu." Lulu plunked down a huge salad bowl beside the steaks and corn.

Rae walked to the awning, turning the crank to roll it back. "That was a long-assed run you took, wolf boy."

Lulu's lips thinned, but she trotted inside the camper, returned with plates and utensils, and set them out.

He lifted a longneck from the cooler, popped the cap, and drank. Why the hell had he kissed her in the first place? He'd been so fucking pissed—pictured her torn apart by the goblins—scared to death for her. That kiss. It wasn't supposed to be like that. Because he couldn't hit her, it was a pissed-off, don't do that again kiss. Instead it became...more. He lowered his beer and forced a smile to his lips. "Needed the run."

The look she darted him was shocked, and maybe a little hurt. Damn, but he'd never meant to hurt her. And here came the outburst. The recriminations.

"I've explained," she said in a quiet, controlled voice. She cleared her throat. "I told Rae and Charlie how the goblins changed after I sang, about the leader's warning and what he said about the wards. We've been talking, strategizing."

Her voice held the coolness of a mountain stream and betrayed not a hint of anger or aggravation. Well, *hell*. She should be feeling *something*. He sure was.

After their meal, they cleared the table and Rae spread out their map.

"Nothing at Smith Spring but trees and water," Rae said as he Xed it out on the map. "No magic. No people of any genre."

"We thought to hike through McKittrick again," she said. "The goblins won't bother us. We could cut off at the Tejas Trail, at the backside of The Bowl. They're long hikes, so we can spend the night at the Tejas campsite and in the morning, turn off at Juniper, then The Bowl trail for a little ways."

"I like it." Plenty of trails led to The Bowl quicker, but this was the smarter move. They'd enter The Bowl from the backside. If they had to hike, and not apparate in, it was a good option. "What about the hidden trail? The one the lead goblin explained to us?"

Rae's finger traced the secret path from McKittrick straight to The Bowl Loop trail. "When sugah here showed us, that got my tingles all a-goin'."

"You don't like it," he said.

"I sure as shit don't." Rae plucked his lip.

Charlie sighed. "It won't matter which trail we take. They'll be ready for us."

Lulu flushed.

"It's not your fault," Alex said. "It's possible they won't know. They said they wouldn't betray us. The trio seemed pretty enchanted by our Lulu after she sang."

Charlie snorted.

"I bet my mother heard my song," Lulu said.

He wanted to touch her so bad. "And maybe she didn't."

"It doesn't matter." She shrugged. "What's done is done."

Alex wished he could see inside her mind. Was she feeling guilt? Sorrow? Fear? Whatever it was, she was masking it hard. "So let's say your mother and her 'friend' *do* know we're on our way. What matters is mitigating that readiness. So we take the long way 'round. We'll make a contingency plan for escape if trouble heats up. And with resting the night at the campsite, we'll be at full strength in the morning."

He feared for her, feared for all of them, but she was the most vulnerable, both to her mother and the physical nature of the hike. "Can you make the trek?"

She nodded, and he doubted the anxiety in her violet eyes was for the hike, but rather the coming confrontation with Maurelle.

"Good. Number one, we need to make sure Lulu's protected."

She puffed out her chest. "They won't hurt me. Mother would kill anyone who did."

In battle, accidents happened. To him it was obvious how much she hated what she saw as weakness. She'd saved them that after-noon with her song.

Her song... "The Song of Sleep."

Lulu's eyes widened, and she grinned. "Of course! Yes, I can do that."

He wasn't convinced it would be enough, but her beautiful joy sparked the air around him. The world stilled to just them, the need to protect her a thrum in his soul. Stars glimmered above, the three-quarter moon silvering her face.

"Lulu." She would run, scamper away like the fawn she was.

Her spine straightened. She tilted her head. "Yes?"

"Feel like a walk?" Where the fuck had that come from?

Oh, Lulu wanted to. She wanted to so bad. But that was dumb. Her first love, Ronan, had been kind and understanding. They'd already broken up when she'd run away, but she'd still left him a letter, telling him what a fine man he'd become and how she would always admire and respect him. Those years in high school when they'd been a couple, he'd never tried to bully her or demand her obedience.

This man, this wolf, he would demand. And she knew herself, knew her tendency for submissive behavior. Even during her rebellious Goth phase with Clea, she'd felt guilty the entire time.

Alex didn't exactly disrespect her. Yet he'd steamroller her, just as her mother had done. And she'd allow it because she wanted him so fiercely. Yeah, she'd finally admitted that to herself in the shower. It sucked.

He reached for her ponytail and removed the tie, her fall of silver hair fanning around her. His eyes glittered as he lifted a lock into his fingers and petted it. "I've wanted to do this ever since you came to sing to me in the bower. It glistens pure as Sterling."

She pulled it through his fingers, away from his hand. "It's different now."

"Yes, as are you. The copper-color was lovely, but this? It's astonishing." Alex's face was taut, as if he were damming a river of words. "Do you like it?"

Heat flushed her cheeks. "I... I don't know. It's evidence of my ten years in the magic realm. I hated it there."

"All of it?"

"There were parts I liked. I gained skills, grew. But I felt robbed, too."

"Lu. Walk with me."

"Thank you, but I'm tired. I'm going to rest up for tomorrow."

She forced her body to stand, her joints stiff with resistance. She *wanted* to walk with this wolf. Instead, she headed for the camper's door. She wouldn't look back. She wouldn't.

She did.

Alex's eyes pulsed once, glowing gold, then he ambled away.

Back inside the camper, Charlie appeared while she was piling the dishes in the sink. "I'll wash up," he said.

"Thanks."

"The alpha's a fine man, you know."

Surprised, she focused on the fae, aware of how she still thought of fae as other, even though she was one. "What made you say that?"

He took a scraped plate from her hand and dipped it into the soapy water. "Frankly, it was rather an odd impulse. The urge came upon me."

She laughed. "You're funny, Charlie."

He smiled. "I am, aren't I?"

Out the window, she spied Alex carrying the trash bag to the bin by the washroom.

He looked over his shoulder, caught her eyes with his.

She chained the powerful urge to look away, and held his gaze.

The words "what if?" came to mind. *What if?*

10

James needed sleep. Without sleep, his body functions declined, his mind dulled, his reaction times slowed. He could go long stretches without it. But too long... He'd tried. In that crappy motel near Indianapolis. While he let Neddy drive, which had gone against his better instincts. When they'd parked at another rest stop.

No such luck.

They'd just driven through Utah's Fishlake National Forest. Stands of aspen, mountain meadows, lakes, streams—the forest reminded him of home. Of Montana. Clea would have loved to see it. He appreciated the beauty, but he *felt* none of it. All he felt were the minutes and hours sifting away, along with Clea's life.

The road had become desolate. That, he liked.

They would have made better time had they gone through New Mexico, but Neddy'd had a good point. They shouldn't be anywhere near Alex and his band.

Throat parched, eyes like sand, he pulled the SUV over to the road's shoulder. The glance Neddy cut him was full of anxiety, but the kid didn't open his mouth. Smart boy. The only thing sleep deprivation amped up was his hunger for violence, the thread near snapping. His skin felt stretched, his blood simmered, and his jaw ached from clenching. The urge to kill chewed at his sanity, the wyvern egging him on relentlessly.

Those Union bastards had designed him to kill. He lusted for it.

"A sec," he said to Neddy.

He left the SUV, trailed a finger across its dusty coating. If he fisted his hand, he could crunch the metal into a tight ball. Satisfying.

The hand he pressed to the car shook. He took a deep breath, filling his lungs with the scents of sage and pine. The screams in his head quieted.

By the time he made it back to the truck and into the back seat, he was calm enough to touch her.

With great care, he unsnapped her safety belts and lifted her head and torso into his arms. He'd been right, dammit. He knew he had been, but he'd had to check.

Clea's lemongrass and cedar scent had changed, soured. Her face was now porcelain white, near transparent, and tight like a mask, widening the crescent scar beneath her left eye. Cadaverous. *Christ*.

Air rattled in her chest, every inhale shallower than the last, with each breath feeling like a monumental victory.

He pressed his ear to her chest, heard the crackle in her lungs, followed by a wet sucking sound.

"Clea, stay," he whispered in her ear. "You must."

He kissed her forehead, lay her back down, belted her in.

Back up front, he texted Alex and Rae.

No answering text.

"We should take Clea to a hospital," Neddy said, voice pleading. "She's gonna die if we don't."

"We can't."

"*Why?*"

He scrubbed his hands over his face. "About a thousand reasons." Beginning with hospital paperwork. Them being traced. Cops. Alerting Tatianne and The Union to their location.

Neddy unsnapped his seatbelt and slid to face him. "She's dying, Larrimer." Tears glazed the kid's eyes. "*Dying.*"

He fisted Neddy's shirt.

And the earth shook.

He leaned over the seats and braced Clea. "Hang on, kid!"

The shaking shuddered and died away. He checked Clea's nutrient bags and lines. None had come out.

He sat back into the driver's seat. Neddy stared out his window, eyes huge.

A face poked inside the open passenger window. Larrimer's Sig flashed in his hand. No body, just a face, the chin resting on the door's windowsill.

What the hell? Was she kneeling? Pretty woman, honey skinned, wide smile. Except orange eyes weren't his thing.

"Hello, Mr. Larrimer," she said. "And you, Neddy boy. Good to see you both again. I'm here to help."

"Who the fuck are you?" James aligned his perfect shot to penetrate straight between those strange eyes.

She frowned. "You don't remember me?"

"We've never met."

"Oh, we've met, big boy, just at a distance."

They hadn't. "You obviously know who we are, so open the door, take a seat. We'll talk."

She wrinkled her nose. "*Who makes it, has no need of it.*

Who buys it, has no use for it.

Who uses it can neither see nor feel it.

What is it?"

"The fuck?" he said.

"Sorry," she said. "Sometimes I can't help myself."

Neddy, who'd gone half Pinky, cleared his throat. "She's, uh, she's not human, Larrimer."

"No shit, Sherlock," he said.

"I mean, I can see her body." The kid gulped a swallow. "She's got wings attached to what looks like a lion. Her boobs are out, too."

A sphinx. *The* sphinx. "You're Sophy, the sphinx who helped us with Tatianne."

"The big guy wins the macaroni!" Her head bobbed a nod. "Sure am, bucko. I'm a little OCD about my riddles, so you need to answer."

What? The creature was certifiable. She'd also helped Clea, and saved their asses. He rolled the riddle over in his mind, looked at angles, saw crevices. Decided he didn't give a shit.

"A coffin!" Neddy said, accompanied by a string of Pinky drool. "That was easy."

"You're full of surprises, kid," Larrimer said.

"Okay, here's another one," Sophy said.

"Stop." His growl caught her attention.

The wyvern chuffed. *Thank heavens. She'll go on with those things forever.*

You knew who she was? he said.

Naturally.

Asshole. "Why are you here, Sophy?"

"For Clea, of course."

No 'of course' about it. "I'll be out in a sec, Sphinx." One look at Clea and he grabbed a towel. She'd begun to sweat. He wiped her face and arms. "Neddy, roll up the window, turn on the A/C." He put a hand on the boy's shoulder. "Can you go human?"

"Sure, but—"

"Do it."

When the boy complied, he stepped outside and leaned in the window. "Get in the driver's seat. If my convo with the sphinx goes south, take off." He tapped his phone. "We're near Cedar City. Get Clea to the hospital there."

"But you said the hospital—"

"I know what I said. Shit changes. Call the den and talk to Erick. They'll help."

He waited until Neddy crawled into the driver's seat.

"Good," he said. "You clear? Got your knife? Your phone charged? Erick on speed dial?"

"Yeah. Yeah, all of it. But I don't want to leave you with her."

"Clea's our priority. Nothing's going to happen, kid. Contingencies. That's all."

Sage and desert grass clumped beside the road, with mountains in the distance. Sophy had parked herself a little ways down from the SUV and stretched out her long lion's body. Her tail swished. On her back, camped like a black spider, sat the long-haired chihuahua from Charleston. The dog gave him the side eye.

If the sphinx wasn't going to say anything about the dog, neither was he.

He sat down cross-legged before her. "So?"

"Took you long enough, buckaroo."

"How did you know we were here?"

She winked.

James rested his wrists on his knees. "Perhaps if I rip the wings from your flesh, you'll understand I don't want to fuck around with you."

She pouted. "That wasn't nice."

He flowed to his feet. "I'm not nice. We don't need your bullshit. Clea doesn't need it." He turned and walked toward the car.

"Viviane sent me."

He whipped around, his gun aimed straight at the beast for a killing shot.

The creature rose on her four paws. "She sent me to help."

"Hard to believe."

"If you hadn't noticed, Clea's dying."

"Is she? How would you know that?"

"Viviane understands what being lost in those worlds does to a physical form. Her husband went away."

"Clea's father."

"Yes." She padded forward on quiet paws. "He was a guardian, and came across another of the chests. Not his. His abilities enabled him to open it, and he fell, much like Viviane described what happened to Clea. But she was able to save him."

"There's more to this story."

"Much. I can help Clea."

"She's *mine* to help." Their fae bond remained, but it had weakened along with Clea's body.

"I know she's yours. But you can't help her as I can."

The chihuahua leapt off the sphinx's back and yipped.

"What can you do that I can't?" he said.

"Take her to the magic world."

He chuckled. "Not a chance."

The sphinx's eyes flared bright. "Her *only* chance."

"Explain."

"I will put her in stasis. There's not enough magic here to do that in the mundane realm, not yet. But there I can spell her. She will be safe, Larrimer. Preserved. Until your comrades find the chest."

"Viviane hates Clea."

"Of course she doesn't. She's always known the truth of her. For many years, Viviane felt jealous of Clea's and Dave Cochran's relationship as student and mentor. That she'd been replaced in Clea's heart by that mage. But she has *always* watched over her daughter, though Clea was unaware of it. Not to mention how their temperaments are similar. Even as a child, she and Clea butted heads."

"That hasn't changed." He holstered his gun. When he mulled it over, he found similarities between the two women, as well as profound differences. Who the hell cared at this point? Clea was dying. Much as he hated to admit it, that was truth. Yet he couldn't hand her over. She belonged with *him*.

The sphinx spread her arms wide. "Viviane wants her daughter to live."

"Thanks for the offer. I believe its given in good faith, but no."

Smoky, multicolored motes spiraled around the little dog. When it dissolved, the mocha-skinned, six-foot Amazon known as Anouk stood before him. A golden eagle shifter, he'd also known her as a panther, a calico kitten, and, apparently, also an annoying chihuahua. A shifter of many parts. Guardian of the Chest of Stone, a former diner waitress, and Clea's alleged champion. He hadn't seen much championing in evidence.

"Where the hell were you when Clea fell?" he said.

She showed him teeth. "Do you think I could have stopped her?"

"You should have anticipated."

"Pot. Kettle. Black," Anouk said.

"Fuck you." James wasn't leaving Clea with two crazy magic wielders. "I'm out of here."

Wait.

That damned wyvern.

They are wise in these ways. Let them help our Clea.

Our Clea, my ass.

Anouk rested her hand on his forearm. "Let Sophy take Clea. It is her chance for survival. Her one chance."

He didn't trust Sophy. Or Anouk. How could he give them Clea?

She was dying right before his eyes. Her face was gray, eyes sunken, lips pale as death. When he held her, he wanted to squeeze her tight. His strong, powerful Clea. If he did that, she might break. "All right. I'll go with you."

Good plan, kemosahbee.

How to strangle a creature *inside* him he'd yet to figure out.

Anouk frowned. "You cannot."

He laughed. "Oh, but I can."

Sophy fluttered her wings. "If you do, you may forever become the wyvern. You want that? Would Clea want that?"

"Didn't happen on my previous visit."

"No," Anouk said. "It did not. But I suspect you are aware how active the wyvern has become. Is he speaking to you in your mind yet?"

Were these lies to keep him away or were they the truth? He ran a finger down his scar. "Give me a minute."

The SUV was running, the A/C cranked when he eased inside and closed the door.

Clea's cheeks were flushed, her breath labored, her eyelids twitching.

"What's wrong?" Neddy said.

"A choice. Give Clea into the sphinx's care or keep her with us."

Neddy swallowed, a thick sound. "How can you give her to—?"

"I know, kid, but..." *Christ.*

"*We* can save her." The boy practically jumped out of his skin. "We'll get her to a hospital, and they'll put her on a ventilator or something. They'll monitor her vitals. Isn't that what they call it? They can give her drugs to help her, too. And the ventilator'll make her breathe better. We'll protect her."

He blindly stared at the road ahead, saw Clea's smiling eyes, heard her laughter. He pressed a hand to the car's dash. *He needed control.* She wasn't here to save him this time. A *snap*. Six inches of dashboard lay in his hand. He fisted it to dust.

"Ouch," Neddy said.

The kid was close, too close. In his space. Crowding him. His hands reached to throttle him. "Move away fast, kid."

The boy jerked back. "Sorry!" But Neddy's eyes pleaded with him. "We can do it. She'll be better off at the hospital."

Would she? His eyes burned. His breath raced. Sweat scored his skin. He knew the right thing to do. The *only* thing to do. Yet his entire being fought against it.

"I'm sorry, Neddy." For both of us.

James scooped Clea from the backseat, walked across the tired earth to the two creatures who waited. Their faces were solemn, and he'd swear Sophy's eyes held tears. He bent his head, touched his lips to Clea's. *Would it be for the last time?*

The wyvern screeched as he placed his Clea in Anouk's outstretched arms.

"I need a way to contact you," he said.

The Sphinx groaned, and tiny hands appeared where her wings met her body, then forearms, and soon fully fleshed arms. "Hold out your hand."

He obeyed, and Sophy placed a large bronze coin on his palm. "Rub it if you need me."

He fisted the coin.

Holding Clea, Anouk slid astride the sphinx's leonine back. Sophy retracted her arms.

"Save her," he said.

"We will try," Anouk said. "Time is her enemy. Hurry."

With that, Sophy launched into the air.

His eyes tracked the sphinx, Clea's long hair flying like a banner, until they disappeared from the cloudless sky.

LULU RESTED her voice and sucked Ricola honey lozenges by the dozen as their troop of four climbed Juniper Trail. A few hundred feet ahead, they'd make a right onto the trail for The Bowl. The air was cooler here, and she was glad she'd worn jeans and long sleeves. The bow and quiver strapped to her back added some weight, but not too much. All had donned their fae cloaks, which blended into the treed landscape as if they'd been woven here, and not in Charleston's verdant realm.

They'd passed plenty of "Trail Closed" signs, climbed over barriers or walked around them. The forest was dense, the magic thick. Rae would periodically shake himself, as if he were crawling with ants. She couldn't blame him. The magic here tasted different from Charleston's. Older. More feral. The elevation, too, might be affecting him and the others. It was her. She was used to Charleston's sea level. At 7,000 feet her breath came in small pants. Alex was the only one who didn't seem bothered.

Once they left the forest to trek into The Bowl, she looked forward to seeing her first mountain meadow, maybe even a bear or elk or mountain lion. She'd never experienced land like this, and she found it exhilarating.

But business first.

Alex held up a hand. They must be nearing the turnoff.

She dropped her pack and pulled out the earplugs she'd been

forced to craft from chewing gum. She'd cleaned the gum, molded it into plugs, and as she passed them out, Rae's raised eyebrows had made her giggle.

Alex pressed close to her ear. "Remember the signal?"

She nodded.

"And our contingency plan?"

"Yes." Her hands instantly felt greasy with sweat. She hadn't had time for nerves while climbing. She took a calming breath and nodded. "Be careful."

His slow and deadly smile made her shiver. "Where's the fun in that?" His lips tickled the shell of her ear.

She hissed back at him. "Nothing about this is fun, you maniac!"

He took her left hand and waved the others forward. "No matter what," he said as they walked. "We'll be fine."

She wished she believed that.

They rounded the turn. Almost atop the mountain near The Bowl.

Lulu moistened her lips and rested her hand on the hilt of her knife, her eyes searching for movement. Massive trees flanked the path, a chiaroscuro of light and shadow. As they walked deeper into the wood, the magic darkened, a feeling of oil dripping down her skin.

Now we're in for it, Rae said in her head. *Be ready.*

She wished she could project back to Rae, but that wasn't one of her gifts. At least her mother had taught her to walk silently in the way of the fae. Her companions' footfalls were equally hushed, but the stiffness in Rae's gait worried her, as if he were slogging through deep snow.

Alex's raised hand brought them to a halt.

The wood's unnatural silence worried her, its creatures perhaps sensing something they could not. She uncapped her water and sipped.

A weight pressed against her. Did the others feel it? That darkness. Impending doom. Heavy, cloying. Her clothes stuck to her body, and even they felt too weighty, her skin so sensitized she wanted to rip them off and scream.

Alex waved them forward. But she couldn't move, wanted to turn and run and find a deep hole to hide in. Fear curled through her like a black viper, sinuous and evil.

Except Rae and Charlie hadn't stepped forward, either. They weren't scaredy cats like she was.

She got it.

Her mother's magic. Maurelle was pressing these horrible feelings onto them. Bully for her. Gonna outflank you, Mother Dearest.

She had a solution up her sleeve. With their earplugs, her companions wouldn't hear her. But they would *feel*.

Years earlier at the Arctos den, several pack members had taught her the wolves' subvocal singing. She'd practiced. The songs of the wolves were just that—songs. Hers were magic. She wasn't the fae's *Sangestre* for nothing. Now, she began a subvocal humming. She projected the waves of sound outward, to encompass her companions. They couldn't hear her song, but the waves should resonate against them, like a natural sonar, to dispel her mother's projection.

As she hummed, she fought the feelings birthed by her mother's magic—the bleak despair. *One second.* Life's futility. *Three seconds.* She pushed on, though she knew there was no point. *Seven seconds.* Of course they would lose. Nothing would...

Her mother's magic broke, along with a sob that burst from her lips. The tension in Rae's body eased and Charlie gifted her with a wink. Alex stepped alongside her. He smelled of the sea and sun, of musky sweat, and that singular scent belonging just to him. Her hand twitched. She ached to touch him, to feel his smooth skin beneath her fingers. He turned his head, and his glowing gold eyes warmed her. He smiled.

He lifted her hand and brought it to his lips. "Well done, Lu."

Her mouth dried, but she somehow managed to utter, "Thanks."

Together, two by two, they strode forward.

Another mile on, a curtain of light relieved the darkness of the trees. They'd almost reached the mesa atop the mountain.

Alex began to trot.

Once they hit the mesa, they'd stick to the tree line until they sussed out the lay of the land.

The closer they got, the more otherworldly the air. Not the same as the magic world—*that* sensation was unforgettable—but closer in spirit and far more intense than the Charleston fae's blending of magic and mundane.

Rae stumbled and fell to his knees. Charlie snugged his arm around the mage's waist and raised him to his feet. With Charlie's help, Rae managed to walk.

She didn't get why the magic was affecting Rae so adversely. He should be reveling in it. Instead, it was crippling him. Fear squeezed her chest.

Don't y'all be worryin' now, I can fight damned fine on my ass.

She bit back her smile, kept up the humming.

They ran on...and she almost crashed into Alex when he stopped.

For a moment, a piercing light blinded her. As her pupils adjusted, she saw beyond the demarcation of the dark wood to The Bowl's acres of sunlit meadow where two rows of camo-clad soldiers stood, spears pointed to the sky, their blades glistening in the sun. The soldiers faced each other to form an alley between them. From tree line to the horizon, dozens and dozens of them.

In the far distance, near-obscured by an unnatural mist, stood a Moorish-looking compound with glimpses of sandstone walls painted red.

Over her shoulder, movement... Oh, no. She turned. On the trail twenty feet behind their group, a dozen soldiers blanketed their path of retreat. Most were goblins, some with red tongues lolling as they grinned. A few fae, and humans, too, from the look of them, all wearing camo, yet sporting those anachronistic spears and swords.

The soldiers seemed unaffected by her song. Her three companions must have realized the same, because they tossed their earplugs.

"Alex..."

"I know. They've been following us for a mile or so. I've been aware of them, but as they made no move, I wanted to see how your mother's set-up played out." His face was grim, as was Rae's and Charlie's, but he cupped her cheek. "Not to worry. You're on Charlie's express apparation train, remember?"

The soldiers appeared frozen, like CGI constructs, until a goblin at the head of the line licked his tusk. She recognized him from yesterday's encounter.

Terrifying, yet they'd prepared for just this sort of thing. Charlie would apparate her out, while Rae took Alex. Back to safety. Back to sanity. They had to go *now*. The army had to be four-hundred strong. It could crush them in seconds.

This wasn't her mother's doing, but her very own terror screaming "run!"

No. Not yet.

They were here for a purpose. Nothing less would do.

"Stick to the plan, princess," Alex said.

She unclenched her fists and released her song.

The lines of soldiers pivoted, their faces grim with intent. They lifted their spears, straightened their arms, and aimed the points straight at them.

Her song hadn't affected the soldiers at all. She allowed it to die, the last note of power sinking to earth like a gentle rain.

The hand she lifted to Alex's shoulder shook. "What should we...?" her voice trailed off.

"We wait."

ALEX COULDN'T BELIEVE this bullshit. With so many mingled scents, he couldn't tell if all the creatures were real, or if some were constructs of Maurelle's magic. That wouldn't surprise him, but those spears looked real enough.

Dust swirled in the distance, moving ever closer. Horses. One white, one black, with two riders. No trumpets heralding them? Where was the drama in that?

When the need arose—he was certain it would—Charlie would apparate Lulu out of there, while Rae would do the same for him. But he was counting on Maurelle's avarice to keep them breathing long enough for them to gather intel before their next foray for the chest. No one expected their quest to be easy.

Lulu stood shoulder to shoulder with Alex. Though her scent spoke of fear, to all appearances she was calm and in control. Good girl. He gave her hand a squeeze.

"Be ready, Charlie," he said.

"I am."

The horses thundered closer, Maurelle on the white and a stranger on the black. They wouldn't run them down. No, Maurelle would go for the big finale and stop inches from where they stood. She was living some theatrical fantasy he found laughable. Yeah, that wouldn't be cool, laughing.

Instead, he set his face in stone.

As predicted, the horses stopped inches from where they stood. Noses snorting, foam covering their hides, eyes wild—their fear scent amped the predator in him.

Maurelle had braided and beaded the white streak in her black hair and she'd belted her crimson robes with gold. But one sniff told him she wasn't their biggest threat.

The man beside Maurelle sat tall in the saddle. His white hair flowed around him, as did his silvered robes. Cloud gray eyes took in each of them, but sharpened as he studied Lulu. He was a powerful mage, maybe even in Rae's category. Not as much magic as Clea, though hers was debilitatingly untrained.

Like the wolves with their alphas, firsts, and soldiers, mages, fae, vampyres, and mundanes had hierarchies of power and abilities. He didn't much like how the odds had changed. In their favor, this dude was a mega-egoist, and most likely a fantasist, too, since he was going for the Gandalf look, or maybe Saruman.

Hell, ma man! Rae's voice bonged in his head. *We are so under-dressed for these folks. Y'all feel me?*

Rae's mental chortle almost wrecked Alex's stoic face. Any minute, he'd crack up.

He bowed. "Maurelle. Friend of Maurelle." A grin split his face. "You're really jonesing on a *Lord of the Rings* thing."

Maurelle's eyes flared, but Mr. Friend smiled. "The name's Avain. I am more of a Harry Potter fan, myself."

"Good books," Alex said, but Lulu's tremble distracted him. Somehow her fear had turn to fury, and he liked it. He'd bet Avain could sense it, too. The guy was a player, Maurelle, for all her power, a pawn.

Rae chuckled, eyes bright. "I know who y'all are. You used to be pals with Tatianne."

Avain smiled. "You know nothing, mage."

"Quoting *Game of Thrones*?" Alex said. "Man, you need to get out more."

"He can't," Rae said. "He's the *former* Key. The council banished him. Power hungry bastard."

According to Rae, while the council had stripped away his Key status, his innate mage powers remained.

Rae didn't stop there. "Avain, how y'all imagine you can still wield a chest is beyond me. You're powerless when it comes to that shit."

"Shut up!" Maurelle leaned forward. "You're coming with us, Lulu."

Lulu threw back her shoulders, eyes narrowed on her mother, and exploded. "My ass. What you did to Clea was horrible. You disgust me. I'm ashamed."

"It sucks to be you," Maurelle said.

"Lulu, you're here for the chest, of course." Avain tilted his head. "How could you possibly retrieve it with this motley crew?"

Alex reached for Lulu's hand and squeezed.

Lulu smiled. "I have secrets."

The man blinked. "Do you?"

"Yes."

With the wave of the mage's hand, Lulu rose in the air.

"Screw you!" Lulu shouted, offering him her middle finger, then whipped up her bow and sent two arrows sailing straight for the mage.

Alex grabbed her ankle and stopped her ascent.

"Kill them!" Maurelle said.

The arrows bounced off Avain.

"Shit!" Lulu screamed.

Alex's sword flashed in his hand. "Charlie now!"

The fae reached for Lulu's ankle, while Rae leapt toward Alex. But a blast of power flung Alex sideways, Lulu's ankle freed. A kick to the head. Alex's blade sliced out, made contact with flesh.

Agony lanced his back, his gut.

Gone.

11

The following evening, Rae poked a stick at the campfire's ashes. He'd done a containment spell—no chance of the flames spreading. He was sick of that propane shit. "We're in a world of hurt, fae-boy."

"Aren't you Captain Obvious," Charlie said. "Have you reached Anouk?"

Rae shook his head, making his dreads quiver. If he worked enough magic, they'd hiss. *Damn.* That was just about how he was feeling right now. "Wherever she is, she's not answering. Whenever I need her, she's runnin' all over hell's half acre. A pain in the butt."

Charlie took out his phone. "I'm going to call Viviane."

"Y'all awful loyal to that queenie who cut your horns," Rae said.

"I have my reasons."

Rae gripped Charlie's wrist in a vise. "You don't call."

"Absurd." Charlie chewed his toothpick. "Lulu's taken. Alex is—"

"Don't you be sayin' what I think y'all was about to say, motherfucker."

Charlie's eyes squeezed tight. He sighed. "I'm afraid I can't see how he's not."

"That shifter's got skills."

"Right. If you refuse to let me call my queen, we need a plan. I managed to hold onto my black knives. They're imbued with the ancient magic and will end Maurelle and Avain."

"That bastard's lower than a snake's belly. We need to get close. Real close."

"We can apparate in."

Dumbest idea the fae had yet. "I can't even stand with all that magic swirlin'."

"That makes no sense," Charlie said. "Why?"

The fae didn't need to know about his prostheses, how in heavily magicked realms, they failed him, how he feared the retwining of the worlds for that reason. Except...

He pulled up his pantlegs to reveal his "fakies" as he called them.

Charlie blinked, the fae's austere face going rigid, his eyes deepening from silver to hurricaine gray. "Oh, I see. But you magicked Clea's finger and—"

"I sure as hell did." He grinned thinking of the beauty of her magical golden prothesis. "Took a lotta mojo to make that finger. These..." He brushed his hand across the metal and wood that graced his legs from the knees down. "Too much magic needed."

The fae's expression brightened. "I could help. Gift you some of mine."

He took a long, deep look at Charlie, seeing beneath layers of obfuscation. "You would do that."

The fae nodded. "I would."

"Let me think on your offer. It's a mighty generous one."

Charlie reached into his pocked and pulled out a silver flask, holding it out to Rae. "Fae Breath of Life. You?"

"Y'all's just fulla gifts tonight. This shit is rare." The sip he took was long and slow. Honeysuckle and clover burst inside his mouth, followed by a kick of Vampyre Tears. "Damn, but that's fine."

Charlie took back the flask when Rae handed it over. His thumb rubbed the silver container that glowed in the firelight. He raised it to his mouth, eyes closed, inhaled deeply, then took a sip. He licked his lips. "A gift."

"From the queen?" Rae said.

Charlie stared at the flask for a long moment. "No. My mother. It serves as a reminder."

"Of...?"

He rested his forearms on his knees, his eyes focused on the flames.

Or so it appeared to Rae.

The fae's eyes filled with poignance and longing. "She was the reason I colluded with the Union and gifted their nanotech creations with a spark of my fae essence. You see The Union held her as hostage. Or so they said. It was all a sham." A muscle twitched in his jaw. "She was long dead."

Rae tried to catch the fae's eyes and failed. "Heard a rumor that Tatianne claimed she could resurrect the dead."

"Aren't you the knowing one." He proffered the flask again.

The cool metal felt good beneath Rae's fingers as he lifted the bottle's mouth to his lips. "That I am." Ah, that taste, the rush. Visions of Elysian flower fields floated across his mind's eye. "Trying to distract me?"

"Would I do that?" Charlie said. "And, yes, Tatianne roped me into that one, too." He held out his hand for the flask, sipped.

"But you wised up in time." The twitch of Charlie's lips was the only indication Rae'd hit bullseye dead on.

"Now, I follow my heart." Charlie rubbed the stubs of his horns and laughed. "It usually results in disaster, but nonetheless, I hope that truth will allow me to again see the kindest woman ever to grace faeland. When I journey to the other side, of course."

"Of course," Rae said. "I'm guessin' you have things to say to her."

The fae shuddered. "I do. Many." He slapped his thighs. "Enough reflection. It wearies my brain. So how will we work this gig, eh?"

Damn, but he liked this fae. "We're gonna sneak up there, on our two legs, and first find that shifter, then get Lulu and the chest."

The fae's soft laughter filled the campground. "And for your next mage trick?"

Before he could answer, a gray SUV barreled toward them in a swirl of dust and small stones.

"Someone's in a rush to go camping," Charlie said,

"That's no camper." Rae walked forward. "That's one crazy-assed dude."

JAMES PEELED INTO THE CAMPSITE, leapt from the car, and stalked toward Charlie and Rae, who looked like crap, not to mention the mage's strange woven dreads. Neither Alex, nor Lulu were in sight. "Well? Have you got it?"

"No," Rae said. "Where's Clea?"

In terse words, he detailed Sophy and Anouk's arrival and departure with Clea. Damn, repeating those words still made his gut clench.

Rae nodded. "Yeah, I get it. Smart move. The only move."

The click of a car door, and when Neddy reached him, he squeezed the kid's shoulder. "You solid?"

"*Solid?*" Neddy said. "Your maniac driving almost got us killed!"

He grinned. "It's not horseshoes, kid."

"Never again." Neddy shook his head. "Never. Again."

"You two want something to eat, come on in." Charlie retreated to the camper.

They'd eaten on the way. Knowing the kid, he could eat again. "After we shower. Neddy, you go. I've got to talk to Rae."

"But I want food."

"You smell, kid, worse than me. Shower. Hair, too."

Neddy grinned, saluted, and trotted off, not a sulk or stomp in sight. The kid was learning.

"Got any bourbon?" he said to Rae.

"Scotch."

"That'll do."

They sat beneath the camper's awning, and it felt good to stretch out his legs. He'd been coiled so tight his muscles had stiffened. Rae poured them a couple fingers, waved his hand, and three sticks of firewood floated from the woodpile to the circle of rock in front of their chairs. Another wave, and a small blaze danced across the wood.

"Nice parlor trick." James sipped the Scotch, relishing the liquor's fiery path.

It was obvious Rae had a boatload to tell him, but from his attitude, action wasn't on tonight's agenda. He'd wait. Listen. Then act.

"Why the hell didn't you answer your cell?" Rae said.

He'd needed his focus for the road, for cocooning Clea deep within, for fettering the beast inside him. His inner demons or the wyvern? Didn't matter. "I had to concentrate."

"Man, y'all's a pain." Rae knocked back the Scotch, poured another two fingers. Then he launched into the mess they'd gotten themselves into.

"So let me get this right," he said. "Lulu's taken. You didn't even come close to the chest. You think Arctos is dead."

Glittering motes darker than night swirled around Rae's hands. "He *can't* be. We're gonna find him. Neddy say anything about Alex?"

"He did not. Interesting."

"There, see? He's alive. The kid would've felt his death."

He nodded. "So we go in later tonight."

Rae shook his head. "Like I said, Avain was The Key, until the greedy bastard went dark as shit and the council stripped his Key powers from his skinny ass. Clea's mentor Dave, he was a Guardian back then, which put him on the council. Come to think, that was about the time Clea was born."

"The point, Rae?" he said.

"Night's Avain's friend. He doesn't much like the light."

"So first light, then."

Charlie's head popped out of the camper. "Did you mention to Larrimer your little problem, Mage?"

Rae glared at the fae, then swigged another dose of Scotch straight from the bottle.

"Rae?" James said.

The Mage's anger poured off him like lava. "My legs don't work so good up the mountain. Too much magic. More than Charleston. Lots more."

Which meant he shouldn't become the wyvern, if he believed Anouk and Sophy.

The "hehehe" laugh that drove Clea nuts erupted from Rae's mouth. *No, big man, y'all shouldn't turn that wyvern loose, not if y'all want to come back to Clea as human.*

If he had one more person in his head... "Stay out of my fucking mind, Mage." Larrimer finished his Scotch, poured another. "Can you work your magic in The Bowl, where they have Lulu?"

"Hell, yeah."

"So shrink yourself."

Rae slapped his forehead. "You've finally gone round the bend, you crazy freak."

He laughed. "Perhaps I have. I've seen you become a woman, a British aristocrat, and an urban streetwear kid. Seems to me you can shrink yourself to a child. I'll carry you on my back."

Charlie joined them at the campfire. "That's a good one, Larrimer. But why don't you simply change into your wyvern form and fly us there?"

"Because." James might have gotten his spark from Charlie, but he wasn't about to tell the fae anything.

"You should at least—"

He turned cold. "That's between me and the reptile. Got it, Charlie?"

Did you just call me a reptile?

Aren't you?

The wyvern chuffed.

Rae rested his elbows on his knees, his chin on his hands. "I'm thinkin' about your idea."

Clea had told him about the loss of Rae's lower legs and his prostheses, and sworn him to secrecy. He wasn't about to break Clea's trust.

And each time Clea entered his mind, he wanted to rend and tear and smash the world to bits. Doing that to Maurelle and her mage would prove enormously satisfying.

Rae peered up at him. "So I'm supposed to become some kid and you gonna be backpacking me up that mountain and into The Bowl. What if we're attacked?"

"I assume we will be." He shrugged. "You've got your magic. The fae's got his sword and knives. And I've got... You know what I've got."

"Yes," Charlie said. "You're a killing machine. What about the boy?"

"He stays," James said.

Rae shook his head. "He's comin'. That boy will follow us if we don't bring him along. He may be a kid, but as his Pinky, he's bad shit."

He could knock Neddy out until they were long gone. Except the boy's nose for scent wouldn't quit. He'd find them or find trouble. The mage was right. "Neddy comes."

Rae's hair morphed into tight curls, a red bandana wrapped around his forehead. "If I'm doing this humiliating shape, we're going to look for the shifter."

"Agreed," he said. "But after we get the chest and Lulu."

"For some of us," Rae said. "There won't be any 'after.'"

If Clea were here, she'd roll her eyes. "Put on your Big Boy pants."

"Didn't you just tell me I was to become a kid?" Rae gave Larrimer the side eye. "Didn't think you had a sense of humor."

From across the campsite, a snort. Neddy.

"Who said I was being funny?"

LULU AWAKENED on a plush velvet chaise the color of puke. It was fitting, since she felt like puke, too. She sat up, dizzy as a hungover barfly. When her eyes cleared enough to survey the room, she gaped. White marble veined with gold. Everywhere. The walls. The floor. The ceiling. Like in a crypt. Creepy.

Wobbling to her feet, she wove down the hall to the bathroom, reached for the gilded door handle, and spewed. A few dry heaves later she got herself under control, stepped over the gross puddle, and staggered into a bathroom fitted with more marble, gilded everything, and a modern sink, toilet, and tub.

She ran the tap, rinsed her mouth, and after removing the plastic sleeve from the toothbrush, brushed her teeth. Nothing but a shelf with towels beneath the pedestal sink, so she wet one, cleaned up her barf in the hall, and tossed the towel into a corner.

After washing her hands, she squinted into the mirror. A scream barreled up from her gut. She bit it back, though it was a close-run thing. Her clothes might be okay, but blood and other...things... crusted her face. Memory slammed her upside the head. The blood wasn't hers. Her companions? Their foes? Alex's?

Oh, gods. Dizzy, she gripped the side of the sink. They'd ordered Alex and the others killed. She'd seen Rae and Charlie apparate. But Alex. What about Alex?

A terrible memory pushed her to her knees. She'd seen a sword pierce Alex back to front, right through his belly. Seen his guts spill, his blood spew. Seen him fall to the earth. Her hands tightened on the washbasin, eyes burning. A moan. She slapped a hand across her mouth. *They* couldn't hear. No one could hear her grief.

Alex wasn't gone. He couldn't be.

But she'd witnessed his fall.

Pain ripped her insides, her vision blackened.

Could there be a world without that beautiful, annoying, fierce wolf?

A sob broke. She stilled. All remained quiet.

He wasn't dead. But...

Stop.

She would *not* be a puppet to her own grief.

But Alex...

No.

Whether he was dead or alive, she had a job to do.

To find the chest. Steal it. Act with deliberation and meaning.

After that... She'd find Alex. After. It had to be after.

She scrubbed her face with the ginormous washcloth, dried it with the billion-count Egyptian cotton towel. Straightened her clothes. That done, she rebraided her hair and tied it off with the scrunchie she pulled from her pocket.

She had to be clever and cunning. She had to succeed.

A whoosh from the outer door. "Darling girl, are you awake?"

Darling girl? She'd never heard those two words out of her mother's mouth before.

"Out in a sec." She'd put some chipper in her voice. She might not have a plan yet, but Clea often went with her instincts. She would, too.

When she reentered the bedroom, her mother glided over and embraced her. Maybe it was absurd, but she'd try one more time to turn things around with her mother. To show her kindness. To cement fractured bonds. To make her see reason. It could change everything.

Maurelle straightened her arms and gave her the once over. "You don't look too worse for wear. Other than that hideous outfit."

"I'm sure you'll find me something." Dear gods, please not some gown that was the *Princess Bride* revisited. "Where's my bow?"

"We've stored it away. Would you like to know about your companions?"

The taunts, the games, she was sick of them. "I heard. I saw."

"Did you?" Her mother's voice held that taunt she hated. "That their apparition failed? That the wolf died? You're taking this awfully well."

"I understand defeat, Mother."

Maurelle gave her a long look and sniffed. "I see. You're right. You are defeated. But let's not dwell on the negative, shall we?"

She took her mother's hand and led her over to the foot of the bed. "Come sit with me for a minute."

Images of Alex gutted her mind. But she could try with her mother. One more try. "Mom, did you know that when I was a kid, I always hoped you'd return."

Maurelle's eyes softened. "No."

"I did. I wanted you back."

She cleared her throat. "Your father was enough."

"He was wonderful, but I missed you. Dad never told me why you left."

"He was weak. I couldn't bear to be with a weak man any longer. I *had* to leave, don't you see?"

She adored her father, who was anything but weak. But his strength wasn't showy, either. She'd respected that. But weak? No. Instead of spitting at her mother, she put on a thoughtful expression. "Okay, I guess I can understand that. But you left me, too."

The blue vein in Maurelle's throat beneath her pale skin throbbed. "I always loved you."

Her heart warmed. Maybe... "What I can't see is why you're doing this? Killing people. Stealing the chest. Building armies. For what?"

Maurelle took her hands. "Growing up with my father was amazing. He reigned over the Charleston fae court, you know. I idolized him. He was loud, boisterous." She flung out her arms. "He was fun! So unlike your father. I was eldest, and while our mother favored Tatianne and Viviane, Father groomed me, adored me, cherished me. I would be queen when he passed to the Far Lands."

"You never told me this, not for all those years we were in the magic realm." Lulu held absolutely still, hoping, praying her mother might be reclaimed.

"But my beloved Father died before his time. He was out hunting with Viv and Tat, and *allegedly* a dragon speared his breast with her tail."

"Allegedly?"

"Viv and Tat knew he favored me. They contrived to have him killed."

Aunt Viv might not be warm and cuddly, but she was fair and just and respected. "And that's how auntie became queen?"

"Oh, no. After Father died, Tatianne left for the magic world. She'd always hated mundanes."

"Do you hate them?"

A smile shined across Maurelle lips. "Why, of course not. They are what they are. Inferior in every way. We should rule them, as is proper. Mother was queen for many years until she began to fade with longing for our father. It was my turn. I would rule. It was my due."

"Um, I don't know much about queens and kings."

"Queen." She sighed, her eyes growing unfocused and dreamy. Her face hardened. "Mother should have respected Father's wishes, shouldn't she? But I did not become queen, did I? No, Mother named Viviane as such, while I was left to lurk in the shadows."

Oh, boy.

"So once I found Avain, I knew what course I should take. He is handsome and strong. Vital. Powerful. My goals are his, and his mine. We will wrest the crown from my arrogant sister, and it will soon lay upon *my* head. See?"

Yes, Lulu saw way too much, including the glint of madness in her mother's eyes. Why hadn't she noticed it before? Was she too young? Or had she simply not looked deep enough?

"You have a great heritage, my daughter." Her mother's face glowed with joy. "You will be queen someday."

"I appreciate that, Mother. But I don't want to be queen. That isn't my purpose or my desire."

Maurelle continued, tightening her grip on Lulu's hands. "We will find you a consort, one who is fitting for your stature."

Her mother hadn't heard a word she'd said, off in her own fantasy world of queens and kings and power. She felt...sorry for her.

Lulu's efforts might be futile, but she had to try one more time.

"Don't do this, Mother. Stop the destruction. The killing. Stop this all, please. You're admired at the Court. Respected. You're—"

The fury in Maurelle's eyes made her jerk back, but her mother clung to her hands squeezing her grip, digging her lengthening nails into Lulu's flesh. Pain batted her, but she forced herself to stay still and not pull away. Bright spots of red oozed from where Maurelle's claws scored her flesh.

She'd tried. Now, she was done. "So tell me about Avain."

Her mother's talons receded, and she reached out her hand to pull the scrunchie from Lulu's braid. She undid the plait and fluffed out her hair. "First of all, Avain prefers hair loose."

She'd nearly batted her mother's hand away, but it was time to return to her original plan to steal the chest. Her failure to make her mother see reason pinched her heart. Onward. "I see."

"He's very much onboard with the faction that supports the re-twining of the worlds. With the chest, he can help it happen, as well as keep it from that monster sister of mine."

"Rae said Avain was pals with Tatianne."

"No longer."

She doubted that. "Ah. I see. Then why not let Clea gather the chests?"

"That girl isn't strong enough. I remember her. Awful child. She would fail, and Tatianne would succeed."

Not the time to point out that Clea had already recovered two of them. "If you don't return the chest to her, she'll die."

"No loss there." Her mother tickled Lulu's nose with the ends of her hair.

"So what's next?

"Avain wishes to talk to you." Maurelle pointed to an alcove. "Go shower and change. I'll set out some things for you. You'll want to look your best."

What she wanted was to get the chest and escape in one piece.

ALEX'S GUT was on fire. Lava streaked through his veins and arteries and into his brain, his fur, his paws, his tail. Move an inch, and it would destroy him from inside out. A howl bubbled up from his throat. He clamped his jaws.

Where was he? When was he? How...

"Wolf."

Pain near drowned out the voice. He had to have shifted while he was out, something he hadn't done since he was a pup. He hung on, lupine eyes ablaze. He would escape.

"Wolf, awaken. You must shift."

More pain. Terrible pain. *Father Fenrir*. He... *Fuck it*.

The world came apart. Reformed. He lay flat on his back, panting.

A hand reached beneath him and lifted his head, tipped cool liquid into his mouth. He drank.

"Sleep now. Heal."

He did.

LULU and her mother left the suite. Outside, two camo-clothed, spear-wielding guards flanked the elaborately carved door. Noise smashed into her, making her head ache as they stepped onto a patio framed by a colonnade of pillars that formed a rectangle around the two-storied building's courtyard. Hundreds of torches and braziers lit the night, the noise clamorous. She faced the expansive center greenspace with its large swimming pool. A monstrous snake writhed within.

Her eyes bugged. No snake, but bodies—live ones, hundreds of them. Humans, fae, goblins. Even a few vampires, the rarest of the rare. They drank and laughed and had sex in more positions than she'd ever imagined. The revelers undulated across the lawn and beneath the trees, surrounding the pool, in the pool, everywhere. Many were naked, some dancing, dangly bits she wished she hadn't seen bobbing up and down to the music.

Her mother leaned close. "We keep our troops happy."

Happy? How did they even function after this?

Except, that was a good thing. Yeah, when the party wound down, they'd be hungover big time.

"Care to join them?" her mother said. "After we meet with Avain."

Was her mother nuts? "Let's see how our talk goes, shall we?" She'd be sharp and canny, like Alex would have wanted her to be. She had no weapons, no shield. All she had was her voice. Nothing else. That would have to be enough to find the chest and escape.

LULU PAINTED ON AN IMPERIOUS FACE, one she'd learned from Aunt Viv. Shoulders back, spine straight, she prayed to the gods for cleverness and smarts in the upcoming confrontation.

Given her mother and Avain's arrogance, when they passed through the archway to the interior, she expected to enter a hall with a huge throne. The room was large, tiled with mosaics, covered with glittering Persian rugs, and lit with torches. And more marble. Couches were strewn beside tables piled with food and drink.

Couples—trios!—were having sex, downing food, drinking, laughing. The center of the room held a dais with... Not more humping. *Gods.* Naked and squirming like a clump of worms, a pile of people went at it. The scents of sex and booze nauseated her.

Her mother calmly led her around the pile and headed toward a corner of the room where a man lounged on a chaise draped with silks that flowed to the floor.

Avain. Barefoot, dressed in jeans and a white button down, he'd swept his white hair back from his face. As they neared, he held out his arms to her mother.

Into her head popped the image of her mother and Avain doing it. She shoved it right back out again.

They held a long, sloppy kiss while she stood there, struck silent. But when her mother lifted a knee to rest it on the chaise, her foot snagged on the silk skirt draping the couch.

Lulu's breath caught. Beneath the chaise sat a small basket of woven reeds.

Whoop! She clamped her teeth so she wouldn't let it out. The chest. Avain was keeping it nice and close.

When the pair broke apart, her mother reclined on a matching chaise, reached for a pitcher, and poured golden liquid into a goblet. She offered it to Lulu.

"What is it?"

"Wine, of course," her mother said.

"I'm going to hold off. Water, maybe?"

Maurelle laughed, and Avain sat up and held out his hands for Lulu. "Come here, child."

No, you come here, asshole. She walked to the chaise, and when she didn't take his hands, he patted the seat beside him. He was young and handsome and smelled of...rotted flesh?

When they'd stripped him of his Key powers, had that taken his longevity, too? How old *was* this dude? Was he decomposing beneath a glamour of youth?

She lowered herself to the cushion at the farthest end of the chaise, which wasn't nearly far enough.

He sat up, bending one knee, and leaned forward. Wisps of white hair fell around him, his gray eyes thoughtful.

"I won't say we're sorry for the loss of your companions. I will say I regret that necessity."

Liar. Rage pumped though her. But that wouldn't help her escape. Smart. She had to be smart. She held her threaded fingers loosely on her lap, lowered her lids, and nodded once, again going for an Aunt Viviane pose.

Avain sighed. "I am The Key, as I have been for centuries." His face tightened while volcanic anger roiled off him. "Until they stole my position from me."

Hello? He sure wasn't The Key anymore. But she'd play along. "They?"

Nostrils flaring, he sighed. But his eyes burned. "The Council. Fools. They failed to see how I was bettering our world and the mundane one. I could have accomplished so much! We would have ruled this realm, as is our right."

"We?'"

He and her mother shared a chuckle. "Magical beings, of course. We are obviously superior—stronger, faster, gifted with talents mundanes only dream about."

As much as she wanted to argue that humans had their own gifts and that there were a bazillion of them, she wasn't that dumb. "All true."

"As The Key, I had accomplished righteous things. My plan would better everyone, even the mundanes. They would be as our children. Guarded, nurtured, cared for."

Without rights, she suspected. Sounded a lot like slavery to her.

"Those sharing my vision see the virtue of my plan. Yet the Council took my birthright away and anointed a sad infant with little magic. A pretender. "

Pretender? *I don't think so, buster.* Did this awful creature share her mother's madness or had he infected her with it?

"Do you not see my quandary?" he said. "I must fight to get it back. I *will* get it back. To do that, we need your assistance." His voice held a gentle plea, his eyes radiating kindness.

All the hairs at the nape of her neck rose, and she took great care keeping her words measured and even. "How can I be of assistance?"

"I have the Chest of Time."

"*We,*" Maurelle chimed in. "We have the Chest of Time."

He gifted her mother with a deferential smile. "Of course, my dear. Just an expression."

Maurelle sniffed. "Do get on with it, Avain. Time, my dear. Time."

He sighed. "The pretender Key has one use. She must activate the chest."

Things were getting interesting. She gave Maurelle a wide-eyed stare. "Why didn't you wait until it was activated to steal it, Mother?"

Her mother sniffed. "I was lucky to escape in one piece from that freak show."

"You did well, my dear." A warm smile graced Avain's lips. "It was my fault, really. I'm afraid I didn't mention that aspect of the chest to my love."

Lulu smirked. "Not the smartest move, Avain."

Maurelle's fist connected so hard, Lulu's head snapped back. Warm blood filled her mouth. She spat it out, then wiped her lips with the hem of her frou-frou dress.

"Nice, Mom," she said. "What happened to 'darling daughter'?"

Her mother loomed over her, fist raised.

In a blink, Avain was standing, his hands around her mother's waist. He pulled her back against his chest and nuzzled her neck. "Maurelle, Maurelle. Your anger's getting the better of you."

"I was defending you," Maurelle said.

"I know, dearest."

The throbbing pain in her cheek felt good and real. It grounded her. She slapped her hands on her lap. "So guys, I ask again, what do you want from me?"

Avain whispered in her mother's ear until she visibly relaxed. She turned to him, and they hugged, her mother resting her cheek against Avain's chest. Lulu could almost believe their affection for one another. Almost.

Maurelle again draped herself across the chaise. "I'm sorry, daughter. Avain and I want this brighter, better world so very much and sometimes my temper gets away from me. Forgive me."

Interesting how no mention of Maurelle becoming queen was mentioned. Lulu nodded.

"And it *will* be better," Avain said, his eyes aglow with fervor. "We will have magic, along with the science and technology of The Union. This coupling will be unprecedented, a mighty conjunction of forces where good will rule and science and magic will blend. No more poverty. No more famine. No more war. Only harmony."

His intensity was such that had she not seen their bloodshed and cruelty firsthand, she'd believe him. Her truthsense told her *he* believed what he was spouting, which made it all the stranger.

Avain leaned toward her, his scent of decay twisting her stomach.

"We'll strike a bargain," Avain said. "A part of Clea Reese's soul rests inside the chest."

She kept her silence.

"Because of that," he continued. "Clea Reese's physical form is withering. Without her soul reuniting, she's dead. Take us to Clea. We will allow her soul's reuniting, and she will activate the chest."

What he didn't say was that once activated, *he* could wield it and use its power for his own gain. The idea of *him* possessing an active chest...

Another wave of his hand. "Her life for the chest's activation. It's simple, really."

It was anything but. Lulu didn't even know where Clea was. But she believed him when he'd said Clea would die.

"I need to think about it," she said.

His smile was almost as unpleasant as his smell. "What's to think about?"

Caution. Careful. Avain was like a sandpit seeded with traps. She stood and began to pace, then twirled to face him and did that hair-toss thing her mother used to hate. "Seems to me only I can bring you and Clea together. She and her friends trust me. So what do *I* get out of it?"

The fake smile turned genuine. "Smart girl. You get to go back to your life, of course. And the pretender Key lives."

Yeah, right, she believed that. Asshole. She'd practiced her fake grin a lot as a teen. Now, it came in handy. "And I should trust you because...?"

He winked. "Because you have no other choice."

She pretended to ponder, tapping a finger against her lips. "All right. I see you've got me hemmed in. So I'll do it."

12

James' chin burned with the sizzle of Texas sun. Instantly awake, his internal clock said he'd been out for a solid twelve. He breathed deep. The hot, dry air told him it was before noon, but not by much. He'd slept in the car, needing to be away from the others.

While getting his Zs, he'd dreamed of a possibility that might give them an edge. A plan had come together.

With time evaporating for Clea and Lulu, he withdrew Sophy's coin from his pocket. He flipped it. Should he tell the others first? No.

THE WOLF in Alex awakened and prodded the man back to consciousness. Alex wuffled a sigh. His body was healing with shifter swiftness, but the extensive damage would take time, something he didn't have. No longer on fire, he moved...a paw? He'd shifted back to wolf again while asleep. The paw ached—a remembrance of pain—but nothing more. Muzzle resting on the floor, he sized up the room. Light poured in from a high window. Ambient noise pricked his ears. Scents of old blood and fresh, too, wine and meat. Meat would be good.

Was that a hint of Lulu?

Anticipating the pull of pain, he stood on four paws and was rewarded with a stab to the gut. It was tolerable.

He sniffed his fur. Disgusting. He needed a bath. Food. More water.

Where was here? Where was Lulu? Were they both captives?

She wasn't nearby, her scent too faint. But he'd seen her taken. She'd fought. Screamed. Rae, Charlie, had they escaped?

Maybe Maurelle and Avain had stashed him someplace. No. Neither of their scents were present.

He swiftly shifted to human, not as painful as the previous shift, but he hurt everywhere. He checked for his weapons. Gone. Where? He needed them, then he'd find Lulu. She was safe and whole. She had to be.

He shook his head, tried to run his fingers through hair matted with blood and offal. Might be good to lick. Father Fenrir, his wolf was doing the thinking.

Damn, the fire in his belly was making him muzzy. He had to clear his brain. Had to think human.

Someone had saved him, helped him. An ally? He had none other than Rae and Charlie.

Footfalls thudded down the hall, outside the door. He knew that scent. *Shit*. He pressed against the wall so he'd be hidden when the door swung open.

A seven-foot goblin stepped inside the room.

LULU BRAIDED HER HAIR. She found her scrunchie and tied it off, then pulled her jeans from the closet floor. She tugged them on, their stiffness and stink grossing her out. Bloody they might be, but she wasn't flouncing around in that stupid dress.

Okay, it was time. Or was it? Should she confront them in the salon, steal the chest from under their noses, and make her escape?

That wasn't much of a plan.

She walked to the window, pushed back the curtain, and peered out. The courtyard was piled with sleeping bodies in a tangle of arms and legs. She'd bet her mother and Avain were sleeping it off, too.

No time like the present, she guessed. Maybe.

Or maybe later, when all those idiots were half drunk and having sex. No, it would be better when they were all passed out. The thought of the chest right beneath Avain's chaise gave her shivers. Why couldn't they stow it in some nice, safe place she could at least attempt to reach? But she figured it went where he went.

Her nerves were like centipedes crawling across her skin. They felt way too real.

Time to try something out of the box. Actually, in another county, it was so far from the box.

Socks on, boots on, scrunchie. Set. No more stalling.

Now all that remained was her crazy hope.

She walked into the bathroom and locked the door. She sat on the closed toilet seat and centered herself. Took a couple sips of water. Because of her mother, she couldn't risk singing, but she hoped a subvocal hum would work as well.

She began to hum, searched inside herself for the exact notes. She cleared her throat, started again and found the Song of Calling. In her mind, she composed an image of the chest. Not the sweet-grass basket, but the one she'd seen when Clea had held it. With her song, she focused on that image.

The chest had "come" to her once. She'd discovered it in the magic realm, and she'd been sure the chest had led her there. A foolish notion? Perhaps, but it *had* felt like that. So she hoped her song would compel the chest come to her.

Had the chests ever come to Clea? Not that she knew. But Clea didn't have the fae song, and this chest belonged to the fae.

Raising her volume a touch, she closed her eyes and dove deeper inside herself where he magic lived. She encouraged it. After ten long minutes, she opened her eyes and looked around.

Nothing. Damn.

She wasn't giving up.

Help me, Clea. Help me.

A CALL. *Didn't understand. So many voices. Young and old, demanding and commanding, pleading and whining. Laughing. Gloating.*

This was different. Spoke specifically. She knew the voice. She loved the voice.

The other ones...asked the impossible. To return. To where? How? Why?

This voice asked for help.

Could she?

Her breath sloughed. The cosmos paused.

Perhaps... Perhaps...

But then the cosmos took her again.

LULU CLOSED HER EYES, sank deep inside herself. She thought she'd felt something, an otherness that reminded her of Clea. Now wasn't the time to give up. She'd try harder, and again began the Song of Calling. *Help me, Clea. Help me.*

JAMES WATCHED the skies with his eagle eyes pointed north.

"We were supposed to leave this morning," Charlie said.

"Tough," Larrimer replied. "We wait."

Charlie threw up his hands. "For what?"

Larrimer spotted an eagle in the distance, high in the sky. The closer it came... Good. Not an eagle at all. As the creature spiraled downward, its tail streaming behind it like a banner, it grew. Larger, and larger still.

"What the hell!" Charlie said, his hand shading his eyes.

He lost sight of the creature, momentarily blinded by the afternoon sun, then caught it again.

"Sophy?" Rae fist pumped the air. "She's comin'!"

She'd confined her large breasts with a band around her chest. Smart move. Across her back, she'd strapped a *kopis*, a curved sword called a "chopper." Other than that, she carried no weapons but her deadly claws. It would do.

Her landing was softer than a whisper. Her face? The word "pissed" worked.

"Took you long enough." Larrimer winked.

"Bite me," she said.

"Sugah, that's *my* job." Rae stepped forward and kissed her. Full on the lips. With tongue.

Larrimer did a double take. Rae had gone from swirly caftan and sparkly cowboy boots to jeans, black t-shirt, and shitkickers. He was taller, too, and broader and bulkier.

He sobered. "Clea?"

"She lives," she said.

But her eyes hadn't met his. He locked down the anger that seethed just beneath the surface. No weakness. Not until his Clea was safe. "We need your help to rescue Lulu and get the fucking chest. Now."

"I CAN SMELL YOU, SHIFTER." The goblin spun to face Alex, a frown stretched across his purple face, a sack held in one hand. "No need to fear me."

The goblin trio's leader. He hadn't been at yesterday's battle. Alex snorted. "I haven't feared your kind since I was ten." His father had beaten his fear out of him. Acid would have been kinder than that man's fists. That last time, he'd made sure his father never touched him or his mother again.

"Not afraid of us?" The goblin smiled. "Must be my *smaller* brethren, most likely." He waved a hand. "Come. Let's sit. I brought food. You will need it."

With startling grace for such a lumbering creature, the goblin seated himself on the floor, cross legged, slabs of muscle flexing as he did so.

When Alex sat, he was reminded by his aching body that he'd recently been chopped meat.

"If you're anything like us, you'll heal faster with food." The goblin handed Alex a foot-long sausage, then withdrew one from the sack for himself. "Name's Cassius."

"Historical."

Cassius chuckled. "True, that. When The Union remade us, they gifted us with new names."

Alex froze. Those bastards had tentacles everywhere. Seemed Larrimer's cadre wasn't the only ones they'd "remade." What else was out there? "Why did you save me?"

The goblin tapped a tusk. "Not to eat you. Too stringy."

"You've hurt my delicate feelings." Alex grinned, producing a gut pain sharp enough to make him wince.

"Sorry." Cassius eyes danced. After a bite of sausage, a lick of his tusk, his face sobered. "We had a deal with you and the singer. We lost the bet. Marcus betrayed that. He'll pay. He's an asshole, anyway. So's his brother, Casca, but not so bad." He pulled two huge water bottles from the sack, along with football-sized loaves of grainy bread and rolls of paper towel. He handed one of each to Alex. Finally, he drew out two double-magnum bottles of Cabernet and thrust one at Alex. "Good vintage."

Man, everything was giant-sized with this guy. Alex took a swig of wine, then another. "Thank you for this, for the healing, and for the rescue." He wiped his hand on a sheaf of towel and held it out.

The goblin clasped Alex's forearm, and Alex mirrored it. When they released, Alex said, "Is she safe?"

Cassius frowned. "You're fond of the little singer."

"I am."

"No, I mean *fond.*"

The need for Lulu rode him hard. He jumped to his feet. "Gotta go."

A hand clamped his thigh. "Wait. You need food and water for fuel. You need to listen and learn."

His sense of urgency was in overdrive. "I can't."

"*Think*," Cassius said.

He took a long breath and uncurled his fisted hands. He sure wasn't using his alpha logic these days. Images of Lu derailed his mind and his common sense. He sat back down, and while he ate and drank, Cassius filled him in on what had occurred during the battle, which had been over pretty quickly.

"Where are we?" he said.

"The 'special' goblins' bunkhouse, the one farthest from the main compound. They don't like us too near."

"'Special'?"

"As a favor to Avain," Cassius said, "those fucked-up Union scientists 'upgraded' five of us, which is what the mage called it. Three of us are left. Avain uses us but doesn't trust us."

By Father Fenrir's balls. "What did Avain give them in return?"

"I don't know. But he's thick with them."

"Are any of their soldiers here?"

Cassius shook his head. "Avain won't allow it."

He snorted, and one of Clea's sayings popped into his head. "Avain sounds like a legend in his own mind."

The laugh that burst from Cassius boomed through the room. "That he is! Whatever he wants from the singer, it can't be good."

"I'm sure it's not." He had his suspicions about how they wanted to use Lulu. He'd bet Cassius did, too. "Nothing about that mage is good."

"See?" Cassius said. "We agree."

"I've got to go." He explained their mission to retrieve the chest.

"Come with me."

The goblin shook his head. "Wish I could. Perhaps... See, Avain has power over me. If I'm within ten yards of him, I must obey his commands. It's too risky for me to go with you to the compound."

Alex nodded. "How did you rescue me, if Avain—"

"Loopholes." Cassius grinned. "I'm good at them. Wait until tomorrow. You'll be stronger. Better equipped to—"

"I can't." He ate fast, downing wine and bread and more meat. He wouldn't leave Lulu with those bastards for one more second than necessary. She'd be terrified. A vise tightened around his throat. She was young and beautiful and Avain might... He had to get to her *now*.

He sprang to his feet. "Weapons?" Both his wolf and half-forms were good, but with a sword and knives, they were better.

"You'll need them," Cassius said. "I have knives, a bow, and a sword for you."

A board creaked down the hall. Stealthy, but loud enough for his shifter hearing. He tossed Cassius a dark look.

The goblin's index finger shot to his lips, then he whispered. "We *should* be alone. Must be Casca or Marcus. I trust neither. Go." He pointed to the window. "Now!"

Weaponless, he shifted to wolf and fled.

How LONG HAD Lulu hummed the Song? Minutes? Hours?

Lulu was dying, the world dimming to black. She had to be. She saw nothing.

She saw *everything*. Caves and crystal balls. Sun rising and Moon setting. Wings and watersongs. Larrimer in gold armor. A wyvern twined around a key. Time spiraling backwards, forwards and...

Pay attention! the voice barked.

Clea?

This isn't easy. Unclench your right fist.

She unrolled her fingers.

Here goes, Lulugirl. Let's do it!

A weight like an anvil on her chest. *She couldn't breathe!*

It gradually lifted. Thank the gods. Something warmed the center of her palm. She blinked her eyes open. A small dust devil whirled in her right hand.

Made of amber-lit motes, the vortex flickered in and out, almost merry, as if playing a game. The motes zoomed and dived and...

Warmth at the tips of her fingers. Clea's fireflies. She giggled. They were amazing. As if it were the most natural thing, she curled and uncurled her hand in a come hither motion, humming her Song all the while. The chaotic movement of the golden lights mesmerized her. Again she dug deep for her magic, and the motes formed the diamond motif that dipped and rose and weaved. They dissolved, and something light pressed her thighs. When she looked down, the sweetgrass basket lay in her lap. The Chest of Time was hers!

Thank you, my dearest Clea.

Hugging the basket, she raced from the room, thoughts scrambled. What next? She skittered around the bedroom, all jerky movements and excitement. *Gods*, she needed to settle. She tied the basket into the large square she'd cut from her dress and double-knotted the ends to a loop of her jeans. Set. She took a deep breath —*gods*, let her plan work—and eased open the door.

The afternoon sun flamed across a courtyard filled with dozing bodies of all species. Mostly naked, sprawled across partners, with wine goblets and hookahs strewn about. The wind changed, accompanied by the scents of vomit, stale wine, and musk. Her guards faced the courtyard. They lolled on their spears near enough to the pillars for her to slink behind them if she was very, very quiet. Could she be that quiet? Or maybe luck would be with her.

Oh, please be with me.

She inched out the door, closed it behind her, held her breath. Neither guard moved.

She could do this.

One guard swiped his face. "You got any weed?"

The other one fished around in his pocket and tossed over a blunt without looking at him. Damn, she needed to see their ears. The guard lit up, took a drag, and turned his head to pass back the blunt.

Yes! They wore no earplugs.

She began to hum the Song of Sleep, except her throat was so dry, nothing came out. *Why hadn't she swallowed some water before trying this?*

After a forced dry swallow and another, she began again.

The guard on the left pivoted toward her. The hairs on her arms stood at attention. But then both of their heads drooped, their bodies slumping against the pillars. One guard's heavy spear began to fall, and she caught it before it clattered to the ground.

She'd take it with her.

No, too awkward.

She laid it down carefully, then glued her back to the building's wall, which gave her some cover. On quiet feet she slid sideways down the columned walk. The farther she got, the more she deftly increased her song's volume just enough to make it to the nearest alcove, but not loud enough for her mother to hear. She moved with stealth, relaxing a fraction when she slid into the shadowed niche. *Booyah!* She drew a trembling hand across her shirt.

Two more guards stood down the perpendicular colonnade that led to a set of double doors. She fast-walked down the aisle, singing sleep to the first guard, then the second. The pile of bodies in the park-like courtyard remained passed out, their snores and wuffles the only sound.

She could do this, she kept repeating. She *would* do this.

JAMES HELD his breath as Rae apparated him to the edge of the clearing. "Poofing," as Clea would call it, and the entire time he imagined ending like that character in *The Fly. Christ.* Charlie, Neddy, and Sophy awaited him, the sphinx having regrown those arms of hers. Instead of him carrying Rae like a backpack, the mage would ride Sophy, an offer that surprised the hell out of him. He readjusted his katanas. His conscience pricked him that Neddy was participating. The boy was already in his Pinky form, no other weapons needed. That didn't mean he couldn't be injured or killed.

Rae carried knives—his black motes his true weapons—while Charlie wore his sword and black fae knives.

A small, but formidable group. They would have to be enough against the hordes of soldiers Rae had described to him, but he wished his brothers and sister were here.

Threads of time tugged him.

He nodded.

They'd agreed Rae should try to disable the wards surrounding The Bowl, whether it alerted Avain or not. It took Rae fifteen minutes and much effort, but he was able to break them. They paused another five minutes waiting for an alert to sound. When nothing happened, Rae slid astride Sophy, and James gave the go-ahead to move. They bent near double and ghosted across the meadow.

ALEX SLIPPED from the screen of trees into the field, surprised no wards sounded the alarm. He padded forward on silent paws catching and separating the myriad scents from Lulu's. *What?*

He froze, double-checking the impossible.

Except his nose told him the scents of Larrimer and Charlie, Neddy and Rae, and one strange and mysterious one were real. They came from just inside the meadow. At a run, he angled to his left. There, his brain didn't believe what his keen eyes saw. Was that a lion with wings, her head and torso like a woman's, and Rae riding her?

Had Cassius given him a hallucinogen?

That was definitely Larrimer and the rest. He angled his body further north, his strides eating up the ground beneath him, to leap in front of that lion thing, shifting to human as he did so.

"Who in Hades name are you?" said the lion/woman, as she screeched to a halt. Rae tumbled off her back.

"Fuck, Arctos," said Larrimer. "I almost took your pretty head off."

Silent cheers all around, and hard-as-hell slaps on the back.

"Next time, y'all just don't do that," Rae said, wobbling to his feet. "Scared the shit out of me." A grin wreathed his face and he took Alex in a swift hug.

"Let's get Lulu," he said.

LULU FACED THE DOUBLE-WOODEN DOORS. The hardest part. She'd have to cross the interior of the building to access the outside. She cracked one of the doors and peered up and down the hall, its width maybe ten feet across. No one to her left, nor to her right. Straight ahead, across the hall, the glass above the double doors showed fluffy white clouds and distant treetops.

Freedom.

There must be guards outside those doors. But she found it odd that none were inside. A "something" bugged her, but she couldn't tell what.

She felt like a competitor on American Ninja Warrior, a show she loved and even watched in faeland on DVD.

On silent feet she tiptoed across the hall to the double doors. One more step and she'd reach them. Someone grabbed her ankle. A magical silent alarm slammed into her.

Damn!

Whatever held her ankle was invisible. Some kind of magical trap. She leaned against the wood, pushed down the lever, and cracked the door, all while trying to shake her ankle free.

She wasn't breaking the grip.

Swiftly, she untied the basket, and with a quick prayer of forgiveness, she slammed the basket against her ankle.

Free!

Except when the grip broke, her momentum flung her against the doors and outside.

The two guards flanking the entryway startled at her abrupt appearance.

She ran.

Zig-zagging helped—she'd seen it in the movies, so what the

hell, that's what she did through the tall grasses plentiful with flowers, insects rising in the air as she passed.

The air ruffled, and a spear flew by an inch from her head.

She zagged.

In the distance, people running toward her.

Crap, they'd outflanked her. But wait, no, she'd recognize that Pinky anywhere. Neddy and the gang. And there, a flag of blond hair flying wild. Alex. Alive. Whole. She whooped, and clutched the chest tighter, legs pumping like crazy.

Shouts, shrieks, a scream of fury. *Screw you, Mother.*

Rae's deadly motes flared around her. Over her shoulder, she saw the two guards chasing her flung into the air. Were those bows they carried? *Gods, had she ever been more terrified?*

The earth shook with footfalls, the air ringing with shouts. Her feet scatted tiny critters and trampled flowers as she pushed herself harder. She might be a damned fine runner, but could she outpace the hordes thundering behind her? Guess Avain had done a quick "come awake" spell. A horse neighed.

Oh, no.

How could she outpace horses? And even with Larrimer at point, she doubted her companions could defeat the sheer numbers of Avain's army.

The Song of Sleep, but... No. She couldn't sing it. Her friends would go comatose, too.

She was panting, her breathing had become labored. Fear, not exhaustion, was slowing her. Close, on her left flank, one of those giant goblins raced toward her.

Exhaustion overwhelmed her. *How could she take another step?*

She stumbled to a halt.

Everything was futile. *What was the point?*

"Run!" screamed the goblin. He was the leader, and he pressed a hand to his heart. In his other hand, he carried a huge, balled-up "thing," and he unfurled it. A giant fishing net?

She was so tired.

Like a hammer thrower at the Olympics, he twirled and twirled, then cast the net even as a row of archers raised their bows.

The arrows would find her, pierce her, end her. She was done.

"Lulu!" screamed Alex. "Run, Lu!"

But why bother?

The hordes drew closer. In minutes they'd reach her.

Alex broke away from the group, shifted, and raced toward her.

The goblin's net sailed lightning-fast across the distance, glinting metal-like in the sun, keening as it pierced the air. It caught the archers, rows of soldiers collapsing beneath it, causing those behind to tumble into them, starting a chain reaction.

Maurelle and Avain kicked their horses flanks, tugged their reins, trying to whirl their animals away from the net, but the sea of soldiers made turning impossible. The net enveloped them all, and they went ass over teakettle in a pile of bodies.

Holy moly! Why was she standing still?

The next thing she knew, the goblin was hauling her forward, Alex on her other side, and they *ran*.

Arrows flew, falling short.

Larrimer shouted "*Aera!*" and began firing missile after missile at her pursuers, while Rae flung motes and Charlie loosed arrows.

Now she and her companions raced together toward the tree line and safety. Arrows rained around them. Rae had turned around, facing the sphinx's lion ass, and his motes flew, knocking the arrows off trajectory and casting them from the sky.

Almost there. Almost... *There!*

She zoomed between trees, and slowed.

"Keep running," someone said.

"I've got the chest," she said.

A bark of joy from somewhere.

They ran, threading through the forest, stumbling down the mountain paths, and finally piled into the campsite.

A pair of campers, mundanes, took a look at them and fled to their pickup. They peeled out leaving their tent and gear behind.

She'd done it! Giddy with joy and slaps on the back, kisses on her cheeks, and laughter. Until she realized why she'd slowed down and halted in the meadow. Maurelle. Her ability to influence emotions had stopped Lulu cold. It made her ashamed. She should have recognized her mother's messing with her mind and tried to counteract it.

Twice she'd succumbed. Lesson learned. It wouldn't happen again, not that way.

"What are you frowning at?" Alex sauntered over, all proud male.

She closed her eyes, shook her head. "Nothing important." When she looked at him again, his eyes were eating her up.

A lopsided grin. "Congrats, kid. You really manned up."

"Woman'd up, you mean." She gave him a sly smile.

He nodded. "Woman'd." He took her by the shoulders, pulled her close, and kissed her cheek.

What? Her *cheek*? I mean, she probably looked awful, but still.

"I couldn't be more proud of you."

"Thanks."

He strolled off to talk to the sphinx, Sophy.

Larrimer materialized in front of her. "You got it." His voice was rough with emotion. He smoothed a hand down her face. His eyes... She'd never seen them more blue, his face taut with emotion.

She handed him the basket. "For Clea, of course."

"Of course," he said, smile wide, laugh lines fanning from his eyes. He crushed her in a hug.

"We've got a *problem* here." Rae's concerned voice broke their embrace.

Everyone turned at the mage's serious tone. Charlie was supine on the ground, blood seeping from his neck.

They crowded around the fae, while Lulu dropped to a knee beside him. Rae, already on the ground, cradled Charlie's head in his lap.

"Stupid," Rae said. "Stupid fae. Shielding Sophy like that with those spelled arrows flyin' every which way."

"Can't you heal him?" Lulu brushed Charlie's hair away from his face.

Through gritted teeth, he said, "I coulda. Back there, in the forest after he got hit in the meadow."

"Didn't want to slow us down." Charlie's labored breathing slurred his words. "Chest too important."

"*You're* important, Charlie." She took his hand.

"Not like Clea."

"Fuck," Larrimer said. "You should have said something. As with all ops, we leave no man behind."

Charlie winked. "But what about..." He took a breath, face white with pain. "A fae?"

"My magic," Rae said. "Took a lotta the pain. Slowed the bleeding. But it's too little, too late."

She'd known Charlie since she'd come to Charleston. The mercurial fae could be kind or mean, funny or dour, but there was a core to him that was bedrock solid. Even her aunt continually forgave him is transgressions. He was unique.

"Stay alive for Clea, buster." Larrimer squeezed his shoulder.

"Would that I could," Charlie said. "Prop me up, James. I'd like a little chat. Alone."

JAMES WASN'T A FOOL, so he handed off the chest to Arctos. "We need to leave," he said to the group. "Fast. You with us, Cassius?"

"I'd like to be."

"Good. You're in. When they come after us, they won't bring their army."

"No," Cassius said. "It'll be Avain, Maurelle, Marcus, and Casca."

"We'll handle them," Alex said.

"Er," Neddy said. "Cassius, you're cool. I mean, you're amazing and all, but you're also big and purple, with tusks and red teeth. Mundanes will notice."

A belly laugh rolled out of the goblin, who changed. His skin turned a chocolate brown, jaws morphing to human, tusks receding. His pointy red teeth squared and changed to white. "Better?"

"Wow," Neddy said. "Neat."

"Ohhh, Cassius," Sophy said. "You're one hot dude."

"Hey!" Rae said, giving Sophy a dark look.

"Thank you, Sophy," Cassius said. "I am, aren't I? I'll stay in this form for our journey. As to the others of Avain's, only Marcus, Casca, and I can change. The unaltered goblins can't shift form. They might bring along a shifter or two, maybe even some of their humans. But they're all pretty low on the totem pole and are next to useless against all of you."

"Okay," James said. "Prepare the truck and the camper. Sophy, you can ride in the camper itself. Alex drives the camper's SUV with Neddy. Rae, Lulu, and Cassius, you take my SUV. That should do it. There's a motel thirty miles west of here. Head there."

"You didn't mention where y'all gonna go," Rae said.

He gave Rae a long stare. Rae knew very well what was about to happen, that James was about to die along with the fae, but he didn't want the others knowing his end was near. "I'll be in back in the camper, with Charlie and Sophy."

Neddy gave him an incredulous look.

"I'm in the mood to chill, Ned." He grinned and squeezed the kid's shoulder.

Rae's brows rose. "I see." The mage didn't say another word.

Smart man. James had stared death in the face in too many ways to count. This was just one more. The final one. A good thing Alex and Rae would see Neddy to adulthood. He didn't doubt the kid would become a fine man.

If he had time, he'd call his nanos. Who was he kidding? The sands had run out. His team knew how he felt about them, who he was. No need for more words.

And Clea? There would never be enough words for all he felt.

"Everybody got it?" he said. "Now break camp."

As gently as possible, he lifted Charlie. Rae handed him a cool water bottle, the mage's eyes solemn with grief.

"Take care of my Clea," James said, then walked around the truck into the shade of the camper.

Cradling Charlie, he pressed his back to the camper and slid to the ground. "Well, here we are." He uncapped the bottle and tipped the mouth into the fae's parted lips.

"Yes, here we are."

"Will I just wink out when you die?" he said.

Charlie's smile turned to a grimace. "Don't know."

"I see. I'm sorry this happened Charlie, to you and to me."

"Clea..."

"It'll be tough. But her soft heart and steel spine will see her through. She'll do okay. The four remaining nanos will rally around her. She's got Lulu, the wolf, Rae." He tipped his head against the metal of the camper and closed his eyes. "Don't you worry." He opened his eyes to peer down at the fae. "Is there anything I can do to ease you?"

"No. Thanks."

James expected the wyvern to shriek at him, but the lizard was curiously silent. What would happen to the wyvern when he died? Too convoluted by half to think about, especially when there was nothing he could do about it.

Charlie began to glow. No clue why. He'd seen other fae die, but they hadn't glowed.

"Did you know..." Charlie's voice was a mere whisper. "I'm Clea's second cousin."

"I didn't."

Several gasps, then he said, "Part of the reason the queen always cut me slack. Not to mention how great I was in bed." The fae's lips tilted upward, a bubble of blood painting them red.

"I'm sure you were." James ran a hand across his stubble. When had he last shaved? "I never thanked you for my life spark. Had you not given it to me, I'd have missed a lot." Like the glory of loving Clea. He wouldn't have wanted to miss that for anything.

"You're welcome. Wish I'd seen this through to the end."

"Me, too."

Charlie's glow increased. He pulsed with light, and it was a beautiful thing.

"See you on the other side, James Larrimer."

"Deal."

With a startling suddenness, the glow vanished. Except a ball of light rose from Charlie's sternum and smashed into his chest.

He roared with agony like no other.

ALEX RACED AROUND THE TRUCK. *Holy shit.*

Charlie looked like an angel, his wound gone, hair to his waist, horns perfect and five-inches long. His face, even more other-worldly than in life, was peaceful in its beauty.

Larrimer still held him across his lap. But he was passed out cold, a mean burn the size of a pancake on his chest. The remains of his shirt flapped in a soft breeze that hadn't been there a second ago.

A chill danced down Alex's back. Was that gentle laughter inside his head?

What the fuck?

Cassius, Lulu, and Neddy crowded around him, staring down at the fae. Lulu fell to her knees and pulled the fae to her. She stroked his hair and rocked back and forth.

"Where are Rae and Sophy?" Alex said.

"Being weird," Neddy said. "Sophy's comforting him because Rae, he's sort of lost it."

"I mean," Alex said. "It's sad and all about Charlie." Lulu had squatted down and was hugging the fae, her tears wetting his hair. "But I wouldn't expect Rae to be so overcome."

Neddy shrugged. "I think we missed something big. Something we don't get. Don't you?"

"Yeah, I do, Ned. I sure do."

Alex carried Charlie, while Cassius picked up Larrimer.

"Careful of the burn, Cassius," Alex said.

"On it."

When they rounded the corner with their burdens, Rae stood by Sophy, head bent, hands in pockets, staring into space.

"Rae?" Alex said.

The mage nodded, remaining oddly quiet.

"Larrimer here could use your help."

Rae's head shot up. "Help?"

"He's got a nasty burn on his chest from gods-knows-what. He's passed out, but when he wakes, it'll hurt bad."

Neddy dashed into the camper, returning in seconds with a blanket. "For Charlie."

He and the boy carefully wrapped the fae. Rae walked over. "Farewell, friend." He ran a hand down Charlie's face, then turned to Larrimer, still passed out in Cassius' arms.

He looked at Lulu. She was pale, eyes huge in her face. "We should go."

"Lu's right," he said. "Do your thing with Larrimer, Rae. Then let's get out of here."

"Change of plan," Rae said. "You drive, Cassius?"

"Sure."

"Y'all drive the SUV. I'll sit in back with Larrimer. Do some healin' on him. Lulu and Neddy with Alex."

Something glinted off the ridge up Guadalupe Peak. It could be nothing or... "We go *now*." They scrambled for the vehicles. Alex stepped toward the camper to stow Charlie's body, which was when he realized the blanket he held was empty.

13

Alex followed the SUV, passing the occasional car or truck. They'd left Sophy sprawled on the floor of the camper, out cold. Snoring. Lulu sat silent in the passenger seat, and every so often she'd peer in the rearview mirror.

"Are they behind us?"

"So far, it's clear."

And then she'd go all silent again.

"He was a good guy," Alex said.

"Sometimes." She smiled. "He was always good to me."

"Are you okay?"

"I am."

"Huh?"

Her lips wobbled. "I thought you were dead."

He wasn't about to tell her what a close run thing his injuries had been. "Cassius saved my ass."

She turned to him, wide-eyed. "He did?"

"Because of you, princess. Our bargain. How are you?"

"Fine."

She wasn't "fine" at all. "Lu...?"

"I'll *be* fine, okay?"

"Okay." The day's events finally sank in. He tried not to relive Lulu racing across the meadow, dozens of soldiers hot on her heels. He couldn't help but see it again. He'd been both terrified and proud. Where had the Goth girl gone? The rebellious teen, one so afraid and yet with such an attitude? Today, she'd been courageous in her actions, determined, brave. She'd stolen the freaking chest right out from under them. He still didn't know how she'd done it. She was incredible. She might have quaked inside, but she hadn't shown it. When she'd stopped, he'd almost lost it—her damned mother's compulsion—but then she'd run like a gazelle, swift and sure.

Lulu pursed her lips. What was going on in that beautiful head of hers? He didn't like that she was so quiet. He preferred when she sassed him, mouthy as hell. That mouth. He wanted that mouth on...

"What?" she said, eyes sparking.

Father Fenrir, she'd be the death him. "You were amazing today."

Her shoulders straightened, as if he'd insulted her. "Only today? I thought I amazed you all the time."

His laugh burst. "You do, princess. All the time."

"I told you to stop calling me that."

He grinned. "Which makes me want to do it more often."

"And here I was glad you were alive." She rolled her eyes. "I'd forgotten how annoying you are."

A slow smile parted his lips. "I always aim to please." A hint of her musky scent tickled his wolfie nose. His nostrils flared.

Her violet eyes widened, and then she winked at him.

Ballsy little minx.

"You think James will be okay?" she said.

Would he? What had gone on with Larrimer and Charlie? That burn was nasty. He admitted to himself that the Frankenfreak wasn't a bad dude. Damn, he shouldn't think of Larrimer like that. Not anymore. They were...friends. Man, he'd never seen anyone come close to the dude's ferocity, not even a wolf. When he'd chucked missile after missile at supersonic speed with unerring accuracy at those troops, he'd scythed down enemies like paper dolls. He was damned glad they were on the same side.

"He'll be fine."

She bit her lip.

He took her hand, the one she'd balled into a tight fist, and kissed it. "He'll be fine."

THE DAY'S last rays touched the neon sign of the motel, burnishing the desert with a golden glow. After Alex registered them, they'd parked around back, and Rae had gone inside a room with Cassius, who still carried a passed-out Larrimer. Sophy had somehow opened the camper door, and she leapt out in all her leonine-eagle glory. Except a couple rounded a corner of the building. His jaw bunched. If they were mundanes, they'd see the sphinx. Or they could be two of Avain's soldiers.

He growled low in his throat. His people were all beat and banged up. Best take care of this now.

He smiled.

Their eyes widened. Crap.

He stalked toward them, caught their scent. Mundanes. He tried to put on a friendly air. "Hey, there!"

If possible, their eyes widened further. They did a swift U-turn and beat it back around the corner.

Lulu let out a squeal. "Alex!"

He flipped around. There was Sophy all right. In human form, and stark naked.

Sophy crossed her arms. "Don't look at me like that. *I* wasn't the one scaring the humans."

Alex growled. "They saw you fucking naked!"

"No, they didn't." Sophy giggled.

Rae waltzed outside, slid his hands around Sophy's middle, and pulled her close. "Put on some clothes, gumdrop."

"Oh, all right. It was just a joke."

He blinked, and a pair of beat-up jeans and a tank top clothed the very shapely, very human-looking sphinx.

Lulu frowned. "The world's ending, and you're joking, Sophy?"

"That's exactly the time we need to play around, sugah," Rae said. "Without the light moments, shit, life ain't worth livin'."

"You're right. " Lulu blew out a breath. "So why didn't that couple react? To you I mean, Sophy."

"They couldn't see me," Sophy said. "I was invisible to them. I'm also able to cloak my true form with a mundane one. The fae call it glamour, a dumb name if you ask me."

"Sophy-girl," Rae said. "You're always glamorous."

She turned and pecked him on the cheek.

Alex scratched his head. He admitted, with the pack's being so long in the mundane world, he knew way too little about the magical one. So why had the couple run?

Lulu rocked back on her heels. "That's handy. And cool. Can all magical creatures do that?"

Sophy shook her head. "Only some. The adult higher forms, like myself. Cousins of mine, the chimera and griffin, can, as well as the Pegasi, or, if you will, the Pegasuses, which sounds dumb. Not so much the Acromantula, Basilisk, or Thestral."

Lulu crossed her arms. "Now you're putting me on. Those are creatures from Harry Potter."

"Where do you think Rowling got them from, eh?" Sophy winked, took Rae's hand, and waltzed into their motel room like they hadn't a care in the world.

"So why the hell did the couple look like they were fleeing a monster?" he said, mostly to himself.

Lulu laughed, the clear sound stirring his senses. "They were."

"What?"

"You went all wolfie on them."

"I did not."

"Yeah, you did. Tufts of hair, lengthened canines, a snout. Ha! You looked like a werewolf from a horror movie."

He rubbed his face. His world had been a lot simpler when he was only alpha to a pack of wolves.

JAMES SCENTED THE ROOM—STALE cigarettes, pizza, and sex. He wasn't dead, then. Why? He should be. Charlie must be alive. How? The fae was done for. A spring poked his back, so he sat up. The wyvern must be sleeping, because he hadn't put in his two damned cents.

He rubbed his chest, an ache bugging him just below the surface. He'd been talking to Charlie, then...pow.

They must be in some cheap motel room. The smell fit, as did the fixtures, the '70s TV, and stained carpet. What the... In a dark corner, Neddy in human form sat with his knees folded to his chest, arms braced around them. Shit.

He walked over to the boy and dropped to his haunches. "Hey, kid, you don't look so hot."

Neddy rested his chin on his knees. "Me? You've been passed out for hours."

"Something's troubling you. So?"

"It wasn't at all like I pictured, Larrimer, when those people were chasing Lulu. Back then, before Clea fixed me, when I was full-on Pinky... My head tells me I killed people, too. But this was...a lot." He plucked at a thread on the shag carpet.

"Yes, it was. You understand they would have killed us."

"Sure. But... I'm not sure I liked it. You... With that crazy grin on your face you just...you just lobbed those things and mowed them down. You were so cool."

"Not cool, Ned. Just what I was created for. Taking lives. Human, goblin, shifter. It's not a good thing, but sometimes it's a necessary one."

"Yeah, I know. But I thought I'd like it more. Seeing each life spark out like that. The Pinky loved it. Me?" He shrugged.

James squeezed his shoulder. "Bottom line, we lived. Is Charlie around?"

"Uh, no. You should talk to Rae."

After he showered, he walked outside. The sun was bright in the sky. How long had he been out?

"Sleep, much?"

He whirled, knives out.

"Jittery, too," Rae said, a grin on his face. "I thought you'd never wake up. Where'd y'all get those things? Thought we'd stripped you."

He sheathed his weapons. "Found 'em. Took 'em. Don't do that again."

"Oooohh. Big bad Larrimer's back."

The mage was stalling. "I need to see Charlie."

"He's dead."

His hands fisted. Not possible. What bullshit was Rae serving up? "Then show me his body."

"Can't. He disappeared like some fae do when they die. He was older than I thought. Way older." Rae walked closer. "Pull up your shirt."

James hadn't a clue what the batty mage was about, but his gray eyes held grave intent. He did as asked. Rae pointed to a scar, a fine starburst of white lines fanned from above his heart across his pectoral.

"Y'all's changed, even more than the scientists who created you calculated. Charlie gave you what remained of his spark when he passed on." The mage's face grew solemn. "It was a great gift, James Larrimer. If I'm not mistaken, y'all's immortal now."

Immortal. Before him sprawled the Chihuahuan desert, vast and desolate. *Immortal.* He shoved his hands into his pockets and walked.

JAMES RETURNED when the day was fading, before its abrupt departure. His mind was no more settled than when he'd strode beneath the searing sun. Charlie would remain a conundrum to him, a puzzle never to be solved. It ate at him like a sore tooth. Deciphering "immortal?" Not possible.

"You've been gone for hours, James Larrimer." Sophy stood in front of his motel room door. "I've been waiting for you, everybody was worried, and I'm starving."

"Let's go, then," he said.

Sophy glamoured herself as human as they walked around the building to the motel's small restaurant.

"Any sign of Avain or Lulu's mother?" he said.

"Not a one," Sophy said. "I'm not surprised. In this fully mundane land, their abilities are decreased."

"Are yours?"

"Nope. Most of us have acclimated a time or two in the mundane world. These cowards? They've never left the magic-imbued spaces." She hooked an arm through his. "Hurry up. They have the best Tex-Mex here I've ever tasted."

ALEX HAD STARTED on his fourth delicious burrito when Sophy and Larrimer walked into the restaurant. About time. Whatever Rae had told Larrimer, he'd gone and had a big think.

They all sat at a round table, eating family style since Rae had ordered heaps of food for everyone.

"Are you all right, James?" Lulu said.

"I am."

Alex bristled at Lulu talking to Larrimer. Man, he had it bad.

Larrimer pulled out a chair and dug in. Sophy nudged Alex to move over, so she could sit next to Rae. Strangest relationship ever.

"I presume Cassius stayed in his room," Larrimer said.

"Crazy goblin," Rae said. "Told me he doesn't like Mexican eats."

The newcomers dug in, and they all vacuumed up the food and sweet tea.

When they'd finished, Larrimer eyeballed everyone with his thunderous gaze. "I leave with the chest in the morning."

"Me, too!" Neddy piped up.

He'd swear Larrimer almost smiled. Wonders never ceased.

"Yes, Neddy," Larrimer said. "You, too. We'll go to the magic world, take the chest to Clea, and—"

"Outside," Sophy said. "This'll cause a ruckus."

Smart sphinx. Alex threw a hundred down on the table, more than enough including a substantial tip, and they reconvened by the picnic tables out back near their rooms. Sophy returned to her sphinx form and hunkered down on the ground.

Her tail swished, puffing a cloud of dust. "You can't come to the magic world, Larrimer. First of all, you'll change."

Larrimer glared at her. "No. I'm in control."

"Perhaps," she said. "Second of all..." She blew out a breath. "In the magic realm, the chest is unstable. They're not sentient, not precisely. But their directive is to conceal until The Key unites them." She glanced at Lulu. "How you discovered the chest, I'll never understand."

"Luck?" Lulu said.

Alex chuffed. "You don't believe that."

She shrugged. "I don't."

"To continue," Sophy said, "within the magic world the chests' directive to conceal is prime. You will lose it."

Larrimer shook his head. "Not going to happen."

Rae snorted. "Sweet Sophy's right."

Affection filled the smile she gave Rae. "Thank you." Her leonine body gracefully rose, and she walked forward, her orange eyes glued on Larrimer. "No, you bring it to the Arctos compound, to the safe room."

"What safe room?" Neddy said.

"The secret safe room." Alex sighed. "Formerly secret."

"You bring the chest," Sophy said. "I'll bring Clea to you."

"This is bullshit," Larrimer said. "Clea needs the chest now." He stood and began to walk away.

Sophy's feathers ruffled. "Don't you dare leave, James Larrimer. You will listen to what I have to say."

"C'mon, Larrimer," Neddy said. "Hear her out."

Larrimer moved so fast, he blurred. Human eyes couldn't track him. He wasn't sure Rae's or Sophy's could, either.

Larrimer towered over the sphinx. "Talk."

"The room Anouk created at the shifter compound provides security for the chests, particularly when they're activated. It's also safer to return Clea to herself in the mundane realm." Her face whitened, her lips thin and tight. She chuffed, and raised up on her hind legs to place her forepaws on Larrimer's shoulders. "Are you that much of a gambler? Are you willing to risk losing the chest, and with its loss, Clea?"

She slid her paws from his shoulders and padded over to sit beside Rae on the bench, looking very much the sphinx.

Larrimer stilled. Alex didn't see a breath or a blink. But, man, did he ever feel him. Violence soured the air. A battle was raging inside that beast. Alex's claws sprang out. If Larrimer lost it... They could take him, but at what cost?

Neddy wrapped his hand around Larrimer's bicep. "Let's listen to Sophy. We should trust her. She's cool."

Larrimer's eyes cut to the boy's, then his hand fisted, and he gave a sharp nod. He stalked into his room and slammed the door.

Lulu let out the breath. "That was something."

"Y'all a good friend to that man, Neddy," Rae said.

"I like him." Neddy smiled.

Rae's eyes warmed. The mage's affection for the boy was obvious, which was just what Neddy needed after numerous family and packmates had dealt poorly with him because of his Pinky form. Alex wished he could travel back to Arctos with them. Not possible. He retrieved a bottle from the camper, poured a couple fingers, and took a sip of Scotch. "I'd appreciate if you'd return to Arctos with them, Rae."

A nod. "Planned to."

"Thank you. Lulu, you'll be going with them, too."

She tilted her head. "That sure sounded like an order."

"It sounded like I'm your alpha," he said. "Which I am."

That lilting laughter made him want to throttle her.

"You're going to get Melike," she said. "Correct?"

Another tack. He needed to do better with this chick, woman, whatever she was. "You should be there when your foster mother returns."

She rolled her eyes. "With James there? And Neddy and Rae? She'll be fine. You need me to go to Charleston with you."

He needed her for something quite different. "No, I'm afraid I don't, princess."

She puffed out her chest. "As you say, I'm a princess, the queen's niece. Without me, they'll cut you up like... Like..."

"So much limp spaghetti?" chimed in Sophy.

"Yes!" Lulu grinned. "Love that, Soph!"

That did it. His growl roared up and out. "This isn't a joke."

Lulu giggled. "Sure it is."

He leapt over the picnic bench.

Oh, shit. Lulu ran, and made it about twenty yards before he was on her. He was so angry he shook with it. He gripped her by the arm and dragged her behind the SUV, out of the others' sight.

Damn him. Lulu would not be dictated to, especially by him. She made big eyes. "Too much? Over the top?"

His jaw clenched. "You will go back to the compound. You will not go to fairy land." The wolf was in his eyes, glowing gold in the darkness.

Gods, Alex was gorgeous in his anger. She needed to talk, make him see reason. Oh, forget it. She was half-Welsh, after all. And her bad-Lulu side knew just what to do.

She drew in a breath, smiled sweetly, and in a well-modulated voice said, "Just because you want to fuck me doesn't mean you get to order me around."

He released her so fast she stumbled backward. "That mouth will get you killed someday."

"It's mine, and I'm keeping it."

His nostrils flared, chest heaving like he'd run a race.

"Why don't you admit it, Alex?" she said.

Moonlight painted his face. Beautiful, compelling. She wanted things from him, felt things for him, things she didn't understand. Not really. It was like that first time she'd swum out over her head.

She stepped forward, ran her hands across his shoulders, twined her arms around him, and kissed him hard and fast.

His arms grasped her hips, and he wasn't gentle, not at all. He tugged her tight against him, ground his hips into hers, his erection tight against her crotch. Her hips answered his, and he deepened their kiss, his tongue flicking, dueling, twining with hers. Frantic and divine.

Sensation drowned Lulu. Her stomach clenched, her breasts grew heavy, and heat arrowed to her most private place. His mouth was everywhere, on her throat, her cheeks, her eyes. Kissing and licking and sucking. He wanted her, desired her. Joy burst, frothy light. Giddy with it, she slipped one hand beneath his t-shirt. His muscles bunched at her touch, and she explored the expanse of his back, finally snaking her fingers beneath his pants, to the curve of his ass.

He nipped her breast.

She was lost.

LULU'S MOAN slipped inside Alex's mouth like melted chocolate. He ate it up. He ate her up. The cream of her flesh, the silk of her hair, the curl of her warm, secret place when his hand delved inside her jeans. He suckled her breast, while he probed her wet folds, his cock an ache only she could assuage.

She was magic and light and air. She was his. He devoured her, breathed her in. Her scent had once been cashmere and bubblegum. The cashmere remained, but now with a hint of honeysuckle, peppered by a heady musk.

He lifted her t-shirt, suckled a breast. His fingers sped up and her hips rotated, hot and fast.

"Don't stop," she breathed.

"I won't, little girl."

"Wha... What?" She pushed away from him, panting, violet eyes glittering in the moonlight.

He fought to get his breathing under control.

Her t-shirt had fallen back down over her torso. She shook her head, arms rigid beside her, hands balled into fists. "That's how you still see me? As a little girl?"

What the fuck? Of course he didn't. They were just stupid love-play words. Nonsensical.

She turned away.

"Lulu, don't."

"I'm not anyone's little girl."

ALEX SAT on a rock in the inky dark, beer bottle in one hand, Scotch bottle in the other. He was alternating between the two. Man, it was stupid. But something had to dull the ache.

The unusually damp Texas night coated his skin with moisture. Earlier, the moon had been bright. Now clouds cloaked the stars, with the pretense of rain. It wouldn't. He raised his face to the sky. Uncertainty clung to him like the moisture in the air. It'd been a long time since he'd felt so unbalanced.

Mostly, he'd taken packmates to his bed. They'd come eagerly, called him a generous lover. He supposed he was. But that spark of love never lit with any of them. That was cool. They'd pleasured each other. Had fun. It was fine. Then he'd met Clea. She'd blown him out of the water. He pretty much worshipped her, was sure he loved her. He loved her all right, except his "love" was a lots of smoke and too many mirrors. The more he knew her, his feelings had deepened...to friendship. They were too alike. Too explosive. He was light to her light. Larrimer? That bastard was nightfall to her sunrise. Once he'd seen them together? The depth of their bond scorched his mind.

His romantic love for Clea had been his own foolish idealization. The real Clea was far more interesting, but she wasn't for him, which hurt his heart, not to mention his ego. What he felt for Lulu? *Father Fenrir*.

He'd always liked Lulu. That contrary nature of hers, all teen feistiness, hid a core of sweetness that both he and his wolf loved. He'd responded to how she'd lost her dad, how she'd come through her kidnapping strengthened, and he'd taken her under his wing. But she'd been a kid. A child. *Hell*, she wasn't a child anymore.

He snorted, shook his head, swigged more beer and whiskey. The burn didn't sear away his confusion. Muffled it, though. Not enough.

He reached for the pack bonds, their faint warmth settling him some. He was eager to leave for Charleston, Melike's capture a hot stone in his gut. Melike was pack, and he'd rip her from the fuckin' fae, maybe rend some of them in the process, which would feel pretty damned good. How dare they kidnap his packmate?

Gods, given Lulu was fae, he should like her people more. It was crystal, that moment in fairyland, lying in that bed, sure he wasn't going to make it, when a mysterious woman had begun to sing. And what a woman. That was the moment his world imploded.

The whiskey bottle clinked against his teeth when he took another swig.

Like water on a stone, his memories of the teen who'd been part of his pack had worn away. True, for a while he'd still seen her as that kid, no matter how her flesh appeared. Yet he'd been powerfully attracted to the *Sangestre* who'd helped heal him, unaware she was Lulu.

No, she wasn't that kid anymore. He massaged his bicep. Not for a good while. She was a woman grown, strong and clever and beautiful. "She is mine."

"Who?" Larrimer said.

"Fuck. How'd you sneak up on me?"

Larrimer slid beside him on the rock. "I'd say it had to do with those two bottles you're clutching. Deep thoughts, huh?"

Alex held out the bottles to Larrimer, who drank from each, then handed them back. The light from the motel splashed across his face. Man, the guy looked like shit, bags like plums beneath his weary eyes. He'd lost weight, too. A fuckin' mess. The dude was worried about Clea. They all were, but it was eating Larrimer from the inside out.

"Calling Lulu 'little girl'?" Larrimer said.

His hand flashed to the other man's throat. "You were watching?"

Larrimer squeezed Alex's wrist until his bones ground. "Tonight, you get a pass, wolf. Never do that again. I wasn't watching, nor deliberately listening. Your voices. The desert air. Think about it."

Man, what was wrong with him? He released Larrimer's throat. "Sorry, man. Fuck."

"The Lulu I knew in Midborough was emotional and warm. Bubbly," Larrimer said. "I'm hoping that girl's not completely gone, but the kid's touchy about the age thing."

Alex showed teeth. "Lulu's not a kid."

Larrimer took the Scotch and gulped, swiped a hand across his lips when he finished. "No, she's not."

"So what the hell am I supposed to do? She's mine."

"Are you hers?" Larrimer said.

"Damned straight I am."

Larrimer laughed low and long.

Alex growled. "You think that's funny?"

"No. What's funny is anyone asking me relationship advice."

"Yeah, well, you know more about it than me."

Larrimer cracked his knuckles.

"And...?" Alex said.

"Apologies are good. Clea likes them. They make her happy. I don't have anything else."

Alex rose from the rock. "Thanks for the chat. Here." He shoved the two bottles toward the other man. "I'm for bed."

Larrimer took the bottles. "Show her that you see her as a woman, not a kid."

"What?" How was he supposed to do that? "I told her—"

"Show her. Take her with you tomorrow."

He shook his head. "No way."

Larrimer finished off the bottles, stood, and tossed them into the recycle bin a good twenty feet away. They landed perfectly, the tinkling sounds of them breaking... Lulu's laughter. Lately, everything reminded him of Lu.

"Take her with you," Larrimer said. "She's proven herself a worthy comrade. Do you believe that?"

"Well, fuck yeah, but—"

"No 'buts.' Show her. If you send her off to the compound, you're doomed."

DAWN'S LIGHT tickled Lulu's face. She'd forgotten to close the curtains. Stupid. She scraped the crust from her eyes. She'd cried herself to sleep, hurt that Alex still saw her that way, yet ashamed at her overreaction, a childish one.

The motel was quiet, everyone else apparently asleep. Reluctantly, she sat up in bed. She needed more sleep, and sure could use...

"What the heck?"

She slid out of bed and tiptoed across the room. Propped in a corner sat a bow and a quiver of arrows. *Her* bow, quiver, and arrows. *How the heck?* They'd been captured with her. She lifted the bow and ran her hand across the limb, the wood velvet beneath her fingers. With care, she examined it from tip to bowstring. Hers. Made for her in the magic world, as were the quiver and arrows. She laughed aloud. However they'd gotten here, she wasn't questioning it. She grinned. Her day was starting out great.

After cleaning herself up, she made a mini-pot of coffee, and sat with her earbuds to listen to the news.

The devastation in the wake of scores of huge fissures opening up in the earth... For long minutes, she listened to the report.

Gods, no! She jumped up, phone and mug tumbling to the ground.

"What?" Sophy said, peering at her through the window.

"Wake the others up."

Sophy disappeared, and she ran outside, spotted Alex asleep on the ground near the camper in his bedroll. "Alex!"

He sprang up, perfectly and utterly naked. "What's wrong?"

"Get dressed. Ugh. You have boozy breath." She raced back to the campsite.

Larrimer strode toward her, face tight. "You okay?"

Neddy peered from the room he shared with Alex. "What's all the fuss?"

"Picnic table," she said to both. "Now."

When they'd gathered, with Alex thankfully wearing clothes, she began. "Those Events Clea's told us about. They... Oh, shit... Giant cracks, fissures in the earth happening around the world at the same time. They're huge. Some fifty-miles long! Ethiopia, Bermuda, Tibet, Arizona, South Africa. I don't remember all the places the news said. More. Thousands dead. The West Coast corridor." She snapped to Alex. "Not L.A. They didn't say L.A."

Horror marked her friend's faces.

Larrimer, grim as death, said, "We're running out of time."

14

They stood by the vehicles, Lulu's restless eyes drinking in each of her companions. They'd be going their separate ways, and she wished they weren't. Worry squeezed her throat.

While Sophy got Clea, Larrimer, Rae, Neddy, and Lulu would drive to L.A. with the chest. Alex would return the camper in Albuquerque, then catch a flight to Charleston.

"Cassius will go with me," Alex said.

Should she let it be or speak up? She knew the answer. "Alex, that might not be the best idea."

His brow furrowed. "Because...?"

She didn't want to hurt Cassius' feelings, but... "Goblins have been the fae's natural enemies for eons. No matter which form he takes, they'll kill him and ask questions later. It'll just make getting Melike harder."

Cassius frowned. "It's true, my friend. The fairies hate our guts."

"So he comes with us." Larrimer stowed his katanas in the SUV's trunk. Over the hood, he gave Alex a long look, then turned to the goblin. "If Cassius is willing."

The wind picked up, rattling the motel's shutters. Cassius' chest expanded, his eyes focused on the Guadalupe mountain in the distance. Was that longing she saw?

The goblin nodded. "Thank you, James Larrimer. I will be pleased to join the California contingent. Though I will miss eating a few fae. Tasty." A laugh boomed from his chest and he slapped a hand on Alex's shoulder. "My friend, we part here, to meet again."

"Count on it," Alex said.

Everyone exchanged hugs, the males trading those manly thumps they loved so well, then donned weapons, stowing the larger ones.

Larrimer pointedly stared at Alex.

The wolf nodded, hands on hips, jaw tight. "Lulu, I'd like you to go with me to get Melike."

She blinked. Had she heard him right? She couldn't believe Alex was counting her in. She kept her mouth shut, though, afraid to break the moment's spell. She stuffed her hands into the back pockets of her jeans. "Good. That's good." She was pleased at the steadiness of her voice, given the fizz frothing her insides. "Be safe, Sophy."

"I will be, little fae child."

"Not a child, Sophy," Alex said.

His words stole her breath.

"I'm older than dirt." Sophy winked at Lulu. "So to me, she is. But I hear you."

Larrimer's granite face softened. "I suspect our Lulu hasn't been a child for a long time. Safe journey."

JAMES STALKED through the Arctos compound carrying the boxed-up Chest of Time. Erick, the pack's second in command, led the way, with Neddy, Rae, and Cassius trailing behind.

On the trip from Texas to L.A., Cassius had proven a solid companion. The drive had been uneventful until they hit L.A. County. Snow. Which turned SoCal's drivers into blithering idiots. They'd barely escaped the demolition derby that had followed hard on the arrival of the first flurries. Clea would've had something funny to ...

Find her! Find her!

The wyvern's screech made him want to rip something apart, preferably flesh. The damned thing had been quiet for so long he'd almost forgotten about it. *Shut up, lizard!*

Why the hell wasn't that sphinx here with his Clea?

A nudge on his shoulder.

He whipped around.

"Chill, ma man," Rae said. "Y'all are glowin'."

He shoved the wyvern back, hard. No way was that thing taking control. A painful shudder rippled through him.

"Where's Sophy with Clea?" Neddy said, his tone plaintive. "I thought she was supposed—"

"She's obviously not here!" James bared his teeth.

The kid jerked.

He was fucked up. "Sorry, kid. I'm...tense."

Neddy clutched his claw-and-tooth necklace. "Ya think?"

A grim-faced Erick's impatient scowl got them moving again. He hoped the damned reptile had gone to sleep.

Fat chance.

Fuck off.

Laughter inside his head.

When they arrived at Alex Arctos' suite, Erick pulled a shiny brass key from his pocket. "Only you, Larrimer."

He'd been here twice before, to Alex's luxe rooms filled with artifacts and a gorgeous rapier on the wall he wouldn't mind owning. The sword hanging beside it was crap, though.

They walked through the rooms to the bedroom's far wall, with its Ansel Adams photo of Yosemite.

Erick set his hand on his hips. "I've tried. Nothing I do will open the door."

James had seen Alex hold his palm to the left of the photo's frame, which caused a door to pivot open. The door was keyed only to Alex and probably Clea. But he carried the chest.

When he'd been with Clea, he'd heard the chests' songs. He'd swear he could hear them now, a reminder of all he had lost when Clea had gone away. She'd looked at him with stars in her eyes. *Him.* She'd made him whole.

"Let's get this over with," he said, voice bitter with memory.

He placed his palm on the wall. The door didn't budge.

After two more tries, he shoved the chest onto a shelf in Alex's closet, only too aware of its vulnerabilities outside the warded room.

Erick chuffed. "That didn't go so well, *compadre.*"

Screams and a shriek had them running.

HIGH IN THE cerulean sky above the compound, a creature shrieked on a wobbly downward spiral. James' enhanced eyes saw what looked like a limp wing and the flap of the opposing one, the only thing keeping the avian aloft.

"That be my Sophy!" Rae said, his hands waving conductor-like as sparks of magic shined from the tips of his fingers.

The sphinx was badly damaged. And without Clea.

Her spiral sped up, her plummet swifter.

"I can't slow her enough!" Rae said.

Gasps. Moans. Sophy's screech.

James waited, waited, focus absolute on the plummeting sphinx. When she was low enough so he could see the crumpled feathers, the blood-coated hind legs, the slashes on her face and breasts, he bent his knees and sprang.

The wind slapped his face as he arced toward her, arms at his sides. When he neared the falling Sophy, he raised his arms. She thudded into him, and he wrapped himself around her lion's body.

And they were falling, plunging toward earth, her huge form awkward. He twisted, turned, but couldn't get his legs under him to take the brunt of their fall.

The watchers on the ground backed up, making a circle with plenty of space for their crash landing.

That would hurt like a son-of-a-bitch. Those stones were damned hard. Broken bones aplenty.

He tumbled.

Below, the circle of watching wolves stretched out their arms, linking forearms, stances wide. There was Erick, Mari, Pilar, Justus, more he didn't recognize, and fucking Neddy.

Fools. They'd get themselves smashed to bits.

Impact!

JESUS, he hurt. James peered into blackness and sneezed. Fur tickled his nose, itched his eyes. Where the hell... Falling with Sophy.

If he lifted her off him, it could damage her further. He guessed she was alive. He hoped so.

And where the fuck was Clea?

Sophy's blood stung his arms, his face, his chest. Not enough that it hurt much, except for his cock, which was bitchin.' How the hell had her fucking blood gotten into his crotch?

Man, he could do without this shit.

HE LAY ON HIS BACK, body itching. He must've passed out. The damned itching from her blood had awakened him. He smelled Sophy and turned his head. She looked like shit and was out of it on the infirmary bed next to his. Rae was there, hovering. The mage was jonesing for the sphinx. How the hell could they do it? Best not to go there.

Rae paced, wearing out the stone-pavers. Too-cheerful sunlight slashed in from the windows.

James felt anything but sunny. "Has she woken up at all?"

Rae tossed him a frown. "No. Soon. She better be wakin' soon. Thank y'all for saving her, ma man."

"Sure." He left Rae to pacing while he simmered, took a shower, which hurt like a bitch, and returned to find Sophy still in the land of Nod.

James gritted his teeth. "If she doesn't wake up soon, I'll—"

Rae halted. "You'll *what*?"

An orange-pupiled eye popped open. "How's a person to get any rest with that point-counterpoint going on?"

"You okay, Sophy-sweetie?" Rae said.

"Where is she?" James was in her face in a flash. "Where's Clea?"

A groan as she shifted her lion's body on the bed. Her fur remained bloody, her brown hair crusted with the stuff, although her wounds were healing. "I lost her."

"*How?*" he barked, his voice combining with the wyvern's bellow of pain. The windows rattled, one spider-webbed with cracks. She'd *lost* Clea.

Neddy and a nurse raced through the door.

"Get out!" He gave them teeth.

The nurse turned tail.

"No," Neddy said.

"No what?" He snarled at the boy.

"I'm not leaving." Neddy stepped forward. "You go all wyvern on us, we'll never get Clea back."

Too worked up to speak, he gave the boy a nod. He was losing the battle. Clea calmed the wyvern. Without her... He pushed until he tamped down the wyvern enough to think, then unclenched his fists with deliberation. Time to compartmentalize, something he'd been expert at before Clea. She was his life's demarcation. He'd almost forgotten how to become the Ice Man. But if he didn't, he'd lose himself to the reptile and would destroy the world with their combined fury.

The chair he pulled beside Sophy's bed almost broke. He smothered himself in another layer of ice and sat. "Tell me, Sophy."

Sophy glanced at Rae, her eyes fogged with pain. "Anouk planned to accompany me. We were getting ready to leave her aerie when she got a summons. The Council. Urgent." Her eyes cut to his. "Fool that I am, I told her to go. She didn't want to. But I was on the council eons ago. You ignore a summons at your peril. I pushed her out like a fledgling, and she said she'd hurry back." Her lips thinned. "I haven't heard from her since."

Rae was pacing again, small black motes drifting from his ears. "Go on, Soph."

"Before she left, she strapped Clea to my back. Anouk understood I couldn't wait for her. Could. Not. With each moment that passed, Clea was fading. We lifted off, and all was well until we hit that unnatural snow." She blinked. "The northern realms in our world have much of the cursed stuff, but this... I couldn't see! What those cloddish mundanes with their clumsy magic didn't realize was that I could still *hear* and *smell*."

"Who the fuck are the 'cloddish mundanes?'" the wyvern said from James' *own* mouth. He wanted to manacle the thing. *You're not helping.*

I am, human.

No, you're not. And I'm about as human as Frankenstein.

Who?

Just shut the hell up.

"Larrimer?" Neddy patted his shoulder. "You're, um, glowing again."

"Little flamey things are comin' outta your nose, too," Rae said with a grin. "Gotta hurt."

James spoke with a calm that belied his fury. "Wiseassing to the wyvern? Bad plan, Rae. So tell me, why didn't you mention the snow was produced by magic wielders?"

Rae shrugged. "We were too busy playing bumper cars to say somethin'. You feel me?"

"No, Rae, I do not 'feel' you." He focused on Sophy. "I assumed the snow was one of those 'Events' Clea talks about."

Her cheeks reddened. "It was *not*. A squadron of airborne mundanes in machines attacked me, using pathetic magic, as if their feeble attempts would bother me. *Me!* Ha! I had little trouble fighting them off until... Until a thing of Power ripped my right wing. I scored it with my claws, and I almost had it on the run, when some pilotless mechanical flying creature—"

"A drone?" Neddy asked.

"I don't know what that is."

The kid dug his hands into his pockets. "They're unmanned aircraft. Also called unmanned aerial vehicles or UAVs."

"I still don't understand," Sophy said.

"They're like flying robots." Neddy splayed his hands. "They can be remotely controlled or can fly with software directing their flight plan. They're very cool."

"This drone thing wasn't cool!" Sophy said. "As I battled the Power, it *ripped* Clea from my back and flew away." Tangerine eyes deep with sorrow peered up at him. "I tried to follow, to wrest her back. But the Power kept attacking me, the machine was too fast, so..."

"You lost her," James said.

"Yes."

"Hush." Rae stroked her cheek. "You did your best. A mighty effort."

One green tear spilled over her lower lid and down her cheek. "But not enough."

JAMES CALLED a war council for that afternoon. Then he called his team.

As the first nanoteched agent for The Union, a consortium of DarkPool's military-for-hire corporation and the government, James had led his team of five other nanotechs since its inception. He'd been the first to go rogue, but it was Rolf's death that had turned the remaining four against them. With the rekindling of James' emotions, they'd asked him to once again lead the team. Only now, their mission was to decimate The Union.

Inside the rooms he shared with Clea, he opened his ops case and distributed five sound-dampening sensors. He fired up his laptop, then set up four tablets, all switched to intricate and obfuscating channels that would scramble the signals.

He didn't hesitate before he made the call, although he wished to do so. Not one of his fellow nanoteched team, three brothers and a sister, would be pleased with his request. It was what it was. He rubbed the back of his neck.

The noisy and lethal Fan and the angelic and equally lethal Pyotr were hunting down Balfour, the former FBI agent and Clea's traitorous boss, who'd seemingly vanished off the face of the earth.

James hoped... He'd see how it went.

He made the call.

Greetings exchanged, jokes, and catch-up from the other four.

"How's it going on the hunt?" he said.

Pyotr's ice-gray eyes darkened. "We've got a lead. Word has it he might have been seen at their base in West Virginia. We're following up."

"Hate that fucking place," Gierr said.

Like James, he despised what he was, what they'd become. That base was where they'd been created. "Agreed. We'll take it out one of these days." He paused. "I have news."

He filled them in on what had gone down in Charleston, not revealing the purpose of the chests or that Clea was The Key. That was her story to tell. Then he dropped the bomb.

"The Union's got her."

After their chorus of "fuck that" quieted, he said, "I'm going in after her. Tonight or tomorrow."

Gierr's ebony-skinned face tightened. "You can't ask this of us."

"No?" The soft menace in that one word should get his point across.

"They still believe the four of us are working on their behalf," Fan chimed in. "This'll give away the game."

He nodded. "Yes, it will."

When he'd last seen them in the flesh, he'd told them exactly what had gone down with Rolf, one of the original six. How The Union had destroyed Rolf's mind and tossed him away like so much garbage, which was when the remaining four chose to turn their might and power against their Union creators. Geirr's rage at the horror and loss of Rolf was echoed by all.

"We've been under the radar, Larrimer," Brina said. "You know that. We've been effective working against them, as we agreed after their betrayal of Rolf."

"I know that, too. But we've also been lucky. We should be the ones to shove the truth in their faces, rather than them discovering it on their own."

"Can't she extricate herself?"

"She's unable to do that," he said.

"It's too big a sacrifice," Fan said.

These people are fools, said the wyvern. *You don't need them.*

Shut up.

If he was to penetrate The Union and extract Clea, he needed more than the shifters and their motley crew. He needed his fellow operatives. They understood The Union's tactics, knew how to combat them. How much to tell them about him and Clea?

"Are you with me?"

The silence deafened him. Except Brina held up a finger. The paleness of her albino face often hid her emotions. Yet she was the most intuitive of the bunch. "This woman means much to you."

"She means the world."

Brina's eyes widened.

"That you are doing this will again make you their prime target," Fan said. "They will hunt you."

James nodded. Each understood what it meant to be hunted and punished by The Union, with their infinite resources and megalo-maniac desire to steal magic and control the evolving world. How, without thought for the individual, they'd transformed six humans into monsters. They all knew what had been done to him when he'd rebelled, that he'd been tortured and his emotions stripped until he was more machine than man.

Taka had spearheaded their transformation and handling, but she was done, reduced to ash by the wyvern. He suspected that

Balfour played a key role in the organization, which was why it was crucial they found Balfour's location.

"They might hunt Larrimer," Brina said. "But if Fan and Pyotr continue their search for Balfour, they'd remain under the radar. If you don't join in, Geirr, we will still have three covert operatives. They don't understand our bond."

"I don't like it," Geirr said.

"Neither do I." The pencil Pyotr held crumpled to dust.

"It's a risk and a sacrifice," Larrimer said. "I'll give you an hour to talk it over amongst yourselves." He moved to close his laptop.

"Wait." Brina's eyes sparkled. "I don't need an hour. I'm in."

Geirr rolled his eyes. "Brina, you fool."

A emory board appeared in her hand and she began to file her nails. "Oh, get a life, Geirr."

Geirr slammed his hand on the arm of the couch.

Fan laughed as it toppled to the floor. "You're sure tough on furniture, asshole."

"Yeah, well, I'm in, too," Geirr said. "Somebody's got to watch your back, Brina."

She winked. "And such a pretty back it is, too."

"Thank you." He turned his attention to Pyotr and Fan. "You two will keep up the hunt for Balfour and remain covert."

Pyotr frowned. "You mean we don't get to join the party?"

"Shut up." Fan's eyes took on a hungry, curious heat. "Losing the safety of secrecy. Shoving our faces onto the bastards' radar. Is this woman worth it, Larrimer?"

"Worth it? She is worth the moon and the stars."

15

Deep in the den, James walked through the cellars, past where the shifters had held him prisoner, to a long oval room banded by rock and stone. Wolves surrounded the table. He pulled out an empty chair near the head and sat. Justus and Mira, parents of a murdered child Clea had helped; Pilar, with Comanche blood like his; Carlos, Melike's mate; and Erick, who in the absence of Alex had taken the alpha's seat. Neddy and Cassius were at the table, too, and next to Rae sat Sophy, beat up but whole, breasts bobbing, tail swishing across the floor with a susurrating sound. They only waited on Geirr and Brina.

Would they show? He'd bet his favorite quarter horse on it.

James refilled his coffee cup, trying to contain the vicious energy coursing through his body, while the rest drank coffee and tea, and ate bagels and pastries.

Tension a berserk current inside him, he leaned back in his chair. The muscles he forced to relax didn't want to obey. Yet the beast within was oddly quiescent. Concerning. The dimming of his and Clea's song, even more so.

That day so long ago when he'd first seen Clea... She'd been covered in blood, but stayed composed. He'd been impressed. That was when their song had first stirred. That moment rang so clear his heart thumped with longing. To push past the ache, he tried to go back further, to those memories before he'd been remade. To his fine mother—he knew she was fine, but he couldn't see her face. Nor his dad's. Couldn't picture his beloved horse, damned ornery creature, nor the house where he was raised, the land he ranched with his parents. The scents of sage, the sounds of cattle lowing, the glitter of a trout on his line. They were all vapor, as were his special ops missions for the FBI and DarkPool. The blood in Afghanistan, the guts of comrades spilling into his shaking hands.

The memories remained in his head, the knowing, the facts. But the explosion and his nanoteched recreation had stolen the images, the experiences, the scents and sounds and sights, the *feelings*, leaving only the awareness of their existence inside the monster he was today.

And she'd lay into him, his fierce woman, for calling himself that.

Gierr and Brina sauntered in as if they owned the den, bristling with power and arrogance.

"Tone it down, guys," he said, allowing his eyes to speak of friendship and shared battles.

The massive male's bellowed laughter rang out, which prompted the petite albino to elbow him in the ribs.

Gierr snorted, taking a seat to James' left, and rubbed his side. "She's gotten meaner."

"Not possible," James said.

Brina's lips tugged up.

"Everyone's here." The room quieted, and he began. "Brina, Geirr, and I will lead and control the op to retrieve Clea." His heart might be iced with fear, but his words rang with fire. "The fools used a drone, which is a neon arrow from her abductors straight to The Union and DarkPool."

"How can you be so sure?" Mira said, the shifter's voice tight.

"They've been hunting Clea for years, long before they knew exactly who and what she was. Remember, I was their property. The drone, coupled with their somewhat incompetent magic users, all point to The Union. They've co-opted magic users before. Given their attrition rate, and the weakness of the magic used, I suspect they've got a new crop of fools who seek power with the combining of the worlds." They'd used Charlie that exact way.

Smoke swirled in the doorway.

James leapt to his feet, knife in his right hand, SIG in his left. Geirr and Brina—equally prepared—appeared beside him.

Magical motes in purple and orange coalesced into a giant bird-thing with a gold body topped by a mountain lion's head the size of a balance ball. The creature's front legs bore feathers that rose to cover its iridescent purple wings, with its back legs furred like a lion's. All four legs bore massive talons and the thing nearly spanned the conference room.

The din of shifters' growls as they changed assaulted his ears, as did the buzz of Rae's swirling motes and Cassius' bark when he morphed to his goblin form.

Above the cacophony, Sophy shouted. "Cousin! Yeah!"

Cousin? James lowered his arms, but didn't release his weapons.

"Quiet!" He had to bellow it twice before the room finally stilled. The odd creature stared at him with a feline smile. Christ almighty, Sophy had one weird-assed cousin.

"Fine!" Sophy rolled her eyes. "You've made your entrance, my dear. Now shift."

The thing's dark laughter accompanied the smoky magic enveloping the creature, which dissipated into...

Six-foot-eight of woman stood before them, her deep purple hair cropped into a bob. Cinnamon eyes, tip-tilted nose, and full lips wearing purple lipstick and a smile that revealed overlong canines. Her breasts rivaled Sophy's, but on a bigger scale, her bountiful body covered in amethyst leather, with legs that went on forever clad in thigh-high, spike-heeled boots.

She looked like something out of a porno space opera.

His eyebrow arched. "Why are you here, Sophy's cousin?" Which sounded awkward as hell.

Sophy's sigh was belabored. "*I* asked her to come." She gave the valkyrie-creature the side eye. "Ziz always has to make a grand entrance."

Ziz waved her arms. "*Nyet!* I'm just doing *me.*"

James sat and placed his weapons on the table within easy reach. "Russian, Sophy?"

"Of course I'm not Russian. She's not, either. She just likes to put on the accent when in human form. It's very annoying."

"I do not annoy." Ziz drew out a chair, removed her epic sword from its harness, and plunked herself in the seat. With an odd gentleness, she lay the plain sword in front of her. It spanned the table.

When he glanced at his companions, he'd never seen so many goggle-eyed creatures in his life.

Ziz was *something*, that was for sure.

The wyvern laughed.

Not now.

Her real name's Zissel, which means sweet. Rich, don't you think?

You know her?

Of *her. Some call her a Ziz, others Anzu, Simurgh, still others Gryphon. Whatever she is, she's legend.*

Ziz leaned toward James and sniffed, then proceeded to smell Brina and Geirr. "What *are* you three?"

"Different." He wiped his hands across his face. The day was a fucking circus, while Clea's life was bleeding away. His temper boiled over.

The fist he slammed down cracked the table. No more racket. Flame spurted from his nose, while his eyes speared Sophy's, which were round as coins.

"Why *the fuck* is she here, Sophy? We have other shit to tend to."

Rae puffed up. "Y'all don't talk like that to my girl."

James vaulted to his feet, chair crashing to the floor.

Brina clamped a hand on his forearm. Geirr's hand banded his wrist.

"Temper," was all Geirr said.

He blinked—Clea, she'd bring him down, calm him. But she wasn't here. He needed to rip someone's head from their torso, blood spurting, body twitching.

The hold on his arms tightened.

Brain freeze, so cold he ripped his arms free, slammed his hands to his head. And saw flame.

Cascades of noise. Shouts. Pain.

James. James...no.

Clea?

Calm, my James.

A spike of cold inside him. *Clea, where are you?*

Love you. The words fading.

Clea! "Clea!"

But she was gone.

He staggered, opened his eyes. The others in the room ringed the table. Former table, since it lay in pieces, ripped apart by... He stared at his hands. Shit. Not hands, but red-gold scaled fingers with curled black talons at the end. He fisted them and watched them gradually change back to human.

"What the fuck was that, Larrimer?" Brina said.

He shook his head like a dog shedding water. He'd been a freak show for years, but this...this was a special kind of monster.

Clea had *talked* to him, mind-to-mind. He pressed his thumb and forefinger to his eyes. Nothing else mattered but finding her.

"Apologies." He looked at Erick. "I'll replace the table."

"No worries, man," Erick said, eyes wide with something like awe. "You coulda busted out of that jail cell anytime you wanted."

No point answering the obvious.

Erick shook his head and sat. The others followed his lead.

James righted his chair and did the same. At least he hadn't hurt anyone. Curious that nobody had tried to stop his rampage.

That creature, Ziz, wore a shit-eating smile.

He didn't like that smile. "*What?*"

She licked her lips. "We finally meet, Wyvern. Yum."

Christ. "Sophy! Let me repeat, why did you call Ziz?"

"She could help us with Clea," Sophy said.

Ziz cut her off. "Sorry, cuz, not happening. I may have found Anouk."

Sophy took in the room. "Anouk's gone missing. See?"

"I don't see," Pilar said.

"Who gives a shit?" Gierr said.

"I give a shit, you *idiota kusok*!" Ziz stood. "She is my child."

"Many times removed," Sophy said.

"Shut up!" Spittle few from Ziz's mouth. "I will not be able to extract her on my own." She slapped her palms together. "So! Who will help me get my *rebenok*?"

"She's my best friend, Larrimer!" The feathers on Sophy's wings ruffled.

"I don't give a fuck. We rescue Clea first!"

"Well, you have a point." She sighed. "What about Alex? I bet he and Lulu have gotten Melike by now, right? He'd be—"

"No." He considered sending his other two nanotechs, Pyotr and Fan, but they were undercover, and that op mattered too damned much. "We'll help find Anouk after Clea's recovered."

Ziz rose to her full height and replaced her sword in its scabbard. The roil of animus thickened the air. "Not good enough."

James leaned forward. "Tough."

"Ziz," Sophy said. "Don't go all badass on us."

Ziz shrugged. "It's my nature." And she smiled, those long canines growing. She wagged a finger. "You will all regret this."

He reached for her, but in a tornado of smoke, she was gone.

THE SWORD FLASHED in an arc toward Alex's neck. He twisted right and parried, but not before the fae bastard sliced his shoulder. His eyes darted to Lulu and back to their adversaries.

The fae had surprised them, damnit. *How?*

He never expected retrieving Melike would be easy, but this ambush by the Charleston fae made no sense.

Movement to his right. A brutish bastard gripped Lu's shoulders, started hauling her away, his hand rising to...

Alex slashed another attacker's groin and spun. The brute's fingers banded Lu's throat. She bonked him in the chin with the top of her head and let out a piercing note.

Alex's head split open, brains spilling out.

No, wait, someone was hauling him to his feet. Blurry-eyed, he took in the feminine hand, grim expression, teeth bared in fury. Once she got him standing, she hissed, "Run."

They stumbled, but his head cleared enough to race forward. Lulu was a wraith, threading in and out of trees, around bushes. He shifted mid-stride, became wolf, and galloped.

An hour later, she finally stopped, panting furiously, runnels of sweat coating her face. "That was horrible."

She faced him, chest heaving, and what a glorious chest it was. His tongue lolled out.

She whirled and tapped him on the nose. "Now isn't the time, Alex. Change, please."

He did so and grinned. "It's always the time to admire a beautiful woman."

She punched him in the arm.

"Next time," he said. "What say you warn me about that fucking note."

"Duh. Warning you would've warned them."

He massaged his ears. "Damn that ringing. My head's still not right."

"Sorry, your wolfiness."

"Alpha wolfiness, please." His grin widened.

She laughed, then the violet of her eyes darkened, as her delicate fingers feathered his shoulder. "You're hurt."

"I'll heal." He fell into those eyes, their concern stroking his heart.

"Let me find some—"

"I'll heal, princess. No need to fuss. You saved our asses."

Her freckle-dappled face flushed. He moved closer and clasped her chin. "You were magnificent."

He brushed his lips across hers, tasted the spice of her, the sweetness. He needed more, drew her to him, seeking entry. His tongue danced with hers.

She softened, then nipped his lip, hard.

He jerked back, licked the dot of blood, and smiled. "Father Fenrir, you're a sorceress."

"I try." Her words were light, but her eyes. They burned.

Lulu could melt him like molten gold, and he'd love each minute of it. She was right to bite him. Much as he hated to admit it, she'd reined him in. The whole mating thing was riding him hard and if he didn't get control of himself, he'd get them both killed.

"Why attack?" he said.

"It's strange," Lulu said.

That it was. "Hold that thought. We need to keep moving."

An hour later, they'd washed in a nearby creek. Then in the shade of a broad live oak, they ate sandwiches and drank water they'd taken from their packs. He slapped a mosquito, leaving a bloody smear on his forearm. It was buggy as hell. Bloody hot. And muggy. Even in October, the Charleston weather sucked. Except for the scents—fecund earth, rich with growing things and magic. They urged him to become wolf and roll around in the dirt. A languid breeze attempted to play with his hair, drying the wet strands that clung to him from his dip in the stream.

"So why do you think your fae attacked us?" Alex said around a mouthful of beef brisket and pumpernickel. "Especially since we have a fae in our party."

"Auntie Viviane wouldn't do that. Not to me. Or even to you. As ticked-off as she must be at us for stealing Clea, she wouldn't try to kill you."

"Maybe. Maybe not. But you, Lu? I watched you two. You're precious to her. Something is very wrong in fairy land. Give me a minute." He needed to check on Melike. He relaxed his muscles, smoothed his mind, closed his eyes. As alpha, the threads of his individual pack members were like strands of nerves bundled inside him, ever-present. They murmured, a comforting amalgam of individuals as one. While his pack was far distant, Melike was nearby, her thread easily the strongest due to proximity. He felt her forceful thread, vibrant and alive, but something was off and...

"They won't kill Melike," Lulu said.

"You keep saying that," he said.

"I know them," Lulu said. "Like I know you, Alpha."

He tugged the end of her braid. "Not nearly well enough. That she's in their hands concerns me deeply." Pain speared his wrists, his back. His body vibrated with it. He vaulted to his feet, scattering food and drink. "They're hurting her. I can locate her. We go."

"Trap?" Lulu said.

He winked. "Most likely. I'll buy us some insurance." He pulled his phone from his pocket and texted Larrimer and Erick.

"Insurance?" she said.

A snap of wood ten yards away.

"Go," he hissed and shifted to wolf.

Fleet and silent they raced through woods dappled with purple and yellow and green, Lulu setting the pace. An arrow flashed by his cheek, displacing the air.

"Faster." Lulu picked up the pace.

The whoosh and thunk. More arrows.

Ahead loomed a massive pine. Lulu pushed out a startling burst of speed and he easily matched it. They ran shoulder to shoulder until Lulu blazed toward the pine, took the lead, and...

Vanished.

Alex leapt.

Weightlessness melted his bones, and his wolf scrabbled for purchase, clawed and snarled.

Gravity stole his breath when he thudded hard onto the rocky earth. *Gods blood!*

Took him a sec, but he got his legs under him and stood. The sun bright, too bright. He squinted. Whoa. He was on some kind of promontory, with the wind frantic and the sea crashing nearby. A scattering of gnarled trees, like Monterey pines, pointed toward a craggy peak in the distance. He scented the air, rich with sea tang and mixed with an appealing sweet-biting scent that tingled on his tongue. An alien smell. Through a haze of soft clouds circling another far off peak stood what looked like a jagged town, with spires like cork screws twisting toward the sky.

As Clea would say, they weren't in Kansas anymore.

Lulu stood a good ten yards away, arms wrapped around her waist.

He reached for his Arctos pack.

Gone. Empty. A void where they belonged. His vision blurred, and he swayed. Never. He had never been alone, never been without pack.

His chest heaved. He'd get through this. He must.

On rubbery legs, he trotted toward Lulu, who stood at the cliff's edge overlooking a roiling sea far below. Black waves attacked a shore of alabaster sand. Damn, but those waves would be fine to surf. Problem would be that murder of crows, elephant-sized ones, breaching the waves, catching man-sized fish in their pink beaks. He expected they'd find his wolf a tasty morsel, indeed.

Lulu had led them into the magic realm. Man, that sucked. *Shit.*

He shook out his fur, damp with the sea.

If they didn't return to the mundane world soon, this was where he would die. Not in battle, nor as an old toothless wolf.

His pack's long tenure in the mundane realm couldn't sustain life in the magic one. Plenty of pack histories put forward that unpleasant hypothesis. The long-ago alpha, Ólafur, compared it to an opiate overdose. He believed the magic would flush through their systems, but the too potent incremental buildup would leave no way for an Arctos wolf to offload the accumulation. No Arctos wolf had ever returned from this realm, not in the histories, not in his lifetime.

Dead man walking.

How soon? How much time did he have? Hours? Days? Weeks? Could he and Lu make it back to Charleston before...

His shift was instantaneous, his flow to his human form an eye blink. Alex took the few remaining steps to stand beside Lulu. Her hands were white-knuckled fists, and confusion and fear shined up at him from those beautiful violet eyes.

The magic realm was a tricksy one, its reality shifts infamous. From her worried look, he bet when she'd gone through that tree with an intended destination, she'd landed someplace else.

"I have no idea where we are, and I don't know how to return from here."

"Hush. It's okay."

The fragile hands she placed on his chest trembled.

Never would he tell her that she'd written his death sentence.

He wrapped his arms around her, pressed her close. The smell of honeysuckle and cashmere and *her* made his wolf whine with want. He whispered in her ear. "No worries, princess. We'll find our way."

ON SILENT FEET, James and his companions stole through the halls of The Union's central building, having left Cassius as their lookout at the side entrance. The second team—made up of Eric, Gierr, Brina, Justus, Mira, and Rae—had taken the building's left wing, while his team—Sophy, Neddy, Leon, Carlos, Pilar, and him—took the right.

Now they faced three branched halls. They'd already taken down a dozen guards, scientists, and a weak mage who seemed almost happy when he'd died after attacking them. Another victim of The Union's conscription program, he presumed.

When they found Clea, he'd wind her in bubble wrap, take her to an island, lock her in a safe room, and barricade the door. Maybe plant some IEDs around the perimeter.

"Larrimer, y'all good?"

Rae's voice in his earbud jerked him out of his reverie.

"Hell, yes."

"You be soundin' awful cheery."

"Just do your job, and I'll do mine."

James pointed to the hall on the left and notched his head to Leon and Carlos, who peeled off to take that corridor. He motioned Pilar and Sophy to take the right, while he and Neddy in his Pinky form moved forward.

They entered the central corridor, dotted with rows of doors to his left and right. The neon tube above them buzzed, the corridor's only sound. No guards. Not good.

The first door he opened revealed an empty suite, with steel lab tables, instruments, and a bucket of foul-smelling blood. Neddy sniffed, and a rope of drool fell to the floor. They moved to the door on the right. The corpse of an old man lay on a gurney. He was attached to wires and tubes bubbling with blue liquid. With a swing of his katana, he hacked off the corpse's head. Blue liquid oozed from the stump. For insurance, he chopped the head into pieces, separated the legs from the torso, and backed out of the room.

Two doors down, Neddy waved him over. Soft whimpers came from inside the room.

The kid leaned close, jaws wide. "Lockkk...ed."

Whatever was in there couldn't get out. Or it could be a trap. "Wait out here, Ned."

With a delicacy born of practice, Larrimer picked the lock, eased the door open with a soft push, and stepped inside.

A child wearing brown corduroy pants and plain blue t-shirt sat on the floor. Black ringlets haloed her heart-shaped face as she played with a Barbie dollhouse and dolls in the center of the otherwise empty room, the skylight's faint light that of impending dawn. The kid was painfully thin. Tears streaked her cheeks, and she quickly buried a sob, as if she were afraid to make noise.

The urge to leave, re-lock the door, and continue his search battled with the memory of Clea's voice. *Help her, James. We can't just leave her.*

They couldn't afford the time.

Make time, she'd say.

Dawn was coming. More Union employees and soldiers would

arrive for the workday. He *should* leave the child. His lips twitched. He hadn't anticipated this kind of battle at Union Headquarters.

He reached for the door, intending to leave. Instead, he closed it.

His Clea had not only reanimated his heart, but his human conscience, that sense of right and wrong he'd lost long years ago.

The click of the latch brought the child's head around, her dark eyes pools of surprise.

He hunkered down onto his haunches. "Hello."

Those big eyes widened further.

"I'm James. What's your name?" He kept his voice low and calm.

Her lips pursed, and she shook her head, curls bouncing.

"Would you like to leave here?"

She nodded, eyes bright, and held out her arms.

He reached for her. Pilar and Mira could take charge of her. They'd know what to do, how to handle this small bundle of a girl.

He scooped her up, scattering the dolls, and stood. She raised her head, smiling.

Her lips latched onto his, some kind of venom seeping from her mouth. Needles pierced the back of his neck where her hands were clasped. He tried to snatch his mouth away, but small pricks of suction glued her lips to his as his legs weakened. He dropped to his knees.

She inhaled, his breath, his *essence*. His arms went to push her away, but instead fell limp at his sides. The venom's paralyzing effect made him slump to the floor, the child glued to him. She inhaled again and again.

James battled the paralysis, fought for consciousness, yet he saw Clea. There she was, holding out her hand, smiling at him, wearing a pink ruffled gown. Ruffles?

Not his Clea. No, she wasn't here. He had to find her. Where was the wyvern? He called, expecting an answered roar of fury. Silence greeted him instead.

He was tired. He'd never been this tired. Clea's face appeared before him, beautiful and luminous with love. His eyes closed.

Reality roared through his consciousness.

The child sailed through the air, crashing into a steel file cabinet. It bounced off the cabinet and dropped to the floor in a heap of limbs and bloodied head.

Hands shook him, not gently, and his lungs expanded to swallow gulps of air.

"Kill it," James gasped, sitting up.

Through a dizzy haze he watched Neddy whirl and reach for the creature.

"She'ssss gonnne." Neddy's hiss echoed through the room.

"We found Clea!" Rae's voice blared in his ear. "North corridor."

He clambered to his feet and ran.

16

H ow? Lulu sank into Alex's embrace. *How could they find their way back to the mundane world?*

She had no idea where they were in the magic realm. Not even a hint. She'd really messed up. When she'd gone through the tree with Maurelle all those years ago, they'd arrived in a land-locked meadow near a village on stilts. The village, one of several in the area, stood above the river they'd explored for the chest. She'd traveled that region for ten years, long enough to understand that magical landscape and its people. She could ask them for food and shelter. The villagers would help them find the exit back to Charleston and Viviane's court.

Except nothing looked familiar. Even the time stream could be different here. A minute might be a day or it could be a second. She wasn't skilled enough in the magical arts to navigate a place she'd never been.

She squeezed Alex tight, stepped from his embrace, and raised a hand above her eyes to scan the landscape. Her panic rose. "I wish Charlie was here."

"Likewise," he said.

The blood rushed from her head. She wobbled. Alex snugged her to him, front to back. "Steady, princess."

Toast. They were toast. Pride said not to tell Alex, to brave it out until she found an exit.

She turned in his arms and stared at her beautiful wolf-man. He deserved better, so she explained.

He wasn't angry, didn't rail at her, his face gentle with understanding. "Not to worry. We'll manage."

She didn't see how.

He grinned. "Food. Drink. Information." He pointed to the distant town. "An adventure."

"Thank you." She stood on tiptoe and kissed him.

His answering kiss took her to a place of comfort and heat and desire. She wanted to hang on, shut out the world, hold him, love him. It took every ounce of her will to finally step away. She nodded. "Food. Drink. Info."

"And maybe a warm bed." He waggled his brows. "Some velvet ropes. Black ones."

She laughed. "You're incorrigible! Does your mind always go there?"

"Pretty much." His eyes sparked with a smile.

"Ridiculous man." She hoisted her pack onto her shoulder. "The first step and all. Let's go."

ALEX SENSED THE MONSTER CROWS' intentions, before they dived.

He drew his sword, shoved Lulu behind a rock, and took on his half-form, leaving his sword hand human.

Massive talons grazed him, but he ducked, slashed. No more legs on you, sucka. Hell, yeah!

And the world became a blur of slashing, stabbing, and raking his claws over the bastard birds' chests. Time slowed. The world paused. Sword slicing off a beak, sinking into a breast, claws sweeping across a belly that tried to squash him. His senses said

Lulu was safe, so again and again he slashed and thrust and clawed, until...

A cacophony of caws, and the massive birds arrowed away. He braced his hands on his knees and panted beside the corpse of a crow. Man, he ached.

"Alex!"

He whirled.

A fist connected with his jaw in a resounding crack. His head snapped back and stars lit up the sky. "What the hell!" The blood he spewed dotted Lulu's already-blood-spattered leathers.

Fury arced from her eyes. "How dare you push me behind some rock like a little...*princess* in need of rescue?"

Oh, *shit*.

He stepped backward.

LULU LEAPT AT HIM, her emotions see-sawing between fury at his overbearing tactics and awe for his bravery and fierceness. She slammed into him, wrapped her arms around his neck, and took his lips in a fierce and bloody kiss. Okay, she was crazy, didn't know how to react to his stupid domineering... But he was so good, so gallant, she feared she was lost.

He ate her up like she was the finest meal. She returned the favor.

His lips hard on hers, tongue invading, she invaded back, dueling, sucking, soaring with the pleasure of kissing Alex. His stubble brushed her cheek, his hands cupping her bottom as he pressed her closer. Joy soared through her, heady and potent.

But they had to get out of this magic realm sooner rather than later. Hard as it was, she drew back from his beautiful lips.

"Princess." he said, his voice low, guttural, his face tight with passion.

She crooked an eyebrow, a smile hovering at her lips. "Alpha. Please try to remember I'm a warrior, too. We should go."

He looked poleaxed, as if he had no idea what to make of her. That felt pretty fine, actually.

He squeezed his eyes tight and released her.

As she walked off, careful of her steps, she felt drunk with passion. She raked a hand through her hair, and snagged it on her hair tie. Annoying damned thing. She ripped it from her hair and retied it. Had she really punched him? Kissed him as if tomorrows were irrelevant? The punch she understood, but she'd overreacted to something Alex had done that was part of his nature.

Awareness seeped through a crack in her mental armor. Because her mother had done the same thing, time and again. Except Mother had taken it further. She'd marginalized her. Belittled her. Diminished her to boost her own self esteem

Alex would never do that.

She took her time plucking her arrows from the immense bird she'd downed and struggled to climb the stupid thing to retrieve an arrow stuck in a wing. What was he up to? She snuck a glance at him.

He leaned against the boulder, eyes closed, lines of exhaustion scoring his face. Gods, he looked awful. He was coated in blood and guts, and his arms were scored with cuts. She couldn't tell how serious they were, but the urge to run over and take care of him engulfed her. She jerked out the final arrow, cleaned it on the spare t-shirt she'd been using, and replaced it in her quiver. As she walked toward him, she swung her pack from her shoulder and delved inside for her first aid kit.

She wanted a relationship with Alex with every molecule in her body. For that to happen, he needed to see her as a woman and an equal, not a child or a fairytale princess. In return, she needed to accept that he would always try to protect and shield her. If those two things didn't occur, their relationship would never work.

JAMES PRESSED against the wall nearest to Clea, the other eleven team members doing the same, spacing themselves down the darkened corridor. They'd taken out the two Union guards patrolling the hall without raising the alarm.

Clea was inches away, suspended in a glass prison. He kept his eyes pinned on the dark hall when all he wanted to do was smash through the glass and touch her.

While his team waited, he worked on a plan to extract the woman he loved. She might be The Key to the worlds' recombining, but she was *everything* to him. She deserved more. A home. A family. A couch, for Christ's sake, all of which mattered a fuck of a lot more to him than this "world-saving" crap that had entangled them in its sticky web.

His mind was still scrambled from that creature sucking his life force, his fury boiling near the eruption point. If only...

"Ma man, are y'all ready?" Rae's worried voice through his ear bud helped him tether the crazy and focus on what needed to be done.

Her prison was a twelve-by-twelve room encased in glass walls, no discernible doors or locks. She lay on what looked like a cushion of air, suspended about a foot above a metal table. The dim ceiling lights haloed her, as did her long curling hair billowing around her.

Inside her cell, a man and a woman sat at a table in jeans and polo shirts playing cards. They looked human. He doubted they were. Not knowing their hidden arsenals of power, it was hard to predict how they'd react when his team extracted Clea.

While Clea's "room" was lit, the hall where his forces stood was dark. The pair talked to each other, seemingly oblivious to them.

Long metal tracks ran along the ceiling outside the glass. If trouble arrived, he predicted that steel doors would crash down to further encase her.

He waved Rae over. "Can you teleport inside?"

"I've been feeling out this here prison, delicate like. It's warded. I can go in, but it'll trip the wards."

"Can you take out the two inside without entering?"

Rae shrugged. "I don't know what they are. Can't tell without breakin' the wards."

"I don't see any way we can do this quiet."

"Me, neither."

"I'll bring out the wyvern to—"

"No!" Rae poked his chest. "Y'all *not* gonna do that."

James growled and pushed Rae's finger away.

Rae gave him teeth. "I'm lookin' out for Clea's best interests and yours. Y'all bring out the beast, you maybe can't be puttin' him back again. Hear? Y'all know that. I know that. What's that darlin' girl gonna say when she wakes up to a big red ugly beast and not you, huh?"

Unfortunately, Rae made sense. He'd also given him an idea. In the conference room, he'd expressed only hands with wyvern skin and claws. He nodded, and Rae returned to his position beside Pilar.

Knowing bargains seldom ended well, those hands and claws would be worth a try. If he was in luck, the contrary creature would oblige. The wyvern wanted Clea out of this place as much as Larrimer did.

With his plan in place, he called Cassius back from guard duty, then went to speak into the mic to his team.

A mist formed at the end of the corridor, halting his words. A humming, tra la la, the sound of light footsteps skipping down the hall. The *child*. Fuck. Mira ran forward and scooped her up, a smile wreathing the child's face.

Just as the creature moved to latch her lips on to Mira, Neddy pulled her from the shifter's arms and punched her in the face. The kid went limp. The Pinky reached for the child's neck.

"Wait," James whispered to Neddy. "Rae, do you know what that thing is?" He described what the child had done to him.

"Vampyre. But unprovoked, they're not usually aggressive without cause."

"This one tried to suck me dry." He'd bet terrible things had been done to the child in this place. Since she'd fed off him, he'd swear her bones weren't as prominent as when he first spotted her. Had she been starved into desperation?

"I'm guessin' they've been doin' tests," Rae said. "Makin' her crazy without food. If we give her breath—her food—I can control her."

"You sure?"

"Pretty much."

James wasn't sure that was good enough. He checked the time. The sun rose in thirty minutes. Their assault on the room would set off the wards, signaling Clea's keepers. Stealth wasn't a possibility. Speed was their friend.

An idea swirled in his brain. The little vampyre could be the linchpin to rescuing Clea. He whispered in Rae's ear, then explained his plan via mic to his team.

Clea would hate it. But he could live with her anger, since it would mean she'd returned to him.

"Now," he said to Rae.

The mage took the unconscious child from Neddy. The child stirred. Rae bent close, whispered in her ear. Her eyelids fluttered. When her eyes opened, she smiled.

James didn't get it. If she was vampyre, then where the hell were those long canines?

The child turned her head, as if to reach Rae's lips.

No!

Even he heard the mind-to-mind command from Rae. More whispering. A childish pout that transformed to a shy smile.

Rae nodded to James, then reached for Mira's hand. Hugging the child to his body, Rae, Mira, and the vampyre poofed out.

He then caught the gaze of his nine soldiers who now included Cassius. "Ready?" he said in the mic.

All nodded.

"Go," he said.

Alarms screeched. Steel slammed down from the ceiling to the floor. The shifters, along with Neddy, Sophy, and Geirr raced down the corridor to hold off any attackers.

Set? he asked the wyvern.

Of course.

Red smoke coalesced around his hands. The pain almost brought him to his knees, but he and pain were pals, and he'd half expected this. A little payback for his and the wyverns bargain.

When the smoke dissipated, iridescent red scales ending in lethal black claws covered his hands to his wrists and partially up his forearms.

He curled his talons onto the steel and dug in. Brina and Cassius muscled the steel he freed into a roll, peeling it away from Clea's prison. In seconds they'd revealed enough glass for even the largest of their group to enter the room.

Cassius's booted foot punched through, pounding the jagged edges wider to make a safe entry. Rae was already inside the room, his black motes battling a mucoid substance projected by the male guard, a mage, whose back was pressed against a wall. The vampyre child had latched onto Clea's second guard, a woman, while Mira reached for Clea. She jerked back her hands as if scorched and blew on them, red with welts and blisters rising on her skin.

Gunfire and shouts came from down the hall, and he directed Cassius and Brina to aid the others. He stepped inside the room.

"It burns." Mira held out her hands where some of the blisters had already popped, her skin mottled red.

James frowned, kept half an eye on Rae and the vampyre child, and reached for Clea.

The heat seared through the cloth on the parts of his forearms bare of dragon scales. He carefully wrapped his hands around Clea and drew her from her cushion of air. The burning ceased, though his arms were covered with charred flesh and burst sores. A minor irritation. He held Clea in his arms once again.

She lay limp, and he snugged her close to his chest. His clawed hands pricked the gray fabric of her medical-style tunic and pants. He retracted them a hair. Her lids were down, lashes resting on her cheek, but behind them, her eyes frantically darted left to right. "Clea."

"Fuck," shouted the mage battling Rae.

Rae's grin widened. He was enjoying the fight. Perhaps too much.

"Hurry up," Larrimer said to the Rae.

The vampyre child sprawled across her victim, now a husk of desiccated flesh. The child burped as she sat up, turned her face to him, and smiled.

What the hell were they going to do with that kid? "Finish it, Rae."

Rae chuckled, his hands waving like a conductor's. His black motes tightened around the other mage like mummy wrappings.

Far down the corridor, Sophy shrieked.

The lights in the hall flickered on, then failed.

Erick raced out of the darkness. "Larrimer, you gotta come."

With reluctance, he handed Clea to Mira.

"You can get all of us out of here?" he said to Rae.

Rae drew his motes back into his body, the other mage having dissolved inside the shroud of deadly magic. "It'll take time."

Larrimer kissed Clea's lips and took off down the corridor to engage the enemy.

ALEX WAS A MESS. Three hours later—at least it felt like three hours, time being mutable in this screwed up world—he watched Lulu continue to glide across the dry rocky earth as if her feet didn't touch the ground.

That punch. That kiss. He was so messed up.

He'd hurt her—one alpha move too many—by shoving her behind that rock.

Lulu was profoundly *more* than she'd been mere days ago when she'd run away. The years she'd lived had given her skills and accomplishments. She was brave, too. He'd been sure he'd die watching those crows chase her across the mountain meadow and knowing he couldn't reach her in time. But his prickly, brave girl had made it through.

He was alpha. He would figure out how to leave that kid he'd liked behind and accept who she was now. What was happening between them *mattered*. He knew that with alpha certainty. He shivered, remembering how her cool fingers traced and bound his wounds soothing both him and his wolf.

Now she was all business, determined to find a way back to Charleston and Melike.

Alex should have changed to wolf, the trek easier in his four-legged form, but he sensed Lu needed that connection with his human self. She mattered more to him than pack, than Clea, than his own wicked hide. He'd *always* protect her. The question was, could he relent enough for her to stand shoulder to shoulder with him? Her worthiness wasn't in question, but rather his *perception* of her strength as an alpha mate. She would accept nothing less. Neither would he.

Thick magic tickled his skin like feathers as they climbed along the rocky coast. Except for the birds, and some purple and pink trees, he hadn't seen much that differentiated this place from the mundane. So far, he felt okay. More weary than usual, maybe, but he could chalk that up to having fought off the fae and then those improbable birds.

Every step he took, the sword on his back was a reassuring presence. For the last half mile eyes watched them. Though he'd caught not a hint of predatory scent, he'd bet on it.

Man. What if that nightmare creature they'd battled in the museum, Tatianne, knew they were here? He didn't know what she looked like since she'd worn Tommy's form, but he'd recognize her stench anywhere. He hadn't given her a thought. Well, hell, now that he had, he was prepared.

He chuckled, calling himself on his own bullshit. No way was he ready to face that monster.

LULU'S ANKLE TWISTED, pain spiked her, and she almost went down. Alex caught her elbow and kept her vertical. She'd been deep in thought, not paying attention. Foolish. Admittedly, she was pooped, but the blue-grass earth as they neared the town was so much easier to maneuver compared to the rocky soil they'd trudged for miles.

"Thank you," she said.

He leaned toward her, his eyes questioning. "You okay."

His low warm voice was the worst, as if it held secrets he wanted to explore with her. "I am."

They'd been silent for miles, and she'd had plenty of time to scatter the jigsawed pieces of her life to the winds and begin the process of reassembling them. So many of her disparate parts never seemed to fit together right. She'd begun to dump all the junk from her past and to focus on what mattered, to remind herself of her strengths. She was a *Sangestre*, after all, one who could call the birds from the trees, literally.

A shadow darkened the sun, splashing them in gloom. Alex reached for her, but drew his hand back before touching her.

"Another bird?" she asked. "The crows again?"

"No." Alex pulled his sword from his harness. "That thing is twice, three times their size and there's only one avian up there. Walk, don't run, to that forest."

ALEX COULDN'T BELIEVE the weirdness of this place. Two football fields from the tree line, shifter smoke covered the earth from their feet to the trees. Purple-and-orange motes sparkled in the light, a-shimmer with whirling magic.

Sword at the ready, he grabbed Lulu's arm and pulled her back, but not behind him. He wouldn't make *that* mistake again. The smoke began to take shape, and whatever it was, the thing was monstrous. It fused into a giant bird-lion creature so large he'd have to back up further to take it all in. Except the smoke swirled again, coalescing, reforming to change into...

Holy shit. A tall, muscular valkyrie of a woman dressed all in purple leather. Brienne of Tarth, if she'd been a hooker.

Lulu giggled. Nervous laughter.

The creature's brows snapped together, hands slapped on hips. "You *dare* laugh?"

A Russian accent, except he couldn't think of any magical Russian shifters that fit this Titaness.

Tears streamed down Lulu's cheeks. "Sorry." She hiccoughed. "You look just like my Barbie doll when I was a kid. Really. Except your teeth are bigger."

The woman's purple leathers creaked as she bent to press her face inches from Lulu's. "A Barbie."

"Well, yeah. I used to dress her up as a warrior. I made the clothes myself."

The woman-creature hissed.

Oh, *fuck*.

Instead of biting Lulu, as he'd expected, she patted her head and straightened, face wreathed in a grin that showed lots of teeth and unnaturally long canines. "*Da*! That *iz* all right, then."

"I guess we were supposed to be scared of you?" Lulu grinned back.

"*Da*. That is the more typical reaction."

"Sorry."

"*Nyet*. Were your doll's leathers purple?"

Lulu shook her head. "I did the black thing. Y'know, scary and all."

"That is the more traditional color, but I prefer the complexity of purple. More daring, don't you think?"

His head was about to explode. "Ladies!" He stepped back from the women. "Who are you? What do you want?"

The shifter growled low in her throat. "Impolite wolf."

"Answer my questions or get out of our way."

"Alex!" Lulu said.

"I am Ziz, and you will help me."

"I don't think so," he said. "We're headed for the mundane world."

Ziz opened her mouth, but before she spoke, her eyes darted to the horizon, where a soft yellow glow lit the sky. Flocks of birds headed their way in what looked like manic, frantic desperation before thin blades of lightning streaked the air. Birds fell from the sky and the air soured, smelling of rotted geraniums and cat piss.

The evergreen of Ziz's eyes darkened to black. The shake of her head, and in a blink, she reformed as the colossal avian-lion creature.

"To the wood. Now!" Ziz turned and ran, loping toward the forest at incredible speed.

The sky brightened, and the lightning turned red, like a festering scar.

He sheathed his sword, grabbed Lulu's hand and raced toward the forest.

LULU RAN, yet she had to look back. Like Lot's wife, she knew it was a dumb idea.

Two creatures stood where they'd been moments before. They were something out of nightmare, one a huge wolf-like thing, the other two legged. Both were composed of an oily blackness, of sinew, pointy teeth, and bone, with fathomless black where there should be eyes—hideous shadow things made real. Like gollups, but bigger and creepier.

The wolf-thing sniffed the earth, back and forth, its fleshless black ribs heaving, as a vaporous cloud dripped from the hunched, two-legged creature. The miasma flowed across the earth, seeking, hunting, hungering. The two-legged creature's jaws yawned wide, and it turned to reveal a black chain of fire and smoke that ran from its clawed hand to surround the wolf-thing's neck.

A moan escaped her lips.

The wolf-thing raised its head, abysmal eye sockets focused on her. The pressure of that gaze made her stumble to her knees.

Ziz must have felt it, too, because she skidded to a halt in a cloud of dust and mantled her wings around them. Her leonine nostrils fluttered, and she hissed. "I cannot fly. *She* will see. Nor can I carry both of you."

"*Run!*" Lulu said, her voice breaking as she scrambled out of Ziz's protections.

"Wait!" Ziz's wings fluttered around her again. "They will outpace us eventually. We have nowhere to hide."

"If you leave us," Lulu said, "will you be safe?"

"Yes." Ziz laughed. "Safety has never been part of my agenda."

What to do? Lulu's mind scrambled. She knew of only one "she," her aunt, Tatianne. An eater of souls. A thief who subsumed all manner of beings and their attributes into herself. Her aunt wanted the chests, wanted Clea, wanted the worlds to remain separate.

Lulu's trembling worsened. The idea of becoming *part* of Tatianne, part of her evil... Horrible. She'd kill herself first. She squeezed her eyes, composed herself. She was a *Sangestre*, after all. "I'll sing. The creatures will sleep and we can escape."

"*Nyet!*" Ziz said. "Your song will be a beacon for Tatianne to find us. These are her scouts. She has dozens of them."

Alex's hand snuck around hers and squeezed. "Ziz, fly Lulu out of here. I'll distract them."

His face was tight, and he'd paled when he'd seen that wolf-thing. He *knew* something about the creature. She clenched his hand tighter. "No way, and if Ziz flies, Tatianne will see us."

"Those creatures are deadly," Ziz said. "If they score us with their talons, we will die."

"Why haven't they scented us?" Alex asked. "I smell them, and it's foul."

"Your sniffer is exceptional," Ziz said. "And my wings are cloaking us with the forest's scents. Have you read nothing about my abilities, wolf-man?"

In the distance, the yellow glow drew closer.

"Cloaked in your wings, can we wait it out?" Alex asked.

"Tatianne nears. Flesh-to-flesh, that soul-eater will know we're here."

"It's because of me." *She* was the beacon who'd alerted her aunt. Her stomach roiled.

Alex vibrated with fury, but she felt his sorrow, too. He was going to bolt, try to save them. She just knew it.

Think. Think.

Those things were inching closer, sniffing, rabid on the hunt.

Think.

The forest was quiet, its creatures hushed by fear. Could they climb those pink-leaved trees? No, that wouldn't help. Hurl the party-colored crystalline rocks? Right. Maybe swim the nearby stream, its burbling the only sound breaking the silence?

Gods, what to do?

They needed more time.

Time.

The stream. "Are we near a time stream?"

Ziz's soft laughter didn't carry. She bent low and kissed Lulu's cheek, her fur tickling.

"Brilliant girl!" Ziz said. "Of course. They won't follow into the river. It is but a mile away."

"Too far," Alex said.

What he hadn't said was too far for Lulu. She was fast, but hadn't anywhere near Ziz or Alex's swiftness. If they made the time stream, they'd have a chance of escape. "We have to try. Let's go. You've got to change, Alex."

"With you running on two legs? Ha."

A brush of Ziz's breath across her cheek. "Bravery deserves a reward. Hop on my back."

She shook her head. "I'll slow you down too much."

"A feather like you?"

They'd be in a run for their lives. She had so much to tell him, so much had gone unsaid. "Alex, I..." His kiss was hard and swift, too swift, and then he flung her atop Ziz. She clenched her thighs, pressed her hands to Ziz's neck.

"Go!" Alex said before he changed.

They'd make it. They had to.

An inhuman screech. Close. Too close.

Ziz's body tightened, then exploded into a gallop.

17

J ames raced down the corridor. The darkness wasn't just dark, but stygian, a boiling thing that reached for him. Bring it on. He ran, his taloned hands changing to human. The wyvern asserting its independence. Fuck that. Near the hall's end, a black smoke-like fog clung to his body. He skidded to a halt beside Geirr and the others.

Beyond the fog, a dim light revealed a hall littered with the bloody bodies of Union security guards and lab-coated flunkies who'd paraded as doctors. He despised them all. The fog parted to reveal a massive creature staring back at him. More than six feet tall and almost as wide, blackish green with skin like armor plate coated with barbs. Its arms were unnaturally short, and ended in suckers covered with pointy needles. It might be bald with spikes on its head, but the face. He knew that face. Despised that face.

Balfour. The man who, along with Taka, had turned him into a monster. Clea's former boss at the FBI, an alleged friend, who'd tricked her, deceived her, betrayed her. "Drink some of your own Kool-aid?"

"Tastes good," Balfour said, his grin made up of two rows of short serrated teeth, like a Gila monster's. Once a Gila sank its teeth into you, only cutting its head off would set you free.

"I'm stronger than you now, Larrimer." He held up a hand. "Each one of these babies has poison enough to kill you ten times over, as does this." A thin black tongue crawled from his mouth, the end of which had a blade-like tooth that glistened.

James had been waiting for this a long, long time. "But look at you! More freak than I am, that's for sure."

Those beady brown eyes sparked with humor. "But I can change back to human. More than I can say for you."

Balfour didn't know about the wyvern. He'd keep it that way. Time to dance. He lifted his hands to his shoulders and drew his katanas. Knowing the man well, he did the one thing that would drive him nuts—he laughed.

Balfour screamed and lunged.

"He's mine," he barked to the others. "Get back to Rae! That's an order."

His focus narrowed, his mind ice. Muscle memory directed the machine that was his body. He engaged.

Balfour leapt.

With a swipe of his right-hand katana, he skewered the beast, held him off. His knees bent to where he was almost kneeling, the weight of the creature impossibly heavy. Balfour's barbed chest made contact. If those deadly hands touched him, he was a goner. He pushed his sword higher, so Balfour's venomous hands couldn't reach him.

The tongue swept out, stole the katana from his left hand. Fuck. He wrapped that empty hand round and round the tongue, its tipped blade darting, trying to slice his hand from its wrist.

The wyvern took over his left hand, the pain dampened by adrenaline. Scales appeared, talons extended to shred through the tongue's black flesh.

Balfour screamed.

He shoved Balfour's shoulders upward, his talons parting the fleshy armor like paper.

Balfour pushed, inching himself further down on Larrimer's sword, the serrated teeth closer, his suckered hands extending, reaching for his flesh.

The wyvern demanded to take over, to emerge.

No!

One chance, but he could do this. End Balfour.

Come back to me, James.

Clea or his imaginings?

That minute distraction allowed Balfour's hand to swipe centimeters away from his face.

His muscles bunched, his abs and shoulders crunching tight. Impossibly hard, but... He curled upward, and two-handed, he flung the blade with Balfour on it in a mighty arc.

The beast soared into the air to crash into a far wall, cinderblock and dust raining down on top of it. It roared.

An answering shriek shook the building, so like the wyvern's cry it stopped him cold. Fuck. Had The Union gotten another wyvern?

His wyvern responded with its own roar, an answering battle cry that only he heard.

Not happening today, fella.

A hand, an arm, a face emerged from the pile of cinderblock. "We're not done!" Balfour bellowed.

"Raincheck, Balfour!" He turned and ran.

A massive thud above him. The building trembled.

Christ, what would the denizens of L.A. say about that?

When James plunged through the hole into the glassed room, he stood alone. No Rae.

Blood trickled from hundreds of flesh wounds. Body one big fucking ache, katanas gone, he drew his knives and squared his shoulders, preparing for Balfour's assault. His wyvern had gone deadly quiet, most likely pissed that James wouldn't let him engage with another of his kind.

From down the hall, the thud of Balfour footfalls drew closer.

"What y'all doin' standin' around like a slacker?"

He closed his eyes, shook his head. "Waiting for you, Rae."

Balfour launched himself into the room.

Rae's hand thudded onto his shoulder.

"Later, Balfour."

They disapparated.

THE FEELING of knives scoring Alex's flesh increased. He put on a burst of speed as if the demons of hell were after him. He supposed they were.

Frustration churned inside him. He wished Ziz could fly Lu to the river. He wished he had more time. He wished... He howled. He wasn't done with life, dammit, he and Lu weren't done! Sun dappled the waters, a few hundred yards away. Spittle spewed from his muzzle as he raced, hungry for the river, for safety. His wolf couldn't swim, so he'd change mid-air. Simple.

He tried to erase the image of that four-legged spectral creature and failed. Had Tatianne created it? Not created, not exactly. It had once been a wolf shifter, a brother lost in the magic realm and transformed by the witch. He knew, had felt the spark of oneness between himself and that chained thing. His heart ached with the knowledge.

Icy heat licked his rear paw. Damn, not paying attention would end him. He could turn, rip into the thing that was once pack, but his Alex brain said "no." So he ran on.

Tatianne's creatures were too close. He'd been flanking Ziz. Now he dropped back. Protect the mate.

He slowed—enough so the dust cast by Ziz's leonine hind paws near choked him.

Icy heat rose up his right rear leg to his flank. Better him. Better him.

The earth rumbled, tilted. He kept his footing, though his right leg had gone fully numb. Hell, he could run on three legs. Defiant, his jaws snapped the air.

An arrow flew above his head. Lulu's. A glance back. The arrow plowed harmlessly through the clawed creature a few feet behind him. Man, he was proud of Lu's game.

"Get them!" screeched Tatianne. Too close.

Fuck her. He barked a laugh, as if his useless leg didn't spell disaster.

The waters roared back at the witch.

Sentient?

Anything was possible in this fucked-up land. But the cool water's fresh scent spurred a last effort.

In front of him, Ziz's haunches bunched. She leapt.

Lulu turned. "Jump, Alex!"

But he couldn't. So he ran.

The numbness crept up his back and across his rump to his other leg, his hindquarters failing. He tilted forward, his weight on his forequarters, and continued, dragging his hindquarters like a corpse.

"Alex!"

Vision blurred. But he was close.

Ziz landed in a cascade of water and vanished.

Safe.

His heart stumbled.

Why hadn't the creatures gotten him?

Water. Above him? Higher and higher. Coming toward him. Massive.

Shrieks and howls that snapped out of existence.

ALEX'S BRAVERY AWED LULU. He'd risked everything for them, and now he was going to die. She dived from Ziz's back into the roiling waters. She'd seen him land in the river, watched him sink beneath the writhing waves. Water frothed around her, tossing her like a beach ball as she groped, hunted, reached.

Fur brushed her questing fingers, and she gripped tight and kicked with her legs, lungs burning, pulled the thing toward her. Alex.

Her arms wrapped around his wolf torso and she hugged him tight. She kicked for the surface, kicked and kicked. Where was the surface?

They twisted, turned, and she clung to Alex as they were tossed in a tornado of water, blinding her eyes, choking her mouth. She heaved and kicked, blackness edging her consciousness.

Something thrust at her, spun her, and she rose higher and higher, dizzyingly fast. They burst through the surface. She gasped. Except they kept going, the force propelling them skyward until she was looking down at the river. She wrapped her legs around Alex's hindquarters, tightened her arms on his torso, and buried her scream in his fur. A push catapulted them through the air.

Their landing shook her brains, jarred her bones, pain blasting through her. Sand and grit crunched in her mouth. She spat, wiped her face, and stared at the wolf sprawled next to her. *Who wasn't breathing!*

Hands pressing his chest, she breathed into his muzzle over and over. Was this working? *Alex!*

The wolf choked, coughed. Water spewed into her face. He shivered. But he breathed.

The wolf blinked.

"Alex?" she said.

The barest twitch of a nod.

"Can you change?"

He closed his eyes, which was either "no" or "I'm too tired to answer."

Two purple legs appeared. "*Otlichno.* He lives."

"I could've used some help. What the heck have you been doing?"

Ziz crouched on her haunches. "Making sure we are safe here."

Lulu's snort wasn't pretty. "We weren't very safe at all! Alex and I were drowning. But then the river, um, the river pushed us out. Like, flung us to the bank. We would've died if it hadn't."

"If *she* hadn't." She tapped a long, painted nail against her teeth.

"Ah! Perfect. Now I know where we are. She does that, when she likes people."

"She?"

"Lethe."

"The mythical river of forgetfulness?"

Ziz shook her head, bob haircut twirling. "Mortals have such interesting myths. It's a long, boring story."

"Boring? I don't think so. I bet it's sick."

"Sick? No, Lethe isn't sick."

"Oh, never mind. She got us out of there. Did you see how she saved Alex by curling that wave over him? We should do some kind of offering of thanks. Something meaningful."

"A wise idea, princess."

"Not you, too! Never mind. I don't have much with me, but..." She pulled the knife strapped to her thigh.

Ziz stiffened. "No blood!"

"This isn't for blood." She measured to where her long braid met her shoulders and raised her knife. Its sharp blade sliced effortlessly through her hair. That hurt. But it would grow back. She raised two feet of braid, keeping the loose end pinched. The wet leather felt slimy when she reached into her pocket for a scrunchie, and she wrapped it around the silver braid's raw end. "I hope she'll like this."

When she stood, she gasped. She grew aware of more than Alex and Ziz and the river. No longer did the dark forest and rocky terrain surround them. Her feet sank into sandy soil. The terrain was dotted by rocks and aloe and trees much like weeping willows, except the rocks resembled crystals and the bark on the willows was rusty red, the leaves neon-green.

"Watch Alex, please," she said.

Ziz nodded.

She skittered down the sandy bank to stand by Lethe. She was about to talk to a river. Why not?

"Thank you, Lethe, for saving Alex from those monsters, and for saving both of us from drowning. I give you a part of myself to acknowledge and thank you for your great gift to us. My tribute is heartfelt."

She tossed her braid into the burbling waters.

A funnel-shaped spout rose from the middle of the river, a vortex of water that spun with blinding speed, shooting rainbows across the waters like a crystal in the sun. Lulu squinted. Within the funnel, a woman appeared, small and curvy, with red lips and laughing blue eyes, dressed in a blue gown made of river waters and long cerulean hair to her hips that rose and fanned out beside her luminous face. So beautiful.

"Lethe."

Laughing, Lethe scooped Lulu's braid from the waters and smiled. Lulu's heart danced. Lethe's palms pressed together and she nodded. In response, Lulu pressed hers together, and bowed low. By the time she straightened, Lethe was calm, rippling lazily downstream.

Had that just happened?

Laughter drew her up the bank. Ziz, all smiles. "You are one blessed woman."

She surveyed the soggy mess she was, chewed on how she'd screwed up bringing them to the magic realm, how things had only worsened once here. Her eyes turned to Alex, who was breathing easily, thank the gods, but whose blackened hindquarters scared the bejesus out of her.

When Alex awoke, he smelled bacon. Had to be dreaming. Except...

He went to speak, realized he was in wolf form, and knew he didn't have the strength to change. His nose and belly demanded he follow that smell, but when he tried to rise, his back legs didn't answer the call. Man, that sucked.

Then again, he was alive, and by the looks of it, so were Lulu and Ziz, both munching happily on strips of deliciousness he badly wanted. It made him happy that Lulu loved bacon. Clea was a vegetarian, which made no sense at all.

His yip got their attention.

Lulu placed her plate on a nearby rock, and stalked toward him, on hands and knees, four-legged, as if she were a wolf. He chuffed a laugh.

Her eyes burned bright, and she reached for him, her full-body hug so fine. She buried her nose in his fur, the feel of her warm breath against him, bliss.

Oh, but she smelled good, too. But then that bacon scent...

She raised her head. "You drooled on me!"

Alex's chirp sounded apologetic, at least to his ears.

She kissed his muzzle. "Hungry?"

He nodded.

"I'm guessing you're not ready to change."

Not ready. Right. If he was stuck in his wolf form forever...

"Here."

She'd placed a giant pile of bacon and a roasted rabbit-thing with six legs on a plate in front of him. He cleaned the plate in seconds, tilted his head with what he was sure was a hopeful look.

"That's it, Alex. Sorry."

He licked her face, which was almost as good.

Time to shift.

An hour later, he still wore his wolf form. He was spent, played out physically and emotionally. His pride refused to let him attempt the change in front of Lulu. She'd fallen asleep soon after she'd fed him, and he'd struggled. Man, had he struggled. But he was too wiped out to gather enough energy to change.

They had so much to accomplish, but he finally acknowledged that his body needed rest. His hindquarters remained numb. As soon as he changed, he'd heal. He hoped. He didn't want to think about the possibility of being unable to change.

Lu slept nearby. The jeans she changed into did great things for her ass. Her leathers hung from a nearby tree. Leathers. Fuck. Since they were in the magic world, would his be shredded? Damn. Did he have his pack? His clothes were in there.

That Ziz. She'd gone off for a while. Now she was quiet. Too quiet. She stood near their campfire's flame, looking eastward, eyes intent. Whatever it was that Ziz wanted, he'd have to wait until tomorrow to find out. He dragged himself over to curl around Lulu. She turned toward him and sighed, dug her fingers into his fur, and slept.

He slept, too.

LULU BLINKED open her eyes at the brush of the sun across her face. Every bone in her body ached. That meant she was alive, when she'd been so sure none of them would see another sunrise.

She searched for Ziz, but she was nowhere to be seen. The glimmering light reminded her of California and home. Had Larrimer found Clea? Had she recovered from her fall into the chest? She missed Clea, the kindness and the snark, and the abundant love, something her self-absorbed mother hoarded like a dragon's treasure. Her eyes widened. Where was that ache when she thought of Maurelle? She couldn't remember a time when she hadn't felt the heart pain of her mother's abandonment or the hope of her mother's love. The pain was gone. Like a splinter pulled from a wound, and the relief made her dizzy. For the first time since childhood, her heart felt whole.

Lulu almost laughed aloud, except Alex was snoring peacefully beside her. Sleep would heal him.

Alex's fur and body heat warmed her when she cuddled closer. He'd almost died. She couldn't fathom it. Yet she'd pictured it when he'd raced toward the river, when his legs gave out, when he wasn't breathing. Her fear revealed a truth she'd fought and fought. She loved him. It sang through her bones and blood and heart. Not just now or yesterday, but for many, many yesterdays.

Those surfing lessons, him balancing on the board with such innate grace, his mad smile, hair flying behind him, laughing as a monster wave barreled toward them. The times he'd driven her to dance lessons and stayed to watch. When he'd calmly assumed a helping hand with math, which had Clea frazzled. Or cared enough to piss her off when he'd forbid her to do some crazy teenaged thing.

When had her teenaged crush bloomed into a woman's love? It didn't matter. She saw him. All of him. Her love filled her up.

She needed to speak those words, to get them out into the world. After all, tomorrow the monsters might get them.

Alex stretched, sniffed her. The charred black of his rear legs remained. She bent close. "Alex?"

A long, pink tongue slithered out to lick her ear.

"Stop! Tickles!"

His wolfie cough/laugh warmed her from the inside out. "Time to get up. Time to change."

He ducked his head, looked away.

"Try? For me?"

He bellowed out a breath and nodded. But when he tried to stand, his hindquarters remained limp and unresponsive. Instead, he rose on his forelegs. He towered two heads over her as if he were intentionally sitting. A flash of fear in those gold eyes, instantly masked with his usual bravado and assurance that he was alpha of the pack.

Maybe... Yeah, her idea might just work.

She pressed into his chest, arms surrounding him, and used Voice. "Change."

She released him, and thin tendrils of smoke appeared.

"Change," she demanded.

The smoke swirled, higher, brighter, a golden vortex that echoed his eyes.

Let him be healed.

Flecks of magic merged until he sat before her, Indian style, clothed in his ripped leathers.

She couldn't stop staring at him, while her heart thumped in her chest. The leanness of his build only enhanced his fine musculature. The river's breeze stirred, and she scraped an annoying lock of shortened hair from her face. He sat casually, head erect, broad shoulders back, yet his eyes were weary.

He gave her a tired smile. "For my next party trick..."

She knew what he was thinking, fearing. His muscled thighs and long legs looked no different. But would they work? Could he stand?

Normally, he'd just unfold to a standing position. But today he braced his hands on the sandy earth.

"Wait!" she said.

He cocked his head. "No time like the present."

"I... I love you, Alex."

He tilted his head in a wolfie way, his eyes narrowed.

She flushed. "I just wanted... I needed you to know."

His jaw bunched just before his arms swept around her. He dragged her forward, smashed his lips to hers, his whole body vibrating.

His tongue darted between her lips, hot and moist, hands threading her hair with urgency.

"What happened to your hair?" he said.

"Later. Much later." She pressed herself to him, as tight as she could get, and it wasn't enough, not nearly. Her hands moved, frantic, wanting, needing. His heat burned her, everywhere. He stretched out, pressed her body along his, his erection fitting her cleft, making her pulse with need. She clenched and unclenched her hands, aching for his skin on hers, his lips on her breasts, his mouth delving deeper and lower. She groaned, eyes tearing. This was what she'd been waiting for, needing forever. Him. Every particle and molecule and atom.

He sucked her neck, and oh, gods. Her head fell back, her hands roving to his chest and burrowing beneath his clothes.

"Princess," he groaned. "Ah, don't kill me for calling you that. It's been a long time. Let's take it slow."

"I don't know slow," she said between breaths. "I don't know how."

"We'll do the best we can, then. Yes?"

"Maybe."

"Mine. You are all *mine*, Lu."

She kissed his chin, his cheek, his neck.

He bit her ear, then suckled. "Are you a virgin?"

"Ronan, remember?" she said. "A long time ago. Years, eons, lifetimes."

"Ah, sweet Lu, I'm sorry about the time thing."

The hands she threaded through his long, silky hair tightened. "I'm not. Or you'd be arrested for child something or other."

He froze.

She'd never seen that expression on his face, one of abject terror. Her laugh blossomed. "I'm twenty-four. Or twenty-six. I've lost count. Perhaps the time-stream thing is a backhanded gift from my mother."

If possible, his muscles tightened further. "I'll be sure to thank her before I kill her." He raised her shirt, and his head slid down until his lips captured the tip of her breast. He sucked it into his mouth, teased her nipple with his tongue, nipped. Gods, how she needed. Him. Something. Everything.

She rubbed her hands across his chest, lower still to his abdomen until she was able to rub her palm up and down his cock. She squeezed.

SHE WAS GOING to kill him. Alex was sure of it. His breath caught, and he bit her nipple. Her hands scrabbled with the button on his pants. His body burst with energy, with life. Lulu was his, and he had to finish this, complete them.

Slow it, asshole. He tamped down the feral desire. His Lulu deserved more than some frantic screw. He spread her before him. She was like a banquet he could barely wait to eat. Hell, yeah. "You are beautiful. Like some fairy sprite, you glow."

There was that lovely blush. He undid her shirt, and with each button, he kissed her bared flesh. Her collar bone, between her sweet breasts, her navel. He again took her breast in his mouth and suckled. She'd started to pant, and he nipped the sweet bud, laved it with his tongue, and moved to the other breast. She was perfection, made exactly for him to love her. He battled for control so he didn't go all animal on her and take, when all he wanted to do was give.

Between hitched breaths, she said, "You, too. Shirt off."

Obeying her command, he tore it off, tossed it, and her splayed hands on his chest nearly undid him. She pet his pectorals, his rib cage, and ran her hands up and down his arms. He failed to stifle his groan. He'd been touched by many women, in friendship and as lovers. None felt like Lulu. He was about to lose it.

He unzipped her pants, pulled them down, taking her panties with them. She had a mole on her right hipbone, and he bent and kissed it, swirled his tongue.

The scent of her wove through him, that cashmere and honey-suckle and musk mingled into the finest aphrodisiac. Had to taste her now... He spread those beautiful nether lips with their soft tuft of silver hair and laved her clit.

She jerked, moaned. "Oh, Alex, please come inside me. Please."

LULU WAS A MINDLESS, maddened thing. Alex touching her was different, *he* was different, and she needed him to fill her so very much. No earlier encounters had prepared her for this cauldron of flesh and emotion, a brew so heady she expected to die any minute if he didn't come inside her. "Please, Alex."

He shucked off his pants, and she couldn't breathe. He was magnificent, long and lean, thick with defined muscle and a ribbon of hair arrowing from chest to groin and... He dropped to his knees, and she curled up and wrapped her hands around his penis, thick and long with desire, velvet and steel, with a bead of moisture so tantalizing she had to lick it. All for her. Her tongue darted out to taste.

"No, princess, no, or I'll be a goner."

He pressed her back down, covered her with his beautiful

weight. This was all so strange. It had been so many years. What if she was a flop? What if she didn't please him? What if...

"Lu," he said, staring at her as if she were the sun and moon and stars. "You are perfect. We'll go slow, eh?"

"It's... It's been such a long time for me."

He brushed a hand over her hair. "You're not the only one. Think of this as the first time for both of us. Okay?"

How had he known that was the perfect thing to say? She smiled, and the smile he returned... The beauty of it burned right through her. "Okay."

His kiss was soft and gentle and filled with indescribable care. He wrapped her legs around his hips. The feel of him at her entrance brought shivers. He flexed slowly and entered inch by inch. She felt as if she were dying and being reborn.

ALEX WAS ALMOST unmanned by her uncertainty. Lulu was so much more than he'd ever imagined. And *she'd* been worried? He'd have to show her, prove to her that she was the most wonderful creature in existence. Slowly easing into her flesh, her liquid desire encased him, gloved him so tight he strained to hold it together. The hot sun beat across his back and flanks, and he figured he'd combust any minute. Finally being deep inside his beautiful Lulu felt so damned fine. Her hips flexed, and he was cooked, so cooked.

He couldn't stop looking at her, watching the pleasure flash across her face, her eyes limpid, her lips red from their kisses.

When he moved, she met him, thrust for thrust, her hands clawing his back, and he took her mouth, ravished it, his tongue dancing with hers. She went nuts, her face passion-flushed, her skin slick, her hand furrowing through his hair.

One-handed he cupped her head, kissed her fiercely, while he worked his other hand lower, nearer her nest of curls. There. He dipped a finger across that slick, delicious bundle of nerves, back and forth as he pumped his cock in and out of his beautiful Lu. She tremored. She was so close. He had to bring her *there*. He pinched her clit.

She exploded, her back arching, an exquisite note pouring from her mouth, tears cascading from her eyes.

Father Fenrir. He came, pouring himself inside his mate.

She squeezed him, milked him, and he'd never felt anything like this, better than the best wave, the best hunt, he pulsed and pulsed inside her.

He collapsed to float weightless for long moments before he found the world again. He'd been rocketed to some universe that shattered any conceptions of pleasure he'd ever held. Epic. Monumental. *Fuck*, he didn't know, didn't care.

When he looked into the face of his beloved, she was frowning, her eyes wide.

"Lu, are you okay?" he said.

"Oh, Alex." She cupped his cheek. "I love you. I've never... That was..."

"Beautiful? Incredible? Amazing?"

"So much more." She smiled, and bit his shoulder.

"Ow! So you're trying to get me going again, eh?"

She laughed, chimes ringing. "Maybe."

A shadow, someone approaching. He hadn't heard, hadn't smelled.

He twisted and sprang to face the intruder, a growl ripping from his throat.

18

Z iz, all six-foot-eight of her loomed over them, a shit-eating grin on her face. "Why wasn't I invited to the party, hmm?"

Alex snarled as he tugged on his pants.

"Because it's a party for *two*," Lulu said, smiling sweetly. She flowed to her feet, slipped into her jeans and pulled on her shirt.

"*Two?*" Ziz's long canines sparkled in the sun. "Where's the fun in that, eh?"

A blush raced across Lulu's face. She was irresistible. He dipped his fingers beneath the back of her jeans.

"Alex!"

"Feels good," he said.

"Time to get back to business, *da*?" Ziz said. "And our adventure."

An "adventure" was it? He'd bet a deadly one. The pressure to find Melike rode him hard. He'd never felt so far from home. A glance at Lu. Except wherever she was, that *was* home.

Lulu slid her hand into his, nuzzled his ear, and whispered, "You're standing, Alex."

He *was*, though his legs felt funny, chigger-bites funny, especially the left one. Weakened. Not good. But he was upright. Progress.

Ziz walked closer to the river's sandy bank. She folded onto her haunches, picked up a stick, and began to draw. "You two will assist me on a rescue operation."

That seemed to be the *mode de jour* of late. "We're on our own rescue mission."

Nonetheless, he and Lulu walked down to join Ziz beside the riverbank. A melody played in his head. From the *river*. As if *she* were singing him a song. A pretty song. Soothing. But what the hell was it doing in his head?

Man, he really liked the mundane world better, where he knew what was what. He'd have to get used to the crazy, given the worlds were retwining. But it wasn't going to be easy.

Ziz's smile was that of a predator who perched atop the food chain. "Mine first. Life or death stuff."

Lulu raised her face to his, eyes solemn. "Melike can't be happy, but she's alive. I'm certain the fae won't kill her."

In his mind, he pictured the striking soldier, with her midnight hair, fiery nature, and will of iron. She could withstand a lot, but even the strongest break. The urge to go to her near overwhelmed him. In this magic world, her thread of life was absent, as were all the pack's threads. The aloneness ate at him like a canker.

Ziz stared at the two of them. He knew stares like that, had one himself when his will was immutable. He could fight, except he wasn't a dumbass. One on one, he stood little chance against Ziz.

Lulu made this whole mess better, but, *damn.*

He dug deep into his alpha nature, the bedrock of who he was. If the magic world killed him before he could rescue his packmate... There was always a choice. Except when there wasn't.

Forgive me, Melike. "What do you need us to do?"

THEY RAN FOR HOURS, making their swift bath in the river moot. Lulu was swift and sure, that floating gait of hers easily traversing the sandy soil. Ziz was in "human" form, since she couldn't carry both of them.

He'd stumbled a time or two, his legs weakened, his balance off. He could change to wolf, but he wasn't sure his hind legs would function. He'd never been a coward before, but this... Confident he could still manage a half-form, he dug his heels in and raced.

The further they got from Lethe, the more the soil hardened. The vegetation changed, too, the river's sparse grasses giving way to a dotting of tall purple fronds topped with starburst flowers that waved in the breeze. Scents of mint, spicy dianthus, and thick verdant magic tickled his nose.

They crested a rise, the sun high above their heads. Stretched out before them lay a broad plain blanketed with those purple fronds they'd seen earlier. The plain rose to another, taller hill, upon which nestled a massive stone structure that surveyed the land below. The series of connected buildings reminded him of Al-Khazneh in Petra, Jordan. Imposing and old. Very, very old. The pink face of the building glittered in the sun, as if embedded with crystals. Purple and yellow and green swirls covered the facade and wound around pillars that widened at their bases. He was too far away to tell if the rocks were composed of those colors or if they were painted on.

The three of them skittered down to the plain, his body a bit more in tune, more...put together. He scraped a hand through his hair, greasy with sweat. A shower right about now would be great.

They paused, facing a wall of those purple plants growing a good nine-feet tall. They swayed. Except the air was still. No breeze, no wind, no nothing.

The silence reached him. No birds chirped. No animals skittered. No scents of anything alive, except for the three of them. Deeply disturbing.

Lulu kept blinking, as if clearing her eyes to see what she couldn't quite believe. Ziz stood in a relaxed pose, hands on hips, eyes narrowed.

"Are they sentient?" he asked Ziz.

She shook her head. "Worse. They're directed by Khosrow."

He waited.

"He is on the Council," Ziz said, her anger palpable.

"A guardian?" Lulu said.

"*Nyet*. He works for the Council. Like, um, in your world, a high-level manager."

Lulu reached out to touch a purple frond.

Ziz gripped her wrist. "Not yet! Touch the frond or flower, and he'll know we're here."

Alex surveyed the sea of plants. "Impossible not to touch them if they're between us and your *whatever*."

"*Da!*" said Ziz. "That's the point. It's all in the timing. We seek Anouk."

"Anouk!" Lulu said. "But she was with Sophy, and—"

"She was betrayed." Ziz spit into the dirt. "By Khosrow."

Shock rippled through him. Anouk was the most powerful shifter he knew, a Guardian and an Ancient. He *answered* to Anouk, and only to her. Annoying she might be. Cryptic as hell. But also a friend who'd saved his ass more than once.

Ziz tapped a nail on her teeth and grimaced. "Which is why I didn't tell you before this. You're all in a twist."

"Yeah, I'm in a twist," he said. "Is she in that castle built into the hill?"

Ziz took a deep breath and expelled it. "*Nyet*. Khosrow is away, so it would be far easier to rescue her if she were in that structure. He *buried* her, my *rebenok,* my child, in the earth. And he had help. Wherever she is, her tomb is warded so she can't disapparate out."

Anouk was Ziz's *child*? Wrapping that one around his head sure wasn't easy. What this Khosrow had done to her was horrific. Anouk might be a shifter, but she was primarily of the air, an immense golden eagle. So the bastard had buried her, beneath earth and rock. Was she conscious? In agony? Could Anouk breathe?

"Is she still alive?" Alex said.

Ziz nodded, her cinnamon eyes turning neon orange. "She is alive. As my cousin Sophy told me our Clea—"

"*Our* Clea?" Lulu practically flamed with fury.

"Yes," Ziz hissed. "She belongs to all of us. Not just you, child."

"Okay, yeah," Lulu said. "She belongs to lots of others, but you don't even *know* her."

"I know *of* her. We don't die easily, but we fade, and Anouk is fading, just as Clea is, though for different reasons."

They'd seen up-close-and-personal what "fading" had done to Clea.

Ziz's arm stretched out to wave across the sea of quivering plants. "She's somewhere here. Buried deep. That's why when Sophy mentioned you, I hatched an idea." Her eyes sparkled with self-satisfaction.

He shouldn't even ask, but... "What do I have—"

She tapped his nose. "This. You will scent her. Sophy once said you had the best nose in and out of the Magic and Mundane realms. *You* are the solution."

"Talk about an ass-backward compliment," Lulu said.

He snorted. "While I'm flattered, you just told us if we touch the plants, we alert the bad guy. The field is acres and acres of these things. I can't scent Anouk from here. I'm not even sure I can scent her if she's buried deep."

He forced his mind away from the image of the elegant shifter entombed beneath tons of earth. She was a fricking Golden eagle. An epic. A legend.

If Rae were with them, he could link his mind to Anouk's. "I know this mage. He might help us." As he explained, Ziz only shook her head.

"No, he can't. He refused. They all did."

As Ziz told him and Lulu about her discussion at pack headquarters, a growl rose from his throat. Clea taken by The Union. Worst thing ever. Larrimer must be going ballistic. In addition to being powerfully magical, did The Union know she was The Key? Talk about a whoopsydangit. *Man.*

"Tell us about this bad guy," Alex said.

"A shifter, like you."

"A wolf."

"No, I meant..." Ziz huffed. "All right. He's a basilisk shifter."

"Gods!" Lulu said.

Alex shook his head. "Seriously. A guy who becomes a basilisk. One look and we die."

"Well, no," Ziz said. "One look, and you'll freeze. Then he eats you. As a senior member of the council hierarchy, he should have been loyal to Anouk. Obviously, the *ublyudok* is not. Someone got to him."

Tatianne? The Union? "Will his gaze freeze even you?"

Ziz's cheeks pinked. "I'm afraid so. There's more."

Lulu rolled her eyes. "Of course there is."

The scowl on Ziz's face didn't seem to bother Lulu one bit. He chuckled.

"If we lose Anouk," Ziz said, eyes on fire, "we don't know who the Chest of Stone will choose as the next Guardian. Disastrous if it's one of that *prostitutka* Tatianne's bootlickers."

Reality slapped him. His nose was good as a human, but as a wolf, he caught a bazillion more scents. Man, he didn't want to shift. Did *not*. But without shifting... He'd never find Anouk in his human form. Yeah, he was fucked.

"Stay here." He kissed Lulu hard and fast. In a blink, he shifted, stumbled, his sickly hindquarters threatening to fold. But they held. For now. He found his footing and darted into the field of fronds.

LULU HAD PLASTERED a beatific smile on her face when he'd told her to stay. Stay? Fat chance. He'd need backup, and she and Ziz would provide it.

His orders had been so knee-jerk. Larrimer used to be like that, too. Clea had told her stories. She got it. When you love somebody, you try to protect them. And she did love him so ridiculously much. Clea said love was about compromise and growth. And she most definitely loved her single-minded, paternalistic, pain-in-the-ass protective alpha wolf.

But he was also caring and considerate, concerned about her well being. He wasn't rigid, but a guy with a strong moral compass who never flinched when things went south. He'd take the hard road, if that's what was called for, and he was funny. He could be so damned funny.

He was *her* wolf. Just like she was his fae-mage.

They'd work it out, and the "working" could be fun, too.

Time to ignore his order.

The two steps she took forward were hesitant. She froze. Not *that*, not *now*. She stared at the sea of tall waving fronds, reminded of the time she and her dad had walked through a similar sea, a cornfield, filled with slithery, snakey things. Sweat beaded her temples and upper lip.

She swiped it away, so angry at herself. This was absurd. She'd done worse. Dived into a roaring river for Alex, for gods' sake. But snakes? They'd always terrified her. A mega field like this? Oh, my. When she'd watched *Anaconda*, she'd had to peek through the fingers she'd held over her eyes. Watching it swallow Jon Voigt... She pictured being gulped down slowly into the dark, slimy, undulating...

"Are you coming?" Ziz waved for her to follow.

She stepped back. *Gods.* She had her song, after all, and her bow and arrows and her godsdammed sword. She drew it from its scabbard. Like Clea, she was a woman of action. Pretty much, anyway. "Absolutely I'm coming."

Ziz snorted a laugh. "If you say so, *malyshka*."

"I'm no one's little girl. And, yes, I understand some Russian. Let's go."

Her footstep was firm when she stepped into the sea of plants and took lead.

The plants bent to touch her, the tiny hairs on their leaves moving across her flesh as if eager to taste. The sensation gave her goosebumps. Despite her size, Ziz walked on silent feet behind her as they followed Alex's path through the field.

Each of her senses was on alert, and she breathed in the wrongness of the place, the smell like rotted geraniums, the hush, only broken by the slight rustle Alex made as he dove through the field. Leaves brushed her legs up to her waist, making her tingle through her thick leathers.

Half of her mind continued to worry about Alex and what she'd seen when he'd changed to his wolf. He'd stumbled. Not badly, but enough so that it was obvious his back legs hadn't fully recovered.

He wasn't moving as fast as usual, either. Up ahead, the tips of some fronds would dip. Alex. He still outpaced them enough that she couldn't see him.

Her bare skin—her throat, hands, and face—began to itch. She forced herself not to scratch. Soon, teeny blisters formed where the plants had touched her. When the blisters broke, the plants swayed closer and brushed their flowers across her aqueous skin. Licking her like they were eating her up.

She picked up the pace, weaving this way and that, following the wolf where he'd bent the stalks through what became a maze. The deeper they ran inside the field and the more the plants touched her skin, the weaker she felt. Her legs began to tremble with exhaustion.

A whooshing sound, like a sifting of straw. A hiss.

No, no, no.

If she kept her eyes open and the basilisk found her... But close her eyes, and she couldn't follow Alex.

She froze.

A shove from behind. "Move!" Ziz said. "If you falter, you die."

She forced her legs into a run.

That crunching sound, and the sibilant hissing grew louder.

Stop. They had to stop. If they were to confront the basilisk, it should be on their terms, not on his. She held up a hand and Ziz skidded to a halt.

"I have an idea," she said, a part of her praying Alex was okay, that this would give him time to find Anouk and free her.

"*Run*, you foolish girl."

"No. The basilisk will eventually find us. We have to take a stand

and buy Alex time." She dumped her pack, then rifled around inside to pull out the small mirror she carried. "This will help us."

Ziz wrapped an arm around Lulu's waist and hauled her to her feet, Lulu clutching the mirror and bag. Ziz began to run.

"Dammit, stop." Lulu bobbed like a piece of limp spaghetti. Ziz *would* listen. Lulu punched her in the boob.

"Ow!"

She plummeted unceremoniously to the ground, landing with an *Ooof!* Scrambling to her feet, the plant things were all over her. Screw them. "Stop, I tell you. Or go on without me."

"You are being ridiculous." Ziz waved a hand at the mirror Lulu gripped tight. "What's that little thing going to do?"

"Don't you know the story of Perseus and Medusa?"

"Of course I..." Her eyes widened. "His shield."

"Yes. You hold the mirror so you can see where the basilisk is. It doesn't attack first, you said, but freezes us, right?"

"One of us. It can't freeze both of us at the same time."

"Even better."

"Well then what? One of us gets eaten?"

"No! Of course not, I'll—"

A hiss.

The creature had found them.

Lulu tossed Ziz the mirror, squeezed her eyes tight, and began to sing.

A rustling. A breath on her shoulder. *Godsgodsgods.*

Her sword. She continued to sing the Song of Sleep as her fingers found the hilt. She drew it from its scabbard, twisted her wrists, and held it in front of her in a two-handed grip.

Polished to a high shine that never dimmed because of fae magic, she stared into the sword's blade. Oh, boy, with its head raised to strike, the thing was maybe six stories high. Head of a monstrous snake, with feathered horns gracing the crown, eyes like whirring pinwheels, it was thick necked and legless. Gray scales covered it except for the virulent yellow ones that ran from its throat down its chest.

The basilisk moved, but as if in slo-mo, swaying back and forth, its jaws widening. A pearl of venom formed on its fangs to drop slowly to earth.

Though her song hadn't put it to sleep, it at least slowed the thing down.

When she tilted the blade, she found Ziz's legs, then her clawed hand digging into the side of the creature's head just below one eye, beads of black blood bubbling around it. Ziz wasn't moving. The creature had managed to capture her gaze and freeze her.

Lulu trembled, which affected her song. The basilisk blinked.

She steadied herself, wrestled her song under control.

Her throat felt raw and tight. *Keep singing.*

Now what?

The blade gave her a good sense of where the immense creature was, still behind her, still weaving, Ziz still frozen, still hanging from it by her claws. The creature was again moving in slo-mo, then its head started to bob, as if it were trying to loosen Ziz and flip her into its jaws. So far, Ziz's talons remained embedded in the basilisk's head, all that prevented her from being devoured.

Lulu scooched a little farther away. She dropped one hand from the sword's hilt and used it to loosen her quiver. She let it fall to the ground, then she unfastened her bow and strung it.

If she didn't hurry up, the basilisk would loosen Ziz. Even slowed down, the creature would nonetheless consume her.

Lulu was a good archer. The best. But could she shoot the basilisk with her eyes closed and kill it, while at the same time not harming Ziz?

If only she could be certain.

Maybe if she used her sword. But she was so much better with her bow.

She fell to her knees, took her bow in hand, the quiver beside her knee. Something liquid touched her neck. *Fire. Pain.* Acid carved a path down her back as if someone had taken a knife and gouged our her spine.

Sing. Sing. She could *not* stop singing.

Still on her knees, she flipped around, eyes closed, arrow nocked, and let it fly. A ululating scream. The plants to her right moved. She'd swear the thing's breath touched her cheek. She loosed more arrows until she had one left. Should she look?

No. She waited. A hot puff of air to her left. Her arrow flew.

The earth shook.

Quiver empty, she flipped around again and raised her sword to see what she'd accomplished.

Her arrows peppered the monster, blood running like flows of black lava down its head and neck. But its pinwheel eyes were open, its jaws wide. She'd failed.

The pain of the fire on her back roared into her mind. Her eyes teared, and she squeezed the hilt tighter in a vain effort to fight the agony.

"Foolissshh fae," came a sibilant voice from that yawning mouth. "Your song tires me. You will be my appetizer, while the Ziz promises to be a fine main course. You burn, do you not?"

The fire consumed her thoughts. A plop onto her head. A burning brand.

She screamed.

The basilisk's head reared back to strike in the mirror of her sword.

She rolled away. Not going to be easy prey. But her song was finished.

A screech. A howl.

A scream.

Her fingers scrabbled for the hilt of the sword she'd dropped. She dragged it to her and looked.

A massive eagle had dug its talons into the crown of the basilisk's head, jackhammering its beak into the creature's skull, while a white wolf clawed its way up the monster's side, its teeth ripping and rending scales and flesh as it tore at the creature.

Unable to get purchase on its attackers, the basilisk whipped its head back and forth in a frantic bid to get its assailants off. Its venom flew, charring clumps of the white wolf's fur, but failing to reach the eagle, its screams shrieking through the air.

Ziz's clawed hold broke, and her limp body dropped to the ground.

Holding tight to the hilt of her sword, Lulu bent her knees and leapt, impaling her blade deep into the fleshy part of the basilisk's lower jaw.

The monster reared its head, let out a deafening screech, and slumped to the earth. Dead. They'd done it. Alex changed, and with several swift strikes of his blade, he separated the basilisk's head from its torso. Apparently dissatisfied with his carnage, he hacked out one eye and then the other.

Lulu dropped her sword, too exhausted and in too much pain to do anything but fall to her knees. "You did it!" Her words sounded like a frog's croak.

Ziz moved for the first time since the attack. Oh, crap. One of her arrows jutted from Ziz's thigh. She gave Lulu a dirty look, ripped the arrow out, and tossed it aside. Blood streamed from the wound, grew sluggish, then stopped. "Look what you did, Lulu! Now I have to repair my outfit!"

Lulu fell back on her ass, laughing, even as the venomous pain flayed her head and back.

Alex kneeled in front of her and doused the crown of her head with cooling water. "That should help."

"My back."

He turned her and splashed on the soothing liquid.

"So much better," she said.

"I've got some salve."

"Good thing. This kills."

"You did it, you know. You bought me time to free Anouk."

She glanced over at the eagle. "Why is she still pounding its head with her beak? Maybe she wants to kill it again?"

"Looks like." Taking care with her back, he pulled her close. "Thankfully, that won't be necessary."

THE FOUR OF them sat before a campfire. They were a day's hike from a portal Anouk claimed would land them in the realm of the Charleston fae. The slice of grilled antelope he slipped between his lips was delicious. Add some s'mores and, hell, things would be almost perfect. He couldn't keep his eyes off Lulu. She'd recovered well. That pleased him.

"Are you good?" she said, across the lick of flame.

His smile was jaunty. He made sure of it. "Couldn't be better. Maybe one thing." He chuckled. She'd know just what he meant. "Yeah, maybe one thing."

"*Al-ex!*"

"I'm talking about s'mores!" He spread his arms wide.

Those violet eyes twinkled. "I'd like some...s'mores, too."

He choked out a laugh. Except it was getting tougher and tougher to keep up his front of *joie de vivre* in front of Lulu and the others. Having accomplished half their mission—recovering Anouk—they still had to rescue Melike from the fae.

He'd make sure, with or without him, his companions did exactly that. Because he was going to die. True, he hadn't died...yet. Why? They'd been here for a dozen daybreaks and nightfalls. His legs were weakened, both in human and wolf form from the attack by the shadow creatures. When they left the following morning for the portal, he suspected his transition back to the mundane world would end him.

Had it been worth it? Yeah. But everything had a price, right?

Was he ready for the end? Not even a little.

He couldn't tell Lulu. It would break her. No goodbyes, then. No sweet farewells, no making love one more time, just business as usual.

He raised a hand to the fire to feel its warmth.

The guardian of the Chest of Stone turned those sloe eyes onto him, her penetrating gaze cutting into him like steel into flesh. "Thinking about death, Alex Arctos?"

Shit. "Are you, Anouk?"

She narrowed her eyes. "Interesting how all members of Arctos who traveled to this realm have ceased to exist."

Not gonna look at Lulu. "You don't—"

"Is that true, Alex?" Lulu's eyes stabbed into him.

Man, he wanted to lie. "It's true."

Her hands fisted in his shirt. "You never said a word."

"Didn't see any reason to." He shrugged.

Fury sparked her violet eyes, her face etched with disappointment. Her lips wobbled, tears hovering on her lower lashes. *Fuck.* Worse, much worse.

"How could you not tell me?" She shoved away from him and stalked into the trees.

Ziz shot Alex a dirty look and followed Lulu into the woods.

He rose to go after Lu, but paused. No, he wasn't that big a fool. She most definitely needed to calm down. She'd see he'd only kept her in the dark for her sake. He sank to his heels, poked at the fire.

"Thanks for that." Sarcasm ripped through his words as he stared at the guardian. He couldn't believe Anouk had blurted that out. Maybe he'd crunch the guardian's neck between his teeth. That would be most satisfying.

"You two..." She lit a cigarette, taking her time, inhaling deep, the smoke curling from her flared nostrils. "Why not, eh?"

The muscles in his body bunched with his fury, his jaw rigid, a growl snaking from his clenched teeth. "You're a bitch."

Her body shifted to a panther twice the size of his wolf, except for her head and the arm holding her cigarette stayed human. That was just *wrong.* She took a drag. "Remember to whom you are speaking."

"I don't give a shit. You're an asshole, a cruel one."

She chuffed a breath. "The girl and you are involved. She deserved to know."

"You took care of that just fine, didn't you?"

"Death may still come to you."

"I know!"

With a swirl of smoke, she returned to her human form. "But I do not think it will."

His heart thumped. "Why?"

"I suspect you have acclimated."

"Not possible. This is the only time I've been in the magic realm."

She tamped out her cigarette and lit another, taking her time, drawing things out like she always did. She loved the power that knowledge gave her and used it like a talon, to pick and prick and slash. He settled, used to her waiting games, and tossed another branch onto the fire.

She smiled, moonlight glinting off her teeth. "You have improved your patience. A good thing."

Not going to say a word.

"You spent time in the half-magic, half-mundane world of the Charleston fae. And from the tale you recounted about Texas, the Guadalupes are also a commingled space. As I said, you have acclimated."

He rocked back on his heels. She made a strange sort of sense. "I still have to reenter the mundane world."

"That you do. But I believe it will not kill you."

Maybe. Maybe not. But the spiked band around his heart loosened. Was it possible to have a future? One that included Lulu? Hope, that deadliest and most beautiful emotion, made him light headed.

"What may kill you is the girl, who I suspect is so angry with you she wishes to put a stake through your heart."

"Her name is Lulu."

"So it is."

The trees rustled, and Lulu and Ziz approached the campfire. He stood. "Lu, I—"

"I'm going to bed," she said, addressing Ziz and Anouk. "We need to get an early start in the morning."

"Lulu!"

"I need to think, Alex. Leave me be." Her gaze never moved from the other two. "Are you guys coming with us?"

"*Nyet*," Ziz said. "I said I'd help rescue that Clea person, once I found Anouk." She rested a hand on Anouk's shoulder, almost as if she needed to touch her descendent, to confirm she was real and present. "My *vnuchka* is coming with me. She will be needed. How do you say it? Ah, yes. It's been real. We go."

The two poofed away.

Lulu spread out her sleeping bag, shimmied into it, and turned on her side, away from the fire. Away from him.

FROM THE WARMTH of her sleeping bag, she rubbed a hand over her heart. She hurt. Everything hurt. He was expecting to die. And he hadn't told her. Her back was turned away from the fire. She didn't want him to think even a little bit that she would welcome him. Fury and hurt smothered her. She cried silently, grinding her teeth so she wouldn't make a sound. The worst betrayal of all. If she lost him... She stifled a sob.

The way they lived, especially now, they could die at any time. She knew that. She accepted it. But this was different. What, would he just fade away? Fall at her feet? Vanish?

She understood her hurt was driving her, squeezing her heart so tight she thought it would burst. She was angry, too, so damned angry.

He hadn't told her.

Whether he lived or died, how would she ever get beyond this?

19

R eeling, James slapped his palm on a table to steady himself. The table crashed to the floor. "Fuck."

Rae's arm whipped around his waist. "Y'all's not steady. What? That creature do you in?"

"Balfour?" he said. "No. Where's Clea?"

"Y'all's a mess. You get clean and fixed up before you see our girl."

He found his footing and pushed away from Rae. A whole lot of shifter scents filled the room and the smell of...steak? His belly rumbled.

The room was small and tidy, except for the table he'd destroyed. Stone walls, a twin bed, not much else. Rae pointed to a door. "Bathroom."

"On it." Except James wasn't sure about that. A thousand jackhammers were pounding his body. He felt like shit, and he stank. He turned on the taps and stepped into a shower built for midgets.

The water ran red, then pink off his flesh. The cuts he'd sustained were plentiful, but shallow. His nanoteched body should be sealing them closed. It wasn't. The jeans the shifters had supplied were fine, but a white t-shirt?

He needed to see Clea. Instead, he sat down hard on the closed toilet seat.

Rae peered into the room. "That's not good."

Blood leaked from the cuts, turning the shirt crimson. "Any ideas? They should've begun healing."

Rae shook his head. "Those fuckers at The Union got some bad shit goin'."

"That they do." He couldn't see Clea, not like this.

"Lift up the shirt," Rae said.

He pulled it over his head and tossed it. Rae's hand hovered an inch from a cluster of cuts and a swirl of motes hit his skin.

"Feel anything?" Rae said.

"No."

"Not a damn thing's happenin', either."

"I'll live. Find me a black t-shirt and get me to Clea."

SHE LAY on the alpha's bed. James crushed his instinctive jealousy. Alex and she were friends now, and *only* friends. Clea was a small woman, and the huge bed swallowed her. Her skin was translucent, fragile-looking, as if the life were leaching out of her. Back in that room at Union HQ, he hadn't gotten a good look at her. Now... Veins mapped her body, her lips were cracked, her hands restless.

He balled his hands so he wouldn't scream.

Too many eyes on them. Erick and Rae, Sophie and Neddy, all staring at him as if they expected him to say "Shazam" and she'd rise up out of the bed as if none of this had ever happened.

It had happened.

Her soul was still trapped in that damned chest.

So why was he stalling? Why didn't he reunite her with the chest, get it over and done? A fist burrowed into his solar plexus.

James was drop-dead scared. That it wouldn't work. That she'd never wake up. That he'd never again see the fire light her eyes.

Fuck it. He scooped her into his arms and walked to the hidden door. Pressing his hand to the wall latch, it instantly opened. The Key was in his arms, after all.

He stepped inside, elbowed the door shut before anyone could worm their way in with them. Alone. Just him and her. Like it should be. He ran his finger down that damned scar of his.

Facing Balfour had been nothing compared to this.

The room smelled of incense. Twice before, he'd heard the music, with Clea and when he'd brought the chest. Today the silence felt like a shroud, his breathing loud in the closet-sized room.

He smoothed a hand over her hair, her arm, her face. He couldn't stop touching her. What would she be like when she awakened? Would she smile at him? Would her eyes warm? Would she slide her arms around his waist and hold him, maybe stand on tiptoe like she did and kiss his ear? No. She'd attack his mouth, his cheeks, his chest, as if she'd been drowning for one taste of him. Like he was for her.

Or would she be awake, but not really there? Eyes open, but gone. Mindless from her weeks spent...somewhere. Would she be empty? Or full? Would she babble away, like she sometimes did, full of passion and enthusiasm? Or would she remain silent, unable to form coherent thoughts or words?

James rubbed the back of his neck. Stalling wasn't like him. His was a world of action, where he did what needed to be done. He'd plan and act. No second thoughts.

The stone floor he laid her on was cold. He should have brought something to warm her. She was still as death, except for her restless hands and her eyes behind those closed lids. Some of his blood had smeared on to her white tunic and loose pants. He finally turned to the chest. It sat on its plinth, an unassuming sweetgrass basket. Someone, maybe Rae, had said the chests were semi sentient. Would it know she was only physically present and not transform? Or would the chest try to help?

He lifted the thing, then sat cross legged on the floor.

If this failed...

James threaded his fingers through her limp ones, kissed the back of her hand. "Come back to me, baby."

Clea lolled like a rag doll when he braced her against him, her back abnormally cool against his torso. He lay the basket in her lap. Then he took her left hand in his left one, then her right. He pressed the open palms of her hands to the sides of the basket.

Nothing changed.

A shudder quaked through him.

If he pressed their hands harder against the basket, crushed it beneath their fingers, squeezed it to dust, would she be freed?

He wanted his Clea, not her magic, not her worlds-altering purpose, just her.

Seconds stretched. He forced each muscle in his body to relax, then centered his mind and dug deep. Ignoring the silent wyvern, he traveled to where their song lay quiescent, as it had since she'd gone away. He reached for his song, their song, deep in that magical place that both baffled and awed him. He tried to coax it to life.

What felt like hours later, he relented. His song hadn't responded. Neither had the chest transformed, not even with her touch. "Baby, you've got to come back." He kissed her forehead and finally, he called the wyvern. Who didn't answer. Fucking useless...

Kaleidoscope smoke swirled by the door. Hell!

No one was taking Clea.

In a blur, he placed her behind him and drew his gun and knife.

A shape coalesced in the room, and the tall, mocha-skinned creature stepped forward.

He bullseyed the shifter's left eye with his gun and iced his words. "Get out, Anouk."

"Playing shits and giggles with Clea? Nasty."

He would rip her to pieces. "Fuck you."

She plucked a pack of Marlboros and a lighter from her pocket, lit a cigarette, and took a long draw. She smiled. "Want one?"

"Get. Out."

Anouk's shrug belied the spark in her eyes. "All right. But understand that I can help."

"Can you, now? Exactly how?"

"Oh, this and that."

The room's temperature dropped a good ten degrees. Some idiot banged on the door. Anouk flicked ash into her palm, though no smoke clouded the room. "That mage is a pest. Shall I turn him into a piglet?"

The absurdity tickled him. He was self-aware enough to know she was deflating his rage. Had to give her credit, she wasn't bad at it. He laughed. "You're an asshole. But a funny one."

A slow, deliberate wink. "So I have been told. I will make you an offer."

"How kind."

"You are like a feral dog with a precious bone." Anouk took another drag on her smoke, the tip flaring. "I will help you raise Clea, and then you will thank me and I will leave."

He didn't trust her. Never had. She was tricksy and dangerous.

"Y'all talkin' to yourself, Larrimer?" Rae's voice blasted from behind the door.

"Shut it, Rae!" he bellowed, and notched his chin toward Anouk. "Go on."

"I can raise her song. It will help reconnect her to our world and to you."

Allegedly. Anouk saw Clea as her tool, little more. What would she get out of her offer?

Desperation made his decision for him. He folded himself onto the floor in front of Clea, putting his weapons in easy reach beside him. Mistake or no, he nodded.

She doused her cigarette with two fingers, dropping the butt into her pocket, and kneeled. "Hold her."

He slid Clea again onto his lap, her back to his chest, one arm around her waist, the other bracing her shoulder or she'd flop forward. She was near scentless, his sweet honeysuckle woman. His throat closed.

Anouk reached for the basket and laid it in Clea's lap.

The shifter raised her hands, pressing two fingers of each hand to Clea's temples.

"Lean back against the wall, Larrimer," she said. "Close your eyes."

James did as asked.

"Now find your song and raise it."

The song, buried deep inside him, a thing he hadn't known existed until he'd met Clea. As before, he found nothing, sensed nothing, felt empty.

"Remember," she said. "You have the spark of fae."

He had more now, since Charlie's death. But with Clea, the song just was. He didn't have to call it. He imagined drawing whatever "it" was up and out. His mind fractured. He so wasn't into this magic shit.

But then a quiet bass note chimed with a sluggish energy. He imagined pulling it, amplifying the sound. The melody rose, though it sounded half finished. He struggled to hold it in his mind, to bolster it.

The volume increased, and in his mind's eye a single helix flickered, disappeared, and reappeared, like a blinking neon sign.

Beneath his fingers, Clea warmed.

Faint, distant notes of longing undulated through him. He did nothing, yet the power of his song increased, infusing his being—a twisting half helix, unfulfilled without its matching spiral.

His song collapsed.

He stiffened, pain pounding his head.

Now what?

Clea would laugh. She would. He saw her, hands on hips, toes tapping, as if to say "Get it together, Dragon Dude." His song again stirred, like tiny hairs tickling his belly.

A memory. Perhaps... He forced himself to relax into it.

CLEA LEANS ON A CRUTCH, *and her hand is raised, palm out, her face resolute and tight with tension.*

Is it for him? Or for some unknown threat?

Her body trembles, the crutch shaking.

Gods she's beautiful, inside and out. He doesn't deserve her, but he loves her so completely, half the time it scares the shit out of him. The other half, it awes him.

She is everything.

He leaps the stream and walks toward her, needing her touch so badly his gut hurts. He stops himself, when all he wants to do is... He has to wait. She has to make the move. Maybe she's done with him. After all that's gone before, she needs to own the choice.

His Clea trembles so badly the urge to keep her upright almost over-comes his resolution.

She has to reach for him.

His heart pounds like thunder.

She doesn't move, just stares at him with those questioning green eyes.

Damn. He's still wearing sunglasses. Eyes are important to Clea, so he removes them.

Her eyes widen. In fear? Disdain? Hope?

She licks her lips, they part. "I would hug you, but I'd fall on my ass, so I'll do this instead."

She leaps.

He clamps his arms around her. She is here, alive, real. "I will catch you always, Clea mine." He blasts open his shields, so she can see all of him, feel all of him. So she knows he's truly back.

Her eyes devour him. He's too full. His song rises, twines with hers, almost brings him to his knees. Tethered to her, now, always. Us.

She cups his face, and he holds her tight. She is his sun.

He buries his face in her neck and breathes her in.

THE TWITCH of her metal finger snapped his reverie.

His song, their song, the double helix surrounded them.

On her lap rested the Chest of Time, changed.

A hexagonal crystal box without seams, about six inches in

diameter. The chest pulsed, matching Clea's heartbeat, its face and sides covered in symbols and runes.

Anouk sat back on her heels, gray-faced, lids drooping with exhaustion.

"How do we open it?" he said.

"Take her hand, use it to lift the lid."

There was no lid. Clea had told him it only formed at her touch. And though their song sang, she remained limp and unresponsive.

He lifted her hand, refusing to imagine what he'd do if they failed, and pressed her fingers to the box as if to lift its lid.

The chest yawned wide. He didn't look, didn't know if it could capture him, too.

He gently turned Clea's head, so her face was directly above the yawing chest.

Seconds ticked by.

Her lashes twitched, her eyes flew open, and he forced his muscles to stay relaxed.

She sucked in a deep breath, another, and turned her head. The chest tumbled, but Anouk snatched it up before it touched the floor. Clea's torso shifted, and her movements felt awkward and disjointed. She seemed to want to turn, so he repositioned her legs to one side, freeing her upper body. Clea's arms came around him and she snugged her head against his chest beneath his chin.

"What..." She cleared her throat. "What took you so long?"

TWO DAYS, and Clea slept on. James pressed his threaded hands against the back of his neck. He paced. Once Clea had returned from the chest, his myriad battle cuts had healed. Not that anyone understood why. Now, all he wanted to do was fight. Anyone. Everyone. Bloody his knuckles. Pound somebody to meat. Have someone pound *him* to meat.

More pacing. He'd taken no shit from Rae or any of the others. He trusted no one. She would rest in their room, *not* the alpha's bedroom, for Christ's sake.

Once again he checked her pulse. Normal. Her flesh was warm, and she sighed occasionally as she slept. Her basset Gracie lay sprawled on the floor, mimicking her.

How to wake her up? Forty-eight hours. Too long.

Had he ever felt more impotent in his life?

He flung himself into the chair beside the bed, reached for one of his new katanas and began to oil it in slow, long strokes. The whooshing of the cloth over the blade relaxed him. Down, back. His jaw loosened. Down, back. He could breathe again.

Someone was outside the door.

He stood, katana dangling from his right hand.

The doorknob clicked, and Neddy slipped into the room, looking sheepish and worried at the same time.

Maybe he trusted Neddy. He put down the katana and tried on a smile to reassure the kid he wouldn't gut him.

"Why do you look like you want to cut me into little pieces?" James snorted.

"Were you trying to smile, Larrimer?"

"What if I was?"

The kid shook his head. He scrunched his hands into his jeans' pockets and slunk around to the side of Clea's bed. "I have an idea."

"What?"

"If we brought up some food and held it under her nose, maybe she'd wake up?"

He started to laugh. But, hey, maybe the kid's idea wasn't so bad. "Why not? Got any lobster?"

"She won't want that! I say chocolate cake, fresh baked."

His eyes traveled to Clea. A slight flush stained her cheeks. Now he was worried about fever. No, she was fine. Was she?

"Hello?" Neddy said. "Jeez, Larrimer, pay attention. I said chocolate cake?"

"No. Brownies. With walnuts. Lots of them. And a glass of cold milk."

After Neddy left, James resumed oiling the sword. Maybe Gieri or Brina would be up for sparring. No, he wouldn't leave her, and the room was too small. He could practice his katas. Maybe they'd work off the energy hissing under his skin.

Did Clea's lids just flicker? He lay his sword across the chair, moved to Clea, and ran his fingers over the backs of her hands. "Clea."

She bit her lip. "James?" Her voice was but a wisp of sound.

Heat burned his eyes. He squeezed the bridge of his nose. She needed calm from him. Not the monster.

"It's me." He brushed a butterfly kiss across her lips.

"Tickles," she said.

The fingers he wrapped around her hand still shook. "Can you open your eyes?"

"I'm...not ready."

"Okay. Keep them closed then. I'm going to climb onto the bed."

"Good."

He settled beside her, dwarfing her tiny form, even smaller now, so thin and wan. Her body had been slowly dying. Fuck, she could've left for good. He boxed up his fear before he lifted her into his arms and snugged her against him. "Is this good?"

"Yes."

"Some water?" He reached for the bottle on the bedside table.

"Okay." She parted her lips and tentatively pulled on the straw.

"Not too much."

"No." After a few more sips, she nodded and he took away the water.

He smelled brownies. "Not now, Neddy." He didn't need to raise his voice, the shifter would hear his words.

"But...?" Neddy said through the door.

"Neddy!" Clea's whole body tightened. "Don't let him in!"

"I won't, baby."

She slowly relaxed against him, and he flinched when she patted her hands across her frame.

"Are you cold?"

She shook her head. "I feel creepy. Bony."

"I'll fatten you up." He went to kiss her.

She turned her head away. "Don't. I'm gross."

"Baby, you're my beautiful girl."

"I need a shower."

"I bathed you. You're shiny clean."

"I feel weird, like any minute I could leave again."

"Like hell you will." He smoothed his hand over her hair. Her lips trembled. "Yeah?"

"Never again, babe."

"So you say."

"Yeah, I do."

"Sleepy."

She drifted off in his arms. He should be feeling euphoric. So how come it felt like there was worse to come?

THE ROOM STANK. Where was I? My empath senses stretched and... Ah, there was James' thread, his presence strong in my mind. I relaxed and found funny Erick and sweet Neddy, Rae, Carlos, a ton of wolves, and a few unfamiliar entities. I sighed with relief. Somehow I was home, at the Arctos compound. Hallelujah and hooray.

Was it day or night? And when was it? Ack! My mind was foggy as a night in New Orleans.

Where was James? I listened. Ah, in the shower. Time to surprise him.

I puffed out my cheeks and lifted my lids. The room was so blurry I could barely see. Rubbing my eyes didn't help much. Whatever. I needed to get out of this bed. I kicked off the covers and slid my feet to the floor. Whoa. I was on some crazy carousel ride. Groping, I found the side table and held on until the room stopped spinning.

Guess I'd have to wait on that surprise.

Odd. I was a mess. What had happened? We were in Charleston to get Lulu. And Alex was hurt, and my mother was there, and Lulu... Damn. She was all grown up. A funny little dog and the chest...someone had the chest.

A sweetgrass basket? A pop. I began to shake.

I clamped that down. Later. Much later.

My eyes finally focused and...what the...?

The room was a pit. Gods. A tsunami had swirled through the place. Jeans, shirts, underwear, books lay on the floor and on the dresser, along with the detritus from meals, which was gross. At the end of the bed, atop the redwood chest, sat a gnawed t-bone steak on a greasy blue plate. My stomach lurched.

James was always the most meticulous of men. What had gone on here?

I put aside that puzzle, since getting dressed seemed a doable option. Goal one: get across the room. Goal two: put on clothes.

I wove through the room's mess and slammed my hand onto the dresser. Thankfully, it kept me vertical. Goal achieved.

Panties on, check. Bra...forget the bra. Fresh T-shirt donned, check. Jeans...yeah, that wasn't happening. I'd probably pass out pulling up the zipper. My loose workout pants were in the bottom drawer. With one hand pressed to the dresser, I leaned down and... crashed to the floor, pancake flat. I turned my head so I wasn't breathing in the smelly carpet.

Thundering footfalls, then a naked James strode across the room, his powerful thighs flexing and releasing. Muscles rippled across his chest and shoulders, and his gorgeous cock was... Oh, wow. My mouth dried.

"Shit!" he said.

He scooped me up and snugged me close. "Christ, Clea, are you okay?"

The most beautiful man in the world held me in his arms, eyes dark with concern, forehead furrowed, and I sensed panic beneath that fierce exterior. He was looking at me like some precious teacup that had just shattered. "I'm fine. Better than okay."

He hugged me tight. "Jesus. Jesus fuck."

"Can't breathe."

His grip eased, and was that a shine of tears in his eyes? Oh, my

Dragon Dude. I brushed a hand across his cheek. "Hi, hon. How's it hanging?"

His chest shook, and he bellowed out one of those laughs rarer than diamonds. "Pretty damned fine."

An hour later, I sat in his lap, my head resting on his chest, his strong heartbeat, music. "You've told me what happened in faeland, stuff I can barely remember. So what happened after you left?"

He scowled. "You don't need to know."

"You're paternalizing, James."

"That isn't a word."

"You know exactly what I mean." I huffed. "I do need to know, hon, all of it."

"You're a pain in the ass, Clea."

I kissed his chin. "You wouldn't have it any other way."

He laughed. "No, I wouldn't." He filled me in, though I had to drag some specifics out of him.

"Whoa, I missed all sorts of exciting stuff. Sophy's okay?"

"Just fine."

"After that fight at Union HQ, do you think they'll attack the den?"

"No. Not in the near future. We decimated them. Strategically, they'll need to recoup. That'll take time."

I tried to picture his description of my former boss. Impossible. "I can't believe Balfour. Bob always hated—"

"Freaks? His words, if you recall."

"Only too well. Since we're returning to Charleston, we've got to be back before they regroup."

"We will be."

"I'm glad Cruella got her ass fried."

"Cruella?" He arched an eyebrow.

Such a turn on when he did that. "When I was a kid, that's what I called Maurelle."

His eyes darkened to predatory.

"You're sorry you didn't get to kill her."

"Profoundly."

"She's Lu's mom."

"Irrelevant. She will die by my hand for what she did to you."

I heard the memory of his voice...

"Don't open it," he said.

"I must."

"Wait. Please."

I'd tried to wait, yet I'd failed. And because of that I'd caused terrible damage. "I'm...sorry I looked. It put you through hell. It was my fault. I never should have—"

His eyes gentled. "Don't. Your mother said you're compelled as The Key. Your father fell."

"Da?"

He explained how my father had fallen, and I swallowed tears of longing. I wished I could see him again, my sweet Da.

"I should have fought the compulsion harder," I said. "I hurt you. I'm so—

"That's in the past."

I wrapped my arms around his shoulders, nibbled his chin, whispered in his ear. "Make love to me, James."

A sharp breath. "Ah, Clea mine. You've just awakened. It's too soon."

I deferred. But that refusal was a first, one that made doubt nibble my heart.

HOURS PASSED. I slept. I ate. I was grumpy. Now I sat in the chair, knitting. The yarn soothed me, the stitches grounded me, and with each row, I tried to settle. It wasn't working.

James strode across the room and loomed, a specialty of his. "What's wrong?"

"Lunch was gross."

"Not a fan of the chicken soup?"

I shook my head. "Now a glass of wine..."

He had that determined, feral glow in his eyes. "How about later?"

"Is that your new favorite word, 'later'? I want to see Neddy and Rae and—"

"Perhaps it's too soon."

I wanted to scream.

He sat on the edge of the bed. "How about you lie down?"

"No!" I'd apparently been lying down for weeks. He was treating me like glass. Worse, my Dragon Dude looked worn to the bone, deep circles beneath eyes red with what I guessed was lack of sleep. He must have gone through so much. But for no comprehensible reason, though my muscles were weak noodles, I bristled with energy. Worse, I felt helpless and lost, turned around and upside down. My head was so full, I wanted to stick a knitting needle through my temple.

If I wasn't calm and reasonable, he'd cosset me more. "Is the West Coast corridor really that bad?"

"The fissures killed hundreds here, thousands around the world where the cracks occurred. Property damage is massive. It's bad, Clea. It'll take years to recover. But we've got to sort out our own problems."

I clenched my hands around my knitting. "We have so much to do. We've got to make sure Alex got Melike, we need to bring Lulu back here, we've got to locate Maurelle and her mage lover. The other chests to find! It's too much!" The needle in my right hand snapped in half. *Shit!*

He lifted me into his lap, smoothed the hair from my forehead. "Sshh. We're good. We'll get it all done. Anouk assured me Alex and Lulu are still in the magic realm, which Erick confirmed. He can't sense his alpha there. Anouk said they were safe. And until they return to the mundane, there's no rush."

I looked up at him and I'd swear I saw pity in his eyes. *Pity!* I reached out with my empath senses, and all I felt was a scramble of mottled noise. What was happening to me? "But..."

"No buts. Erick promised to alert me when they return. Until then, we wait. Deal?"

It made sense. All he'd said. Except the world felt so *wrong*. Everything was wrong. I'd lost so much weight. James didn't desire me anymore because I looked so gross. "And you won't even make love with me."

My lips were wobbling and my tears were falling, and I sucked.

He lifted my chin and his lips moved sinuously across mine. His kiss deepened, and I answered, opening to him. His tongue ransacked my mouth as if he were starving.

James was fire and love and everything I desired in this world or any other. He tightened his hold, kissing my cheeks, my eyes, my chin, and he shook with that passion he so effectively buried in daily life.

I wished to be consumed by this man.

My shaky hands raced across his chest, and I scraped my fingers through his hair, pet his face until I ran out of breath. "I want you, James."

He stilled. Our song rose, twining between us, through us. The beauty of it stole my breath. We held each other as the melody cascaded, alluring and unearthly.

And yet...even as he kissed me, he didn't touched me physically in any other way.

20

The following afternoon we were attending a party in the den to celebrate my reclamation. My first outing, and I was pretty nervous-excited. Two-thirds of my clothes were black, but today I wore a Caribbean-colored flowy skirt since all my jeans were too loose, along with a pretty peach floral top that covered my stick-like arms, and I'd chosen those gorgeous earrings James had given me. My dreads hadn't returned, so I tied a turquoise scarf around my crown of wild curls. When I walked out of the bathroom threading the second earring into its hole, things got weird.

My man was ready, and he looked fine. I ached to be skin-to-skin, but pushed that worry deep inside.

Rather than his typical t-shirt, he'd donned a black button down tucked into black jeans. His eyes warmed when he saw me.

The room dimmed, and I saw... *James is wearing a black button-down shirt and jeans. He bends over, tying his left shitkicker boot. The lace breaks. "Fuck."*

I blinked. So weird.

"You're beautiful." Then he bent over and tied his left boot. The lace broke. "Fuck."

Whoa. I rubbed my eyes with my forefinger and thumb. Maybe at the party Rae could explain that little "incident" to me.

"You okay, babe?"

"Super." Right.

He replaced the lace, then walked over and butterflied a kiss to my neck. "You sure?"

"I am." I ran a hand down his chest. "You look delicious."

"So do you." His wolfish smile melted me. "Ready?"

"I am."

I SO *WASN'T* ready for the crush of people in the den's small kitchen-party room. My legs wobbled, so it was a good thing James had his arm snugged around my waist. Rae was nowhere to be seen, but I had a wonderful reunion with Neddy and Sophy. Anouk's arrogance was on full display, per usual, and I loved meeting crazy Ziz who wore purple leathers and a badass sword. James' teammates, Geirr and Brina, were polite and distant, and looked at me as if I were an eggshell about to crack.

They weren't far off.

When I shook hands with Cassius—in full goblin mode with his tusks and red forest of pointy teeth—the memory of the goblin who'd killed my da technicolored though my mind. I slammed that door firmly shut. Cassius was sweet and funny, and when he transformed to human, quite the looker.

My energy flagged around ten, which was when Rae blew into the room in full-on caftan mode. I pulled her aside and told her about "seeing" James tying his boot before it happened.

"You've got to expect that weird shit after bein' so long in the chest, sugah."

"Will it continue?"

She plucked her lower lip. "Maybe. Maybe not. I've got some-thing' to say to y'all, and you'd best listen. Promise me y'all will rest up for a good three days before you go gallivanting off. Feel me?"

"No, I *don't* 'feel' you. You're not the boss of me, as they say."

"Hehehe. You'd best promise, or I'll be turnin' you into a toad."

She laughed, but her eyes were serious, not about turning me into a toad—I didn't *think* she could do that—but about my health. Rae was worried. I loved him-her, in all his many-faceted glory. "All right. It's silly, but I promise."

"Y'all best, sugah." Big grin. "Ribbit."

THAT NIGHT, James and I cuddled in bed, "cuddled" being the operative word. No matter how I touched him, teased him, ached for him, he would not touch me in any way sexual.

The dance we were doing further raised my orchestra of insecurities.

Now, he was wrapped around me, my back to his front, his one arm thrown over my shoulder, his leg bent between mine. I might have been exhausted, but I couldn't sleep.

Finally, I spiraled into a doze.

Clea. I must see you.

My eyes flashed open. The wyvern. Fear throttled me. I'd been lost for so long in the chest. What if I dove into James and couldn't leave? What if I got trapped?

Why are you afraid?

Afraid. Yeah, I was, of everything. A realization blinded me. Ever since I'd awakened, I was nothing but a bundle of fears. My body, Charleston, now the wyvern. If that's how I was changed, it sucked.

Come to me. There's nothing to fear.

There was *plenty* to fear. But I owed the wyvern, even loved him in an odd sort of way. He probably had an agenda tonight. I formed my own, a very personal one, and dived into James' consciousness.

As I plummeted, the strange, unreality of being within James settled. For the first time I could almost see his thoughts, like wisps of white on a background of black. I tasted his emotions, too, as if they were corporeal. Sweet honey, of course, and metallic rock. Licorice like Charlie, and sharp pine, which was all James. The deeper I dove to where the wyvern existed, the more a suffocating pressure built.

Was I within James or was I back inside the chest?

You are here with me. You are safe. A little farther, my Clea.

His voice soothed me, a deep bass timbre different from James' that echoed through my bones. But I didn't have bones, did I?

James' fae spark was a reassuring beacon, entwining his and our songs. Learning of Charlie's death had hit me hard, but seeing James' newly brightened spark—Charlie's gift—reminded me how a part of him lived on.

A glimmer of red-gold through the wisps of white, then emerald eyes aglow with pleasure. The full majesty of the wyvern emerged. His bugle call soared when I landed on the sandy soil to stand before him. His immense head dipped, eyes aglitter, and I laid my palm on his warm hide. *Hello, wyvern.*

You left. I couldn't find you. I needed to see for myself that you had returned. He chuffed, and smoke curled from his flared nostrils.

I sneezed. *Here I am. See?*

He dipped his head lower. Oh, I knew *exactly* what he wanted. Demanding wyvern. When I scratched between his eyes, he sighed with pleasure.

Now do behind my horns.

He laid his head on the ground, and I stood on tiptoe and scratched.

There. Ah, yes.

So basically you wanted me here so I could give you some happy scratches?

He chuffed a laugh. *No, although that's a marvelous bonus. You were gone a very long time.*

C'mon, you've lived for eons. How could those few weeks possibly feel long?

After your sojourn in the chest, do you not now understand how time is relative?

My composure shattered. Where had I been? What had I done? Icicled fragments pinged my mind.

Dawn rises. Watersongs. I dive into them, swimming the time stream alongside Oona the queen, headed toward a bank of caves glittering with crystals. The bright waterstream tickles my skin. Oona turns her head and smiles. We are old, dear friends, yet new again, and I...

Clea!

I was sitting on my ass, the soft sand of the wyvern's lair cradling my butt. How had I... Heat surrounded me, the wyvern's iridescent scales comforting. The wyvern had wrapped his endless tail around me where it spiraled out to form a sea of red-gold scales reminiscent of the endless journey.

You left, he said, voice petulant.

No, I didn't. Or maybe I did. I'm confused.

His lips curled, three-foot-long canines glistening. *Do not go there.*

What if I couldn't help it? But I didn't say that. *No, I shouldn't go there, for sure.* Now it was time to make *him* understand. *You cannot take over James, much as you want to.*

The wyvern blinked, his eyes full of ancient knowledge, arrogance, and a hint of longing. *Can I not?*

No. James is mine.

And I am James, am I not?

I gritted my teeth. *No, you are not.*

An earthquake of laughter. *Can he exist without me?*

I didn't know. I didn't want to think about it, either, except my mind saw a patchworked man made of fae spark and wyvern blood, nanoteched flesh and human brain. *You know I love you, wyvern, but it's a different sort of love with James and I. Ours is complete.*

And ours isn't?

It's not the same.

It will be, he said, his immense eyes full of certainty. *You will see. First, I will gift you my name.*

His name...something he'd once said was too difficult for me to pronounce. For ages, I'd been curious.

In your language, I am Akashagni.

Ak-ash-aqni.

He blinked. *Well said. That's the shortened version, of course. We are now further bound.*

If a wyvern could look self-satisfied, he did.

I rose to my feet, and he uncoiled his tail. I pressed my hands to his muzzle. *Please do not steal James from me.*

A force ripped me from Akashagni and out of James mind. I jolted back into myself, dizzy and reeling.

"What the hell, Clea?"

I heard James, but I didn't *see* him. Instead…

A movie unreels of the wyvern flying across a mountainous landscape, a place I don't recognize, while my lens parallels him. In the distance, the night radiates light and sparks burst in the air like shooting stars. Akashagni's massive wings flap and he nears the light—an erupting volcano.

Why was he doing that? Where was he going? He was so epic in flight he stole my breath. I had no idea how, but I moved closer to the images.

The wyvern flies in a circle, and down below a person is trying to keep pace with him. Once circle, two, then he shoots off again in a straight line, closing on the volcano. Reflected in the volcano's glow, his scales glitter like red-gold gems, his eyes like emeralds.

Two, three, four more beats of his wings, his great head turns and looks straight at me.

Then Akashagni rises higher in the air, arcs his body downward, and dives toward the volcano's yawning mouth.

I screamed. "No!"

"Clea, wake up!"

A naked James stood over me, frantic.

"I'm awake."

"Fuck."

I lifted my lids to see him drop onto the bed, his forearm covering his eyes. "You scared the shit out of me."

I rested a hand on his chest. "I'm sorry. I wasn't asleep. I…" What the hell had *that* been? "Just daydreaming."

He rolled to his side and raised his torso onto his elbow. "Daydreaming. You wouldn't open your eyes and they were doing that fluttery thing, like when you were inside the chest."

I peered down at him. "I didn't mean to scare you."

"Well, hell, you did."

Boy, was he pissed. "You, um, you haven't released the wyvern again, have you?"

"Why would you ask that *now*?"

"He called me."

His body compressed, and he was suddenly sitting up, legs crossed, muscles tight, hands fisted. "And?"

"I visited him."

"While I was asleep."

"Yes."

Ice crept across his eyes. I sat up and scooched closer, pressing my hands to his cheeks. Normally, he'd wrap his arms around me and pull me to him. He didn't. "James?"

"You shouldn't have done that."

"Why not?"

"I find it disturbing."

"I'm sorry, James. He called. You haven't become the wyvern since I was gone."

"I said 'no' already." Shadows skated across his eyes. "My hands only."

"You can do that, partially become the wyvern?"

His face tightened. "If he permits."

"Oh, he can be such a pain in the butt."

He chuckled. "Agreed."

That's not nice, Clea.

I am NOT doing a three-way. Go to sleep.

The wyvern's laugh boomed.

"What's he laughing about?" James said.

"Just being *him*." I threaded my fingers through his hair. "I can't lose you to the wyvern."

A smile, all the way from those beautiful lips to his gorgeous eyes. One of those special ones he only gave me. "I'm not going anywhere."

I *knew* that. We were safe. *He* was safe.

He hugged me to him, kissed the top of my head. I rubbed my cheek against his bicep, warm, human. The wyvern would not steal James. *Ever.*

THE BED WAS soft and comfy, and I didn't want to get up. I planned to activate the chest that day, no matter how it scraped my nerves. Since I'd promised Rae I'd wait, we had two more days before we left for Charleston.

A tap on our door, and before the words "ten more minutes" made it to my lips, James' hand was on the knob.

"Who is it?" James said.

A muffled answer.

"Tell them to wait a sec." I pushed up on my elbows, then rolled out of bed. Minutes later, I'd brushed my teeth, showered, and dressed, which was more than I could say for James.

"Why are you growling?" I said.

"Never mind."

"Yes, mind. How long have you been up?"

"Couple hours. Paperwork." He pulled on his jeans and lifted one of his katanas from the dresser. "The little vampyre girl wants to meet you."

"Okay." Should be interesting.

He ran a finger down his scar, opened the door, then sat in the bedside chair. Mr. Casual, except for his eyes focused on the pair who entered. He reminded me of a hawk who'd spotted prey.

Neddy stood in the doorframe holding the hand of a child who barely came to his waist. Someone had tied back her black ringlets in a ponytail and put a butterfly barrette in her hair. Though her eyes were dark, rather than violet, she reminded me of a young Liz Taylor.

"Come in." I smiled. "Welcome. You're...?"

"Isobel," she piped up. "But I prefer Izzy. It's more hip." So serious. She couldn't be more than eight.

Neddy grinned.

"Why did you bring the child, Ned?" said James, the Ice Man. "Clea's still recovering."

"She wouldn't shut up about it." Neddy rolled his eyes.

"I'm glad they came," I said.

"She's a child, Ned," James said. "*You're* supposed to be in charge.

"I am in charge. Mostly."

I laughed and hunkered down in front of the adorable little girl. James' vibe soared to the stratosphere, but he didn't move.

"Do you like it here in the den?" I asked her.

She nodded, so very solemn. "I...do."

"But...?"

"Um, sometimes kids call me 'vamp.'"

Neddy frowned and leaned down. "Izzy, I told you to tell me when the pups talked trash."

She thrust out her bottom lip. "I'm not a tattletale."

Time for a subject change. "How come you wanted to see me?"

She latched her eyes onto mine, and I began to float in warm soothing waters.

When I surfaced, my bum was on the floor, my legs out straight. James was holding the child, whispering in her ear. Neddy looked on, his expression going from guilty to embarrassed and back again.

I folded my legs, yoga fashion, fascinated by the tableau they presented. I saw James holding another child. *Our* child. A raven-haired, Pacific-blue eyed infant. The wonder of it pinwheeled through me.

James set Izzy down, and she kneeled in front of me, hands on her knees.

"Oops," she said with a frown. "I sort of stole you for a minute. That's what Neddy calls it, and I'm not supposed to do that. It was an accident. I'm still learning control. Right, Neddy?" She looked back at the boy.

"That's right, pumpkin," he said.

I smiled and took her hand in mine. So small, her nails painted a perfect pink with red hearts on the index fingers. My empath senses told me she was both sugar and spice, but beneath that lay a deep hurt and much longing. "No harm done. Now, you wanted to see me because...?"

She fisted her hand and raised a tiny index finger. "One, I wanted to meet you. Neddy talks about you *a lot*."

My heart squeezed. Sweet Neddy. "I talk about him a lot, too. He's pretty terrific."

She held up a second finger. "Two, I have to go."

"Why are you leaving?"

Her head shook, ponytail swinging. "No, silly, I mean when *you* leave, I have to *go*."

"When we go to Charleston?"

She giggled, those pearly white canines lengthening. "Nope. You'll see." She leapt to her feet and raced out the door, with Neddy following hot on her heels.

James held out a hand. I took it, and he pulled me to my feet and into his arms.

"That was interesting," I said.

"Izzy is everything interesting and terrifying."

"Do you have a clue what she meant?"

"No."

"Me, neither, but I found her enchanting."

His eyes narrowed. "She'll enchant you, all right."

"I meant I liked her."

"She's deadly."

"So are we." I laughed. "I figure that's why you like her, too."

I kissed his pectoral, but his smile didn't reach his eyes. He released me and stepped toward the bathroom. "You see right through me, babe."

Except I didn't see him. Not this new, dispassionate James who barely touched me.

"I'm going to shower," he said.

I didn't wiggle my brows, didn't cock my hip or lower my lids. But I still hoped he'd ask me to join him.

"I brought you some muffins, eggs, bacon, and coffee." He gestured to the side table where a thermal pot and plate with a domed lid awaited.

"Thank you."

"I've finished up my paperwork." He shucked his jeans and pulled out a pair of loose training pants from the dresser. "After my shower, I'm going to spar with Geirr and Brina."

"Sure. Great."

He showered and left, while I shoved food into my mouth, determined to regain the weight I'd lost, to get strong again, to hold James' interest. All the food did was give me a bellyache.

I RAN the cloth over my shrunken breasts, across my too-visible ribs down to the ridges of my hipbones. Over my legs and back up across my prominent chest ridges and collar bones. I scrubbed my face. Finally, with great reluctance, I brushed the cloth across my pubic area and genitals.

Hollow. Empty. I ached.

After a thorough rinse, I dried off, dropped the towel in the hamper, and walked back to the bedroom.

No reason I couldn't activate the chest on my own, while James was sparring.

I froze.

James had returned to our rooms. He faced the window, looking outward toward the courtyard, his hands clasped behind his back. He wore only his sparring pants, and he stole my breath. He was beauty personified, his long, raven hair almost brushing his shoulders, his defined muscles sculpting the V of his back. He peered over his shoulder. For the first time in...ever, I covered my breasts and pubis.

"I didn't know you were here." Why did I sound so breathy?

He turned to face me. Sweat glistened on his chest and arms.

I swallowed, and went to scamper back into the bathroom.

A hand on my arm stopped me. He pulled my shoulders back against his chest. He burned. Tears bit my eyes like gnats.

"Let me go, please?" I said in a light voice that only wobbled a little.

"I can't."

I wanted to turn invisible. "Please."

"Waiting's been hell."

Waiting? "For what?"

"For you."

21

James turned me in his arms, his erection pressing into my belly. I held my breath.

With his thumb and forefinger, he tilted my chin up, so our eyes met. "Why are you crying?"

I bit my lip, couldn't say it aloud.

"Am I hurting you?"

I shook my head, then pressed my cheek to his chest, right where his heart beat strong and sure. I wrapped my arms around his waist.

"Then why the tears, my beautiful Clea?"

Could I say it? I was so afraid to say it. "I thought you didn't want me anymore."

He peered down at me. The muscles in his face were tight, his jaw bunched, his eyes filled with longing. "I want you so much it hurts."

He lowered his head slow, so slow, until his lips were an inch from mine. His breath tasted of cinnamon and him. "So. Much."

His kiss was like none other, filled with longing and need, desire and pain, its fury leaving me breathless.

We landed on the bed, him atop me, and I gloried in the weight of him, the feel of him. I clenched my arms around his broad back, desperate for more, always more, my love greedy with want. In a blink he'd shucked his pants. In another, his cock probed my entrance, and he moved it back and forth, moistening me when I was already gushing.

He kept his eyes open, and I did, too, as he flexed his hips, and in one slow, torturous glide he entered me, slid deeper and deeper until he filled me completely.

"Home," I said.

"Home." His brow furrowed, and he squeezed his eyes tight. "You were gone so fucking long."

Hands on his shoulders, I curled up and kissed his eyes, his cheeks, his chin. "I'm here now. *You* brought me back."

"Clea mine."

"Always."

He latched onto a breast, swirled his tongue around and around, bit my nipple. Sensation shot straight to my belly and clit.

He moved. Our song rose, and I clamped my legs around his thighs. He thrust and retreated, thrust and retreated, and I matched him, our rhythm perfection. The double helix tightened, as did I, clenched by passion and love, our breaths raw, our skins slick, our song ever rising. The power of him pounded into me, and he ate my mouth, sucked my breasts, his hands stroking, touching, greedy. I frantically squeezed his back, pet his shoulders, dizzy with need and want, my core clenching him tighter and tighter. I was rising, spiraling, close, oh gods, so close.

He slowed.

What? No! Faster, harder.

His hips swiveled, another angle, a twist, he sped up again, pistoning into me, pounding that sweet spot. Oh, gods yes.

"Can't hold..." he said.

Faster still.

Please, please, please.

There. I gasped. A thousand fireworks, our song crescendoing, cascades of pleasure, orgasmic waves echoing again and again. He pumped twice, froze, strained, his liquid heat pulsing inside me as he barked his completion.

We collapsed, muscles useless, gulping air, sweaty, his head tucked into my shoulder, his chest rising and falling like a bellows.

I stroked his damp hair again and again, so damned happy I giggled.

He raised his head, joy in those beautiful eyes, and growled. "Funny, was it?"

I cupped his cheeks. "Oh, yes, hilarious. Couldn't you tell?"

He grinned and went to roll away.

I clung to him limpet-like. "Don't you dare."

"I'm crushing you."

"I like the feel of you on me."

"I need to—"

"What?"

"If I don't roll off, I'll love you again. You're fragile—"

"As titanium." Feeling him harden again inside me was bliss. "If you don't do me, I'll bite you."

His chest rumbled with laughter. "How about both?"

"Deal."

UNUSUAL, but I woke before James from our nap. We'd worn ourselves out, and it felt grand. That dear face, scarred and beautiful—I could stare at him forever. His raven hair glistened in the soft light that poured in from the window. Each time I saw him, I loved him anew. The thrill that sang through me when he walked into a room never dimmed. I shivered when he spoke in that honied-granite voice of his and heated with desire when he challenged me. The complexity of our relationship was a spider's web of threads that I would gleefully remain entangled in forever. I'd never know all of him, but I reveled in exploring his nooks and crannies, mining the deep crevices of the man I loved. He was the most unexpected joy of my life.

"You're thinking awfully hard, Clea." His eyes flashed open. "Where are you, babe?"

"You. I'm with you. You are my dreams fulfilled."

"*Jesus*, Clea."

Those exquisite carved lips beckoned. I leaned in, brushing a kiss over them, stealing his breath, his love a living thing that surrounded me.

I flopped back on the pillow. "I hate that I'm so bony."

"You're *all* Clea, which is what matters."

We needed no words as he touched me, and I, him. As day turned to night, we made slow exquisite love again. It felt so good to be home.

"I want to chain you to this bed," James said.

My lips twitched. "Getting kinky in your old age?"

"Probably."

His soft laughter wove through my senses. Already, I longed for his lips again. "Charleston. Are we ready?"

"Yes. Erick's coming with ten additional packmates, Neddy, too, and Cassius."

"I have a feeling that Ziz person left out plenty when she told us the story of the magic realm."

He nodded. "Agreed. For all we know, Ziz is winding us up. She's adept at that. We'll go soon. What do you say we wait another week?"

"Tomorrow night. I'm serious, James. I'd leave today if I hadn't promised Rae I'd wait."

His eyes darkened to inky shadows.

"It was hard on you, with me gone, wasn't it?" I said. "First, I lost you emotionally, then you lost me. It's like a greater force is pulling us apart in an endless cycle."

He took my left hand, wrapping me in comfort, and uncurled my fingers. His head dipped, and he pressed his lips to the finger I'd lost, the one now made of gold.

"*Nothing* will keep me from you, Clea. You know that, right?"

I nestled in the crook of his shoulder. "You always sound so certain."

"I am. Some things I know. That's one of them. Love you, Clea mine."

He dipped his head and licked my breast, followed by a sweet nip that shot straight between my thighs. Again, we lost ourselves to the wonders of the flesh.

WE'D DOZED SOME MORE, and when I awakened, James was gone. I stroked a hand across the still-warm sheet where he'd slept. Getting food, I presumed.

A gibbous moon splashed its light through our window onto the maple floor boards. In several days, the moon would be full, and the pack's excitement for the coming monthly hunt in Griffith Park streamed into my consciousness.

I checked my phone. Thirteen minutes to midnight. A fine time to activate the chest.

Our door opened, and James strode in carrying a bountiful plate of nibbles, with a bottle of wine clutched in his other hand. He eased the door closed with his foot and placed the food and drink on the nightstand.

"Brief raincheck on the food," I said.

He arched an eyebrow.

"I need to do the chest now."

"How about we eat first?"

I shook my head. "It's the witching hour, James. The right time."

ONCE INSIDE THE small between-worlds room, my eyes locked on the third plinth, the one that held the sweetgrass basket I was to activate.

Images and sounds assailed me, comets zooming out of chaotic blackness.

James rested his hands lightly on my shoulders and leaned forward. "Do it fast."

"Yes." Before I stepped forward, I turned my head and kissed him in the event everything went south. "You have the case?" The black one Anouk had crafted. Inside it, the Chest of Time would rest after I'd activated it. While the room was heavily warded, the cases were yet another layer of wards to guard the chests from magical or mundane seekers.

I took that final step, and my hands framed the basket. I didn't touch it. Not yet. A faint tremor slid through me, but the chest's call was dampened by James' arms banding me just above my breasts. The warmth from his torso seeped into my back.

I didn't want to touch the Chest of Time. Yet I was dying to touch it. Flashes of memory strobed my mind—of Queen Oona's warmth, the waving rowan trees, and the scent of heliotrope. I tasted a dark fleshless presence, eager to subsume me. "I don't want to fall again."

"I will catch you," James said.

Our breathing grew loud in the small room.

"Doing this," I said.

A kiss on my temple.

I placed my hands on the chest. Feathers touched my flesh, then roiled up my arms. My wrist spiral glowed, and my fireflies seeped out from where my hands and the weave of the chest connected. The chest's power snapped onto me like Godzilla's teeth. My back bowed. Prickles danced across my flesh.

The crystal box took shape, its runes and symbols flowing across its face and sides.

I stuttered in a breath, the chest's melody stealing all thought, all feeling.

I realized my eyes were squinched tight.

If I looked, I'd feel the euphoria, see that divine beauty, smell those exquisite scents. My soul would join the other soul-fragments occupying the chest—I pulsed with the desire to return.

I could be there, inside it, with them.

I tried not to breathe, but jasmine surrounded me, infused me with the promise of that infinite and alluring darkness.

I opened my eyes and lifted the lid.

Now I could explore realms upon realms. I'd never tire, never weary of the endless sights and sounds and scents. No more eternal hunting for the chests. Responsibility banished. Complete surcease from pain and worry and fear.

The chests were wisps of remembered power and desire, of magic and mystery, of long forgotten kings and queens, and of She who created them. They were beyond my ken. They were worlds without love.

Those worlds weren't mine.

A melody hummed, bright with promise, one I knew intimately. *Our* melody. Real. Here. Pairing the two of us, sweet and deep and *alive*.

If I again fell, I would lose James. And all the others I loved. For love did not exist inside the chest.

Trite, yet true—I would always choose love.

"Now." I pressed my will.

A snick. A click. Activated. *Alive.*

A picture formed. No, not a picture, but the reflection of one. Moving. Flicker, flicker, like an old-time movie reel. Lulu and Alex lay naked, asleep on their bellies. A monster made of smoke took shape, no, *two* monsters. The creatures towered over them, black and oily and evil, open mouthed, with sharp-bladed teeth. Mucus dripped from the creatures onto Alex and Lu's skin. Their flesh sizzled and bubbled and burned. The monsters reached, stretched tentacled arms, and pulled Alex and Lu into their mouths.

I screamed "No!"

"Clea!"

James slammed the lid closed.

He took the chest from me and placed it into its ebony box, then set it on the plinth. "What happened?"

"I saw them. Alex and Lulu. They're in terrible danger. We have to leave for Charleston tonight!"

He stared at me for a good five seconds. "Real or not, we go."

TERROR NEARLY STRANGLED LULU. It had taken them another day to reach the portal's location. Now, the mundane world lay just ahead, through an indentation in the lava-like rock beside a waterfall sparkling with amber light. Anouk made a point of telling them not to swim in the alluring stream. Microscopic fish would swim up their noses and into their brains, and grow and grow until they consumed them. True, the fish would ultimately die, but so would they. Lulu didn't know if the guardian was joking or not, but she wasn't about to test it.

Would she and Alex talk? Have a heart-to-heart? Profess undying love before they entered the portal?

"Let's go," he said, inches from the portal. She rushed to his side, and they stepped through shoulder to shoulder. That he might die gutted her.

The black void smacked her, twirled her, and she lost contact with Alex's shoulder, lost all sensation until she tumbled into a forest she knew well. They'd returned to Charleston faeland.

Alex lived. He was bent at the waist, hands on knees, but he hadn't collapsed, hadn't *died. Gods, thank you.* She dammed her tears. No time for her going all emo, especially when the wolf was all business.

Since his big revelation a day ago, he'd given her plenty of beseeching looks, but he hadn't tried once to talk to her, damn him.

They stood behind a huge live oak dripping with Spanish moss. Had they lost time in the magic realm? Gained it? Or did it correspond to the mundane world?

He stepped away from the tree, as if scoping the path to their left, and staggered, bracing a hand on the trunk. She wanted to ask how he felt. No, she wouldn't do that.

Alex looked back, his smile breathtaking. "I feel them." Wonder lit his voice.

"Who?"

"My pack, very faint. And Melike." He pointed toward the path. "She's that way."

"That path leads to Aunt Viviane's home, her seat of power."

The skin beside his eyes tightened, his jaw muscles bunching. "I should feel her energy more. She's either sleeping or..."

"Or what?"

"They've hurt her so badly, she's dying."

"Well, come on then, let's get this over with so you and she can get out of faeland."

His eyes implored her, but he said nothing.

Whatever he wanted, she didn't have it to give.

He stiffened. "Let's go."

THEY RAN DOWN THE PATH, their feet falling lightly on the soil. His legs weren't right, but that was the least of his worries. He was fucked. He was so fucked. He'd seen Lulu angry before, but she'd never turned away from him so thoroughly, like an ice maiden.

If he didn't tuck away his fears about losing Lulu, he'd go mad. Now was for Melike. Later... They'd work their way out of this and be fine.

Up ahead, the queen's home stood silent, a one-storied, elegant structure with swooping wings that seemed a part of the living trees woven into the building like spires.

The roofline of the queen's palace poked through the trees. Yet it was too quiet. No murmur of people going about their daily tasks. No song, that sense of music which always hummed the air in faeland. No small rustlings of wild animals, nor insects abuzz.

The atmosphere disturbed him. He scented the land. Few fae scents reached his nose, but the air was rank with another familiar smell. Goblins. His lip curled. He raised a fist to halt their progress, then hauled Lulu off the path.

"There are goblins in the queen's home," he said.

Lulu caught her breath. "Cassius?"

"I can't tell, but there's no reason for him to be here."

"Maybe James and Clea came for Melike?"

He shook his head. "No scents of Larrimer or Clea, either. Something's really off."

Her leathers creaked as she sat on a large rock. "Agreed, but I can't imagine what could be wrong."

"Melike's in there, of that I'm sure, and she's not doing well."

"It's better if I go in alone."

That sucked as an idea. "Why?"

"My aunt won't hurt me. There's only two of us, Alex. One of us should stay hidden."

"So I'll be the one to go in." He nodded.

"No. Here, I stand a better chance of not getting killed if something bad's going on inside."

Every instinct, every fiber of his being rejected the idea. She looked up at him, her face a pristine mask. Was this some test she'd dreamed up? He walked away, needed to clear his mind, which was never easy in Lulu's presence. Yeah, okay, he'd let her go in...those thoughts. They were wrong. He'd said she'd be his partner. His equal. You didn't "let" your equal do anything. She'd proven herself again and again. Hell, she'd fought off a basilisk. She was smart and capable.

And hers was the better plan.

A slight rustle of the grass. Was she leaving on her own without his agreement? He whipped around.

She'd simply taken a few steps to move out of the sun and stand beneath a tree.

She was so fair, a beautiful woman. The ever-present heartache sucked. "A good plan, Lu. I'm going to shift."

"You think that's better?"

He hated this whole scenario, but his gut told him it was the best move. "They won't be expecting the wolf."

She nodded, released the clasp holding her bow. "Okay." She stepped forward toward the path.

He grasped her by her shoulders and tugged her against him.

She didn't pull away. Not unaffected, then. He leaned close, his breath fanning her cheek. "Kiss me," he whispered into her ear.

She slipped out of his grasp. "I love you, Alex. But imagine if our positions had been reversed, if I thought I would die. How would you feel if I hadn't told you? I know it's hard for you not to roll me in bubblewrap. I'm not used to having someone look out for me. And it mostly feels pretty nice. So I'm really trying to become more accepting. Better at it. But I want us to fit together right, and not have you steamroller over me."

Steamroller? "I was trying to protect you from hurt."

She brushed her fingers down his cheek. "I know. It's your nature. But loving means sharing the bad, as well as the good. Knowing you might die just because we were in the magic world crushed me, Alex. That you hadn't told me made it worse. Don't you see I could have eased your fears? Softened them? Helped? Let me be there for you as you are for me. I admire your strength, and I lean on it sometimes. Can't you do the same for me?"

Lulu raised her face and took his lips in an all-or-nothing, blistering kiss. Then she smiled, winked, and walked down the path at a swift pace.

22

L ulu found no guards in the outer courtyard, which was strange. Stranger still, none stood in the inner courtyard, either, only a man idling beneath the porch roof, a murky shadow concealing his face.

She went to pull an arrow from her quiver.

"No need for that."

Double damn. She released the arrow back into the quiver. Avain stepped into the light, his gray eyes alight with pleasure. That creepy mage. Really?

Behind her, the courtyard's doors whooshed closed and locked. She didn't need to see the goblin who'd sealed them in, she smelled him.

Damn. Alex would find a way inside. But they'd thought they would have to deal with the court and her aunt, who loved her. Not freaky-deaky mage Avain. And her mother. Yup, she'd bet a dragon's hoard dear old Mom was here.

Avain moved off the porch with a bouncy step. Gone were the billowing Gandalf robes. Instead, he wore fae clothes, his silver tunic molded to his lithe muscled form and his leggings gleaming gold. She bit back a giggle. Gold? He really did look rather ridiculous.

"We've been waiting," he said in a sing-song voice. "Your mama misses you." He held out a hand. "Don't be afraid. I'm not going to kill you. As long as you behave, that is."

She was shaking, and he'd mistaken her fury for fear. She wasn't the same girl he'd first captured, not even a little. The less said to this asshole, the better.

Her arms remained at her sides, but his fingers wrapped around her upper arm, giving her the creepy-crawlies.

"Shall we?" he said.

She pressed her lips together and allowed him to escort her inside.

No surprise he didn't lead her to Viviane's welcoming living room, but the more formal throne room where the queen held court. Fae lined the walls, many manacled, but what drew her attention were the bolts in the floor at the center of the room attached to thick chains imprisoning a naked and bloodied Melike, crouched on hands and knees before the assembly. A bowl of water sat on the floor just out of reach. Her dull eyes hadn't moved when they'd entered the hall.

On Melike's right, Iron Heart was chained in the same matter. He, too, was naked and bloody, long strips of flesh missing from his back, arms, and thighs.

Oh, no. Swallowing the bile erupting from her belly, Lulu sprang forward.

Avain tightened his grip. "I don't think so."

Her eyes lifted to his too-handsome face. Within her, fury and disdain battled for ascendence. How to play this? "Ah, so you're in charge."

"I am, as the prince consort."

She whirled, for the first time focusing on the throne.

"Mother." The word tasted sour on her tongue. This woman had born Lulu, but it was her father who'd raised her, thank the gods. She forced a smile. Avain kept his grip firm as she approached the throne. Her mother wore her aunt's crown and held her scepter. To Lulu's eyes, she looked like she was playing dress up, possessing little of the power or wisdom of Viviane. "How good to see you."

"Is it, you ungrateful child?"

"Of course. And the queen is...?"

"*I* am queen."

Murmurs filled the hall. A fae stepped forward, and was swiftly checked by one of the goblins. She recognized Casca from the Guadalupes, one of the three Union "improved" goblins.

When she finally stood before her mother, she evened her breath so her revulsion didn't spill out and widened her smile. "Where is Aunt Viviane?"

Her mother waved a hand. "Somewhere."

"Alive?"

Maurelle eyes shot to Avain and she frowned. "For now."

The "queen" wanted Lulu's aunt, her own sister, dead. Apparently Avain had stilled her hand. "And did the fae *choose* you, Mother?"

She cleared her throat. "I am the older sister."

"Oh? But I didn't think that was how it worked in fae."

"You're a foolish girl. You fail to understand—"

"Haven't you noticed I'm a *woman*? I believe I understand pretty damned well." She laughed and held out her wrists. "Do I get some pretty bracelets, too?"

"Of course not." Maurelle smiled.

Massive arms banded around her, while rough hands wrapped tape around her mouth. She didn't fight them; that would come later. But she sure wished she could poof out like her mother could.

Avain stripped her of weapons, fingers deliberately brushing her breasts and inner thighs.

"Stop it, Avain!" barked Maurelle.

He smirked. "Stop what, my dear?"

Her mother ground her teeth, but it was she who dropped her

eyes first in their dual of wills. Then Maurelle turned her head to stare at an unbound fae male, an acquaintance of Lulu's named Eldon. Maurelle crooked a finger.

The fae pushed off the wall and kneeled before her mother on the dais. His jeans were ripped, and blood smears darkened his white t-shirt.

"Drop them," her mother said.

The fae's eyes burned with fury, but without a word he unzipped his jeans and pushed them down, exposing naked flesh.

Her mother pet his thigh, then cupped his balls, her thumb brushing back and forth across his penis.

"My queen, does he please you?" Avain's smile was cruel, his voice flippant, his eyes laughing. "He's yours."

Maurelle kicked Eldon's chin, and he fell backwards. He recovered, and with silken grace, spine straight, he pulled up his jeans and returned to his place along the wall. He was a fae warrior of exceptional skill, yet he'd done nothing, said not a word.

Fae warriors filled the room, and Lulu guessed that their utter submission to Maurelle and Avain meant the pair had somehow imprisoned their wives and husbands, their children and the elderly, and their queen. The warrior fae were protecting their loved ones the only way they could.

How many creatures had Avain and Maurelle brought with them? Apparently enough to subdue the powerful fae. How had they gotten here? Perhaps they'd traveled through the magic world from Texas, entering faeland through a portal, as she and Alex had just done.

Her mother stood. All the fae bowed, but their hate-filled eyes promised retribution. Avain flicked a finger at two of the goblins, then he gripped Lulu's upper arm. Maurelle nodded as she stepped down the dais and took the lead. They walked beneath an arch covered with living branches and down the hall.

So the fun begins.

THE CLOSING of the gates signaled trouble. In his wolf form, Alex could easily jump the six-foot wall, but the inner courtyard was mostly bare of trees and foliage. On silent paws he padded through the canopy of trees that filled the outer courtyard, filtering out the numerous smells of unknown fae and goblin so he could identify ones he recognized. He already had a bead on his wolf warrior— Melike was within the compound, a fading presence that made him blaze with fury.

His paws didn't make a sound as he continued to circle the compound. His back leg caught on a downed branch, and he stumbled, once again aware of his wraith-born injuries. Damn them.

There. That scent. His Lulu. He froze, his lips pulled into a snarl. Goblin stench was everywhere. For the first time, Avain's and Maurelle's scents stung his nose. *Fuck.* Lulu had said her aunt wouldn't kill her. But the vicious couple they'd battled weeks ago were an entirely different tale. His wolf demanded he charge in and protect his mate.

He held on tight, refusing that call with a struggle that made his sides heave as if he'd been racing. No, he needed to trust his clever Lulu, to wait and form a plan and execute it. But, man, that sucked.

Faint scents of iron and mulberry tickled his nose. Iron Heart. He tasted the joyful healer, Ozille, now reeking of fear. Her scent mingled with a dozen or more other fae he didn't recognize. But the paramount scent was the bitter, astringent one of an anger so fierce it burned his tongue.

Man, if he could only turn into a puppy dog, maybe a Chihuahua, and sneak inside. Anouk had. For him, impossible. Instead, he followed the burble of a stream until he found a small brook flanked by willows. The bank was mossy and muddy, and he rolled around in the mud, coating his fur. He'd be less noticeable. Scruffier. Less threatening.

He drank his fill, the cool water invigorating.

Avain and Maurelle were tough—filled with magic and dangerous as shit. Their goblin soldiers only worsened the odds.

He cursed, wishing that he'd insisted Ziz and Anouk come with them. No help for it now.

The weariness in his hindquarters forced him to sit on the bank for a moment, his sensitive nose wrinkling at the smell of skunk cabbage.

Too far away to call on the pack, except...

His plan took shape.

Long minutes later, he leapt the six-foot wall and stilled. No approaching sounds. Slinking on his belly he crept around the structure, noting exits and the fae who guarded them. He had little cover, yet they appeared not to notice him. Deeply strange.

Before he put his scheme into motion, he needed to be assured of the players' positions. He sniffed deeply. Lulu rang siren clear, and he smelled her rage and a hint of pain. Damn them! He continued circling the building.

Shit! He willed himself to blend with the earth. A goblin approached the fae guard directly in front of the entrance before him, not ten feet away. The fae guard angled his body. If Alex didn't know better, he'd say the fae was screening him from the massive goblin's sight. He recognized the goblin with the bruiser nose, one of the trio he'd met the day he'd first encountered Cassius.

The goblin waved his arms for a good minute, yelling at the fae. He finished with a wicked punch to the fae's gut, laughing as he walked away. The fae hadn't even drawn his knife. Why? The goblin might outweigh the fae, but they were fast and clever and strong, each with his or her own magical attribute, much the way Lulu's song held magic.

The fae was a warrior, but something cowed him. Whatever it was might also compel him to reveal Alex if he made an overt move. It would be good to have an ally, but it wasn't worth the risk of exposure.

Alex continued his creep around the perimeter until he again sensed Melike's thread. Someone had bruised and abused her. She was damaged, her thread thin and weak. But she was also pack and her closeness strengthened his resolve.

He tightened his muscles, preparing to spring through the glass windows into the room holding his packmate.

Words slipped inside his head. He froze.

A jumble, words repeated over and over. It took long seconds, but he finally caught them.

We are coming.

AVAIN PUSHED Lulu inside a small room holding a chair banded with leather straps and coated with what looked like dried blood. Her stomach flip-flopped.

As Avain pushed her down into the chair, her fist flew. She got his chin with a solid right cross hard enough that he staggered backwards. Her smile might be muffled by the tape, but he'd catch her eyes laughing at him.

He worked his jaw back and forth, blood dripping from where she'd cut his lip. He spat in her face.

She gave him a one fingered salute, which she also shared with her beloved mother.

While he held her down, her mother strapped her into the chair.

HOLY SHIT. A thrill seared Alex's body. Had he heard right?

We are coming.

Erick. With the might of the pack behind him, his packmate's "voice" grew louder by the minute. Using pack magic, Erick had drawn on the pack as their de facto leader while Alex was away. No, it was more than that, and he'd bet dollars-to-donuts Rae was boosting Erick's signal.

We are coming.

Well, hell, yeah! No way to tell when or how, but soon enough for them to reach him mind-to-mind. Man, so good. He was energized, charged.

He revised his plan. He'd try something risky, something that would weaken him.

How long would it take for his pack to arrive? Fifteen minutes? Thirty? Two hours?

Did he dare it?

Melike might be damaged, but if he poured his strength and that of the pack into his soldier, there'd be two of them kicking ass, instead of just him. It wouldn't last for her, not for long, but it might be enough to free her from any bonds that constrained her. The two of them could wreak havoc on the goblins, Avain, and Maurelle until help arrived.

The odds sucked but, man, they were worth it. Except it would take extra time for him to get to Lulu.

The wolf pressured him, pushed him.

He wrangled down the wolf. He was in charge. Lulu was competent. She would understand, would fight her captors. He said a prayer to Father Fenrir and began gathering the bonds.

WHEN THEY FINISHED STRAPPING Lulu in, Avain circled the chair. He tapped a finger to his cheek, and when he faced her again, he nodded to her mother. Maurelle drew a bejeweled knife that shone in the watery light filtering through the high window.

They didn't know about Alex. He was out there, somewhere. She was so glad he hadn't entered the palace alone. They'd have killed him right off. True, she could be dead in the near future. But she had faith either she or Alex would get her out of this pickle.

"I'm removing the tape," Avain said. "You start to sing, you die."

A lot of what she said would depend on their truthsense. Her mother had little. Avain? But hiding her words from someone's truthsense was one of her gifts. It worked on her aunt, so it would work on them. She hoped. She nodded, and he ripped the tape from her mouth.

"Who came with you?" he asked.

"Nobody."

"Where are the others?"

"What others?"

"Don't play stupid, girl," her mother said.

She gave her the stink eye. "I'm alone. If you mean my companions in Texas, they returned to California"

Maurelle tapped the side of the blade against her chin. "Not all. What about Charlie the fae?"

"He's dead."

"You were with the wolf in faeland a week ago."

Days had apparently passed in both realms. Not an exact match, but close enough. "Alex...died."

Avain's lip curled. "I don't believe you."

She shrugged, as much as she could bound to the chair. "Like I care what you believe? Ask Melike. She'll tell you that the Arctos wolves have been too long in the mundane world to exist for long in the magic one. The overload of magic kills them. We were there for weeks, not hours. He...he died."

"If that were true," her mother spat, "then why didn't you immediately return?"

She watched them closely, their faces full of avarice and cruelty. How much to tell? As much of the truth as she could, which is what Clea had told her once when she'd done something stupid and lied. "Before Alex died, we met Ziz there—"

Eyebrows raised, Avain chuckled. "The famed Ziz? My incredulity grows. You'll have to do better than that."

"She was on a rescue mission to find Anouk," she said. "She conscripted us. It took days before we found her."

"I don't like this," Maurelle said. "Anouk was supposed to be taken care of."

Avain's soft laugh filled the small room, his fingers caressing Maurelle's chin. "You don't really believe her dear, do you?"

Maurelle raised the dagger and plunged it into the arm of the chair, a hairsbreadth from Lulu's wrist. "Unfortunately, I do." Her mother thrust her face an inch from Lulu's. "Are they here?"

The temptation to spit right into that cruel face almost overwhelmed her. "No." She opened her mouth, about to say "we." She clamped her lips shut.

The bands on her wrists and ankles were turning her hands and feet numb. The powerlessness of her position chafed big time. But she'd been honed to sterner stuff by the woman staring at her. Maurelle had called it tough love. Lulu knew it for what it was, a love of cruelty. "I don't know where they went after Alex died."

Avain's face whitened, his nostrils flaring. "All right. Where is the chest?"

"I don't know."

Her mother's eyes narrowed. "She's lying."

The knife in her mother's hand again, the point moving closer to her face. Lulu's muscles tensed. Where would her mother cut her with the knife? "Your truthsense sucks, Mom."

The blade came closer, and her eyes glued to the tip that shined with a promise of pain.

"Sweetheart," Avain said. "We don't have time for this. Where is the chest?"

"I have no idea." She couldn't keep her eyes off the knife. So sharp, with tiny serrated teeth.

The blade moved ever closer. She held her breath. Knowing. The point pierced her flesh, her cheek, scraped bone. Pain blazed. She grunted, hands fisting, toes curling.

Cascading tears mingled with blood. Vision blurred, she watched Maurelle's smile widen, her eyes aglitter. Then pain splintered down her cheek as Maurelle carved into Lulu's face.

Her nails dug into the chair arms, her back bowed. Teeth clamped tight, she made horrible, animalistic sounds, but she wouldn't cry out. She wouldn't.

The knife's passage slow, impossibly slow, her face afire. She ached to scream, to cry, to release the pain. *Don't! Don't scar my face!*

She squeezed her eyes tight. She didn't want to stare at the monster anymore. So she pictured Alex, his beautiful, wonderful face breaking into a smile, pictured her hand touching his cheek, his hair. *Gods, it hurt so much.*

Lips tight, she bottled her screams. But she couldn't stem the flow of tears, or how those salty tears sharpened the pain on her wounded flesh. *Alex. Alex.*

The pressure eased, the knife lifted. The pain remained. It seared her skull, her brain, throbbing, biting. Warm blood coated the side of her face and slid down her neck, dripping onto her shoulder. Drip. Drip. Drip.

She lifted her lids and stared at the woman who'd cut her.

Avain glanced at her mother, then focused again on her. But Lulu hadn't missed the shadow of disgust that had darkened his eyes. "Tell us where the chest is, Lulu."

She had clamped her jaws so tight, it took an effort to make them work again. "Think, you fool. Charlie died, we split up in Texas, and the others took the chest. Alex and I came here, to fae. How should I know where it is?"

In a lightning move, the her mother's blade again pierced her cheek.

She screamed.

Avain slapped Maurelle's knife hand away from Lulu's face. "Stop!"

Lulu sucked in great gulps of air.

"Why should I? Her beauty offends me. She offends me. Such a disappointment."

He squeezed Maurelle's wrist until she dropped the knife. "Gods, woman, enough! Get yourself together. This isn't about her or you." He grabbed a dressing from the small table littered with medical supplies and dabbed it across her face. "She doesn't know!"

Lulu suspected her teeth were ghoulishly red, but it would only add to the smile she forced to her lips. It hurt so much. "Took you long enough to get it."

Her mother's fist.

A haze, and reality snapped shut.

THE ROOM SMELLED of antiseptic and anger. She awakened bundled in soft down with Avain kneeling beside her. He was looking toward the door. Her eyes were blurred, but they finally found focus. Light seeped through half-a-dozen high windows, revealing a luxe carpet, two red leather wing-back chairs and an immense flat screen. Viviane's den.

She'd only been out long enough for them to move her.

They'd put her on the large black leather sofa where her aunt most liked to lounge. Wrapped as she was, at least her blood wouldn't stain Viviane's favorite piece of furniture.

They'd again taped her mouth, and wound the tape entirely around her head.

Her cheek felt tight and hot, like someone had taken a branding iron to it. Every few seconds, pain pulsed behind her eyes. She'd bet it was Avain who'd bandaged her. She raised a hand to her face, which felt blimp-like. Gods, what a mess. She wouldn't think about what she'd look like after this was all done. That was if she lived to think about anything.

Mommy dearest was nowhere to be seen.

Something warm and vibrant washed over her, and she made sure not to react. As it cooled, it hardened to a protective shell. Not her doing, but...whose?

Avain gently tugged her hand away from her face and held it. "I wish she hadn't done that."

Bastard. He could have stopped Maurelle from her carving expedition any old time. He'd made sure to wait until she was mutilated.

A gentle finger brushed her chin.

Her stomach seized and she almost hurled. She raised an eyebrow.

"Your mother is playing with her boy toy." A smirk. "Or should I say fae toy?"

She tilted her head. This non-speaking crap sucked.

"If I remove the tape, will you promise to not open your mouth except to answer my questions?"

She nodded. Idiot. Of course, she'd lied. If she got the chance, she'd sing her brains out. All she needed was a distraction. It took her song a beat or two to catch the minds of others. Too bad she couldn't just open her mouth and wail away.

He leaned over her, his fall of white hair swirling around her, eyes wide and hungry, but he hadn't removed the tape.

A spike of fear. What if he raped her? She controlled her panic. Barely. She dug for that "don't give a fuck" attitude. If he raped her, she'd deal. She had no choice.

Clea, how do you manage this stuff?

His hands wrapped around her shoulders, tight and painful. "I want to remove this, sweetheart. I wish I could trust you."

She glared at him.

Avain opened his mouth, his fingers resting on the edge of the tape. He cut the tape and pulled it up, so her lips were exposed. "Where is the Chest of Time?"

He was using Voice.

The powerful vibrations undulated inside her and hit that shell encasing her. They bounced off. She had no compulsion to answer him. None.

Gods, don't laugh.

She sucked in a huge breath of air, then shook her head.

His jaw hardened and his cheeks grew flushed. "Speak, dammit. Where is the Chest of Time?"

Nope. Didn't affect her one bit. She shrugged, making sure her eyes were wide with cluelessness.

His hands bit into her shoulders. "You know where it is, girl. Stop fighting and answer me." He shook her like a rag doll.

A shriek from down the hall.

He tilted his head.

Silence.

Avain sprang to his feet. As he moved away, Lulu plucked the sheathed knife from his waist.

Thank you gods!

Lulu hacked at the tape until it parted, and she ripped it off her face, taking the bandage with it. Pain sliced her cheek again.

She opened her mouth to sing.

ALEX HAD GATHERED the bonds meticulously, thread by thread. When the pressure inside him peaked, he exploded, sending waves of power across the bond and into Melike.

Depleted, he staggered for a second, gathered himself, and crashed through the window.

Screeches and shouts, growls and howls.

Shards of glass flew around him when he landed on his forepaws, his hindquarters collapsing.

A howl shattered the silence. Melike's. She surged to her feet, raised her arms, and pulled, eyes on fire, lips a feral grin. The chains stretched taught and broke. But she had to break her leg chains, too.

Maurelle darted into the room and pressed her back against the wall.

A goblin strode toward Melike. Alex got his hindquarters beneath him, said a quick prayer to Father Fenrir, and leapt.

He slammed into the goblin's back, knocking him sideways.

"Kill them!" Maurelle commanded.

Riding the goblin, he dug his claws into its shoulders, while his teeth ripped into its neck. *Yippee-ki-yay*!

The goblin thrashed back and forth, trying to dislodge him, its clawed hands reaching for his sides.

Blood filled his mouth, almost choking him. He slipped, hung on, claws digging deeper and deeper into its meaty flesh. The goblin's hands reached him, and its talons scored his ribs. The pain pushed him to clamp down harder as he whipped his head back and forth.

Another howl from Melike, then a shriek.

Powerful arms banded around him, squeezed, and pulled.

He clenched his jaws tight, and as he was tossed off the goblin, the creature's spine snapped. He flew across the room, thudding into a wall. Agony radiated outward, head dizzy, vision strobing to black.

If he passed out, he was dead.

Ribs broken or cracked, it didn't matter. He slumped to the floor, spat goblin meat and blood, and panted, barely able to catch his breath. Blackness crept closer. He stumbled to his feet. Didn't make it.

Done. Except he had to get to Lulu. Where was she? He struggled to rise. Fuck. Darkness almost took him.

A roar in his ears.

He blinked again, knowing too well he was fodder for the second goblin.

Except the roar continued. Not in his head. *Someone* was roaring. Man, he was half out of it. The fae. Some moved around the room, releasing fellow fae from their manacles.

Two goblins sprawled in the center of the room. Well, not two *complete* goblins. The one he'd killed lay facedown in a pool of blood. The other was in shreds.

His eyes found Melike.

Maurelle was raising her knife, while Melike kneeled before her, weeping. Why the hell was the fierce... Fuck! Maurelle could affect emotion and drown the receiver in sorrow, anger, whatever she wanted.

He had to break it. Had to, or Melike was dead.

He barked a command, while jerking the pack bond between he and Melike. Her head flew upward, just as Maurelle's knife plunged.

Melike sprang back, screaming epithets.

He kept the bond tightened and infused what little strength that remained to him into Melike.

She sprang forward and buried her claws in Maurelle's chest.

Pain rippled across Maurelle's face and she held up her hands. "Back!"

Another pulse from him.

"*Non!*" Melike said, and dug her claws in deeper.

"Die!" Maurelle said, even as she fell to her knees.

"*Non, you* die." The clawed paw dug deeper still and with a powerful pull, she ripped Maurelle's heart from her chest. She bent over the dead woman, ripping Maurelle to pieces.

He howled a command.

She hesitated, finally turned, her eyes seeking him out.

He howled again.

She gave him teeth, but stood and limped across the room. She kneeled beside him. "You look like shit."

His toothy grin brought an answering smile.

"Thanks for the boost, Alpha." The hand she lay on him trembled.

"Need some help here!" Neddy shouted.

Neddy? What the fuck?

Crashes! Wood, glass, and metal rained around him.

23

_____

Avain whipped back around, slamming one hand across Lulu's mouth while his other tore the knife from her.

He slapped the tape over her mouth again, wrapped one hand around both of her wrists, and began to drag her from the room.

She fought, kicking, twisting, but the stupid mage was strong as a goblin.

Using her as a shield, his right arm thrust forward, he splayed one hand outward.

He was going to shoot his deadly needles.

She dug her nails into his wrist, got one hand free, and squeezed his balls so hard she hoped they'd fall off.

"You bitch!" Bent almost in half, he backhanded her. "I shielded you from your harpy mother! I would have been good to you. Taken care of you. Now we've got company, and you're excess baggage. Die!"

She flew over the chair and thudded against a wall. He flung his raised hand upward and out.

A barrage of steel needles arced toward her with deadly purpose.

Lulu curled into herself, shielded her head with her hands,

knowing that was faint cover from the death arrowing toward her.

Time slowed, as if the world held its breath.

Alex. She wanted Alex. To see him one more time. To kiss him. To hold him and feel his warm flesh beneath her fingers. To love him.

Just once more.

She straightened. If she was going to die, she'd do it staring at her killer. She filled her eyes with burning fury, with arrogance and disdain. So he would know that defeat would find him.

A shower of golden motes flew into the room, forming a cabled "crossroads" stitch. It became a fisherman's net of light so bright Lulu had to narrow her eyes. The brilliance grew, encompassing Avain's steel needles in a blazing seine.

The net dissipated and the needles fell to the floor.

"I'm rusty, dammit!" A voice from the corridor, one she knew. Her heart hitched. *Is Clea really here?*

"You can do this," growled a second voice in granite tones. Larrimer.

Avain flipped around to face the doorway, flashing hundreds of needles.

Her heart caught, then thrilled when the net reformed, all dancing cables and shimmering light capturing Avain's needles.

Lulu pushed to her feet, the head rush making her sway.

The needles fought the net. As Avain's face purpled, the tendons in his neck stretched tight.

A woman stepped into the room, petite and thin, blonde hair crazy as always.

Clea! Joy shot through her. Clea was *back*. She'd been the one to shield her from his Voice.

She wore a small smile, her eyes focused on Avain. "Having issues, Mage?" she said in that sultry voice of hers.

Lulu almost giggled.

Avain drew his knife and launched himself at Lulu's former guardian.

While Clea's right hand held Avain's captured needles, she

raised her left and more motes appeared. She froze him, just *froze* him mid-leap. *Holy macarena!* Awesome didn't describe it.

"Aw, poor Avain," Clea said. "You've been outgunned."

Larrimer appeared behind Clea. "Feeling a little redundant here."

Clea tilted her head. "Never, babycakes."

"Dammit, Clea, don't—"

Cassius barreled into the room. Behind him, a filthy, bloodied wolf charged through the door and leapt, barreling into Avain, the two hovering mid-air, the creature's jaws wide, teeth a-glisten, blood frozen mid-drip from its maw.

Clea fisted her hand. With a thud, the pair dropped to the floor, biting, clawing, stabbing.

Alex.

"Don't fucking kill him!" Larrimer's barked words were ignored as they rolled across the floor.

Lulu sprang toward the pair.

Before she completed her jump, Larrimer ripped Avain away, while Cassius wrapped his arms around Alex's torso and pulled. Flesh from Avain's forearm dangled from Alex's clamped teeth.

Alex howled in fury, while Avain's scream of pain almost deafened Lulu.

Larrimer clocked Avain, effectively shutting him up.

Lulu ran to Alex, who snapped at her. She wasn't having it, so she pressed her hands to each side of his wolfie jaws and captured his eyes.

"I'm okay." She rubbed her nose to his. "We're both *okay*."

Sentience slowly appeared in his eyes. He sighed.

Cassius placed him on the floor and released him. Alex's hindquarters buckled.

His wolf's tongue snaked out and licked her good cheek, then his body gave out.

How injured was he? She sat beside him and he lay his head on her lap. His eyes closed, and he slept.

I TOOK A DEEP BREATH, fisted my right hand, motes vanishing. The adrenaline receded, and I slumped back against James. I was light-headed. I might have been practicing at the den, but the real thing had wiped me out.

"You okay, babe?" James said.

I nodded and folded my legs to sit on the floor beside Lulu. What had they done to her? I stared at her ruined cheek. *Bastards.*

Cassius swiped one of James' katanas.

James roared.

"Cassius, no!" I hollered.

The blade arced down and Avain's severed head toppled to the floor.

The goblin stared at me with dark, implacable eyes.

I reached for Lulu, who wrapped her arms around me, hugging me in a death grip. I squeaked.

"Sorry! Oh, Clea," she said through a sobbed breath. "You're back."

"And none too soon, it appears," I said.

Lulu laughed and straightened, one hand still stroking Alex's head. The other lifted my hand and pressed it to her good cheek.

The deep gash scoring her from temple to chin oozed blood. My eyes burned with fury and sorrow. "I'd like to bring that fucker back and kill him again."

She wouldn't meet my eyes, just shrugged.

"Your scar will match James's," I said. "Pretty damned dashing, if you ask me."

She smiled. "Love you, too."

CHARTERED PLANES ROCKED. Lulu sat on a leather couch, half her face covered in bandages. Beside her sprawled Alex, his head resting on her belly. She'd bathed him in his wolf form. He hadn't changed back to his human one, which worried her. He'd tolerated his bath, but he wasn't himself, wasn't really present.

So much joy. So much sorrow. The fae had lost more than a

dozen men and women in the days since Avain and Maurelle's arrival. The pair had been smart. They'd first captured a young fae child and used her as leverage to take Viviane prisoner. Once they'd bound and imprisoned the queen, they threatened the fierce fae warriors with their queen's and the child's deaths unless the fae put down their weapons. To insure the fae's complete compliance, they'd imprisoned the remaining children and the few elderly next, binding them with spells Avain had stolen in the magic realm.

When Clea, Larrimer, Rae, and the pack first arrived, they'd freed a sadly weakened Viviane. They'd left Rae breaking the other-worldly spells that held the children and the others, while the rest had taken out the two-dozen creatures Avain and Maurelle had brought with them. During the fight, they'd lost another fae, as well as Alex's third, Leon and one other wolf. Viviane had reascended her throne. She was wobbly, as were the rest of the fae, but they'd recover. Iron Heart had survived, a steadying presence, as had Ozille. The fae were like gristle, tough through and through.

Every time Lulu thought about her mother's death, she pushed it away. There could have been so much good between them, so much positive, so much love. There hadn't been any of that, but it would take years for her lump of sorrow to dissipate.

Thank the gods for Clea's love.

Her aunt had wanted Lulu to remain in Charleston, but home was with her loved ones—Alex and Clea, Neddy and Larrimer, Melike, Rae, and the pack.

Lulu smoothed her hand down Alex's fur. She wanted him to wake up, to change to human, to talk to her. Forcing herself not to push, she let him be. The deep sadness she sensed within him worried her.

Would his injuries be permanent? Would he ever regain his full strength? Could a crippled man be Alpha?

Neddy flopped down beside her on the couch holding a double deck of cards. "Wanna play Spite and Malice?"

Alex didn't even twitch.

"Love to. Prepare to face your doom."

THREE MONTHS LATER, I walked down the corridor toward Lulu's rooms. The den smelled of honeysuckle. It wafted in from the trellises by the huge glass sliders overlooking Griffith Park, the pack's playground. I'd been busy since our return from Charleston. Everyone had. And my fingers had only recently resettled on the pulse of the den. I was unhappy with much of what I felt.

Something was coming. I'd had one of those weird fugue states, where I felt and saw stuff. Huge, distorted shapes attacking, a winged creature shadowing the sky, the fabric of time ripping, and a woman and child on broken pavement, bloodied and dead.

Where? When?

That was the problem—I had no idea.

Lulu and Alex... Things weren't good, and I needed to understand why. Alex had only recovered the partial use of his legs, but I knew my Lulu. She didn't care. She loved the guy. He loved her, scars and all. Nonetheless, the two of them danced around each other like circus performers, never touching, yet always in the other's orbit. Their dance was making the entire den twitchy. No one said a damned thing.

Time to find out why and see if I could help fix things.

I carried my precious copy of *The Once and Future King*, my mentor's last gift to me. The perfect bribe to gain entry to Lulu's *sanctum sanctorum*.

My alleged business today with Lu revolved around our new cottage. James and I had leased it from the den, two doors down from the main compound. Two bedrooms, one of which Neddy occupied most nights, a sweet great room-kitchen, and a tiny den that housed our computers. The garden out back was where James was building a hut, hauling rocks, and doing other mysterious things. Beyond that spread the wildness of Griffith Park.

Small and perfect, it was all ours. Given Neddy's appropriation of our second bedroom, the great room thankfully sat like an oasis between the two bedroom suites. We'd just moved in and were painting. Neddy and Lulu helped, and even little Izzy gave it a go, though she got more paint on herself than the walls. But Lulu was locked down tighter than a Brinks truck, and I was done with that. She might be all grown up, but I still considered myself her de facto mom.

I rounded a corner, lifted my hand to Lu's door, when raised voices echoed through the corridor. Melike and Carlos. *Again.* I tried to ignore it. I really did. But when something breakable smashed against a wall, I turned in time to see Melike slam the door behind her and race down the hall. Shit.

Carlos. He'd become a problem. A big one.

Knowing their son Bron was in school, I knocked on their door. "Carlos?"

"Fuck off!"

In for a penny, as they say. I pressed down the handle and entered.

Whoa. Carlos' emotional fury pounded me. I beelined for the leather sofa and planted my ass. Anger and fear, disgust and shame battered my empath senses. I slammed up my shields and took a breath.

The once-pristine apartment lay in shambles. Ripped books and broken ceramics were scattered across the floor. Dings and cuts dappled the wall decorated with wood carvings and weapons, some of which were missing. Spider-webbed cracks covered the exquisite glass-topped coffee table that sat on a Turkish rug dappled with... blood? Beneath the destroyed glass, broken carved trout lay flat, where they used to swim in a gorgeous 3-D rendition of a stream. Damaged, but not beyond repair I hoped.

A red-cheeked and fuming Carlos paced across the room, glaring at me—T-shirt ripped, jeans stained, so unlike his usual carefully curated self. He'd cut off his gorgeous blond locks into a skull-hugging buzz, and in his hand he fisted a ten-inch knife that glistened in the light from the sliders. "Get out."

His growl didn't scare me, though I wasn't thrilled about the knife. Sure, I could fend him off with my fireflies, but would I be quick enough if he started to self harm?

"I'm feeling a little dizzy here, Carlos. Give me a sec."

His face tightened. "I'll get you some water, then you leave."

In minutes, he thrust a glass at me, water sloshing over the sides as I took it with a "thank you." I patted the sofa. "Why not take a load off, eh?"

"Anything for you, *amiga*," he said, his sarcasm vicious. His lip curled, but he sat. "I know you. You want me to pour out my troubles so you can fix me up with a bandage of your words. Fat chance."

"Are you broken, Carlos?"

"Fuck, no."

"So then if we're friends, why can't we talk?"

He sneered. "Because you're *her* friend, my *puta's*."

Bitch? Whore? *That* was what he'd called his beloved wife? I'd heard rumblings of this. Typical Melike, she wouldn't talk about it, either. She told me she'd handle it. Obviously it wasn't being handled.

"Melike was not raped."

His eyes glowed with the wolf. "Lies. She should just admit it. Those fae touched my woman. Fucked her. I know it."

"Let's just say they had. Why should it matter, Carlos? She was their prisoner."

He reared back, grabbed my book, and threw it. My precious book zoomed toward the carving of their family, the one that included their dead child, Paul, to smack into Melike's sculpted head.

Fury bubbled inside me. I retrieved my book and brushed it off. The spine had detached from its binding. I glared at him.

He stormed over and spat in my face.

A calming breath later, I said, "You have some level of truth-sense. All the wolves do. It shouldn't matter, but Melike was not raped. You must be able to tell I'm not lying."

For a moment, the burn in his wolf eyes cleared. I read confusion and sorrow and near unbearable pain. Was it the wolf producing this rancid point of view? I didn't think so. Something inside Carlos had broken with their son Paul's death. He hadn't been able to save his son. Nor had he been able to prevent Melike's capture, which had only widened the break. His pain had finally overruled his rationality.

It wasn't in Carlos' power to do anything about either of those events. I knew that. He knew that. Everyone knew that.

All of which was immaterial to Carlos' point of view.

He banded a hand around my upper arm tight enough to bruise and hauled me to the door. "It matters. It is her fault and yours, too. You allowed her capture."

"Melike is a soldier. You—" His hand on my arm tightened. Pain squeezed my lungs. He could snap my arm in two.

"It was your fault," he said, eyes wild. "And our alpha's."

"If that's how you see it, let's go talk to Alex."

"Oh, I'll go see him all right." He laughed as he opened the door and shoved me outside hard enough to slam me into the opposite wall. My head rang and my arm throbbed. After a few seconds composing myself, I headed for Alex's office.

"Clea!" James walked down the hall toward me, a frown writ large on his face. "I've been looking for you, babe. Are you in pain?"

"I'll be all right."

"There's been another Event, one in Italy."

Was that the "something coming" I'd been worried about? "What happened?"

"There are these circular houses in Italy, with these conical roofs—"

"The trulli? I know of them. They're amazing."

He swiped a hand across his jaw. "Overnight they and the inhabitants were covered in vegetation and vines. Seemingly unbreakable vines."

"People hurt? Dead?"

"We don't know. We assume so. I'm heading out with my team to investigate and offer support."

I took his hand and sighed. "When will you be back?"

He smoothed my hair. "I don't know."

A WEEK LATER, I sat at a small table at The Coffee Bean in Los Feliz nursing my cocoa. The Union had been quiet, although a shiver rippled through me at the thought of Balfour and his agenda. "Creepy" was an understatement for the transformation James had described. Thankfully, Tatianne hadn't sent any of her minions after us, and I hoped the debilitating loss of my brother had crippled her in the mundane realm. Since the Italian Event, no other Events had occurred around the world until this morning in Germany.

My gut knew something *else* was coming. Too bad I'd failed Psychic Predictions 101.

James had just set down at LAX. He'd been gone for a week—a *very* long week, indeed. When he phoned that he'd landed, he'd asked if I'd be greeting him at home wearing my lacy bits.

I'd planned on it. Longed for it.

But this morning's Event in Germany shocked the world. Held in Hohenstein-Ernstthal, the German motorcycle Grand Prix final was reaching its climax when the entire stadium full of enthusiasts rose into the sky and disappeared. The contestants on the track were unaffected, and it actually took them a while to realize what had happened. When I heard the news, I'd been driven to come here and listen to the tenor of what mundanes were saying, unfiltered by news broadcasters or the web.

The coffee shop was cheery, with positive energy. Mundanes filled the popular spot, with a sprinkling of wolves and a fae I didn't know.

Terrible and strange as it was, I wouldn't call Germany a Big Event, not like the huge fissures that had opened around the world when I'd been "gone." But it was the prime topic here at the coffee shop. Customers were asking lots of questions, not to mention pundits opining, preachers talking End of Days, and everything in between.

When would anyone make the announcement to the mundane world that the magic and mundane realms were retwining? Apparently no one from the magic realm, which knew all about it, had uttered a peep. Neither had any mundane government, many of whom I presumed knew. Why had no one in a position of importance done so?

"I'm scared, Roger," said the pale woman sitting a table over from me.

Roger chuckled. "Revelation? End of Days? It's probably some movie stunt."

"No." The woman stabbed at her croissant with a fork. "It was real."

"That's not what the networks are saying."

The official media was spin doctoring. Why?

These Events reminded me of pimples. They would spring up, pop, then everything seemingly went back to normal.

"What about all those awful fissures seven months ago, huh?" she said.

He took a sip of his latte. "San Andreas fault? Hello?"

"You never take this stuff seriously." The woman's face turned mulish.

Roger shrugged. "I'm up for a part as the starship captain in that pilot they're shooting next week."

She twirled the pastry on the end of her fork. "Big deal."

Roger tossed some bills on the table and stood. "Couldn't you for once be supportive?" He stalked out.

James walked in, the guy giving him a wide berth. Joy cascaded through me. He was safe. He was here. I was happy.

He didn't look so happy, though, his face carved in taut lines.

"How did it go?" I said.

"It went well. Better than expected." He slipped into the seat across from me, and I pointed to the roast beef sandwich I'd ordered for him.

"Then what's wrong?" I said.

He glanced at the food, leaned forward, and took me in a long, hot kiss. Our song began, and much as I hated to, I hastily ended our lip lock.

"You should have met me at home," he said.

His growled words had a few patrons looking our way.

"I explained why. I've learned a lot sitting here."

He grunted, and took a bite of his sandwich. "Did you get the couch? I'm tired of sitting on camp chairs."

"No, I didn't." I crossed my arms, narrowed my eyes. "We have our new bungalow, and it deserves our making choices as a couple. Like normal people."

He smiled, his snort of laughter attracting even more attention.

"Fine," I hissed in a low voice. "We're not that normal." *But I'd like us to be.* I didn't say it, but he knew that was behind my insistence on renting a home of our own, getting furniture, planning a vacation.

Those Pacific blues softened. He rose and held out a hand. I took it, and he pulled me to his side, his arm wrapping around my shoulder. He kissed the top of my head. "Okay. We'll get a couch today. On one condition."

It felt better than good to be tucked under his arm. "What's that?"

He bent down so his hot breath tickled my ear. "That we make love on it first thing."

I melted. "Deal."

We stepped toward the door just as Lulu flew inside. "Clea! Larrimer! I need you!"

TWO MEN SQUARED off in the pack's huge basement gym.

One stood erect leaning on a cane, the other with his fists clamped on his hips, chest heaving. Alex and Carlos.

Lulu had told me what had passed between them, and about Alex's injuries in the magic realm, which had worsened after his battles in faeland. His recovery, both physical and spiritual, had been imperceptible, even with Rae's healing help. He rarely laughed and shadows often darkened his eyes. He despised using the cane. I rubbed my forehead. Now *this*.

Melike stood beside Carlos, her mate. Lulu hovered next to me, and her compulsion to stand beside Alex tickled my flesh. But she wouldn't act on it. She and Alex had barely spoken in the months since our return from faeland—Alex's damned pride. It was killing my Lu. I wanted to kick the dumb wolf in his butt. He'd shut Lulu down, effectively closing that door with a finality that made Lulu despair. So she stood beside me, shaking with fury and fear.

"*Non, mon amour!*" Melike said, facing her husband with her legs akimbo, arms on Carlos' shoulders. "Do not do this." Her accent had thickened, an obvious sign of her distress.

Impossible to forget the conversation I'd had with Carlos. He blamed Melike for the alleged rape, blamed me. Most of all, he blamed Alex. But I had no idea what had precipitated this confrontation.

I wanted to stop it so bad I could taste it.

The pack surrounded them, giving them plenty of space for what was to come. James had cleared a path to the front of the crowd for the three of us, and given James' dominance, no pack member had protested. Erick stood beside Alex, presumably to act as his second. A wolf I didn't know well, Bart, stood next to Carlos, on his opposite side.

"*She* touched her lips to my boy's chest," Carlos said to Alex.

Christmas. This was about Bron and Isobel. The pack had pretty much adopted the little vampyre girl after Izzy had been taken from The Union's clutches. Always a serious child, she helped out, willingly did chores, laughed only occasionally, and remained very "other." That was okay. I was plenty "other," too, as were several pack members. I liked her a lot, and she was learning civilized behavior—a girl who wanted to be good, having known little but torment in her young life. She and Bron were of an age and playmates. Izzy knew to never touch pack, and obeyed, mostly.

"Did Izzy hurt your son?" Alex said in a low, reasonable voice.

James' fury slapped my empath senses. I stood on tiptoe and whispered. "James, where's this going?"

He leaned down, close enough so the wolves wouldn't hear. "Carlos is going to challenge Alex for Alpha."

"But Alex can't!"

His hot breath on my ear. "He must."

"Answer me," Alex said, his voice a command, though his tone remained low and even.

"No, she did not harm him," Carlos said. "But that isn't the point. We agreed that she would not touch our children."

"No harm came to Bron," Alex said. "She's a child, and children make mistakes."

As clear as day I read Alex's thoughts about three of the pack's children, one of whom was Carlos' and Melike's Paul, who'd sadly made fatal mistakes less than a year earlier.

"You will get rid of her," Carlos said.

This was all posturing. Carlos knew Alex would do no such thing. Lulu squeezed my arm. She knew, too.

"I will not," Alex said. "She is pack now, and no threat."

Carlos took a step forward. "Challenge."

Alex's fury boiled over me, hot enough for me to dig my nails into James' forearm. The two-hundred-plus wolves in the room reacted, too, many with growls of anger at what Carlos was attempting with their injured alpha.

"Carlos, my friend," Alex said, "think about what you're setting into motion."

When Alex had returned home from Charleston, he took the pack's consensus. Not a vote, really, but rather a drawing on the pack to choose whether he should continue as alpha or not. Except for Carlos and a few others, they stood behind him one-hundred percent.

Carlos' challenge was more than a simple insult, but one aimed at the whole pack. Yet any pack wolf above the age of eighteen could challenge the alpha. Everyone knew his indignation about Izzy was simply an excuse. Carlos' anger was all about Melike, and her perceived violation.

Alex waited, and I suspected he was hoping Carlos would withdraw his challenge. He cared for Carlos. He cared for all his pack.

Carlos stepped closer and spat at his alpha's feet. "I repeat, Challenge."

"Accepted," Alex said.

Carlos smiled. "*Hasta la muerte.*"

"No!" Melike said.

For a moment, I was pounded by Alex's anger. He didn't *want* to fight Carlos. He didn't want to have to kill him. More growls and murmurs from the crowd, but theirs was all about the fear of losing their alpha.

"Can Alex call upon pack bonds to help?" I asked James.

"Not allowed."

"What can we do?" Lulu said.

"Nothing," James said. "This is pack business."

Lulu puffed out her chest. "We're pack."

James nodded. "Which means you can't interfere. Rules, Lulu. Rules."

"Forget it." She tossed her head and stepped forward.

I laid a hand on her shoulder. "Lu, don't. Alex wouldn't want it. You know that. This is his business as alpha."

She quieted. "For now."

Alex handed his cane to Erick, who whispered something in Alex's ear. Alex snapped him a nod.

The crowd was restless, unhappy. They loved their alpha, who'd led them well and long. They didn't want to lose him. But to a wolf, they wouldn't interfere.

The alpha's eyes glowed that gorgeous ancient gold, wolf ascendant. "Are you sure you wish to the death, Carlos?"

Carlos raised his arm toward Alex and fisted his hand. "I *demand* it."

They ripped into each other.

24

They fought as wolves. Carlos's growls and snarls rang through the gym. Alex was deadly quiet. I'd seen the wolves fight before, in training exercises and at play. This was different.

Claws and fangs ripped and tore. They broke apart, sides heaving, open mouthed, teeth red with the other's blood. Carlos' chocolate fur made it difficult to tell how badly he was injured. Alex's white coat was streaked crimson. Each was injured badly enough that their blood dripped to the floor, where it began to pool beneath them.

They rose, clashed, each going for the other's throat, but at the last minute, Alex twisted in an impossible move and sank his teeth into Carlos' flank, then snapped his head upward, flipping Carlos onto his back.

Alex leapt, except his back leg collapsed. He stumbled, tottering to the left. Carlos took the moment to twist onto his feet. He backed away, sides heaving.

Alex's wolf was limping and long red runnels stained the flanks of his coat as he circled the other wolf, who appeared no worse for his injuries. This was bad. Very, very bad.

I swallowed, throat dry. My heart constricted. I might actually lose my friend, a man who'd stood by me so many, many times. I wanted to rub my chest, but forced myself not to. Alex could die. He could really die. Until this moment, that hadn't seemed possible.

I wanted to close my eyes and turn away, unable to bear the pain of watching my dear friend's death. But I would never do him that disservice.

The crowd's emotions, their fear, buffeted me. I wobbled. James snugged me to his side, and his sea of calm reached out to me. I steadied.

Carlos leapt for Alex's throat. Slowed by his injuries, Alex didn't move fast enough to avoid Carlos' jaws as he soared through the air.

LULU'S MUSCLES locked at the relentless, unending pain. When they'd cut her face, scarred her, that hurt less than watching this.

Clea's hand squeezed her shoulder, and the pain receded enough for her to think.

She had to stop the fight. If she didn't, Alex would die. They were fated, even if since their return he'd pushed and nipped and harried her away. She'd swear it was due to his injuries, him thinking he was lesser. Or maybe it was something else, something she'd done. She didn't care. She loved him. He'd said she was his mate. Said so.

Carlos leapt into the air.

No! Oh, no, please.

She'd sing them to sleep. All of them. And then she and Alex could leave, go somewhere, be together, love one another.

Lulu parted her lips to sing.

Clea clamped her hand behind Lulu's neck. "You can't," Clea said.

She was panting like a wolf. Clea was right. Of course she couldn't sing. Alex wouldn't want that. Not even a little. But he was her one-and-only. And he was about to die!

Carlos, airborne, jaws wide, arced toward Alex's throat. To end him. Unacceptable.

She couldn't feel the bond. So what. She fisted her hands, gathered all her strength, and imagined it flowing into Alex.

Carlos' jaws snapped over Alex's throat.

Except Alex gracefully slid away, so Carlos only ended up with a hunk of fur between his teeth. Carlos' momentum caused him to tumble forward. Alex flipped around and leapt. He plowed into Carlos' side, tipping him over, to cover the brown wolf with his larger body, jaws spread wide around Carlos' throat.

"No!" screamed Melike.

Alex hesitated.

Carlos stilled. Then he lifted his jaw inches higher, exposing more of his throat, and nodded.

THE HUSH of the crowd nearly deafened Alex. It was obvious Carlos wanted death-by-Alpha. He stared at that bare, submissive throat, and saliva flooded his mouth, Alex's wolf hungry for the kill.

Too fucking easy. Carlos had once been a good man, stalwart and fair. Tragedy had twisted him into this. He might yet be salvageable. Alex's wolf fought him, demanding the kill. But any good shifter was more than his animal, even one as exceptional as his.

Mind-to-mind he told Carlos to stay. Victory was his, and Carlos wouldn't test him again.

It took Alex two tries before he finally struggled onto his four paws. Standing, his head wove back and forth, surveying the crowd, gold eyes dimmed with pain and sorrow, but his gaze held the might of an alpha.

He was exhausted, half-dead. Would anyone else challenge him?

Not one pack member moved.

He gathered the pack magic, and carved the rune of transformation into Carlos' muzzle with a claw on his right paw. Because of the magic, the wound would scar both the wolf and the man. An ancient ritual, seldom used.

Carlos never moved.

Alex then howled a cry of victory.

The pack joined in, both those in wolf and human form, while each and every pack member kneeled and bowed his or her head, including Melike. Carlos began to rise.

Alex cut his eyes to the wolf and demanded he stay put, which he damned well did. He began to sing the song of the pack, the others joining in. When the last note dissolved, Alex nodded, and the crowd rose.

He backed off the supine Carlos, changed, and towered over the wounded wolf. Injuries scored Alex's body, his blood dripping like a metronome onto the other wolf's belly.

"Change," Alex commanded.

With a startled look, Carlos transformed to his human form. He braced his arm on the floor, as if to rise.

"Stay down," Alex said.

"What the—"

"Do not speak." His eyes panned the crowd, their mumblings and mutterings a symphony of confusion. "Silence."

He raised a hand. "You Carlos Arctos have earned death by challenging your alpha and failing to win the challenge." The crowd hushed, and he prayed he'd made the right and proper choice. "Rather than give you the death you seek, I banish you from the Arctos pack."

"No!" Carlos shouted, stumbling to his feet.

"Yes. I have marked you with the rune of transformation. We are Arctic wolves, after all, and we retain some of the old ways." He focused on the defeated man. "This is your turning point, Carlos. Your choice. To trust and believe and become the better you. Or to travel further down your path of destruction."

Alex's legs were beginning to fail, and it hurt to dig so deep for the power to remain standing and to perform the banishment. His Lu was there, lending him her strength. He wondered if she knew, or if her giving was unconscious. He straightened to his full height and fisted his hands, and with his wolf ascending he burned his eyes into Carlos'.

With a rip in his heart and a profound resolve he said, "You are banished!" and cut the thread tethering Carlos to the pack and to himself.

Carlos screamed, his back bowed, his face a rictus of agony.

Alex and his entire pack gave Carlos their backs, faces tight with the pain they also felt at Carlos' severing.

Except Melike. From the corner of his eye he saw her move toward her injured mate.

Would she deny him? Or would she leave alongside him?

Long minutes passed, the mood in the room darkening.

Carlos finally spoke. "Come with me, *querida*."

Silence. Shuffling feet.

"Come," he repeated.

Alex felt Melike's tug on their Alpha-pack bond. She wanted his witness. That, he could do. He turned to face the couple.

Carlos' arm hung loosely by his side, his ripped and scored flesh bleeding onto the floor. The banished wolf's chocolate eyes had deepened to black. They held a question.

"Come." Carlos raised a hand to Melike.

Melike smiled. "Ah, so you now want damaged goods, *non*? A woman who's been had by another. *Oui*?"

"No," Carlos said. "I will try to get past th—"

"Will you now, mate of my life, father of my children? Bah! Whether I was raped or not, you should have cared for me, loved me, cherished me. Instead, you broke trust with me. Me! Your mate! Your love! *Non*, I will never again utter those sweet words or hold you or comfort you. You are not worthy. *Tu es mort pour moi et Bron*. Dead to us. Now and forever."

Melike wrapped her arms around herself and screamed.

His packmate's pain slammed into Alex. Melike had just cut her mate bond to Carlos.

The banished wolf's eyes rolled back in his head and he collapsed to the floor.

ALL I COULD THINK WAS Alex would live. He would live. Thank the gods. Woozy from the emotions buffeting the room—the crowd's emotional avalanche—I swayed.

The arm James snugged around my waist steadied me. "Whoa. Better. Thank you."

Carlos was banished. I couldn't believe Alex had won. But at that last moment, when Carlos had been about to grab Alex's throat, I'd felt Lulu's power pour from her body. Had that done it? Given Alex the strength to escape Carlos' deadly charge? I suspected we'd never know.

Melike marched from the hall, spine rigid, head held high and proud, when I knew she must be dying inside. I stood, planning to go to her.

"No," James said.

"But—"

"She needs time and privacy, Clea, for herself and for her son."

I sighed. "Of course you're right." I sat back down as two shifter soldiers lifted Carlos from the pool of blood where he'd collapsed and carried him out a different exit from the one Melike had taken.

The whole thing was awful. Unnecessary. A waste of good people whose pain now saturated the air. I struggled to understand Carlos and failed.

Alex's eyes bored into James, held his gaze. Alex nodded. James returned the nod. Murmurs and surprise, then cheers blasted through the gym.

"What just happened?" I said to James.

"Alex asked me to join the pack. I accepted."

"Holy cow." Unprecedented. He kissed my temple.

"Tonight we party," Alex said. "To renew pack bonds, to remember a man who once was a vital member of our pack, and to welcome a new pack member."

Amidst more cheers, the pack swarmed their alpha.

AN HOUR LATER, Lulu marched toward the infirmary, determination in every stride. Alex would talk to her. He would face their relationship. He would admit he was crazy about her.

No. That wasn't productive. Instead, she'd use a logical approach to enumerate the reasons it would be smart for Alex to reopen their communication channels. She wouldn't mention how her heart was dying by inches. Or how he'd been behaving like a stubborn ass. She was convinced for some wacko, alpha reason he saw himself as "less." She had to make him see that he was so much more than the physical to her. Infinitely more.

She turned a corner and entered the infirmary. She expected to see at least Carlos there, but five empty beds met her eyes. Banishment must also mean instantaneous. Alex wasn't there, either.

That wolf. Of course he wouldn't go to the infirmary. Too public. She made a u-turn for his rooms...and faced Melike.

"Oh!" she said.

Melike's swollen eyes narrowed. "You."

"Um, yes?"

Melike's right hand turned furry, long black claws springing from flesh. She raised the paw to Lulu's eyes. "Maybe your boyfriend would like a matching scar on your other cheek, eh? If you hadn't run away, all would be different."

Lulu fought the urge to touch her scarred cheek. Clea called her ravaged face a badge of honor. Perhaps. Either way, she'd own her scars, every last inch of them.

Except the one on her heart hurt so bad. Where was that damned wolf?

At the best of times, Melike was frightening. Now, with her teeth bared and her claws centimeters from Lulu's face, she was a lit stick of dynamite. And she was in such pain. Lulu wrapped her hand around Melike's paw. It was huge and warm, tipped with three-inch claws. "Would it really have ended differently, Melike?"

"*Oui! Non.* Perhaps." Her eyes flared. "You cheated. You helped the alpha."

"Honestly? I tried." She'd tried so hard, but she doubted she'd been successful. Their bond hadn't formed. Not from her end, at least. "We're not mated. It was desire and nothing else."

Melike scraped a claw down Lulu's unblemished cheek, her eyes shadowed with confusion, as if she warred between hatred and sorrow.

"You're hurting and angry," Lulu said. "But is it at Alex? Or at me? You lost your mate because he failed to believe in you. I was there in fae, remember. I know the truth." She stood very still, her fingers twined together, shaking. "But whether you'd been raped or not, Carlos should have loved you and trusted in you. He didn't."

Melike's face darkened.

"And you chose, Melike. You made the tough choice to break the mate bond, and it was a righteous one, though it must hurt like a son-of-a-bitch. You deserve more."

Melike's face turned inhuman, canines and jaw lengthening. "You dare?"

She flinched. "No, not really. You're scary. I'm a bit of mess, too. But that's the truth."

Her eyes flashed with her wolf. "Where's the alpha?"

"Here."

Alex stood behind Melike, one hand resting on a bone-handled cane. His eyes glowed bright with compassion and strength. He was alone. Vulnerable. Black-and-blue, with cuts on his face and arms. Melike, a far stronger fighter than Carlos, could take him out.

Lulu gasped, wanted to protect him. By not killing Carlos, Alex had forced Melike to choose. Weakened by the fight, alpha or no, Melike might go for revenge.

He wouldn't appreciate Lulu's interference.

Alex pulled his powerful dominance to the fore and rested a hand on Melike's arm. "Why don't we go talk."

Beneath that commanding gaze, Melike softened. Her hand, no longer clawed, took his.

"Alex, I..." Lulu said.

When he glanced at her, his eyes dulled.

With a look, he'd shut her down. "Never mind." Lulu ghosted away.

THE DAY AFTER CARLOS' challenge and banishment, the sad, gloomy weather was driving me nuts. Where was L.A.'s summer sun when I needed it? Something was coming, something big, that jittery feeling increasing hour by hour. Pressure built inside me, like before a thunderstorm. It was coming soon. And I hadn't the faintest idea of who or what *it* was.

The Union? Tatianne? An unknown enemy?

I wished we could be more proactive with our foes, rather than having to hunt for the next chest. Three obtained, two to go.

I trusted my gut, and I'd told James, Alex, and Rae. I'd even left a message for Anouk. They needed to know that something big was about to happen.

Now I was at loose ends, so I sat in our living room threading my new yarn through my fingers. The wolves had taken some of their combed fur and had it spun with merino. They'd gifted me more than a dozen incredible skeins. Some were chestnut, others gray, two black, and one white. Alex's. The feel of the yarn soothed me as few things could.

Outside, metal clanged against metal, breaking the quiet. Sprawled on her new dog bed, Gracie perked her ears. James was pounding away at the forge he'd built in our garage. He'd told me when he was a kid, he'd dreamed of becoming a farrier. We had no horses, but he'd satisfied part of his childhood dream with the forge.

I drew a long length of gray yarn from its skein and began to cast on. Knitting a cowl would be like eating comfort food, but without the calories. I used to worry that I'd run out of yarn when I did a long-tail cast on. Now, I had bigger worries.

I cast on and on and on, placing stitch markers every fifty stitches. An endless process when knitting a cowl. Calming as it was, my funk wasn't lifting. A text pinged.

Ozille! A perfect antidote for my gloomfest.

How are you? she texted.

I texted back, *Great. You?*

We are making progress. Your mother is incredible.

My thoughts ran in a somewhat different direction, but I kept them to myself. She was a good queen.

I'm glad you're well! she wrote. *You had a challenging time. Please tell James I found the metal he was seeking.*

Ozille, always serving, always caring, and full of surprises. Sweet, joyful Ozille was the Chest of Time's guardian. I smiled. Who'da thunk?

I'll tell him right now, I wrote.

I would have texted him myself, but I wanted to hear how you were doing. Be well, Clea.

You, too, Ozille. After sending her a heart emoji, I set aside my knitting. What metal was James seeking from the fae? Interesting. I stood.

My body became a cascade of needles piercing my skin. I swayed. Black shards of memory, of future tomorrows and past yesterdays, stabbed my mind. *No, no, no.*

Muscled arms banded me from behind. I blinked. The scents of honey and pine and musk. Warmth and strength.

I was here. I was now. I was home. I tilted my head back against James' chest. "Hey, fella. You're all sweaty."

"I'll go shower."

I touched his forearm. "Stay."

He sat on the couch, with me on his lap. I rested my head on his chest.

"Deep thoughts?" he said, breath warm on my neck.

"Too many."

He twirled a lock of my hair around a finger. "How did it go with Melike and Bron?"

"Okay, I guess. They're hurting so bad, even after I smoothed their internal shards of sorrow. It helped a bit, enough for them to get by. Grief's an emotion that needs to be processed. Losing a mate is profound. So is losing a dad."

He nuzzled me. "Like you did. Colorado better help her fast. We need her."

"Alex thinks it will. Me, too. Being away from the pack, from Alex... Ile Iachau's a healing place, with wolves, big cats, and other shifters as pack. It sounds beautiful, a unique sanctuary. A good place to sort stuff out and maybe come to accept the loss."

"Was Carlos always a shit?" He grunted. "I'm going to get some water."

I swatted his arm as he rose. "He wasn't a shit. He was a good man before Paul's death and Melike's capture."

"Sorry, babe. I don't buy it."

"I'm glad you accepted the pack."

His snort produced a woof from Gracie. He returned in seconds, placing two glasses of water on the redwood coffee table, one plain, one with ice for me. He picked me up and cuddled me back on his lap. A long kiss later, I surfaced feeling hungry. For him. I reached for my glass and took a sip.

"I almost didn't," he said.

"Accept?"

"Yeah. More responsibility. I've got the nano team, the pack, Neddy. You." He chuckled. "Not sure how I went from lone wolf to this."

"I'm rubbing off on you," I said.

"You feel everything." The kiss he planted on my temple warmed me from the outside in.

"It's *moi*. What can I say?"

"I don't have to like the way it hurts you."

"Nope. You just have to like *me*."

"I think we've established that." His soft laughter gave me goosebumps.

"I'd say so." I rubbed a hand across a buttery couch cushion. Made of leather, a rich distressed chestnut, I'd adored the sofa on sight. James' had gone utterly still when he'd checked the heart-stopping price tag. But he'd looked at me, perhaps seen the virtual drool on my face, and grinned. So we'd splurged. Yet another of his little kindnesses.

My phone buzzed, and I swiped it off the table. Maybe Lulu... No, the text was from Neddy saying he was off to play pickup basketball.

James took the phone and typed. *Remember to square up before you shoot, Ned!*

"He'll get there," I said, unable to stop my sigh from slipping out.

"You haven't heard from her." He handed back my phone.

"Lu's been spending hours in her room at the den. Alone. She's totally disinterested in pack doings."

"I agree."

"She's devastated by her distance from Alex."

"Nothing we can do about it, babe."

"Isn't there?"

His eyes sparked with danger. "Cle-a."

"All right. Maybe. But I want them to have what we do. I'm so lucky to have you. Blessed."

His arms became bands of steel, and he nuzzled my neck.

"Can't...breathe." They instantly loosened.

"You wreck me when you say that stuff. I'm the one who's lucky. You...fuck, I stumble over words that sound inadequate to what I'm feeling for you."

I leaned back to peer into his beloved face, combed my fingers through his long hair. My chest squeezed so tight, I buried my head in his shoulder, but not because I feared showing him my tears, which were making his t-shirt even soggier. James had no idea, no grasp of how much he gave me. I'd felt so alone until he thundered into my life. He was such an honorable man, loyal, steadfast and true to his marrow. He'd given me strength when I'd needed it, made me laugh, especially when I needed it, and gifted me with his strong heart. He valued me, saw me warts and all, just as I saw him. He was my partner, and I, his.

And if I said those things aloud, he'd scoff. "You know it's far beyond our fae twining. I love you."

"Which continues to amaze me. But I'm keeping it. Keeping you, babe. Love you, Clea mine." He whooshed out a breath.

"What?"

"Scares the hell out of me. I never used to worry."

"And now you do."

"About you, for you. Constantly. It's not so easy for me to box it up like other stuff." He grimaced. "As you noted, something wicked this way comes."

"It's been too calm, and I've got the jitters. I can't believe that after three months, I still have no vibes, messages, or hints about the two remaining chests."

He drew in a deep breath. "Small gifts. Time for us."

"Yes indeed."

"Agreed, the pressure cooker's about to explode. The world's falling apart. Our enemies are planning something big." He turned my shoulders so I faced him. "We'll handle it. You'll stay safe."

I drank in his emotions sparking with warmth and protection and desire. "We will."

"With no intel," he said, "we can't do much. Let's enjoy these small gifts." His face, ice-man serious, while his Pacific-blue eyes danced with mischief. "For example, with Neddy gone, a joint shower would be welcome. You can scrub my back and I'll scrub yours."

"Oh, that wicked grin. I suspect you'll be scrubbing a lot more than my back."

He lifted me in his arms as he stood. "I suspect you're right."

I winked.

TWO WEEKS AFTER CARLOS' banishment, Alex prowled his rooms trying really hard not to throw breakable shit at the walls. It might be satisfying now, but it would only piss him off later. He didn't know what to do, which felt unnatural. Hell, he was alpha, after all. But he'd been an ass. A fool.

Lulu was gone. She'd moved in with two cheetah shifter girls over in Hollywood, away from the pack and him. She'd told Clea where she was. Erick found out and told him. But he'd refused to ask Clea about her. Pride. His damned pride.

Allowing his injuries to fester into feelings of inadequacy where Lulu was concerned had been dumber than dumb. He'd navel-gazed, so fucking self-absorbed in his personal pity party. He'd battled their bond like a cage fighter, refusing even to acknowledge its existence.

Now, he feared it was too late. She was gorgeous, intelligent, kind. She'd meet someone who'd appreciate her. They'd fall in love and...

How the fuck would he get her back?

After their return from Charleston, he'd been pleased that Erick had done such a fine job. The pack was good. He almost smiled. Yeah, his wolves were somewhat needy, and then there was that little vampyre kiddo who'd landed in their laps, but that was all good, too. He'd been busy, too busy for Lulu. Or so he'd told himself. He'd rebuffed her again and again. Then Carlos... That clusterfuck had damaged him emotionally, not to mention how it had hurt the pack. He'd had to bandaid a bunch of bonds until they healed.

Why couldn't he share the bad with her, along with the good? What was his problem?

He'd almost said something the day he'd found her talking to Melike. But he was limping, had his damned cane. Melike needed him.

More excuses. Since when had he started making excuses for himself? *Not* the behavior of an alpha. He was an idiot. An asshole. Blind to the one person who needed him most. The one *he* needed more than breath.

He spotted the blue jar some other alpha had given him. Ugly as shit. He flung it across the room where it shattered into a satisfying cascade of shards.

Good.

Fuck.

She'd sequestered herself from him, from the pack, even from Clea.

For Christ's sake, she'd taken a job at The Grove. The Grove!

He had to fix things. Make them right. Time to hunt, which got his blood bubbling. Tactics. He had to blindside her, or she'd hide, refuse to see him, take off.

If he asked her to visit the den...? No. They'd have hundreds listening, observing, critiquing. Gossipy, nosy wolves.

Her apartment? He wasn't up for an encounter with two cheetah girls. The Grove, then. His lip curled. Pathetic. But maybe necessary, unless he wanted to corral her in some back alley.

Did he enter the store, get in line, wait patiently? No. He'd storm in and drag her ass out of there.

Brilliant, Alex, just brilliant. That would go over big. He flung open desk drawers and slammed them closed, finally spotting his ancient iPod. He'd take this, say it needed work.

But she could just pass him off to a repair guy.

He sat down hard on the end of the bed and laughed. He knew just what he was doing. Avoiding action. He'd sunk pretty low for an alpha. For any wolf, in fact.

Shame made his skin tighten, like he was wearing somebody else's flesh.

What if she was done with him? Had excised him from her heart?

He limped over to the bedside table, swiped a hand across his face. Man, he...yeah, he had to man up.

The navy blue box he pulled from a drawer fit in the palm of his hand. It had been his mother's and so was precious to him. A bribe? Hell, yeah. A bribe for Lulu to accept his heart once again. It felt right.

He grabbed his damned cane and left.

As the manager opened the doors, Lulu peered out the windows of the Apple Store. The Grove was pretty empty this time of day, with only a few customers trickling inside.

Two long weeks had passed since she'd implemented her "clever" strategy of getting Alex to remember what they'd had together. She'd distanced herself from him and the den. It was one of the hardest things she'd ever done. She missed her home, missed Clea and Larrimer and Neddy, missed all the crazy-wild wolves. Most of all, she missed that alpha wolf who saw himself as less because of his injury. Alex was her sustenance, her breath, her heart. Without him, she felt half alive.

Her plan was an epic fail. She hadn't seen or heard from him.

How could he not know she adored him?

She and Clea had agreed her vanishing act would bring His Stubbornness around, and together they'd devised this plan. Right. Had he even noticed her absence?

When she'd met Clea for lunch, she'd been hopeful. She'd learned that Alex had been in a foul mood, his bad temper increasing on a daily basis. She was sure he'd come for her. He hadn't.

Now she'd go to him. She'd told her cheetah pals that she'd be leaving and given notice at the Apple Store. When she returned to the den, she'd take up her Sangestre duties, launch that children's choir as planned, and teach any of the talented how to use their song as a tool and a weapon. It might not be the same as with the fae, but the wolves had their own unique song gifts.

And she'd pursue that damned wolf with all her heart and soul. No longer would he deny her, deny them. She'd make it happen.

An employee cleared her throat and notched her head toward a customer. Her woolgathering had attracted attention. She approached an old man in a suit and tie who was being ignored by the other specialists, which was odd. She helped him pick out a new iPhone, and after he'd purchased it, she guided the customer, Ian, through the steps of turning the phone on and off, accessing his contacts, and then through some of the phone's other goodies. The elegant old man peered at her, spectacled eyes wide, confusion writ large on his face.

She wrote some numbers on her card and handed it to him. He seemed at ease with her. He might ask her questions. Anyone else? She doubted it. She knew she shouldn't give him her number, but the guy was proud, almost noble, and he'd crash and burn without having someone to help him through his first smartphone's maze of wonders.

"Thank you, dear," Ian said, taking the card. His blackberry eyes twinkled, reminding her just a bit of Clea's grandmother, Bernadette. She'd adored that cranky old woman who'd saved Lulu's life and died as a result. Which was why she found the Apple Store soothing. No death. No loss. But given what was happening in the world, it was a false comfort.

"Miss?"

She gasped. "Sorry! I'm happy to help."

"You're being kind to this old man. You're not supposed to give me your phone number, are you?"

It was easy to smile back at him. "Your choice if you use it or not."

He tapped the card against his lips. "I did buy AppleCare, you understand."

"I do." As good as that was, the steps of customer service would frustrate him, too. He needed the personal touch. "I don't mind if you phone or text me with a question or two." She bent and pressed a finger to her lips. "Hush, hush."

A laugh burst from his mouth. "You're a dangerous child."

If only he knew.

A shock wave rippled through the store. She straightened, her breath catching.

She hastily patted Ian's shoulder. "Enjoy your new phone!" She turned, but the old man's hand caught hers.

No no no!

He raised her hand and kissed the back of it.

A roar ripped through the store. Hope blossomed in her chest.

The few customers turned to stare at the tall man stalking toward her, cane fisted in a white-knuckled grip, face a grimace of anger.

Ian slipped to the side and pushed her behind him.

OMG, it was getting worse! She dashed in front of Ian. "It's okay. He's a friend."

"Friends do not look like that," he said.

Mine do. "I'll be fine."

"I'm going to get the manager," he said.

"Not necessary!" she said hastily, her eyes focused on Alex stalking through the store as only he could.

Her heart sped up. He was here, with a determined look on his face that made her heart sing. Her eyes locked on his as he stepped in front of her, his body vibrating with fury he was barely keeping contained. His tanned face had paled, his eyes narrowed and blazing with the wolf. He spread his legs, his hands resting on his cane, which was front and center. She got the oddest image of Fred Astaire.

"He touched you." Alex ground out the words like ragged glass.

She shrugged. "Lot's of men have touched me." That was stupid.

"No, they haven't."

"How would you even know?"

He tapped the side of his nose.

That damned wolfie sense of smell. She was all nerves. How to play this? Leap into his arms? Play it cool? He was tinder, and one match... Cool it was. "I'm working, Alex."

The hand that gripped her wrist was firm, yet gentle. His eyes softened to warm. They asked questions she wanted to answer.

The manager bustled up. "Everything okay here, Lulu?"

She smiled at Eva. "It is. It...it will be." Her smile broadened to take in Ian. "Thank you, too, Ian, but everything's okay. Promise."

Ian's suspicions seemed to remain, but Eva snapped her a nod, rested a hand on the old man's shoulder, and said, "Let's go over to the Genius Bar, shall we?"

She shot Lulu a final dark glance as they departed.

"After all this time," she said to Alex. "Um, it's good to see you."

He began to thread his fingers through hers. She pulled her hand away. She was hot and cold. Up and down. Hopeful and worried. All nerves and icicles. "Why are you here?" Her voice had stumbled. She was terrified. But she hoped.

"You." He retook her hand.

It was just the two of them, surrounded by a fog of intimacy. Wrapped in themselves, as they'd been so often. Alone. Private.

"Cut it out, buster." The security guard slammed Alex's shoulder hard enough that he stumbled, lost his balance, and fell.

She was horrified, but masked it fast. Few things were worse than an alpha's public humiliation. It was devastating for the man she loved, another small hurt on top of all the others. He'd rise using his cane—gods forbid she offered to help him—and he'd politely excuse himself. Would he leave? Or would he punch the guard and *then* leave?

Either way, she'd lose.

The red-faced security guard peered down at Alex. He held out a hand to help Alex rise. Alex didn't take it. No, of course he didn't. He did just as she'd expected and used his cane to stand.

"Sorry, Mister," the guard said. "Didn't mean to topple you. But you shouldn't handle the lady. You feel me?"

Alex's eyes glowed wolf. "You're right. And I apologize."

What. *What?*

He snared her with eyes filled with shadows. "I am not as I once was."

There were so many layers to those words. So much meaning. "No you're not. You're better. Alex 2.0."

A faint smile ghosted his lips. Though his gaze never left hers, he spoke to the guard. "But you see, she's mine."

A thrill raced through her.

"She is my heart." He braced his cane on the floor. "She makes it beat. She's the reason for each breath I take. She is my love. And I am hers."

Her mind flatlined, her mouth gaping, fish-like.

"I have been an ass. And she may not forgive my assholery. But I would ask her to. I would apologize. I would tell her that I have abundantly seen the error of my ways and how my hubris has come between us."

"Your what?" said the security guard.

"Hubris," Lulu said. "Never mind. Just go away, please."

Alex took a step toward her.

She raised a hand to her mouth because her lips were wobbling. She was on the precipice of tears, but she so didn't want to cry here in the Apple Store amidst people waiting with baited breath for Alex's next words and her reactions.

His gaze stroked her. "I would ask that she forgive me. That we talk out what's happened. I will listen to her words, and I will promise never ever again to let my ego come between us."

Oh, she wasn't buying that one. But that was okay. He believed what he was saying. She could work with it.

He offered her a self-deprecating smile. "Maybe that wasn't totally true."

She giggled like a teen. When had she last giggled?

"For all our tomorrows. Shoulder to shoulder. Together." He held out a hand.

She stared at the box. Oh, this was scary as all get out.

His arm was steady, his eyes patient. She knew this Alex. He'd wait forever until she took it.

The love in his eyes blazed crystal. He was everything she wanted. Everything she hoped for. Everything she needed. Here. Now. Her Alex.

She reached out her hand. "For all our tomorrows."

And the world buckled.

25

She and Alex raced down the aisle, through the doors, onto the pavement.

People screamed—shrieks of children and the helpless and desperate.

The ground beneath her rose and rose, splitting like a rotted tomato. She tottered, like the first time she'd ridden a wave. Years ago. Alex teaching her to surf. She knew this. So she rode the rising earth as if she was surfing the waters.

Someone careened into her back, lifted her, and leapt. They soared above the earth as it collapsed into a maw. People toppled into the blackness of the sinkhole, their screams filling the air.

They crashed to the ground, missing a jagged piece of concrete by inches. The rumbling continued as he pulled her to her feet, the earth liquid beneath her.

"Move," he said. "Into that arched doorway."

She leapt over rubble, terrified the gaping hole would widen and swallow her, too.

He shoved her against the doors, the old man's body now young and tall and strong. "Ian?"

Alex! Where was Alex?

She searched the crowds racing like hamsters in a maze, not knowing which way to go or how to get there. *She couldn't find Alex!*

The rumbling subsided to tiny tremors that sent chills up her body. This was no earthquake. Not a natural one, anyway. "I have to find Alex."

"He's safe," young-Ian said.

"How do you know that?"

"I know."

Steam billowed out of the gaping hole that had formed in the middle of the Grove's walkway, the trolley tracks broken into Twizzler shapes. The steam shimmered with light, casting mini rainbows within the cloud of vapor.

Those in one piece helped the injured, while still others whipped out their phones. Thank the gods The Grove had been mostly empty this early in the day.

She leapt over a pile of rubble to help a woman struggling to stand.

"Wait!" Ian shouted.

She lifted the woman to her feet. "Are you okay?"

The woman nodded and stumbled off.

Lulu was jerked backward and dragged over the rubble by Ian toward the wall. "I said to wait."

Her "screw you" died on her lips.

Out of the gaping hole crawled monstrous creatures, ones she'd never seen in the magic realm, but more like monster mashups from *Alien* or *Guardians of the Galaxy*. Pink and red and blue. One-eyed and three-eyed. Multiple armed, four-legged, all bristling with teeth and suckers and...

If mundanes hadn't known about the magic world's retwining, they would now.

She needed weapons. Didn't have her bow or sword. She could sing these people and creatures to sleep. But her magic wasn't as strong in the mundane world, and what if these strange creatures weren't affected? What if only the mundanes were? To sing would sign their death warrants.

Where could she get a weapon? The antique store. Not three storefronts away. They sold swords and bows and...

She ran, but was jerked to a halt by Ian's hand clamped on her arm with the iron grip of a man in his prime.

"What are you?" she said.

"Tired."

His self-effacing smile didn't fool her. She'd bet a bundle he was masking his power. He was obviously no mundane.

"I need to find Clea Reese," he said.

"Good luck with that."

He tightened his grip.

She was emotionally spent, physically tired, and not putting up with this crap. She whirled, elbowed him in the gut hard, and dashed away.

"I know..." his choked voice boomed, his words somehow reaching her over the cacophony of chaos.

She blocked him out of her head and raced to the antiques store. It took her long minutes to slither through the canted and broken wood doors to the interior. The smell made her retch. Someone was dead in here. Or someones. *Don't think about that.* It looked like a giant had swiped his hand across all the treasured antiques that lay smashed in bits on the floor. She searched through broken boxes and cabinets, splintered glass and figurines. Time was passing. People were dying. Monsters were wreaking havoc. And she couldn't find a damned sword. She climbed a pile of crumpled counters flattened like cardboard, scraping her knee on some glass, and leapt to the other side. Resting on a pile of trashed stuff lay two headless people. The guy had one hand wrapped around the handle of a sword.

She reached down—*Forgive me*—and pried his fingers open. She lifted the weapon, the handle still dripping blood, and wiped it clean with her shirt. Seconds later, she raced back out to the promenade gripping the sword and a Bowie knife like the one Clea carried.

On the erupted pavement in front of her, Alex in his half-form battled three creatures. He was holding his own. But for how long? To her right, Ian kneeled by the wall, hands arcing in orchestral waves, his chant rising above the cacophony. Bodies, pieces of flesh, and puddles of viscous glop were strewn about the walkway and on the twisted trolley tracks.

She leapt over rubble and into the path of two snake-like creatures slithering toward an elderly woman frozen with fear. She beheaded one creature, then the other.

"Run," she said to the old woman. "Go!"

The woman tottered away, and Lulu turned back toward the hole, which seemed smaller, even as more monsters erupted from its maw.

"Herd them back toward the hole," Alex shouted. "The dude's trying to close it."

She slashed and stabbed, got clawed, and something bit her ankle. She kicked it away. "Did you call the pack?"

"Yes." He grimaced, clawing out the throat of a tentacled creature. "But L.A. traffic's a bitch."

A six-foot monster leapt in front of her, three-eyed, jaws wide. A knife from somewhere flew into its mouth and it toppled backward.

Thank the gods.

The scene was a nightmare, but most of the mundanes were either dead or gone.

She twirled in a circle, her blades flashing, and began to sing. Several creatures dropped to the ground, while a few slowed, and others swayed to her music.

But a half-dozen of the creatures remained fighting. At least the hole was shrinking. Out of the corner of her eye, a blur, and a four-legged glutinous thing stretched toward her. She jumped to meet it, slipped on some goo, and tumbled to her knees. She raised her sword and managed to impale the creature as it fell upon her, its body pushing lower and lower on her blade, jaws snapping closer and closer to her face.

Die, you idiot!

A knife sprouted from one of its eyes, and the thing crashed on top of her, a suffocating gelatinous blob.

Pressed beneath the monster's weight she couldn't breathe. She struggled, clawing at what felt like Jello. Its flesh slipped through her fingers, but she couldn't move it.

Her gasp got her a mouthful of glop. *Can't breathe!*

The creature vanished, and she sucked in a huge breath as she watched its corpse fly toward some rubble.

"You've been slimed," Alex said, holding out a hand.

Up she went, to stand on shaky legs. She coughed, her voice a rasp. "Thanks for the assist."

He winked and whipped around, his half-form's massive legs launching him toward a hulking green-scaled, six-armed *thing*. He flipped midair, punched it backward with his feet, and did an airborne roll, to stand on the hole's edge as the monster tumbled inside.

The hole snapped closed.

Alex fell to one knee. His chest billowed and blood dripped from a dozen wounds. Lulu stumbled over and hunkered down beside him.

"Alex?"

"What's up, princess?" he said between pants. Smoke swirled and his form became fully human. His wolf-gold eyes slid to Ian, who wove toward them like a drunk. After several heartbeats, Alex shoved off the ground with one foot, pulling her to a stand beside him. He tugged her arm behind him and took her in a wet, bloody kiss.

Held in Alex's arms was where she belonged.

When he broke the kiss, she was the one panting. He slid his lips to her ear. "And your answer is?"

What? All the muscles in her body locked. Oh, shit, *that*. She was instantly terrified. But there was only one answer. "You're my heart, too. For always. Yes." She gave him a saucy look. "Unless you screw up again. Or I do."

"We'll both screw up," he said. "Then we'll fix it." His chuckle was low and sexy and ignited a molten heat that arrowed straight through her.

"What are you thinking about?"

He grinned, looking a little guilty and a lot happy. "Make-up sex."

"Alex!"

In one of those swift shifter moves, she found a ring on her finger, a glorious ring in the shape of a graceful flower, its petals a multitude of gems sparkling in the sun.

"My mother's."

"Oh, Alex, but I'm all bloody and slimy and..."

He shushed her with another kiss.

"Are you two sappy cretins done yet?"

Alex pushed her behind him and growled.

Her very own, crazy-assed alpha. He'd always do that, always try to protect her, shield her. But it was okay. They'd be okay. She wove her fingers through his and stepped beside him. "This is my place."

"It is, princess, but sometimes I forget. Sorry." His crooked smile set her world afire.

Ian raked a hand through his now-shoulder-length mahogany hair. "I need to find Clea Reese. *Now. You will tell me where she is.*"

Voice. Lulu recognized the compulsion, and compulsion it was. *How dare that bastard use Voice on them.* Yet her mouth opened, as did Alex's to answer the question.

"What're y'all doin' here, kid?"

The words sliced the compulsion in two. She stumbled backward, only to be steadied by Rae, who led a horde of shifters, Clea, Larrimer, Neddy...the whole crew. And wasn't that little Izzy, the vampyre girl?

Her family. Seeing them arrive amid the carnage and the horror eased the vise around Lulu's chest.

Except the monsters' corpses were igniting in raging flames.

Rae and Ian simultaneously barked, "*Stamató* !

Lulu froze, as did everyone else. The flames halted, too, some mid-air. The two mages lugged three creatures and some body parts away from the others and into a pile. Then in concert, their hands wove what looked like a spell over the lumps of flesh.

"*Viografiko!*" Rae shouted.

She stepped forward, unbalanced by the abrupt ability to move. Alex swore at Rae. The creatures' remains ignited, all except the pile separated by the mages. In seconds, the flames turned flesh to ash.

"That was close," Rae said, narrowing his eyes on Ian. "I'm gonna ask y'all once more—what the hell y'all doin' here?"

Ian snarled, his upper lips curled. "You know *exactly* why I'm here, *Grandfather.*"

Lulu froze. Rae's grandson?

"You were to come to me first, child!" Rae said.

Ian sniffed. "That's what *you* wanted. Not what *I* felt was necessary."

The now-young mage pivoted to face Clea, whose sorrowful eyes sparked with anger as she surveyed the carnage. He bowed. "Clea Artemis Reese. I've been looking for you."

Alex was organizing shifters into clean-up troops. Why weren't police and firemen swarming the place?

Larrimer was folded onto his haunches, using a pencil to poke the creature pieces that remained. "Lulu!" he said. "Come here."

She hesitated, wanting to hear what Ian had to say to Clea.

"Now Lulu!" Larrimer called.

She trotted over and crouched down beside him. "What's got your panties in a twist?"

"You fought these things, yes?"

"I sure did."

"How did they get here?"

She pointed to the scorched and blistered circle where the hole had once yawned and explained.

He nodded, scraping a finger down his long scar. "Okay. Replay it for me. The whole incident."

"The earth trembled..." The warm breeze licked her face, yet she shivered as she recounted the tale. Her eyes sought the bodies of the dead mundanes. There must be a dozen or more. They hadn't burned. Before her lay a teen with a huge Afro, a man in a business suit, and a little boy whose hand was held by his dead mother. The teen would never again listen to hip hop, nor the man laugh at his spouse's joke. And the child and mother. He'd miss baseball or ballet. His mother would never smother him in kisses again, never watch him graduate grammar school. None of them would ever again feel love or sorrow or joy. She was so sad. She was so angry. For what purpose had their lives been stolen?

She ground her teeth, even as her tears fell.

"Let me have your sword for a sec." Larrimer took it and poked at a fat green tentacle lying flaccid on the ground, all that remained of the creature itself. With a single stroke of her blade he split the thing down the middle, like deveining a shrimp. The halves flopped to the pavement, the gelatinous blue innards glistening in the light. "Alex! Come here!"

Alex reached them in seconds, obviously annoyed. "This better be good. I've got a shitload to do."

"See that?" Larrimer had poked more of the tentacle's flesh apart with the tip of Lulu's sword. A thread, what looked like shiny metal, wove down its midsection.

Alex kneeled and sniffed. "Steel, mixed with something. Another metal of some kind and..." He drew closer, inhaled again. "Smells faintly like you, too."

"Fuck," Larrimer said. "Those are nanos you're scenting. This wasn't an eruption from the magic world, an Event, or whatever we're calling them. This was The Union's work."

"This makes no sense," Lulu said. "The creatures came out of the earth. They had the look of inhabitants of the magic realm. Except I didn't recognize any of their species. When I think about it, that's odd. I lived there for ten years. I saw lots of weird creatures. But none like these."

"That's because they only *look* magical. As intended." Larrimer stood, hands on hips, and frowned. "Obviously The Union had electronics inside them to ignite them after the battle and turn them to ash. But I'm sure plenty of images were taken by smartphones."

"They're shrewd bastards," Alex said. "Without remains, no one could prove they were constructs."

Larrimer smiled, a very scary one. "Good thing those two mages stopped the burning. We've got The Union by the balls. Knowing them, they'll wiggle out of it. But this will hurt them."

"At least something good came out of it," she said.

Alex nodded. "I'll have my guys bag them and bring them back to the den. Our techs and forensics guys are good. They'll go over the remains with a fine-toothed comb."

"I've recalled Fan and Pyotr," Larrimer said. "Pyotr's a tech wiz and intimate with The Union's devices, including their biotech creations."

"Much as I regret the carnage and loss of life," Alex said. "We can turn this to our advantage. Damage The Union for once instead of the other way around."

Lulu stepped aside when Alex struggled to stand, then wrapped an arm around his waist as he barked fresh orders to the shifters. When the cleanup crew arrived, Alex leaned close and brushed his lips across her cheek. "Thanks, princess."

"I won't let you fall."

He stared at her for long moments. "I know. Nor I you, Lu. Not while I breathe."

Their trio walked over to Clea, who was listening with rapt attention to Ian, a man who now resembled a mahogany-haired Jaime Lannister from *Game of Thrones*. Like grandfather, like grandson.

Larrimer swung an arm over Clea's shoulder, and she gave him a warm smile.

Clea and Larrimer supported each other, shared things, were partners in such a great way. Someday, she and Alex would be like that. "Hey, guys, we're engaged."

She hadn't meant to blurt it out but wasn't sorry she had.

Amidst cheers and whoops, she leaned closer to Alex. "Did I say that right?"

"That you did, princess." He took her in a long, hot kiss.

I COULDN'T BELIEVE IT. In the middle of this shitstorm, Lulu and Alex had gotten engaged! I needed *all* the details. I hugged Lulu and then Alex, and a huge pressure on my heart lifted. They'd be great together. Better than great.

I stepped back and let others congratulate the happy couple, aware that some of my tears were due to what Ian had told me. I'd have to leave them, all of them. Soon. Which spawned a soul-deep ache inside me. But I was so damned happy for Lu and Alex. So I brightened my smile and watched the others crowding the couple, wishing them well. I squeezed James' hand. "We need to talk, hon."

He led me away from the group, and we climbed over buckled concrete and shattered doors. Glass from blown-out windows crunched beneath our feet, and my heart thumped when we walked around one of the bodies someone had draped with a blood-dappled cloth.

Their deaths were so unnecessary, detritus from some stupid op cooked up to further The Union's agenda. I hated them with a scary amount of passion.

We stopped beneath the remaining half of an awning, and James tucked a finger beneath my chin. "Well?"

"That Ian person says he heard mutterings of the Chest of Fire. According to him, he's been on the hunt a while, at the behest of his grandfather, Rae."

"The relationship's a stretch."

I blew out a breath. Why couldn't we have just a couple more weeks? "He believes it's in Iceland."

James nodded, his eyes serious. "All right. Worth following up."

"I agree. He said his sources were good. As Rae's grandson, I presume he's trustworthy. We'll talk to Rae, of course, check him out. But we should start making arrangements."

His eyes heated and he tugged me to him, resting his chin on the top of my head. "I've liked this, living like regular people. Having a house, doing the small stuff together, making love in our own bed."

"And in the kitchen and in the living room and at the forge."

His soft chuckle made me sniffle a smile. "Those, too." James handed me a green polka-dotted handkerchief, and I blew my nose.

He stiffened, muscles turning to granite beneath my fingers.

"What is it?" I said.

"The wyvern's talking to me. That other creature, whatever it is that attacked Sophy. It's on its way here."

I pulled him closer, rejecting his words, knowing that meant more fighting and more death. "Is Akashagni sure?"

"Yes. And she's not alone. The Union forces are with her."

I stepped back, throat tight. "All right. Let's tell the others."

He shook his head, ran a finger down his scar, eyes unfocused, as if listening to an inner monologue. I guessed I should call it a dialogue. Face tight, he got that determined look in his eyes. His hands clasped mine. "We go. *Now.*"

"But wait. No. We can't go now."

His eyes, cold and implacable, said both he and the wyvern were in accord.

"James, we can't run out on them."

"It will save lives."

I didn't want to leave. Not yet. We weren't ready. We had good-byes to say, preparations to make, a team to gather for the next stage of our quest. Lulu had just gotten engaged. We would cheer her and Alex's union, celebrate and make toasts. We needed *time.*

"All of that," he said. "All that your thinking. None of it matters. You're the target. Even going now, they'll pursue us. I know these people. They won't bother with the mess they created here." He rubbed the back of his neck, his eyes suddenly weary. "We really have no choice, Clea. I must change."

"Into the wyvern? No!"

"It's the one way we can escape them."

"I'd rather fight."

His one eyebrow arched. "Many of our people will die. The creature is a female dragon. She's arrogant, projecting her thoughts the wyvern's catching. It's you they want. You."

"But the danger of you changing...it terrifies me." I pressed myself into him, heard our song rise, the incandescent melodies melding into one. He was mine. I was his.

James bent, and his lips touched mine, brushed once, twice, butterfly caresses. Then he kissed me deep and hard, and I opened to him, his lips and tongue plundering my mouth, our breaths mingled, our hearts pounding. We were better together. Always better. I clung to James. I'd reason with him, make him see my point of view. I stepped back.

"Dragon Dude, no. It's not wise. We will fight. We'll win. Please." The words tasted bitter on my tongue.

"It'll be all right, Clea mine. You are my salvation. Christ, you're my sanity. No one can get to you again. That's the one thing I can't handle. I'm sorry, very sorry, but I've made my choice."

"James, wait!"

But even as he pushed me away, red-gold smoke licked with flame curled around him.

"No!" I screamed.

The massive swirling funnel totally obscured the man I loved as it rose ten, then fifteen feet into the air.

I screamed. "Get out of the way! Everybody move back!"

Instead, Rae, Alex, and Lulu raced toward me. "I said run!"

"What the fuck, Clea?" Alex said.

"The Union's coming. They want me. James and I have to leave. They'll follow us, give you time to prepare if they come back." I stood on tiptoe and kissed his cheek. "Be happy, Alex." I hugged Rae, then pulled Lulu to me in a fierce hug. "I'm so sorry I won't be here to celebrate with you. You're amazing. Remember that. I love you, Lu!"

"Love you, too!"

"Sugah, I'm so damned pissed I could spit," Rae said.

"Please don't." I chuckled as I released Lulu.

I took them all in, along with Neddy and Izzy and the others. My family. "We'll be in touch. Count on it."

A roar loud enough to pop my ears shook the pavement and

buildings still standing. One glass door of the Apple store fell off its hinges and crashed to the ground. Green flame shot through the whirlwind to scorch another storefront.

The smoke dissipated.

And James was no more. Akashagni stood proudly, chest puffed as he arched his sinuous neck. Fifteen feet high, twenty feet long, his emerald eyes glowed. He tossed his head, and his two golden horns glinted in the sun.

From behind me came screeches and oohs and ahhs. The pack's first glimpse of the wyvern. He preened, his jaws opening on two rows of sharp serrated teeth, the longest the length of my arm.

Like an aftershock, his powerful wave of magic hit me, and I shuddered.

He roared his challenge to The Union forces, smoke and flame shooting from his immense maw and flared nostrils.

The heat of it seared me. I was so damned mad at The Union I hoped Akashagni would fry them all. At least my sweat hid my tears. It was done. James was gone. My heart cracked as I accepted our fate. For now. Our fate *for now*. But James was here, within Akashagni. I must never forget that. The wyvern roared again.

"Stop showing off," I said.

His chuckle set my teeth on edge.

"I mean it!"

Akashagni swiveled his triangular head, dipped his long neck, and stuck his snout in my face.

We must go. Now! Hop on.

Another first. The wyvern held out a wing, and I slung my pack onto my back. I sure didn't have much inside. My keys, wallet, an extra pair of underwear, my phone, and my small Glock. At least I had a half-dozen knives plastered to my body, along with my katana. Better than nothing. Alex gripped my waist and tossed me high. The apex of Akashagni's leathery wing caught me and lifted me parallel to his back.

I leapt on, landing near his neck, in front of his spinal spikes. I scrambled forward on my belly.

Grip my wing where it meets my body. Hold a scale with your other hand and tighten your thighs.

I did as instructed, though I worried that as soon as we were airborne I'd fall off.

We'll get you a saddle.

"For another day." I turned my upper body to capture the eyes of my fellow warriors, my dear friends, my family.

They come. We must go.

"Not yet. I..."

A thump at my back. What the... I twisted my torso around, but the wyvern's muscles bunched beneath my thighs, and I death-gripped the wing and scale just as we launched toward the skies. I might have let out a small screech.

The gods' breath! the wyvern said.

"What?"

He didn't answer, but flew, bulleting upward.

Two voices directly behind me yelled, "Whoohoo!"

What idiots had climbed on the wyvern's back? I felt like I was in a wind tunnel. I didn't dare turn, but pressed myself against the wyvern's luminescent scales, hoping and praying I didn't slide off as the gale tore across my flesh.

Tiny people far below stared upward, while distant specks in the air grew larger by the second.

"Who the frig is hitching a ride?" I said, voice raised to carry over the wind's howls.

"You weren't going anywhere without us, Clea!"

Neddy!

"Who's 'us', Neddy?" I screamed. "Who did you bring?" I'd shoot him. Garrote him. Flay him.

No answer. So I shrieked, "Neddy, *who*?"

"Izzy! She said it was prophesied. She *had* to come, Clea!"

Great. Just frigging great.

26

"Izzy's an eight-year-old child!" Maybe we could set down, get the two of them to safety. I tightened my legs and clung like a barnacle to the wyvern's wing and scale before I peered over the side.

Crap. The distant specks had grown larger, closer. They flew beneath us, but were gaining altitude, an immense blue dragon in the lead. On its back, a grotesquely large rider. *We might not be going so far, Akashagni.*

The wyvern's laughter echoed in my head. *Of course we are, my Clea. Very far.*

As we rose higher, so did the dragon.

I still couldn't see her rider's face, but a long pipe-like thing rested on his shoulder. He raised its snout in our direction. *Why wasn't he using dragon fire?* The man-creature jerked as a ball of flame burst from the weapon's mouth.

"Neddy hang on tight to Izzy!" I screamed.

Where's the trust? Akashagni chuckled as he evaded the first ball, banking fast and hard to the left. Then he banked right, and a second and third burst whizzed past us. Yet the dragon with its weaponed rider grew closer and closer beneath us.

I had to do something. Already pressed on my belly, I clamped my thighs even harder to the wyvern's neck and tightened my left-handed grip on his wing. I needed to release my right hand to fire-fly. I feared it, knowing I might topple from Akashagni.

I'd never sent my fireflies this distance before. But I could do it. I bit my lip hard and raised my right hand.

A fourth and fifth burst spewed from the weapon's muzzle. One flew past us as Akashagni soared upward, but then he shuddered, a vibration so powerful my grip loosened and I was torn into space. He twisted, and I thudded onto his wing, grabbed onto scales, the ridge of his wing.

Whomp. Whomp. Whomp.

The flapping of his wings bounced me, and with each passing second, my grip slipped. My body shook with terror, which wasn't helping. I pushed my toes against his hide and tried to inch closer to his back.

Which is when I spotted the blue dragon soaring *above* us. It turned. The blue dragon was going for the kill shot.

If I released one of my hands, I'd fall to my death. But if I didn't try, we would all die.

I fought the wind as I angled my body, dug toes into the wyvern's wing, hoping that would help. My hair tore with the wind, half blinding me.

And in my peripheral vision at my right, a hand reached across the wing toward me, huge and pink-skinned with patches of gray fur. Neddy held his Pinky hand out to me. *Oh, boy.* I was scared down to my bones.

"C'mon!" Neddy yelled, flicking his claws.

I banished thought, released my right hand, and pushed off my toes for the boy's clawed hand. It slammed around my wrist, my fingers wrapping around his.

"Swing me!"

Neddy yanked, and I was flung into the sky, anchored only by our wrists.

Holy shit! Izzy was holding Neddy's ankles.

I soared upward, then downward, arcing toward Akashagni's deadly spikes.

Twist demanded Akashagni.

I know!

"Let go," I screamed to Neddy.

The instant he released me, I twirled, arms and legs tight to my body—thank you, ballet training. I split my legs and landed with a whomp between the wyvern's first two spikes.

My private parts throbbed, and not in a good way, but I hugged the spike in front of me like a long-lost lover. Why hadn't I sat like this in the first place?

Relief made me giddy. Seconds later, I found the blue dragon, raised my right hand, and aimed.

A face grinned back at me, bristling with rows of teeth, close enough for me to make out its features. *Gods, no.* Was I seeing right? I stared at the warped visage of Bob Balfour, my former FBI boss and friend—a betrayer who'd transformed into a nightmarish monster colored a sickly blackish-green with what looked like barbed armored plates covering his flesh. *Was* it his flesh? Sucker-like things bristling with red needles tipped the ends of his oddly shortened arms. Hideous. Balfour had *hated* James because he'd been transformed from human to a nanoteched man with a fae spark and a wyvern's blood.

Look at you now, bastard. You're *ug-ly*!

I poured every ounce of strength and will into my Flow and unleashed my fireflies on Balfour. Sparkles of light surged from my palm toward the dragon and her rider, forming the Gothic Arches knit motif. A first. They'd work beautifully.

Balfour laughed.

He had no idea.

My swarm of fireflies stretched and grew, a giant net of glowing, pulsing energy. The distance was so far, but I was sure I could do this. I poured on more energy as I curled my fingers inward to tighten the net. If my suspicions were wrong, we'd fail. But if I was right, I'd buy us the chance to escape.

The net hovered over Balfour. But it didn't reach, my strength waning. I screamed, digging for a last ounce of energy, and I tugged the fireflies closer until they mantled Balfour. Almost spent, salty sweat pouring into my eyes—*Now.* I whipped my arm across my body and wrenched the net toward me.

The world froze. Nothing happened. Shit. My fireflies began to dissipate. *No!*

Then Balfour flew off the dragon's back, his screech growing faint as he plummeted toward earth.

The blue dragon dove, tearing after her rider. Her master? I suspected so.

I collapsed against the spike as we soared through the sky accompanied by Neddy's and Izzy's whoops of joy.

Well done, my Clea.

Warmth trickled from my nose and ears, and my mouth tasted blood. Yuck. I spat. *Are you all right, Akashagni?*

Peachy.

I laughed. He'd picked that up from me, and I, from an old friend from my "before" life.

Akashagni is way too long, I said. *I'm going to call you Ash.*

Humph. An undignified nickname.

But one that suits, don't you think?

Perhaps.

With a massive burst of speed, Akashagni arced upward.

Far below, I watched Balfour land on the blue dragon's back. With his enhancements, I'd bet Balfour lived, more's the pity, but he wasn't in any shape to catch us now. I sighed.

The dragon and the distant dots that were The Union forces grew smaller until they evaporated from the blinding blue sky. We climbed higher still, toward the stratosphere. My adrenaline rush receded. Exhaustion drilled my bones. Cold slithered beneath my leathers and down my collar. I began to shiver.

"You got 'em, Clea!" Neddy whooped. "I knew you would. This is gonna be so cool!"

The vampyre child giggled.

Our next hunt should prove interesting. The Chest of Fire was the province of the vampyres. I'd met few, and with the exception of Izzy, they'd all tried to kill me.

Ash swooped upward. I laughed while Neddy and Izzy whooped. The teen was right. Flying on the back of the wyvern *was* cool.

We are headed to my homeland, Ash said. *I haven't been there in millennia. I wonder if its changed.*

Ya think? But I didn't want to hurt his feelings, so I remained silent.

I tried to talk to James' mind. He didn't answer.

The wyvern's wings beat. Whomp. Whomp. Whomp.

Two more chests. My gut tightened. Two to go. We could do this. We *would* do this. Then the combined worlds would harmonize. James and I would finally have our time.

I closed my eyes and pressed forward against Ash's spike, warm beneath my fingers. I pictured James and myself snuggled on our living room sofa, watching some flick while we sipped bourbon. I squeezed my eyes tight. *He wraps his arms around me. I lay my hand on his chest, and he takes my glass and puts it on the table. Then he clasps my chin, turns my face toward his. Those Pacific blues of his burn bright as he leans down for a soul-searing kiss.*

Clea!

Ash, in my head. *Don't shout!*

Are you all right?

Just nifty.

Good. And those hitchhikers?

I gripped Ash's spike as I looked over my shoulder. Izzy was asleep, Neddy cradling her in front of him. *They're swell, too.*

Fine. He grumbled something about parasites, then said, *We need to make a small detour.*

You're the pilot.

His laughter echoed in my head.

James... I missed him already. I felt half finished, lacking a limb, our song missing its bass line. I made a vow. I'd done it before. I'd do it again. James would return. *I would make it so.*

THANK YOU! AND NEWSLETTER

Thank you for reading *Chest of Time*!

Reviews are an author's lifeblood. If you enjoyed the book, leaving an honest review would mean so much to me.

Would you like a free book? I'd love for you to sign up for my newsletter and receive my bonus novel, *Body Parts*. My monthly newsletter contains info on the Afterworld Chronicles novels, and lots more yummy stuff.

Come visit with me... VickiStiefel.com
Facebook • Instagram • Twitter • Ravelry

ALTERED—EXCERPT, THE MADE ONES SAGA

BOOK 1, THE MADE ONES SAGA

The Eleutians are dying out, one female at a time. To save their species, the powerful Alchemic Clan conscripts women from parallel worlds, altering them into the perfect breeding stock.

Kitlyn, a retired circus equestrian broken in both body and spirit, awakens on a strange world in her own much-younger body. She has been transformed into a Made One, but the gift of youth and the promise of a new life come at a terrible price.

Rafe, the Wolf Clan's warrior champion, vows to find the cause of the species' decline. He's certain the Alchemics' bid to save the Eleutians is but a thin veneer masking a dark purpose.

That vow becomes hard to keep with the threat of an inter-clan conflict and the arrival of the proud Made One named Kitlyn.

To save herself and those like her, Kit must carve a dangerous path in this new reality and make a choice that may cost her her freedom, her life, and the life of the Eleutian warrior she's come to love.

ALTERED—coming early 2019.

Prologue

That sunny August day in Maine, the sharp serrated blade of death inched ever closer. Kit and her two sisters, Vivi and Bree, struggled to hike the Flying Mountain Trail, canopied by the forest of pine, to the top of Acadia's St. Sauveur Mountain. The air was thick and close, muffling bird song and the skitter of small forest animals who objected to the three sisters' presence. The towering trees prohibited all but a thin strip of blue above their heads, but the sun felt good, life-affirming.

Kit slapped the mosquito biting her thigh. "Damn you! And damn me for not wearing pants."

Her breath came hard as they climbed. Every single moment came hard. But Kit would not die today, though she fantasized staving off death's blade by choosing her own demise.

She wouldn't suicide. None of the sisters would. But the temptation was there, that longing for a swift death rather than the one creeping toward them from that cursed aberrant gene which was leeching the life out of them.

They might all be in their 50s, but she and her sisters wished for more years with their families, more time with new loves, more days to explore new paths.

And they *were* explorers, especially Kit.

Kit paused to look back at her two sisters, their heads bowed as they scrambled up the mountain behind her. "Hurry up, lazybones, keep up! I'm the gimpy one here. We might be dying, but we're not dead yet!"

But it was close, so very close. Her muscles hurt, her joints, too, and her head pounded. She released the clip that bound her long gray-streaked auburn hair. That helped. She'd be damned if she'd think about her aches and pains, wishing she could could practice her martial arts and hike the same day without collapsing.

She jerked to a halt. How odd. The path came to an abrupt end before a vast yawning crevasse where far below a river raged.

"How is this possible?" Kit said to Vivi and Bree as they stepped beside her.

Which was when the granite bank where they stood vanished.

Kit clamped her teeth tight, refusing to scream as she tumbled toward the raging river hundreds of feet below.

Chapter 1

Kit sputtered awake surrounded by calm turquoise waters while snowflakes drifted from the gunmetal sky. Rounded boulders protruded from the sandy bottom she could almost touch with her toes, while towering rock walls the color of burnt sand reared high above the circular pool. Shaking and dizzy, she tried to swim, only to be hindered by the flowing amber tunic that covered her neck to ankle, shoulder to wrist.

But... She'd been wearing shorts and a tank top when she'd fallen.

How was she even alive?

She scanned the pool. Except she'd fallen down a crevasse into a *river*.

Her sisters... Where were her sisters?

"Vivi!" she screamed. "Bree!"

Panic choked her. They'd fallen, too. She saw neither of them, though she searched the circular bank, then dived back into the pool. The chill water was clear as she swam, her body beginning to shiver as she searched the pool's depths.

Hands and feet gone numb, she scissor-kicked to the surface. They weren't here, and that inner sense the sisters had always shared told Kit that Vivi and Bree were not nearby.

Were they dead? Alive? How...?

Snow drifted down around her. If she didn't get out of the water she'd die.

Using the rocks as handholds, Kit tugged her way to the bank and collapsed. Gathering her strength, she finally crawled out of the pool, her efforts earring her bloody knees.

She pushed herself to sit. Walking along the bank would be useless. She saw no exit, no path or steps.

Body half frozen, she trembled as the snow continued to fall from a leaden sky. With dread, she peered up the cliff face. Could she climb that? Would she make it? Did she have a choice?

Hand over hand she scaled the rock face, made awkward by the drag of the tunic. Given the weather, she couldn't afford to remove it. Adrenaline gave her the juice to put one hand above the other, one foot after another pushing her upward, finding hand- and foot-holds, scraping knees and breaking nails.

When she'd clawed her way onto the summit, she collapsed, panting with relief. How had she done that with her crippled side? Once she caught her breath, she lay prone as her eyes scanned the terrain for shelter. All she saw were jumbles of rocks and a dead leafless tree, a skeleton reaching into the snow-burdened sky.

It didn't really matter. She was done, so exhausted she couldn't even pull herself beneath the dead tree's limbs. *No.* She would try. She stretched out a hand and curled her toes, attempting to push and pull at the same time. An inch. Then two.

Her shivering worsened, and yet something inside her was growing warm, comfortable even. Wasn't that what they said happened when people died from hypothermia?

Kit would have liked to see her daughters one last time. Her grandchildren. Her sisters, too, and her late husband, Adrian. Maybe his stern face would greet her on the other side. Or maybe...

Radulfr was royally pissed. First off, he wished he'd ridden his mistral Nightfall for the retrieval, rather than driving the hovercraft into the Pellopine mountains, an unforgiving wilderness. That was on him. But the second was on his father, who'd pulled his Alpha card and ordered Rafe to do cleanup for the farking Alchemic Clan's mess.

They'd brought over a Made One to the *wrong* convergence

point. Even using the coordinates they'd given him, he'd been scouring the mountains for hours.

Where the fark was she?

If he failed to find her before sunset, she'd die. A priceless treasure, and the wild country would take her. They should have had teams out searching. Legions. But the Alchemics insisted on him, *only* him. While he was the Wolf Clan's best tracker, he wasn't magic. He prayed the Fates would guide him. So far, they hadn't listened to his plea.

All this covert crap was to keep the Alchemics' mistake under the radar. The entire lot, a bunch of fools and egoists.

A discordant glimmer of light snagged Rafe's attention. Oddly shaped ice glinted on a shelf near the mountain's peak. His keen eyes took in the long, shiny thing high above. It didn't belong.

He slipped from the hover carrying his binocs and raised them to his eyes. A frozen object lay within a giant cocoon of ice. Unnatural and strange.

His blood fired. Maybe...

He retied the strip around the end of his braid, then hauled the coiled rope from his hovercraft and slung it over his shoulder. He locked crampons onto his boots, then strapped his claws onto the palms of his hands. What if the goddarts found her? The semi-sentient simian predators were the bane of the Pellopine mountains. Which was why at the last minute he shoved his laseblaster into his shoulder holster.

His mobile chimed. "Hush!" he said, silencing the annoyance. He peered up the rock face, learning the best foot- and toe-holds, then began to ascend. Inching up the frigid mountain he tried to imagine her. What would she look like? Would her voice be low or high? Her hair blonde or blue? Her smile warm or chill?

His imagination failed, so he climbed faster.

Rafe stared down at the six-foot length of ice that was melting beneath the sun's warmth. Not fast enough. Dropping to one knee he examined the thing again. Encased in the ice lay a woman, clothed head to toe in golden-yellow, lying on her belly, arm outstretched. Dead.

His heart thundered. A tragedy of epic magnitude.

Even so, he would never leave a Made One in her icy prison.

The laseblaster would release her in seconds, but it would damage her flesh, and that he wouldn't do. The task called for delicacy.

Rafe's strapped-on talons ripped apart the icy upper layers, then he slowed, taking care not to touch her flesh with his claws. Gradually, the woman was revealed as auburn haired and lovely, her face heart-shaped, with high cheekbones and plush lips, and he somehow knew she smiled often. *Had* smiled often.

He worked with even greater care, unwilling to injure her, though she *must* be dead. He found that intolerable.

It began to snow again. *Fark*. He'd better move it. Once she was fully revealed, her thin gown clinging to her lush curves, he shucked off his coat and wrapped it around her.

A sound disturbed the silence, not a natural one, maybe fifty yards to the east. He settled her over his shoulder and began his descent.

She deserved at least a pyre to send her on her way to the Other land.

Three quarters of the way down the cliff, an arrow zinged by his cheek. *Shote*. Those farking goddarts. He returned fire, then plunged the remaining distance, landing with a thud, knees bent. He slung the woman off his shoulder and into his arms, then leapt into the hovercraft. As he did so, he noticed an arrow had pierced his arm. He hadn't felt it, but the thing hurt like a bitch when he pulled it out. He reached for a handkerchief and staunched the bleeding. Damn those creatures. Thankfully they never left the mountains, but they caused destruction wherever they went.

He lifted the Made One over the console and into the passenger seat. So lovely. Her looks were atypical, with that bold aquiline nose and wide mouth. Enchantment stole over him. He tried to picture the color of eyes that would never again light and lips that would never again smile.

Had she been determined or soft and pliable? Determined. Yes, a woman firm in her viewpoints. Stubborn, even. Yet she'd embrace others with warmth and laugh easily. Her curls might be frozen, but he pictured them springy and soft.

He reared back. He was a practical man, pragmatic even. What the Fates was he doing, spinning stories in his head about a dead woman?

The snowstorm's intensity increased, and his climbing rope flapped in the wind. He'd come back for it later.

Rafe pressed the start button, his craft rose, and he turned up the heat. He was chilled, but unwilling to retrieve his coat from the woman. He pushed the nav's Home button, leaned back, and further pumped up the heat. After a couple swigs of warming troff, he fell asleep.

Kit opened her eyes. Exhaustion like leaden weights dragged at her lids, her muscles. Movement felt near impossible. What felt like a shearling coat was wrapped around her, over that tunic thing. Both were dry, and the chill was beginning to leave her bones. Her brain was slowly coming back online, too.

Everything felt strange. Even the air smelled odd with a scent she couldn't identify.

Where was she? How was she here? *Why* was she here?

Lucky stars, what was going on?

She was in a vehicle, albeit one with a strange-looking convex window. Outside, a snowstorm raged.

Snow? She and her sisters had been hiking in the middle of August. Her time in the pool and the climb flooded back to her.

As the dense pine forest slipped by, she saw protrusions in the road, like big rocks, and deep ruts filling with snow. Yet the strange car ride remained smooth. She froze. She wasn't alone. Of course she wasn't.

She turned to see...

To be continued.

Altered, coming Early 2019

ACKNOWLEDGMENTS

Thank you, my readers! You give me energy and inspiration each and every day. You're the best.

I offer thanks to so many for helping me see *Chest of Time* through to the finish line. To the amazing Rosemary Hill who not only aids me, but inspires me. To Debi McCarthy, for her invaluable Beta critiques and friendship. To my beloved writing partner, Camille Cotton and her daughter, Lorelai. Your smiles make my day. To Tiffany and Robert Freund—your editing skills saved the day. I so appreciate it. To Paula Munier, agent extraordinaire.

To my brilliant cover artist, Dagmara Matuszak—you're amazing. I adore your art and *CoT*'s cover like crazy! To SenshiStock for my Archer's cover pose. To Grace Draven, Tiffany Roberts, Mel Sterling, Monica Enderle Pierce, RJ Blain, Amy Cissell, Elizabeth Hunter, Kimberly Trochesset Ladd, Pilar Williams Seacord, Nancy Trochesset, Genevieve St Yves, Colleen Vanderlinden, Cate Rowan, Alicia Treat, Emma Hamm, Parris Afton Bonds, Joy Ross Davis, Jeffe Kennedy, Tameri Etherton, Susan Emans, and Colleen Champagne, who inspire me with their warmth, humor, and magic.

To Wayne Page, whose friendship means so very much. To Monica Lin and Kiona Stowers, who always cheer me on. To Norah,

Ro, and Karen, for their friendship, support, and knitting expertise. To Sheila Ryan, for her lasting and beautiful friendship, and Marc Ryan, who continues to inspire me. To Andrea Urban, Suzanne Hendrich, Pat Murphy, Donna Cautilli, CJ Williams, Linda Windels —love you. To Cindy's Knitters for the many stitches we wove together. To Betsy Bair, Georgi Mueller, and Karen Waxman for your love and friendship. To Cynthia Michaels, who continues to cherish my dear Cranberry.

To Peter, Kathleen, and Summer—your enduring love and profound support means the world. Love you! Finally, and always, to my beloved boys, Blake and Ben—for all that you are, for all that you have gifted to me, and for all your abiding love. I'm the luckiest mom in the world.

I don't write alone in some crystal tower, but with the support and help of everyone mentioned above and so many more. Thank you!

Please know that any errors or screw ups are mine alone.

ABOUT THE AUTHOR

The Afterworld Chronicles launched with *Chest of Bone,* followed by *Chest of Stone* and *Chest of Time* in the five-book series. My mysteries —*Body Parts, The Dead Stone, The Grief Shop,* a Daphne du Maurier winner, and *The Bone Man,* a du Maurier finalist—are now in ebook format. Tapping into my love of knitting, I wrote *Chest of Bone The Knit Collection* (with Karen Clements, Norah Gaughan, and Rosemary Hill) and *10 Secrets of the LaidBack Knitters* (with Lisa Souza). My late husband, William G. Tapply, and I ran The Writers Studio.

Currently, I'm playing with my pup, Penny, going wild in L.A., and pounding the keys on, *Chest of Fire,* as well as my new sci-fi/fantasy romance series that begins with *Altered.*

Come visit with me...
www.vickistiefel.com • vicki@vickistiefel.com

ALSO BY VICKI STIEFEL

The Afterworld Chronicles

Chest of Bone

Chest of Stone

Chest of Time

Chest of Fire (2019)

Tally Whyte/Homicide Counselor Series

Body Parts • The Dead Stone

The Grief Shop (Daphne duMaurier Award winner)

The Bone Man (Daphne duMaurier Award finalist)

Nonfiction

10 Secrets of the LaidBack Knitters

Chest of Bone The Knit Collection

Visit with Vicki:

Website • Facebook • Instagram • Twitter • Ravelry

www.ingramcontent.com/pod-product-compliance
Lightning Source LLC
Chambersburg PA
CBHW050900250626
47155CB00001B/38